The Lover's Charm

Jack and Priscilla strolled along the darkened walkways of Vauxhall Gardens, the distant music drifting on the air, its sweetness pierced by a feminine gasp or murmured words of masculine passion.

"What are they doing?" Priscilla whispered of a couple entangled on an arbor bench.

"Kissing," Jack said, and tried to lead her away.

"Why? Is it amusing?"

Jack paused, staring down at her. "Don't tell me, Miss Wilcox, you have never been kissed."

"Not like that I haven't. Just—you know. Like this." Priscilla lifted her chin and pecked at the air.

"Would you like to be kissed that way?" he asked.

She shrugged. "I have a certain scientific curiosity."

She stood very still as Jack's fingers found the edge of the mask she wore and raised it. He brushed her mouth with his. She put her arm around his neck, clung to him, mouth parting in a sigh. She held on to him, hesitant and yet willing, in the most arousing way. The very intensity of his desire sobered him.

"We have two choices now," he announced. "We can return to the pavilion, or—"

"Or?"

"Or," he said, dipping his mouth to her, "we can go on to finish what we've begun."

Dell Books by Sandy Hingston

A Most Reckless Lady
The Lover's Charm

The
Lover's
Charm

Sandy Hingston

A Dell Book

Published by
Dell Publishing
a division of
Random House, Inc.
1540 Broadway
New York, New York 10036

This novel is a work of fiction. Names, characters, places, and incidents
either are the product of the author's imagination or are used
fictitiously. Any resemblance to actual persons, living or dead, events,
or locales is entirely coincidental.

If you purchased this book without a cover you should be aware that
this book is stolen property. It was reported as "unsold and destroyed"
to the publisher and neither the author nor the publisher has received
any payment for this "stripped book."

ISBN: 0-440-22371-7
Printed in the United States of America
Published simultaneously in Canada
Design by Carol Malcolm Russo/Signet M Design, Inc.
February 1999
10 9 8 7 6 5 4 3 2 1
OPM

For Jeannette Brogley,

my dog's best friend.

The desire of the moth for the star,
Of the night for the morrow . . .

—Percy Bysshe Shelley
"To_____: One Word Is Too Often Profaned"

Castries, St. Lucia,
British Windward Islands

"Roll over," Jack commanded, and she did, panting eagerly, legs thrust high into the sultry air of the tropics at noon. He put his hand to her white belly, fondling the golden curls there, while she gazed at him adoringly with her liquid black eyes. He took a grape from the basket at his elbow and held it just above her mouth, which was parted in ecstatic anticipation. "Not yet!" he said sternly, and she shrank back, whimpering with frustrated desire.

"Mon Dieu," Camille drawled lazily from the opposite side of the bed, "stop teasing that poor creature. I need to speak to you about Antoine." Jack shrugged and tossed the grape to the spaniel, who caught and crunched it, a thin wisp of juice escaping her jowls. "And *don't* let her drool on the bedclothes," Camille begged, pushing a cascade of jet-black hair behind her naked shoulders with negligent grace. Jack reached across to her and rubbed his thumb

against an umber nipple. Camille slapped his hand away. "I need to speak to you—"

"I know, I know." He flipped another grape over the edge of the bed, and the spaniel leaped down after it. "Tell me about Antoine."

Camille stretched for the fruit bowl, one long leg curving over his bare thigh. "He is stealing from me. I watched last night through the peephole. Mrs. Enderly tipped him two quid. Half of that is mine."

"He deserves two quid for putting up with Mrs. Enderly," Jack said with a shudder. "Or perhaps *you* deserve it, for *watching* him with her. How can you stand to?"

"Business is business," said Camille, and sucked the skin from a grape.

"Let him go, then," Jack suggested.

Camille made a pout. The expression pulled her light-brown skin across her fine cheekbones and puffed her full lips up delectably. "How would I replace him?"

"Ah, you have me there. Antoine is a great favorite with the English ladies." He pressed a grape to her mouth, enjoying watching as she devoured that one, too. "God, you're beautiful. The most beautiful woman I ever have seen." He edged toward her, fingers catching in her hair. "Let's," he said, his voice hoarse with desire.

"First I must settle this matter of Antoine," she told him primly.

"Fuck Antoine."

Her green eyes widened. "Do you think that would do it?"

"Christ, Camille! I didn't mean—"

She laughed. "It might, though. Keep him honest, that is."

"Having you hasn't kept me honest." He stroked her throat, his breath coming faster.

"You are all *too* honest. That is what they ought to call you—'Honest Jack.' "

" 'Devil Jack' has a finer ring to it. And I've grown used to it. Besides, *you* gave the name to me. The first night we met. Do you remember? I'd been in St. Lucia for two weeks when I strolled in and saw you dealing vingt-et-un at the table in the corner downstairs. You were wearing white. Your hair was piled up—so." He raised it with his hands, let it tumble downward. "I fell for you then and there."

Her mouth curved. "You were young. So terribly young!"

"Nineteen!" he said defensively.

"You were a babe. You didn't even know I could be had for a quid. You sent me chocolates—in August. They melted in the heat." Her smile intensified at the recollection. "Still, all in all, meeting you was the best thing that ever happened to me."

"The sentiment is mutual." He nuzzled at her breast.

Firmly she pushed him away. "Not now, *chéri*. I must decide what to do about Antoine."

He was growing impatient. "What's to decide? Let him go, or let him steal. What's a pound a night, with all he earns for you?"

"It is a matter of principle. He knows the rules. And if I let him cheat me, what is to keep the girls from doing so as well? I cannot, will not, allow chaos to reign in my house. I've worked too hard for what I have."

Jack knew that was true. In the decade that he'd been her lover, Camille, with sheer determination and his financial backing, had risen from the lowly post of dealer to own the Hôtel de l'Isle, the finest brothel in all the Caribbean. What irked him more and more as the years went by was that all she had never seemed enough to make her forget her outcast mulatto status, or the scorn heaped on her by the more proper citizens of the island—when, that is, they were

SANDY HINGSTON

not frequenting her establishment. He wished sometimes—
what? That she were less driven. More easygoing. Not quite
so—self-centered? But then, he reminded himself, she
would not be Camille.

"Do you want for me to talk to him?" he asked with
a sigh.

Her green eyes glowed. "Oh, *chéri*. Could you? Since
he is a man, I cannot help but think it would come better
from you. And you must make clear to him, absolutely clear,
that withholding from the house will not be tolerated."

"How am I to explain that I know he is cheating you?"

"He has a new set of clothes—a suit by Forgéres. He
couldn't possibly afford it on what I pay him. And a pal-
metto hat."

"If you know all that, why do you need those blasted
peepholes?"

"If Monsieur d'Alliverd had had the peepholes," she
noted, "he would have seen and heard us plotting to buy
the Hôtel de l'Isle out from under him. Don't you spy on
the overseers for your plantations? The captains on your
ships?"

"No," Jack said bluntly. "I hire the best men I can.
Perhaps if you showed more trust in your employees, they
would reward you—"

"What a fool you can be sometimes, Jack."

He was tempted to retort in kind. But the room was so
hot, the sun pouring through the shutters so blinding, that
instead he lay back on the clean white pillows, closing his
eyes. That was the trouble with the tropics—they stripped
him of energy. He heard Camille shift on the bed and was
surprised when she began to stroke him.

"I did not mean that," she whispered, her hand closing on his rod.

"It doesn't matter." And it didn't, not so long as her
skin, the shade of coffee stirred with much rich cream, was

pressed against him and her torrents of black curls fell over his chest. The trouble was, one could not spend one's entire lifetime in bed. Still, so long as they were here now. . . . He pulled her to him, sighing as she wriggled lower. God, the tricks she knew!

"*Mon coeur*," she murmured, her throaty voice, the foreign words setting him all on edge. "Mmm. Ah . . ."

The spaniel had leaped onto the bed with them. Jack tried to push it away, but it lapped at his face with fervent affection. "Why must you keep dogs, Camille?"

"The English ladies have spaniels," she said evenly, and then called out: "Esmé!"

The white door to the bedchamber opened, and her maid, a small, dark woman in neat apron and cap, entered, took in the situation at a glance, and scooped up the dog. "Come, *ma petite*. I have a bit of bacon for you."

"Thank you, Esmé," Jack said gratefully. "Though it's a wonder that dog isn't the size of a horse."

"Now that I am here," the maid went on, "I may as well say there is a man, m'sieur, to see you."

"Send him away," Jack murmured, entranced by the way the shafts of sunlight were playing across Camille's skin.

"Better yet," his mistress offered, "send him to try his luck downstairs."

"I suggested that. He was most offended."

"Really?" Jack's curiosity was piqued. "Did he give you a card?" She brought it to him. He scanned the name, shook his head: "I don't know him, I don't think."

"He says he has a letter for you. Of the utmost importance."

"A creditor, no doubt," Camille said dryly.

"I don't owe anyone money," Jack objected.

"*Everyone* owes someone money," Camille said.

Jack looked again at the card: *Bennett Shropley, Esquire*. "What a proper, pious name. And he was offended at the notion of playing cards downstairs." Mouth curving in the expression of demonic amusement that had first prompted Camille to dub him Devil Jack, he reached for his robe, tossed Camille's to her. "Esmé. Show him in."

Camille was pouting again as she pulled on the robe. "Why must you meet him now? Why can't it wait? Why must it always be business?"

He looked at her and yanked his robe shut. "You're a fine one to talk, *chérie*." She spun away from him, and he rolled his eyes, knowing she would punish him for that moment of frankness, and knowing how.

"If you will come this way, M'sieur Shropley?" Esmé said, appearing in the doorway.

"Actually, I'm not—" The young man behind her entered the bedchamber, saw Jack and Camille still sitting on the bed, and blanched. "God! I do beg your pardon!"

"I don't know for what," Jack responded, as Camille flounced to her dressing table and began to brush through her hair. "Mr. Shropley, is it?"

"No! No. I'm merely his messenger." He started to look toward Camille, looked away, then let his gaze wander back. "Perhaps I should return at some more . . . convenient time."

"This is perfectly convenient for me," Jack told him.

"I only mean—" Camille's robe had slipped off one delicious shoulder; the young man resolutely turned his eyes to the ceiling. "My instructions, milord, were to speak with you in private."

"I have no secrets from M'amselle Déshoulières," Jack said briefly, trying hard not to laugh. "Go on, man! Speak your piece."

"Very well, milord. I have a letter here for you from Mr. Shropley." He reached into the pouch he carried, plucked it out, and laid it gingerly on the bed. "I'll wait outside while you read it."

"If you like," Camille said, turning to flash Jack a glare and then bestow on the young man a slow, devastating smile, "after I dress, I can show you downstairs. There are any number of *divertissements* to be had there."

"I never gamble," the young man said stiffly.

"Pity. But if you are come from England, you have had a long, *lonely* journey. Perhaps some feminine companionship—"

"Certainly not!"

Camille sighed. "Esmé. Take m'sieur to the parlor, and bring him tea."

"I'd be most grateful for tea," the messenger said with relief, and escaped hastily.

"*Mon Dieu,* what a prig!" Camille said in disgust, taking up her brush again. "I have a mind to go and try to seduce him, just for the—" She broke off, seeing in the mirror that Jack was absorbed in the letter, paying her no mind. "What is it?"

"My brother . . . is dead."

"I did not know you *had* a brother."

"Well, I did. A twin, actually."

"*Vraiment?*" Camille asked, intrigued. "Was he like you?"

"To look at. That's all."

"How did he die?"

"Pneumonia, this Shropley fellow writes."

"I don't wonder, in England." She peeked at him through her lush lashes. "My condolences, Jack."

"Oh, we weren't close. Hadn't been for eons. Actually, it was because of him I came to St. Lucia." His stomach tightened, even now, with something of the impotent rage he'd carried here from England ten years past. Still, it was a shock to think of Robert dead—to think of anyone dead, at their age. Despite the heat, he shook off a cold shudder at this stark reminder of mortality.

Camille got up to take another grape and peered over his shoulder. "That is a very long letter just to say he is dead."

"There's more to it than that. You'll recall my father died five years past." She did; he'd had a letter then, too, and hadn't grieved overmuch at that news, either. "It seems Shropley's the family solicitor. He wants me to come back."

"Back to England? Why should you?"

"He writes that the Avenleigh affairs are in chaos. That it's my duty as the new earl—" He stopped. Camille had sucked in her breath.

"You, Jack? An earl?"

"Well, yes. With Robert dead, and my father—"

"An earl!" She laughed delightedly. "I, with an earl in my bed!"

He smiled and crumpled the letter, tossing it to the floor. "Have you ever had an earl before, *chérie?*"

"No, never! At least, I don't believe so. I wonder will it make you better?"

"What could make me any better than I am?" he demanded, catching her wrist. But as he plied her with kisses, he sensed her mind was elsewhere, working busily. "What are you thinking of now?"

"Just that perhaps you should go."

"Why? What do I need with an earldom?"

"But if your family's affairs are in disorder—"

"If they are," Jack said shortly, "that's due to Robert's idiocy. My family consigned me here to St. Lucia. I'll not go trotting back to England at their beck and call."

Camille wriggled out from under him to take a passion fruit from the bowl. "There could be money in it," she mused, slicing delicately with a little knife.

"I've all the money I need. Unless—is there something you desire?"

"Only you." She offered the fruit to him. "Still, where

is the sense in throwing away such opportunity without even finding what it is worth?" She licked a drop of juice from the side of his mouth. Surprised—he'd expected her to hold back from him for a fortnight at least, for what he'd said about her and business—he turned to meet her tongue, and she thrust it inside him, pushing against his teeth in a way that drove him wild.

"Practical Camille." He grunted as she finally drew back. He recognized what she was angling for with this unexpected display of affection and decided to call her bluff. "Would you come with me?"

She stared. "Come with you? As what?"

"As what you are. My lover."

She thought a moment, shook her black curls. "No. Think of the stir it would cause."

"As if you have ever been afraid of causing a stir! If not as my paramour, then how about as my wife?"

A longer pause. "You . . . have never mentioned marriage before," she said at last.

"There's never been any cause to. But if it would make a difference, if it meant you would come with me to England, why not?"

"I can think of one obvious reason," she noted dryly.

"You mean that you are French."

She giggled. "Idiot. I mean because of my skin."

"I adore your skin," Jack told her, and caressed her breast. "It is one of the things I love most about you, in fact."

"I daresay your family would not agree with your sentiments."

"I've already said—my family can go hang. Anyway, there's little enough of it left. With Father dead, and Robert, and Mother long since gone, there's only my father's sister Bertrice and her exceedingly dull offspring. I vaguely recall a cousin or two."

There was a glimmer of longing in Camille's green eyes. But then they glinted, went hard. "What would I do there in England? Sit and embroider? Write bad poetry? Ink little drawings of spaniels?"

"You'd do what you do here. You would make me happy."

"You make it sound so simple."

"There's no reason it shouldn't be."

But Camille knew better. "There are ten thousand reasons why not. How would you introduce me at—what is the name of the place that has the dancing? Almack's. 'This is my wife, the Countess of Avenleigh, former proprietress of the finest whorehouse in St. Lucia'?"

"No one need ever know about that."

"You are wrong," she said vehemently. "Sooner or later, someone would know me, recognize me. And imagine the scandal!"

Jack's eyes, a blue so clear and bright it was startling, considered her curiously. "If I didn't know better, I'd think you were intimidated by the prospect of English society."

She stiffened. "What I am afraid of is being bored out of my mind. Here, I have my business. You have yours. We have our separate lives."

"We have a life together as well. At least, I thought we did. Ten years, Camille. It is time we thought of the future." He let his fingers slide up her thigh.

She did not even notice. It was the face of her character that irked Jack most, that ability to switch her sensuality on and off as if it were a gaslight. "I think you should go back. You should see what is left you, take what you can and then return to me."

"Aren't you the least bit worried about losing me to some winsome English lass?"

She snorted. "I do not think it likely."

"Mm. Nor do I," he told her, arching above her.

"Will you go back?"

"Christ, Camille. No. I don't want to."

She had her knees clamped shut. "And I say that you should. An earldom, *chéri*! Think of it! There must be jewels, and silver and gold—"

He shook his head in bemusement. "Greedy thing. You realize, I'd be gone for months. Maybe so long as half a year."

"But what a homecoming I would give you," she whispered, drawing him down at last.

He groaned as he thrust inside her. "Oh, Camille. Oh—"

"Will you go?" she asked, her long brown legs wrapping around his waist.

"No."

"Not even if I . . . beg?" With a sudden motion she reversed their positions so that she straddled him, her heavy breasts hanging against his chest, her palms at his shoulders. "Please? And bring me back jewels and gold?" She raised herself up, lowered her loins against him, moving in slow, tantalizing circles. His breath was coming faster. "Jewels and gold and gowns from London—and hats. Plenty of gorgeous hats."

"Don't ask me this, Camille," he said hoarsely. Her black curls swept his throat as she bent down to kiss him, achingly tender. "Oh, God. Oh, Camille—"

"Go." She sighed, pushing hard against him, withdrawing. "Go. Go. Go—"

"Oh, God. Oh, God."

"Say you will."

"Christ! I'll go!" The words burst out just as his seed did. For a few moments longer she pressed her sleek brown body to his; then she fell back on the bed, a smile curving her lips. She nestled close to him, catching her fingers in his hair, stroking the side of his face. His eyes were closed; within minutes he had drifted into sleep.

She eased herself away from him and down off the bed. In the corridor she found Esmé, shaking out fresh linens. "You heard?" she whispered, and the maid nodded. "You must go to Maman Gris-Gris. Tell her I have need of a *charme d'amour*—a strong one. That will last for many months. Do you understand?"

"*Oui*," Esmé said. "You were brave to tell him he should go."

Camille wrapped herself in one of the sheets, going to the window. "What choice did I have? I am losing him, Esmé."

"No, no, m'amselle!"

"I am," she repeated, almost to herself. "What we share, he and I—it is sufficient for a young man, for the man he once was. He is at an age, though, when he will want something more. I feel it in him. He grows restless with me."

"All the more reason not to send him away!"

"Ah, but if I do otherwise, when he realizes his dissatisfaction, a year, two years, five years from now, whom will he blame but me? A little holiday with those chilly English ladies, in that chilly land—that is just what he needs. He will go. But with the help of Maman, he will return. And he'll be rich. Richer than I ever imagined. An *earl*, Esmé!"

The maid still looked dubious. "*I* would not take such a risk with my lover."

Camille turned on her sharply. "No. You would not. That is why I own this house, and you work for me."

"Camille?" Jack's voice, groggy with sleep, from the bedroom.

She pushed the maid toward the stairs. "Go now. The strongest she has. Never mind the expense."

"Camille?"

"I am here, *chéri*." Camille went back into the room, reassured by her reflection in the cheval mirror—tall, lithe, brown, her hair a tumble of rich black curls, her eyes the green of the Caribbean sea. Let him go now, while she had her looks, while she could still twist him around her finger. He'd spoken of marriage; that barrier was breached. When he returned, in the first passion of their reunion, she would accept his proposal. She would be a countess. An *English* countess. And then Mrs. Enderly and all the others could go hang.

"What are you smiling about?" Jack asked lazily from the bed.

"The notion of you an earl," she said, and laughed out loud.

Chapter 1

Jack was bloody freezing. There was snow on the roof, snow on the wheels, snow edged up in little shifting mountains along the carriage windows, snow in his beard, in his teeth, in his ears. Every time he moved on the frozen leather of the seat, his breeches crackled. They'd turned to ice in his effort—successful after God knew how many tries—to help the driver push the heavy coach out of a wayward drift.

He banged at the window to clear away the snow and stared out at the bleak, barren Lincolnshire winter he'd thought never to see again except in his uneasy dreams. "Almost there, m'lord!" the coachman called with unwelcome cheeriness. Jack pulled a flask of rum from his waistcoat and took a long swallow. The liquor tasted sweet and warm as the island sun.

God, what a misbegotten adventure. Two months' passage in the worst bloody weather, lacking only a hurricane to really brighten his mood. The awful rush and clamor of

London after Castries' lovely, small felicity. The English winter, unspeakably drab, while in his mind lush tangles of jasmine and passionflower stretched and curled their tendrils over a balcony that now seemed only a dream. *Was* there a St. Lucia? Was there a Camille, fragrant as jasmine, more beautiful than the blossoms always set beside her bed? He might have been with her now, relishing the smooth curves of her body, feeling her open beneath him like the slow, sweet petals of a moonflower. . . . The force of the image was startling; he realized that his manhood was at stark attention just as the carriage lumbered through the pair of iron gates that led to his ancestral home.

They jolted to a stop. Jack braced himself against the sides of the coach. He was a tall man, more than six-foot-three; anyone shorter could not have spanned the two sides with his hands. He felt a sneeze coming on, and thought he'd conquered it until the footman flung the door open to the blinding cold. "Your Lordship!" he cried. "Welcome home!"

"Aaah—choo!" Jack said, and shuddered in his frozen clothes.

He climbed stiffly down the stairs and staggered toward Avenleigh House. The footman was babbling about how glad they all were to see him, how sorry they were the circumstances should be so unfortunate— "Open the bloody damned doors!" Jack snapped, hands wrapped around his chest. The fellow did, and he entered, hacking and coughing. He felt for his handkerchief, blew an enormous blast, and cursed the folly of his return.

The butler had come forward. "Mrs. Gravesend awaits you in the green parlor, milord," he intoned with gloomy hauteur.

"God, Bellows, you antique. Are you still here? To hell with Mrs. Gravesend. I want a bed."

"Your Lordship's rooms have not yet been prepared.

You must be aware, we had no notion when Your Lordship might be arriving, what with the inclement—"

"You listen to me, you bloody stuffed shirt. You show me to a bed now, immediately, or I'll—I'll—" Jack's threat was subsumed by another huge sneeze.

"As His Lordship wishes," the butler murmured, with a handsome bow. "Won't you come this way?"

The image of pillows, down quilts, blankets, was nearly as seductive as that of Camille. Jack stumbled forward in the butler's wake, heading for the stairs. He'd nearly reached them when a door off the entrance hall burst open and a plump, short woman with a tangle of brown hair shot with gray emerged, tripped toward him, and caught him in her arms.

"Cousin Jack!" she exclaimed.

Jack fell back, perplexed. "Aunt Bertrice?" he postulated.

"You silly thing! As if I ever could be! Don't you recognize me?"

"No," Jack said with utter honesty.

She giggled. "Oh, Jack, you always were a funner. It is I! Agnes!"

Agnes *who?* he wanted to say, but had a sense it wouldn't sit well. "Well, Agnes!" he said instead, heartily—and then erupted in another sneeze.

"Oh, you poor dear!" she cried worriedly. "You sound absolutely wretched! We must be terribly careful, mustn't we, that you don't suffer poor Robert's fate? Bellows, take His Lordship to his rooms. Light a fire, and see that a warm bath is sent up. Is there anything else you would like, Cousin?" she asked anxiously.

"A hot rum toddy would be highly welcome," Jack said between sniffles.

She looked at him askant. "Rum? Oh, we haven't got that."

"Just send up lemon and sugar and hot water, then," He was still searching his mind, trying to place her. Suddenly an image fixed itself. "Agnes! Aunt Bertrice's daughter Agnes! Of course! I pushed you into the millpond!"

"It was one of the highlights of my youth," she said with disconcerting sincerity. "But I must not keep you any longer from your bath. Mamma is very particular about having supper served at six, and it is almost five now!" She embraced him again; through his stuffed nose he caught a whiff of violets. "We are all so unspeakably grateful that you've come at last!"

"Ahhh—choo!" Jack said, and escaped after the butler, up the stairs.

The bath helped, though Jack was appalled by how suddenly the water turned frigid. Spurred from the tub by its chill, he dressed in his usual soft breeches and white shirt, waistcoat and jacket, combed out his hair and ran his fingers through his beard. The looking glass in his bedchamber showed an unfamiliar reflection: the beard had been an afterthought, born of his journey on ship, when shaving every morning seemed worse than extraneous. The dinner bell sounded just as he'd settled down in front of the fire with the toddy he'd concocted himself.

"Damn," he said, and seriously contemplated not responding. But the snow piling up outside the windows propelled him from his chair. The sooner all of this was done with, the sooner he'd be warm and safe at home. He headed down the stairs, still sniffling, noticing that the appointments of the ancestral manor appeared a good deal more shabby than he had recalled.

"His Lordship, the Earl of Avenleigh," the butler, Bellows, intoned as Jack reached the dining room. Already seated at the table were three women: Agnes, another no-longer-young lady, and the grimmest old hag he had ever seen. He recognized her by her eyes: little and black and gleaming with malice, just as he recalled from his boyhood days.

"Aunt Bertrice," he said, approaching the gnarled, glowering woman. "How absolutely splendid you are looking!"

"Don't you sweet-talk me, Jack Cantrell," she snapped, so vehemently that he took a step back. "I can't *imagine* what you were thinking of, to keep us waiting so long!"

"I came as soon as I heard the bell," Jack told her, bewildered.

"I believe," Agnes said delicately, "Mamma is making reference to the delay in your arrival here. But, Mamma, pray recall, Cousin Jack was *thousands* of miles away!"

"That's no excuse for such indecency toward Robert." Aunt Bertrice snarled. And all three women looked at him, Bertrice glaring, the still unidentified one goggling, and Agnes appearing very nervous indeed.

There was soup on the table. It had steam rising from it.

"A thousand pardons," Jack said, "if I have somehow offended you, Aunt Bertrice. It was not easy to book a passage in the dead of winter. I have been these past two months in transit. I came the moment Mr. Shropley's messenger arrived."

"Pish,"said the nasty old woman. "I've spoken to Shropley. You didn't even *leave* St. Lucia for nearly a month after you were informed."

It was turtle soup, Jack's impaired nostrils told him, perhaps laced with sherry. "I had affairs to attend to. . . ."

The other spinster unexpectedly giggled. Aunt Bertrice shot her a withering look. "Nonetheless," she said very roundly, " the fact remains that your brother has been buried without the traditional handing-on of the family title."

"I haven't the least notion, Aunt Bertrice, what you mean."

The cousin who wasn't Agnes gave a heartfelt sigh. "Hand to hand," she said in a soft, wispy voice.

"Precisely, Sephrina," Aunt Bertrice snapped. "For five hundred years, the heir to the Avenleigh title has been present at his predecessor's deathbed. *You*, of course, could not be bothered."

"I didn't know he was dying," Jack said shortly. "And let me remind you, it was your brother, my father, who sent me to St. Lucia in the first place."

"You sent yourself there," she retorted, "with your dishonorable behavior."

Jack had had just about enough. He sat down in his chair. "Is that turtle soup?" he asked, hoping to distract his aunt.

"It should have been you that died."

"Mamma!" Agnes exclaimed in shock.

"Well, it's true, by heaven! Who would have mourned *his* passing?"

Jack had his mouth open to speak his mind, but the sight of the three haggard women in their outdated frocks and hopelessly unfashionable hair arrangements made him curb his tongue. Perhaps they were all genuinely grief-stricken by the loss of his brother. "I am sorry, Aunt Bertrice, that I was not here for Robert's death," he said contritely. "I hope I can make it up to you somehow."

"You can," Sephrina said suddenly. "At the memorial service." He glanced at her. Her eyes were blue, like his, but glassy, glazed, unfocused somehow.

"So there is to be a memorial service?" Somehow he'd feared there would.

"Naturally," said Aunt Bertrice. "We were only waiting for you to arrive. Now—*at long last*—I shall send word to Bishop Wilcox. He can arrange matters in the blink of an eye." Her tone implied the contrast to Jack's tardiness. "However steeped in grief his household may be."

Jack nearly choked on his first sip of soup. "Steeped in grief? A bishop? Over Robert's death?"

"Naturally," said Aunt Bertrice. "His only child was betrothed to your dear late brother. I'm sure Robert wrote you of it."

It was on the tip of Jack's tongue to say that Robert never wrote him, and with damned good reason. But the news his brother had been betrothed at all, much less to a *bishop's* daughter, distracted him. "My heart goes out to Bishop Wilcox at his daughter's loss," he said with suitable aplomb. "I say. A bit of sherry would go down very well with this soup."

"Avenleigh is a dry house," Aunt Bertrice noted darkly. "Liquor is, after all, the bane of the working class, just as Bishop Wilcox says. And it is up to us to set an example."

"Just as dear Cousin Robert did," Sephrina said with another odd giggle.

"Precisely," said her mother. "So long as *I* reside in Avenleigh House, there'll be no drinking here."

There was even less rum in the flask than he'd remembered. Jack, sprawled bootless in the hard horsehair chair in his bedchamber, was seriously contemplating trekking to the tavern in the village when a timid knock came at the door. "Cousin Jack?" It opened a crack, and Agnes peered in with anxious eyes, a mobcap covering her scattered curls. She had a bottle and a glass on a tray.

Jack abruptly sat up. "If that's lemonade—"

"Brandy," she whispered. "Amontillado."

He arched a brow. "I never would have guessed you for a secret tippler, Agnes!"

"Don't be absurd," she said, blushing. " 'Tis from Robert's store. Mamma knows nothing about it, of course. She doesn't approve of spirits. Bishop Wilcox's influence. But

Robert had a secret closet in the cellar just filled with the stuff."

"Did he really," Jack said, trying to reconcile this information with his brother's betrothal to the bishop's daughter. It was all most confusing. She laid the tray at his elbow. He went to pour, then paused. "What is your opinion, Cousin Agnes, of the temperance movement?"

"Well." The blush deepened. "I apprehend, of course, the evil that spirits have wreaked among the working classes. In that respect, I support the bishop wholeheartedly."

"But?"

"But?" she echoed, flustered.

Jack hid a smile. "Would you care for a bit of brandy, Cousin Agnes?"

"Oh, I'd *die* for a drink!" she burst out—then clapped a hand to her mouth.

Jack let the smile show. "My sentiments exactly. Here, you take the snifter." He filled it liberally.

"But what will you do?" For answer, Jack winked and raised the bottle to his lips.

It was damned good brandy. Jack stood, offering her the chair, but she chose the ottoman instead, perching on its edge. "I—I really mustn't stay," she stammered. "It isn't at all fitting."

"On account of what a rake I am?" Jack inquired, feeling in his waistcoat, finding what he was seeking. "Care for a cigar?"

"Oh, really, Cousin Jack!"

"But you don't mind if I smoke?"

"No, no! Of course not!" Then she added, as an afterthought, "Though you'd best open the window. Mamma would have conniptions."

"We mustn't have that," Jack said gravely, getting up to do so, and she giggled again.

"Oh, you are just as terrible as everyone says!"

"As who says?" he asked, leaning back in his chair, inhaling brandy and cigar fumes.

"Well—Robert, for one. 'Devil Jack,' he told us they call you in that place you came from. Odd, isn't it, that you should look so alike and yet be so different?"

"What makes you think we are—were—different?"

"*He* would not have offered me brandy. And he never made me laugh." She took a delicate sip from the snifter, gave a gratified sigh, then took another. "Still, he was very good to Mamma and 'Phrina and me."

"Did you see a *lot* of him?" Jack inquired.

"Oh, no. Hardly ever. He was nearly always in London or someplace else, on business." Jack nodded. He'd had trouble picturing his brother making his home among these sad, aging ladies. "Though we looked forward to his visits with great pleasure," Agnes added defensively. "He brought us lovely gifts. Well, once he did, anyway. A box of Turkish delight for us to share, and a shawl for Mamma. A real Norwich shawl."

That reminded Jack of something. "I have gifts for you, too. No Norwich shawls, alas."

"I suppose," Agnes said timidly, "you have not much use for them in St. Lucia. It is very warm there, is it not?"

"Very." A frigid wind was howling through the open window. Jack stood up, going to his trunk, rummaging in its depths and bringing forth a paper-wrapped parcel. "This is for you."

"For me?" his cousin squealed, so excitedly that he felt a pang of shame.

"It is only a token. . . ." But she'd torn the wrappings off and was staring in amazement at the gift he'd brought.

"Oh, it is lovely, lovely!" She held it up in her hands. "What exactly *is* it?"

"A cowrie-shell necklace." He'd meant that for Aunt

Bertrice, and the ear-drops for his cousins. But Aunt Bertrice hadn't brought him brandy.

"Cowrie shells," she breathed. "They are the loveliest things!"

"The natives on St. Lucia used them as money. Many years past, of course."

She was still contemplating the necklace with awe. "It is quite the prettiest gift I have ever been given. Oh, I shall wear it always!" And she fastened it around her throat as proudly as if it had been diamonds. Jack suddenly wished, somehow, that it had.

She glanced up at him, smiling, fingering the shells at her neck, and he realized with shock that she was a handsome woman, fine-boned and well-bosomed beneath the dowdy mourning clothes she wore. He wondered why she'd never married—then remembered her dragon of a mother. How old was she? He vaguely recalled her coming out when he was six or seven. So, not yet forty. What a crime that she should waste her life away here, attending to Aunt Bertrice's whims.

"I really *am* so very glad you've come," she said in a whisper. "They *all*—Mamma and Mrs. Blathersby and Bishop Wilcox, everybody—kept insisting you wouldn't. But somehow I knew you would." For the first time, Jack was somewhat pleased he'd made the journey, merely for the sake of having proved that gloomy company wrong. She swallowed the last of her brandy and hurriedly stood up. "But I must be going. Mamma's an early riser, and breakfast is at seven."

"Not for me it's not," he told her, puffing out cigar smoke.

She tittered. "Oh, I suppose I should mention—if you hear noises in the night, someone moving about—it is only Sephrina. She tends to wander. I thought it best to warn you. In case you are the sort to believe in ghosts."

"I'm not, ordinarily. But even if I were, I likely would have thought it was just Robert, seeking to keep me from his brandy stash."

She laughed out loud at that. "Good night, Cousin Jack."

He stood and bowed, certain she'd enjoy the nicety. She did. "Good night, Cousin Agnes."

"Sleep tight!" she said almost gaily, and vanished through the door. Jack fell back into his chair, felt the draft from the window, and defiantly got up to close it. Let Aunt Bertrice have a conniption. It would be richly deserved.

Some hours later, in the dead of night, he awakened in his bed, chilled to the bone. A harsh wind was tearing wildly around the crumbling corners of Avenleigh. How, he wondered sleepily, had the place fallen into such a state of disrepair? His father had always been diligent in keeping up the family manor, despite the considerable expenses that entailed.

Christ, what were the pillows stuffed with—potatoes? He beat the lumpy things down, turned them over, finally pushed them off the bed, his fist curled around the golden charm he wore on a chain around his throat, that Camille had lowered over his head as they stood, embracing, on the quay. *Keep this with you always*, she'd whispered. *Never take it off. Never look inside, or the spell will be broken.*

"What is it?" he'd asked, bemused but touched. He knew how she believed in tokens, portents, superstitious things.

My love for you, she'd told him. And then she'd pressed her amazing body against his one last time. . . .

On the verge at last of sleep, he abruptly straightened in his bed. There were footsteps in the corridor outside his room, slow, shuffling footsteps. Then the long, soft creak of a door opening, and another grating creak as it closed again—*click*. More footsteps, so hesitant that it was agonizing to wait for the next one. *Creak!* Another door. *Creak. Click!* And then that odd, hobbling pace. . . .

The wandering Sephrina. It was a damned good thing Agnes had thought to warn him, or he'd surely have burst into the hallway with a bludgeon. With excruciating slowness, the footsteps and clicks and creaks moved on. Jack shivered, not entirely from the cold. It was true he did not believe in spirits, but even so he would not wholly discredit the possibility that Avenleigh House was haunted. It would be just like his twin to refuse eternal rest merely to spoil Jack's sleep.

$\mathcal{D}$ressed in black, dwarfed by the great Gothic splen-
dor of Lincoln Cathedral, Jack watched as the teetotaling
Bishop Wilcox delivered a memorial oratory to Robert
Cantrell, fourth earl of Avenleigh, that was highly moving
and utterly astounding. The bishop lauded Robert's good
works among the poor and downtrodden, his many charitable interests, and above all his dedication to the temperance movement. At this last, Jack could not help but glance
along the pew to Cousin Agnes, who was dabbing her eyes
with her handkerchief.

He'd been set beside Sephrina, who had Agnes to her
right; then came Aunt Bertrice, stolid with public grief. Beyond his aunt was a tiny figure he did not recognize, her
face shrouded in veils—the bishop's daughter, he supposed.

For such a virtuous sort, Robert didn't appear to have
many friends. The company was extremely thin: only the
family, the bishop, the chit in the veils, the landholders
and servants, and one extremely attractive auburn-haired

woman in midnight-blue satin and a cunning feathered hat that Camille would have loved. Jack could not help glancing at her as the bishop went on and on, and once, as he did, she met his gaze with a nod and a quick half-smile. She was so stunning that he contemplated approaching her when the service finally ended—he could always say he wanted the name of her milliner. But when the bishop finally wound down, Jack's progress was blocked by Cousin Agnes, who stood in the aisle embracing the small, veiled figure and kissing her fondly. By the time Jack could work his way past, the woman in the hat had hurried back through the cathedral and out the doors. Since he could hardly race after her, Jack offered his arm to his aunt instead. "Tell me, Aunt Bertrice, who is the girl in the black veils?"

"Your brother's betrothed, of course. Miss Priscilla Wilcox," she said mournfully.

Jack let out a sigh. He would have to pay a call on her, he supposed; no getting out of that. "And the woman in the feathered hat?" he inquired curiously.

But Aunt Bertrice was distracted by Sephrina, who had sidled up to several landholders and was eavesdropping on their conversation. "'Phrina! Come along!" she said sharply. "This is neither the time nor the place for your dithering!"

They went home, to a dreadful luncheon of overcooked mutton and turnips and carrots. The ladies were even more dreary than usual, dwelling in doting detail on the deceased. Jack listened for as long as he could stand to; then he cleared his throat. "Tell me, Aunt Bertrice. When will I meet the executor of the estate?"

"Soon enough, you mercenary creature," she spat at him. "You just can't wait, can you, to get your hands on his fortune?"

"Really, Mamma," Agnes said with a mortified blush.

"I believe Cousin Jack is simply anxious to return to his business in the islands."

"I know all about his *business* in the islands," Bertrice said sharply, while Sephrina occupied herself with spooning up salt from the cellar and letting it fall back on itself over and over again.

Jack was not about to let his aunt's comment pass. "I'll have you know, Aunt Bertrice, that the income from Father's holdings in St. Lucia has increased fifteenfold since I took charge of them."

"That was not the business to which I referred," she told him quellingly, which left Jack in little doubt as to the substance of Shropley's report. For an instant he was heartily glad Camille had not come here with him; then the pent-up longing in his loins convulsed him, and he wished to hell she had. Absence *does* make the heart grow fonder, he mused; it had been a long time since he'd thought of his lover so incessantly—even while in her company.

He wondered what she might be doing now. The images his mind formed were not reassuring. She had been true to him, he was *nearly* certain, for the past ten years. But he had never left her before, not for more than a few nights at a time. He knew well enough there were men in Castries who ached to be her lover—indeed, a number *had* been, before he arrived on the scene. He tried not to picture her sprawled across her—their—bed, negligently naked, reaching for fruit across another man's body. After the meal he went to his rooms, took a sheet of vellum and a snifter of brandy, and wrote to her, poured out his strange renewed passion:

> *I think of you constantly. You consume my mind. I adore you, Camille—now and forever. I see you every-where, in everything—your black hair, your smooth skin, the fire in your eyes as I take you. I miss you to madness. Do not forget me, chérie.*

The brandy had made his handwriting nigh illegible. How odd, he thought. I long for her more now than I did when I had her. And his fingers crept unwillingly toward the love charm she had given him. Could it be? Then he laughed at his own imaginings. It was only the gloomy company of his aunt and cousins, with the drear winter weather, that made him pine for her so. He signed his name, made the seal, and crawled wearily into his chilly bed, while the Lincolnshire wind beat at the rattling windowpanes.

"Jack Cantrell," Jack started to say, and then corrected himself: "I mean, the Earl of Avenleigh. To see Miss Wilcox."

"Won't you step this way?" the bishop's dour butler intoned. Jack followed him into a house so big and bleak, it made Avenleigh seem downright cozy. The only pictures on the walls were grim reproductions of Christ's agony; the furnishings were hard and dark, angular, no cushions or frippery anywhere. He perched on the edge of a most uncomfortable sofa and waited, waited for a long time, while he pondered why in God's name Robert might have chosen the bishop's daughter to wed.

When the door opened, he sprang to his feet. But it wasn't the diminutive fiancée; it was her father, as hard-edged as the sofa. He had a cold, austere face, a magnificent head of swept-back white hair, and eyes of flint gray.

"Lord Avenleigh," he pronounced in the round, rolling tones of a man used to hearing himself speak publicly—and to enjoying the sound.

"Bishop Wilcox."

They stood sizing one another up, like wary beasts. Then: "You've shaved off your beard," the bishop remarked in surprise.

Jack rubbed his chin and nodded. "Just this morning, actually. Got to be a bit of a bother."

His host let out a harrumph. "May I offer you some refreshment?"

Jack had already noted that the sideboard was vacant of bottles. "Perhaps some tea?"

"Tea for His Lordship," the bishop directed the butler, who bowed and disappeared. He gestured Jack back to the sofa, then did not sit himself, but stood in front of the cold hearth, arms folded over his chest.

"I thought it only proper," Jack began, "to call upon your daughter."

"Very kind of you," the bishop retorted. "I am sorry to inform you that she is not here." He was staring at his guest with something akin to fascination; it made Jack most uneasy.

"What a pity. Perhaps I might come again, at some more opportune time?"

"Forgive me speaking so plainly to you, Your Lordship. But I think it would be best if you did not."

Jack flushed. "I suppose you've heard all manner of nonsense about me, sir. Permit me to assure you, the reports of my dissolute nature are *somewhat* exaggerated."

"Oh, no doubt, no doubt!" the bishop said hurriedly. "That isn't my concern. It is just that you are so very like your brother. Especially now, without the beard. A remarkable resemblance."

"We *were* twins," Jack said dryly.

"Yes, of course. Still, I did not expect. . . . I might almost be speaking to poor Robert."

"But you're not."

"*I* recognize that. My daughter, however, who is so enrapt in grief at her loss—I cannot help but feel concerned that she might transfer the affection she had for your late brother to *you.*"

"Good God," said Jack, and swallowed. "We mustn't have that!"

"No. I'm glad to find you agree. She's very young, my Priscilla. Sheltered. Naive, one might almost say. And girls her age are so susceptible to fancies, aren't they?"

"I understand your apprehensions completely," Jack assured him. The servant had come in with a tray. Jack took the teacup he was offered, nodding three times for sugar, while the bishop watched.

"Your brother," his host observed, "drank his black."

"However alike we may have been externally, sir, we were very different at the heart. Since you would prefer me not to call again, I shall, of course, respect your wishes. But you will, I trust, convey my heartfelt condolences?"

"Most assuredly."

Jack had the peculiar notion that the bishop wanted him gone from under his roof as soon as possible. Accordingly, he swallowed his tea and then rose from the sofa; after all, he had no inclination whatsoever to stay. "And permit me to add, sir, my devout wishes that your daughter will soon recover from her grief."

"No doubt she will. Youth has its own resiliency. Not, of course," he added sonorously, "that one can imagine her ever entirely getting over the loss of your brother. He was—a most remarkable man."

"Remarkable," Jack agreed politely. "Would you be so kind as to refresh my memory, sir? How long exactly had my brother and your daughter been engaged to marry?"

"I believe it was three years."

Three *years*? "Well! I had best be going," Jack said apologetically. "Lots of loose ends and what-not to tie up back at Avenleigh."

"I'm sure there are. Your aunt informs me you intend to return to the islands just as soon as it is practicable."

"Absolutely," Jack said with vehemence.

"In that case, I don't imagine we will see one another again. Permit me to wish you bon voyage, milord."

"Many thanks, sir, for your kind attentions to my aunt and cousins. It is good to know they are in the hands of such a . . . such a *stalwart* spiritual leader. Again, my condolences to your daughter." He escaped gratefully.

On the ride home, atop a spindle-legged black mare—Avenleigh's stables appeared to have suffered along with the house—Jack shook his head in bemusement, still unable to reconcile his memories of Robert with the upright soul the bishop had lauded. But none of that was Jack's concern, not really. Just as soon as the solicitor, Bennett Shropley, returned to Lincolnshire—he was, most inconveniently, in London at the moment—Jack could sort out the details of the inheritance and be gone, back to Castries.

A sudden movement in the underbrush of the pasture beside the road engaged his eye. A fox, he thought, watching the sere branches flutter and shake. No, bigger than a fox. Perhaps a badger? Slowing the horse— which wasn't difficult; its normal pace was less than lightning-fast—he caught a glimpse of drab brown among the bushes and then a flash of pale gold, like the feathers on a hawk's back. And then, as the mare gave up plodding entirely, a low, desperate wail of anguish floated into the air: "Oh, damn it all! Damn!"

Jack sat in the saddle and stared as a small, bedraggled figure in a muted brown cloak emerged from the thicket. She—it was definitely a she—had a wicker basket in one hand and a short spade in the other. Completely unaware of his presence, she trudged across the pasture in the direction from which he had come. The pale gold had been her hair; the hood on her cloak had fallen back, and she was covered in mud and brambles. He caught only the merest glance at her face, but that was enough to make him *nearly* certain the girl was Priscilla Wilcox. And from her woebegone expression, she appeared to be in great distress.

"Miss Wilcox?" he called, ready to offer his aid.

She raised her head and turned to him. Their eyes met across the wintry field. She looked at him for a long, long moment as he sat atop the sorry nag. Then she let out a scream of unholy terror, dropped her basket and spade, and ran off in the opposite direction as if she'd just seen the devil himself.

Good God! "Miss Wilcox! Wait!" Jack spurred the horse, which didn't move. Cursing briefly, he leaped down from the saddle and started to pursue her. She glanced over her shoulder, saw him following, and screamed again, redoubling her frantic efforts to escape. Jack halted where he stood, perplexed. "I didn't mean—I'm not—I beg your pardon!" he called after her. She plunged on through the snow and weeds, the wind whipping her muddled hair. Jack watched until a culvert hid her from his sight, then headed back to his horse.

"Well," he told the nag, who was staring at him vacantly. "There's something new. Never had a chit run from me in terror before," The horse snorted impolitely. "You can believe me or not," Jack said crossly, "but it's true." He climbed back into the saddle and gave the mare a nudge with his boots. "Get on, you miserable creature. God alone knows what nonsense Robert told her of me, to frighten her so."

The mare snorted again, with an unmistakable air of derision. Then it resumed its swaying, unhurried progress back to Avenleigh.

"Cousin Agnes," Jack began, pouring her an extra-hearty helping of Robert's brandy. It had become a nightly ritual, her visit to his rooms with the bottle and tray. "Tell me about Priscilla Wilcox. What sort of girl is she?"

"Mm." Agnes sipped, sipped again. "A very proper, decent young lady."

"I understand the betrothal had been in place for three entire years."

"Had it been that long?" Agnes said vaguely. "It seemed shorter, no doubt because Robert spent so little time here. But—three years. That would be right. Eighteen months or so after your father passed on."

"How did the happy couple meet, do you know?" Jack asked, tongue firmly in cheek.

Agnes settled herself on the ottoman. "It was at the Blathersbys' Christmas ball, I believe. Or was it Lady Ashton's? You know, I can't recall. It's a terrible thing, getting old."

"You aren't old, cousin," Jack said gallantly. "In fact, I was only now thinking how very fetching you look in that wrapper."

Agnes paled abruptly, rising to her feet. "I hardly think—"

"Oh, do sit down, Agnes! I am not about to make a pass at you, whatever poison Robert and your mother have poured into your ears!"

She sat, with a slow flush. "I beg your pardon. But I *have* heard some things—"

"From Shropley," Jack said evenly. "What exactly did he tell you?"

"Oh, not me! It was Mamma. She wormed it out of him, and 'Phrina overheard—she tends to do that, you know—and then she told me. That you have a—a special friend." She paused, the blush deepening.

"The woman I love," Jack said resolutely.

"Oh," Agnes said quickly, "I was sure of *that*! And I really don't see why it was any business of Mamma's. After all, you're a grown man. You can do as you please." There was wistfulness in her voice. Jack wondered briefly, sadly, whether she had ever been made love to. It seemed unlikely. What a waste, a shame. "But," she went on with new briskness, "you asked about Priscilla. Whichever ball it was, it happened very quickly. Love at first sight, you know."

Jack peered into the brandy bottle. "Why do you suppose their betrothal never progressed to marriage?"

"Well," Agnes said, faintly flustered, "perhaps because she was so young."

"What age is she?"

"Twenty-two, I believe."

"Seems old enough," Jack noted.

"Yes, it does, doesn't it? You know, I'm really not sure. . . .No doubt there was *some* reason. I know Robert had great plans, big plans, for some investments he was making. He told us about them on that same visit—the one when he brought the Turkish delight and Mamma's shawl. And then he became betrothed to Miss Wilcox only a few weeks later. It was all quite sudden."

"I went to visit Wilcox Hall today," Jack mentioned, "to call on my brother's bereaved fiancée."

He was taken aback by her reaction; her eyes went wide as twinned full moons. "You visited Priscilla?"

"Miss Wilcox was not at home. Her father received me."

"And how did your interview progress?"

"He was most cordial," Jack allowed. "He was also extremely anxious to be rid of me."

She fluttered a hand. "Priscilla is his only child. Her mother died when she was very young. I imagine he feels— uh, protective. You *do* have a reputation, you know."

"If he is so protective, why would he have agreed to marry her to Robert?"

"Oh, Cousin Jack. You mustn't speak ill of the dead!" Agnes said in true shock.

"I beg your pardon." Of course, no one here knew what he knew about his brother. They only knew the stories about *Jack*—stories, he thought bitterly, that Robert had had ample opportunity to hone and embellish through all these years. "I merely meant—Robert was not, when I knew him, an especially religious man."

"No," Agnes said thoughtfully. "But they do say love conquers all."

Does it? Jack wondered. The strong wine had gone to his head. He went to raise the brandy bottle, and it clinked against the amulet beneath his waistcoat. That suddenly, he was visited by a piercing image of Camille in their bed, her black hair tumbled like a waterfall, her skin smelling of jasmine. He felt his manhood rise to attention and quickly hid the fact with the bottle. "I suppose so," he said off-handedly. "Would you be so kind now as to excuse me, Cousin Agnes? I have a letter I must write."

"To *her*," Agnes trilled, voice throbbing with excitement. "Your special friend. You write her all the time. 'Phrina sees the letters on the console. *Mademoiselle Camille Déshoulières*. I think it is so *romantic*." She rose to her feet. "It's a pity, isn't it, you couldn't bring her here?"

"You know . . . she isn't English," Jack felt compelled to say.

"Yes. I do. Mr. Shropley told Mamma. But I say, so what if she is French? You are so very far removed from the war over there, aren't you? Half a world away. So what can that matter?" She went out, leaving Jack astonished that the family solicitor had apparently shown some vestige of tact in not mentioning the color of Camille's skin.

*J*ack slept late the next morning, in no rush to rise from the bed that had come to seem his only refuge in that cold, grim house. He'd been awakened in the dead of night once again by Cousin Sephrina's wanderings, had lain and listened as her excruciatingly slow explorations moved down the hall and then finally away.

The room was beginning to heat up a bit, at least enough to melt the ice that each night collected inside the loose window glass. Oh, God, what he would give to be back in Castries! He rolled over, hand on the amulet at his chest, and fell asleep again, to an alluring recollection of one sultry evening when Camille and he had bathed together in her huge copper washtub; he did not rouse until Bellows, with a knock at the door, entered and informed him that he had a visitor.

"Mr. Shropley?" Jack asked eagerly, throwing off the bedclothes. "Returned from London at last?"

"Nay, milord. Miss Wilcox." The butler's voice was

oddly cautious. Jack was about to send him off with a polite excuse—after all, he wasn't even dressed—when Bellows
added, "It would, of course, be the height of impropriety
for you to receive her, since neither your aunt nor your
cousins are at home."

"You don't say." Jack grinned, reaching for his
breeches. "Ask her to attend for a few minutes, then, by all
means. And offer her a drink—I mean, tea. Kindly offer
her tea."

The butler departed with such a scowl of disapproval
that Jack was still grinning a quarter hour later when he descended to the drawing room. "I do beg your pardon, Miss
Wilcox," he said to the small creature, still wreathed in
black veils, who was perched on the sofa with a tea tray at
her elbow. "I was occupied upon your arrival with—ah—
with family business. And it appears my aunt and cousins
are not at home."

"No," Miss Wilcox said. "I only just now realized they
would not be. They attend Bible studies with Father every
Tuesday, from eleven till one."

"Ah. That must be most enlightening for them. I see
Bellows has brought you tea."

With a start, she turned to the tray he indicated. "So he
has," she noted wonderingly. "Would you care for a cup?"

"I would, very much. Thank you." Jack took a seat
himself, at a distance. "No lemon or cream. But three sug-
ars, please." He reached to take the cup and saucer she
held out to him, noticing that she was peering at him
covertly from beneath her veils. She seemed paralyzed
with shyness. "Is there something I can do for you, Miss
Wilcox?"

"Oh, no. Not at all. I just . . . I felt I owed you some explanation for my—my *peculiar* behavior yesterday," she
began haltingly. "I'm afraid you caught me by surprise by
taking off your beard. You—you look so *very* like your

brother. And when I saw you there, I rather thought for a moment you *were* he." Her voice was extremely low-pitched for such a diminutive thing, and vaguely musical—as if she'd spent a lifetime listening to church bells. But of course, she had.

"I suppose he told you all manner of nonsense about me."

Beneath the veils, he could have sworn, her mouth curved upward. "Oh, my, yes. He was filled with stories of you. From what he'd said, I had imagined an eyepatch. And dueling scars. And perhaps some sort of a pox."

Jack bit off laughter. "I *do* have dueling scars, let me assure you. But in unmentionable places. The bas—my *opponent* caught me running away."

"How very . . . interesting," Priscilla Wilcox murmured, and busily poured her own tea. Jack *almost* thought she'd had to stifle a laugh herself. But no. That couldn't be.

He eyed her curiously. She truly was small, barely five foot, he estimated. Her figure seemed in proportion, though, despite those outlandish mourning clothes—waistless, made of dreary black serge, and as lumpen as the pillows on his bed. Her feet, he noticed, were remarkably dainty, clad in practical black boots that wore a wash of mud. Camille had large feet. While he adored every toe, she was extremely sensitive about that fact. He found himself wishing he could have another look at Miss Wilcox's face.

Just then she raised her veils, to sip the tea. Jack glanced away quickly; it seemed the suitable response. Her pale eyes were still red with tears, and her nose was ruddy as well. In fact, her whole visage was swollen and flushed. She took note of his tact. "You are probably wondering how your brother could bear the sight of me."

"No, no!" Jack said quickly, heartily. "You're quite a—quite a splendid girl!"

"I sneeze and swell up something frightful every winter and spring." She shrugged. "Dr. Allison says 'tis a form of cyclical catarrh."

Jack raised one black brow. "I supposed you to be steeped in grief over my brother's death."

She stared at him for a moment, with eyes the gray of a dove's wings. Then: "There is that," she agreed. "I am certainly unlikely ever again to find such a man."

Jack took a deep sip of tea, eager to turn the subject; he couldn't imagine discussing Robert with her without letting his sentiments toward his late brother slip out. "Do tell me, though, Miss Wilcox, what on earth you were doing traipsing about that pasture in the dead of winter."

"Did Robert never mention to you that I am a lepidopterist?"

Jack blinked. "I *assumed*, naturally, that you were Church of England."

Unexpectedly, the girl before him did erupt in laughter. "Oh, I say, that is rich!" And she spilled her tea. She didn't seem to care, though; she went on laughing. "Lepidopterist— Church of England!" Then she noticed, belatedly, Jack's blank blue stare. She steadied her cup. "I do beg your pardon. I thought you'd made a jest."

"It must have been a good one," Jack said enviously. "Would you care to explain it?"

"I study lepidoptera," she told him, much more humbly.

He waited and, when nothing more was forthcoming, prompted: "Which are . . ."

"Butterflies and moths, of course."

"Ah! I see," said Jack, who didn't. "Bugs, you mean."

"Precisely. It is my ambition to capture and catalog every species in Lincolnshire."

"Butterflies," he echoed.

"I love 'em," she said with great enthusiasm. "Always

have. From a child. Your brother always showed the utmost respect for my avocation. Allowed me free rein to pursue my science. Encouraged it, in fact."

"Well!" Jack exclaimed. "How very . . . fortunate for you."

"You are being ironical," she said, her small backbone stiffening, "The typical reaction of the unscientific mind."

"Not at all!" he protested weakly. "I like butterflies. We have butterflies on St. Lucia. Gorgeous butterflies!"

Her pale gaze abruptly lit up. "Have you? What kinds?"

Jack was distracted, noting how her gray eyes had suddenly taken on a sheen of stone-green, how her swollen face glowed with an intensity that almost made one overlook its deficiencies. "Uh—yellow ones. White ones. With red stripes. Big brown ones, too. Nearly this big." He held his hands apart.

"Those are lunar moths," she corrected him matter-of-factly.

"On St. Lucia," he said in a hasty attempt at regaining her esteem, "their wings are crushed into love potions." Her eyes—they were really very fine eyes except for the blear, huge and almond-shaped and the shade of storm-ridden oceans—widened in fascination. "Well, that's what I've heard, anyway. From Esmé. My mistress's maid."

He regretted that as soon as he spoke it. But she didn't seem a whit offended. "Do you think you might write her and ask her to confirm it?" she demanded urgently. "It would be highly useful for a paper I'm preparing for publication. Under a pseudonym, of course. A male pseudonym."

"I'd be delighted to."

Her gaze turned mournful. "But no doubt you won't remain in England long enough to receive an answer."

"Probably not," he acknowledged. "I'm to have a meeting with Robert's solicitor, Mr. Shropley, just as soon as he returns here from London. Once that business is concluded, I'll be headed home." She looked so stricken that he quickly added, "I promise you this, though—I'll be sure to inform you of what Esmé has to say of the matter, one way or another."

She set her teacup down and curtsied in an awkward way. "I'd be ever so grateful if you would. Good day, Lord Avenleigh. And again, my . . . my apologies for my rudeness to you yesterday. It was only that I believed for a moment your brother had come back from the dead."

It did not occur to him until she'd gone that screaming and fleeing in terror was a rather odd reaction for a woman to show upon the sudden resurrection of her own true love.

Chapter

4

$\mathcal{B}$ennett Shropley, Esquire, finally returned to Lincolnshire later that week from London, with profound apologies for this tardiness in answering the new earl's summons. He was a wiry, red-haired fellow perhaps thirty years old, far different from the elderly, stuffy figure Jack had pictured—though he seemed strangely nervous.

"Well?" Jack said with a grin. "Let's have it! What exactly am I heir to?"

Shropley dabbed at his brow with his handkerchief. "Milord. You have no notion with what profound regret I impart this news. But there *is* no inheritance to speak of."

Jack stared at him. "What do you mean?"

"I mean, milord, that at the time of your brother's death, he was deeply in debt. There were substantial gambling losses, at White's and a number of other clubs, to various individuals. Not to mention the tabs run up at restaurants and clothiers. I believe the overdue amount at

Halleby's alone"—He consulted his papers—"stands at a thousand pounds."

Jack gasped. So much for Camille and her jewels and hats. "You must know, sir, it is my intention to return to St. Lucia as soon as possible," he declared.

The solicitor paled all around his freckles. "But you cannot, milord! These debts must be paid!"

Jack pondered it, briefly. "I'll sell Avenleigh House."

"You cannot," Shropley retorted. "It's entirely mortgaged."

"So what if it is? That's not *my* problem."

Shropley cleared his throat. "I'm afraid, milord, in a manner of speaking it is. Your brother named you executor of the estate. By law, you are responsible for settling his debts, and have a year in which to do so."

Damn you, Robert, thought Jack. *So this is your final revenge.* . . . "But that's unthinkable. That I should stay in England for a *year*—I have my own business interests in the Caribbean that I must attend to." *And I have Camille.* . . . "Can't you handle all of this for me, as my solicitor?"

"That could constitute a breach of professional ethics. You see, I am one of your brother's debtors. He owes me several hundred pounds for past services." Shropley drew a mountain of paper from the satchel he'd brought, laid it on the desk, and pushed it toward Jack. "It is all right in here."

A year in England! Jack shuddered, thrusting the papers back. "I can't do it. I *won't* do it." *By God, I paid Robert's debt once before*, he thought furiously. *I won't be forced into it again!* "What," he asked tentatively, hopefully, "if I just leave? This is England, after all. I'm a free man. No one can make me stay."

Shropley's hazel eyes clouded. "Unfortunately, the Crown can. That is the business which took me to London. Your brother also had been negligent in paying his taxes. Those are now your responsibility. Unless you can come up in ready cash with the sum of"—he paused to consult his account book—"twenty thousand pounds, there is the— ahem!" He glanced toward the closed door of the study, lowered his voice. "The prospect of debtor's prison."

Jack rose to his feet. "What the hell sort of solicitor are you, anyway? To permit the bloody idiot not to pay his *taxes*—"

"Your brother," Shropley said quietly, "had engaged fifteen different solicitors in the five years since your father's death. I was merely the one unfortunate enough to have been employed by His Lordship at the time of his demise. I urged him throughout the exceedingly brief course of my tenure to curb his spending, pay his debts, reduce his standard of living. He would not listen."

"How long *were* you employed by my brother before he died?"

"Just shy of three months."

"Christ," said Jack, and sat back down again. "Christ. You poor bloody fool."

"Precisely," Bennett Shropley declared, eyes glinting. "I had already drafted my letter of resignation. It's there in the pile. My housekeeper, who is extremely scatterbrained, neglected to post it for me."

Jack laughed. "A fellow victim of circumstance!"

"Quite," Shropley agreed, with a ghost of a smile.

"Twenty thousand pounds, eh?" Jack was a rich man, but by Caribbean, not European, standards. And his wealth was inextricably tied up in his holdings, in the Hôtel de l'Isle, in his ships and sugar fields, in promissory notes for cargoes the delivery of which were months and perhaps years away. He wished like hell he'd never come back to England. Remembering Camille's seductive urging gave a twist to his heart. *Go and see what is left you, take what you can.* . . . And here is what he'd got: headaches, a year mired in creditors' proceedings, and, just to top it off, the prospect

of debtor's prison. "Would you care for a drink?" he asked
Shropley abruptly, who let out a sigh.

"Tea, I suppose. . . ."

"God, I mean a drink, man!"

"I was under the impression Avenleigh was a dry house."

"Not anymore it's not."

Once he'd poured liberal helpings of brandy, Jack
looked at Shropley over his glass. "And if I were to stay the
year?"

"You should be able to set up a schedule for repaying
the debtors," the solicitor said with more confidence. "The
fault never was the income from the estates. Only your
brother's inordinate spending precipitated all of this."

A year. Twelve months. God. It seemed a lifetime.
"And if . . . if I should just return to St. Lucia, ignore the
debts?" he began.

"Your aunt and your cousins—who, I might mention,
remain incognizant of the family's circumstances—would
be reduced to certain poverty. They would lose their home,
their furnishings, everything, to the creditors."

Considering Aunt Bertrice, Jack was sorely tempted.
But Agnes, poor Agnes, who had shown him such kindness, whose face had lit up so at his cowrie-shell gift . . .
could he abandon her to that disgrace? And Sephrina, who
clearly was mad as a hatter—what would become of her,
left to the fate of a deranged pauper? She'd be sent to a
bedlam, one of England's institutions for lunatics, so infa-
mous that his and Robert's nurse used to threaten them
with the mere word. How would he *ever* lie quietly again in
Camille's arms if he left his relatives in such straits?

He took a long, long draft of brandy. "A year, then,"
he said slowly, reluctantly.

Bennett Shropley blinked at him. "I beg your pardon?"

"I'll stay the bloody year, man! I'll do what needs to be
done."

The solicitor cleared his throat. "You will? You *will*! Well, that's very good news, milord! Very good news indeed! I would not have mentioned it, of course, unless you'd reached that decision, but I stood a fair chance of landing in prison myself, for malfeasance in your brother's tax affairs. You can imagine I am much relieved!"

"You sound much surprised," Jack noted dryly.

"No, not at all. Naturally, I assumed the heir to Avenleigh would perform his duty."

"The hell you did."

Shropley laughed at last, nervously. "Well, perhaps I harbored *some* qualms. Considering what your brother said about you, I am a *tad* taken aback to find you have a sense of family honor."

"So am I," Jack told him with a rueful grin. "Believe me, so am I." He pulled the stack of records toward him. "May as well get at it, I suppose."

"Quite so, milord," said Bennett Shropley, humbly and gratefully.

𝒜ll that day and into the evening, the two men huddled over the voluminous accountings of Robert's profligacy. Jack had believed, to that point, that nothing his brother did could ever shock him. But the incredible trail of spend-thriftness detailed in the papers left him breathless. "Christ!" he exclaimed at one point. "What else could the bastard have done but die? I'm astonished it wasn't suicide!"

"He hadn't much of a head for money," Shropley admitted, paging through a file stuffed with vowel notes for gaming losses. "And I believe he had taken to drinking quite heavily."

Jack looked at his brandy snifter and pushed it away.

"Still," he noted as the dinner bell sounded, "there's

no question what you said is true. The income from the estates is more than adequate, if properly directed and invested, to make up the shortfall in a year's time. With luck. And if prices hold. The war with Napoleon might seem, on the face of it, to work against us. But there *is* still the American market."

Shropley stared at him. "We are, milord, at war with America as well."

Jack smiled slowly. "Ah, but I have ships to get cargoes anywhere in the world. We can route them through some neutral land—Portugal, perhaps, or the Antilles."

The solicitor coughed discreetly. "That would be illegal." He paused. "But altogether a great help, considering the circumstance."

"You're a man after my own heart, Shropley."

"And you, milord, are the answer to a desperate soul's prayers."

There was one file remaining untouched. "What's this?" Jack demanded, reaching for it.

Shropley glanced at the cover. "That would be Lady Harpool. You'll see I've attached a summary of payments—"

"*Holy* Mary Mother of God!" Jack stared in awe at the figure. "Who exactly is Lady Harpool?"

"The widow of a minor Welsh lord. Her husband died suddenly some three years past. He had a son by a prior marriage who inherited the estate. Lady Harpool was left with the widow's third. She used it to purchase a modest residence here."

"I'm surprised Robert didn't buy the house for her," Jack said, running a finger down the pages of the ledger. "He bought everything else. Look at this! Right down to her unmentionables!"

"She is, as they say, a lady of fashion."

Jack grinned at him. "Or a lady *of* a fashion. I like you, Shropley. I like you very much indeed." The dinner bell clanged again, and he grimaced. "I don't suppose I could inveigle you into staying for dinner. No doubt you've a family awaiting you at home."

"I am a bachelor," Shropley said a bit stiffly—then returned the grin. "But while I am grateful for the invitation, I think it more prudent I return home and write directly to the agents of the Crown that you intend to satisfy their demands. I've never been in prison, and I have hope tonight, for the first time in many months, that I never shall be."

"Let us shake on that, then," Jack told him, offering his hand.

The solicitor pumped it with enthusiasm. "You are very different from your brother, milord, are you not? Despite the remarkable resemblance . . . May I say again how *extremely* grateful I am for your devotion to your family."

"And may I say, Mr. Shropley, how grateful I am for the tact you showed in describing Mademoiselle Déshoulières to them."

The solicitor's blush nearly consumed his freckles. "Well, milord. That was really none of their business, was it? Nor even very much of mine."

Jack had warmed considerably to this unexpected ally. "Very good, Shropley. We'll go at it together, then. Mop up the mess, eh?" He was already thinking of the letter *he* would have to write, to Camille, explaining he'd be gone for another twelve months. Well, damn it all, it was her own bloody fault!

Bellows appeared at the door to the study. "Milord. Mrs. Gravesend wishes to know whether you ever intend to present yourself at dinner."

"You may inform my aunt," Jack began testily—then caught Shropley chuckling as he gathered his papers. That made Jack burst out laughing. "You may inform Mrs. Gravesend," he said, when he'd regained some control, "that I will be directly down."

Chapter

5

"*Y*ou'll see, Jack, that we have a guest for dinner this evening," Aunt Bertrice announced tartly as he entered the drawing room. "And that guest—along with all of us—has been kept waiting quite some time."

"I beg your pardon. I was engrossed in conversation with Robert's former solicitor regarding the affairs of the estate." He acknowledged Agnes with a smile, nodded to Sephrina, who was unraveling the trimmings on the draperies while humming to herself, then turned to the visitor seated by the fire.

"This is Lady Harpool," Aunt Bertrice announced.

"Lady Harpool!" Jack came close to choking.

"How do you do, Lord Avenleigh?" said the lady in question, extending a gloved hand. Jack bent and kissed it, glancing up beneath his lashes. Her face was perfectly composed in its frame of rich auburn curls. It was an extraordinarily beautiful face, and he knew her instantly as the woman in the feathered hat who'd attended Robert's memorial.

"How do you do?" Jack struggled to regain his composure, having only moments ago perused the bills of account for the unmentionables this woman still, no doubt, had on. "You—ah—you were at the cathedral for the service, were you not? I regret I did not have the opportunity to introduce myself to you there."

"You don't remember me, do you?" she asked. Her voice was light and breathy, girlish, though Jack judged she must be nearly his age. Her eyes were a light olive, sparkling and gay, and her cheeks and mouth bore a hint of rouge. Her complexion was flawless, pale as porcelain. She was wearing blue again, but a pale blue this time, cut and draped to show every curve of her extremely curvaceous body.

"Should I?" Jack responded, noting that she had a gorgeous bosom.

"Well—" She gave a pretty little laugh. "I hope I have not changed so much . . . Jackie."

He looked at her more sharply—at the pert upturned nose, the olive eyes, that full mouth with its alluring half smile. But it was the auburn curls that finally placed her in his recollection—though the last time he'd seen them, they'd been cinched in blue bows. "Vivienne?" he said in disbelief.

"None other," she told him, eyes aglow. "So you *do* remember!"

"Vivienne Lessing!" He could not hide his astonishment. "After all these years!"

Her red mouth turned down. "Oh, Jackie. You always *did* know how to flatter a girl."

"I didn't mean—that is—" Jack realized he was stammering, and clamped his mouth shut.

"It doesn't signify," she said in that breathless voice. "It *has* been a long time."

"I regret to interrupt the reminiscences," Aunt Bertrice said dryly, "but I'm sure that by now the roast is ruined."

Jack could not stop staring at the woman whose gloved hand he held. "I beg your pardon! Had I known it was you, I'd have sent Shropley packing! You ought to have told me of our guest, Aunt Bertrice."

"I called quite unexpectedly," Vivienne Harpool, née Lessing, murmured. "I was riding, and my horse's shoe worked loose just at your gates. When she heard of my plight, your aunt most graciously extended a neighborly invitation to remain for dinner."

Sephrina abruptly let fall the draperies. "Are we ever going to eat?"

"Let's go in," Aunt Bertrice said, and waited for a good minute until Jack came to his senses and offered her his arm. "Agnes, *do* come along."

"Squire Lessing's little girl," Jack murmured as their guest attached herself to his free elbow. He caught the scent she wore, something rich and exotic, redolent of jasmine.

"All grown up," Vivienne said sweetly, with a toss of her auburn hair.

I should say! Jack thought as he escorted her and Aunt Bertrice to the dining room, the cousins tagging along like afterthoughts. Vivienne Lessing! Who ever could have imagined that the mud-splashed squire's daughter would have turned into such a remarkable beauty! "You have changed," he told her as he pulled out her chair.

"I learned to scrub my knees, that is all," she said placidly, spreading her skirts in a flourish of that evocative perfume.

The servants brought in the first dishes. They were the usual overcooked muddle, but Jack hardly noticed, so engrossed was he in contrasting the poised, elegant woman seated to his left with the urchin of his memories. As the daughter of the local squire, Vivienne Lessing had been the *only* neighboring child with whom he and Robert had been permitted to associate. God, what a hellion she'd been! He vividly recalled having lost to her in a bout of wrestling when he was, perhaps, eight. She had trounced him into tears. Hoping she didn't share that particular memory, he said heartily, "So, Vivienne!"

"Lady Harpool," his aunt noted squelchingly.

"Forgive me. Lady Harpool. Tell me about your life!"

"Oh, no, Jackie." She smiled in dismissal. "There's so little to say. I'd far rather hear about *yours*."

He took it as a hint. It was entirely possible that Aunt Bertrice and the cousins knew nothing about her affair with Robert. So he obliged, recounting amusing tales of life in the tropics. All the while, though, he could not stop thinking of the sums of money his brother had squandered on this woman. They made the investment he had put in for Camille's purchase of the Hôtel de l'Isle positively negligible in comparison. Was she worth it? he wondered, contemplating the curve of her neck into her lily-white throat, the delightful rise of her bosom. Probably she was.

"But I've monopolized the conversation," he said with sudden crispness. "You must tell me of yourself, Vi—Lady Harpool. I have heard you are a widow?"

The olive eyes discreetly dropped. "Yes, alas. My late husband, Lord Harpool, died quite unexpectedly. We had been wed less than two years."

Sephrina, who'd been busy polishing her flatware, let out a guffaw. "Unexpectedly? Why, he must have been nigh eighty!"

"'Phrina!" Aunt Bertrice said sharply.

Agnes, who'd been unaccustomedly silent, jumped into the conversation just then. "Were there any surprises, Cousin Jack, in your meeting with Mr. Shropley?"

"A few," he acknowledged—then added, just to let Vivienne Harpool know what he knew, and see what she did with the knowledge, "The estate is not exactly up to snuff. Robert seemed inclined to spend more than he had."

Her reaction was to shake her head sadly. "Poor Robert. But that's so common, isn't it, these days?"

"At least," Aunt Bertrice noted bitterly, "your brother had some sense of family honor!"

Jack could not help glancing at Vivienne Harpool. She shot him a gaze from beneath her dark lashes that was blatantly pleading. *Not now*, her olive eyes seemed to say.

"Here's the roast, burnt to a crisp, just as I predicted," Aunt Bertrice announced with satisfaction as Bellows bore in a haunch of venison. "Jack, you may as well carve the remains."

He took the knife he was offered, saw Vivienne look down again at her plate, and felt a burst of pity for her. Robert's mistress—Lord, no amount of frippery could have made that post enviable. Still, he could not help wondering whether at that moment she was wearing the red Chinese silk chemise and underdrawers he and Shropley had noted with such dismay.

"This end's quite rare yet," he said, a slice poised on the fork.

"I like things rare," Vivienne Harpool responded in her little-girl voice.

"Then this is for you," Jack said, and put the meat on her plate.

*D*espite her persnicketiness, Aunt Bertrice had not, up until that meal, stood on the ceremony of the ladies withdrawing. This night, though, with nobility present, she stood in a bustle of black and said briefly, "Lady Harpool, shall we?" Followed by the cousins, they departed for the drawing room, leaving Jack staring in their wake. Absentmindedly he lit a cigar.

Bellows, supervising the clearing, made a rumble in his throat. "Mrs. Gravesend forbids smoking in the household."

"It's my household now, much as you may have enjoyed being the man of it during my brother's absences," Jack said curtly. "Oh, and by the way, Bellows. I want you to order in a quantity of rum. Go through Mills Brothers, in London, and mention my name. You'll get a more than fair price."

The butler straightened where he stood. "Mrs. Gravesend forbids the consumption of spirits in her—"

"I'll also need lemons—say, three dozen a month. I'd suggest the fruiterer on Hollingshead Road in Lincoln whom Father always used."

Bellows's jowly face bore a look of horror. "Am I to understand, milord, that you intend to prolong your visitation here?"

"For one year, I am. After that, we shall see. For now, you may go down to the cellars and fetch me up a bottle of my brother's brandy. Oh, don't pretend you don't know it is there! He may have hidden it from my aunt, but *someone* had to clear away the empties."

"Very good, milord." The butler trundled off, his shoulders drooping in resignation. Jack sucked on his cigar. He'd forgotten to mention ordering more of those.

Bellows brought the brandy, poured it, and retreated with the air of a man who expected Armageddon at any moment. Only seconds after he had closed the door behind him, it popped open again. "Jackie?" a soft, small voice said.

Jack straightened in his chair, nearly knocking over his snifter. "Vivienne! Won't you come in?"

"Only for an instant," she breathed, glancing back into the hall and then shutting the door. "The stableboy sent word that my horse was reshod, and I do hate to impose any longer. I just felt I *must* have a further word with you."

"Would you care for a brandy?"

"Oh, Lord, no! There isn't time for that. I merely wanted to—to thank you. For not . . . exposing me."

She was draped in a silver-blue wool cape trimmed in ermine, which Jack happened to know had cost his brother three hundred and twenty-six pounds at Madame Descoux's, in London. "Exposing you as what?" he asked, admiring the way it hung on her. The French really did have a hand for fabric.

"As Robert's . . . friend." Her voice had dropped to a whisper.

"They don't know, then?"

"No, no. No one did."

It was on the tip of Jack's tongue to note that a good many jewelers, mantua-makers and milliners must have, not to mention assorted purveyors of other costly goods. But before he could, Vivienne Harpool covered her face with her hands, slim shoulders shaking in sobs. "Oh, Jackie! I am so ashamed!"

"Of what?" he asked, resisting an impulse to put his arms around her trembling figure.

"Of what I let him do!"

There flashed through Jack's mind vignettes of certain proclivities Camille had reported to him, having observed them through the peepholes. "And what exactly was that?"

"Spend all that money on me!" she burst out in despair. "Oh, I know it was wrong! Especially when I could see with my own eyes how Avenleigh House was crumbling! But he *insisted*, Jackie! And I was so sunk in doldrums, so engrossed in grief over my husband's death. . . ." She raised her tear-stained face, lovely even in such straits. "He—he just kept *giving* me things! Things I never asked for! And I knew well enough, if it ever came out, what people would say!"

Two thoughts occurred to Jack: one, that she must be

the finest actress who had ever drawn breath, and, second, *Oh, my God. Knowing Robert for the idiot he was, it could be true.*

"One red Chinese silk chemise and underdrawers, forty-eight pounds sixpence," he said slowly.

She colored wildly. "As if I'd ever wear such a thing!"

"Do you mean to tell me they were *unwelcome* gifts?"

"Entirely unwelcome! How could you believe anything else? He was betrothed to that dear, sweet child! 'Marry her,' I told him time and again. 'Spend your money on her!'"

"Vivienne." He waited until she'd raised her gaze to his. "I've only just tonight been over the accounts with the solicitor. Robert may have been a numskull, but his agents kept excellent records. He spent over *ten thousand pounds* on you in the past three years. If you expect me to—" He stopped. Her porcelain face had gone sheet-white; she staggered on her feet.

"Ten thousand—" She gasped for breath. And then she swooned. If Jack had not dived around the table to catch her, she would have fallen to the floor.

"Vivienne!" He patted her cheeks, unfastened the ermine-trimmed cape. "Vivienne, can you hear me?" He was about to summon help when her lashes fluttered; she stirred in his arms, sending a waft of that marvelous fragrance, so reminiscent of the tropics, up against his nose. "God, you frightened me!" he said, seeing her eyelids open.

"Oh, dear! Oh, Jackie!" She buried her face against his waistcoat. "What you must think of me!"

The ermine was tickling his chin. "You might have sent them back," he noted, still far from convinced.

"But I *did*!" she insisted. "I sent back *everything* he gave me! He only sent it all to me again, with more added! Jewels and gowns and—and—"

"Unmentionables," Jack suggested wryly.

"He wore me down," she confessed, clinging to his shoulders. "He would not believe I did not want his love. In the end, it became easier—simpler—just to accept what he sent me. I had no more will to fight." She crumpled into tears again. Then she collected herself, pushed back from him, foundered for her handkerchief. Jack politely offered her his. "I don't mean to speak ill of him, Jackie. Honestly I don't. But he was—like a man obsessed."

That hint of jasmine still hung in the air, reminding Jack inexorably of St. Lucia. "What about his fiancée?" he demanded.

"I bought my house here only shortly after they became betrothed." Vivienne was more steady now, speaking of factual matters, outside the realm of emotion. "When dear Chester died, I thought, what better place to find peace of mind in the midst of my grief than in the country of my childhood?"

"Was he really eighty?" Jack interjected.

"No!" she said hotly. "He was fifty-six when we married. And age meant nothing to me. I had found, at long last, a man, a true man in every sense of the word! Oh, you have no idea what wretches parade themselves before a—a reasonably attractive girl and make offers—not always of marriage! Many, many men spoke of love to me before Chester did. But he was the only one I believed." She sought for breath, found it, continued bravely. "We were unspeakably happy together. His death—so unexpected, so damnably *unfair*—was the end of my life, too."

Jack could not quite restrain his cynicism. "Still—a lord, Vivienne! For the daughter of a mere squire! He must have seemed the very limit!"

She pulled back from him entirely, drew herself up. "I had offers from a number of suitors with more money, greater titles, more impeccable pedigrees. Chester was the one I wanted." Her mouth curled into a dreamy smile.

"Having known me as a grubby, skin-kneed child, it is no doubt difficult for you to imagine. But in my seasons in London, I was all the vogue. The fashion was for redheads then."

"I don't mean to diminish you—" He paused. "Your accomplishment, Vivienne. But you must understand my position. I came here, at my family's behest, to settle Robert's estate. I imagined it would be a simple matter, resolved within weeks at the most. Now I find my late brother has bled Avenleigh so dry that I must stay a year, at least, just to avoid debtor's prison. And a sizeable proportion of my brother's expenditures went to *you*."

"To my very great shame," she said softly. "I was not so . . . strong as I ought to have been. But you, Jackie, of all people, must know how entirely *devoted* your brother could be to the most hapless causes, how single-minded in pursuit of his goals!"

Jack did. That was what had sent him, after all, to St. Lucia—his brother's unbridled dedication to standing alone in their father's regard as the eldest, the heir. It had been the theme of their twinned lives for as long as he could recall—and his memory went back nearly to the cradle. His brother's voice—dunning, blaming, calling for retribution for the most accidental bump or bruise, accusing him of the broken vase, the pasture gate left open—still haunted his sleep. *Jack did it! It was Jack! You know I never would!* For so long as their mother had been alive, Jack had been spared; she'd had a keen sense of fairness. But her death when the twins were eight had put an end to that.

This train of thought was leading him into resentments he had thought long past him. He shook his head to clear it, picked up the guttered cigar. *I never should have come back.* Nothing had changed. There was only Aunt Bertrice now, instead of his father, to tell him he was unworthy, a cad, not deserving of the family name.

He looked to Vivienne, who was still crying quietly into the handkerchief he had lent her. Who was to say what was truth when it came to Robert? Their own father had misjudged his son; why shouldn't a poor widow consumed with grief?

Her olive gaze slanted toward him. "You must hate me," she whispered.

"No. No, Vivienne. It is as you said. I, of all people, should understand."

"The jewels," she whispered. "I—I have them still. I'd be only too glad to give them back. Robert wouldn't let me. But you are different from Robert, aren't you?"

I hope to God I am. "Keep them," he told her gruffly. "They're a drop in the bucket compared to what he owed in gaming debts. And I am sure they suit you more than they would Aunt Bertrice or Agnes or 'Phrina anyway."

"And Miss Wilcox?"

"Who?"

"The girl he was betrothed to."

"Oh, yes. Of course. Well. I have met Miss Wilcox. And frankly, Vivienne, I cannot picture her in jewels—or in red Chinese silk unmentionables."

"Neither could Robert, I suppose," Lady Harpool said with a sigh. "I often think, of nights, that if I hadn't purchased that house, Robert would have married her and had an heir by now." She gathered her cloak around her. "But no doubt you do not regret as much as I my return to Lincolnshire. After all, you are earl now."

Jack burst out laughing. "I'd trade the earldom in two minutes for—" For what? Contemplating the pouf of her red mouth, he'd forgotten. Then he remembered. "For the chance to be at home on St. Lucia. That is where I belong." In Camille's lithe arms . . .

"No matter what you say," Vivienne Harpool declared,

"I intend to return those jewels. You can give them to your lover back on St. Lucia."

"What makes you think I have a lover?" Jack asked, startled.

She gave him that slow half-smile. "I've known you since you were five, Jackie. That's long enough to recognize when you are happy. And you are happy now—or would be, if only you were there." She unfastened the ear-drops—emeralds surrounded by pearls—that she was wearing, and pressed them into his hand. "We must see that you return to her," she said gently, wistfully, "just as soon as we can." She gathered her cloak and vanished through the door in a whirl of ermine, leaving the sweet scent of jasmine lingering in the air.

Chapter

6

Though the sun was still high in the early-summer sky, Jack could sense the dinner hour approaching and began to add up the column of figures in the estate book yet again. His stay in Lincolnshire had become a tight contest between which would come first: achieving his financial goals or losing his bloody mind. But the sum at the bottom of the page soothed his fears. Twenty thousand pounds was what Shropley had said he'd needed. He had nearly half that now, after only four months, thanks to a spring of near-perfect weather for the crops and sheep—not to mention the tidy sum he'd made trading on the 'Change in futures on wool and tobacco and rum. He allowed himself a brief, satisfied smile and lit up a cigar. Then he rang for Bellows.

"Yes, milord?" the butler, puffing, asked as he arrived.

"I trust I am not being overly precipitous, Bellows. But sometime very soon, I hope to book passage to St. Lucia."

"You'll forgive the initiative, milord, but I have had every shipping schedule sent me since the day you arrived."

Jack laughed. "Can't wait to be rid of me, can you, Bellows? Well, guess what?" He leaned forward. "I can't wait to be quit of you, too!"

"I'll bring the schedules directly," the butler murmured as he withdrew.

The cigar was half gone to ash when Agnes stuck her head through the door. "Cousin Jack! Is it true? Are you leaving us?"

"Now, how in the world would you have found that out?"

"Oh . . ." She blushed. "'Phrina overheard Bellows telling Cook you had asked for the shipping schedules, and she came to report to Mamma. She eavesdrops, 'Phrina does."

"I see. Well, Cousin Agnes, it is true. It appears I will be leaving Lincolnshire sooner than was expected. Within the next two or three months, perhaps." He nodded toward the brandy decanter. "Care to toast my departure?"

"Perhaps just a drop. . ." But then she shook her head. "No. I can't bear to. The fact is, I'll miss you horribly."

"Now, Agnes. Everything will be fine, you'll see! You'll have the house to look after, and your mother—just the same as before I came!"

"That is what I'm afraid of," she said morosely. "Oh, dear. I did hope somehow that you would make a change."

I have, Jack wanted to say. *I've saved you and your mother and sister from ruin.* But he hadn't told her, of course—hadn't told anyone how close the earldom of Avenleigh had come to disaster. He'd been *that* sure he could turn the family fortunes around. He smiled at her wan face. "You've come to mean a great deal to me, Agnes. I'm sure you recognize that."

She hardly seemed to have heard him. "Just as it was . . . God. What an awful thought. We'd thought to enjoy the pleasure of your company through the autumn, at least."

"I have pressing business in St. Lucia."

Agnes nodded knowingly. "She's stopped writing you, hasn't she? Mademoiselle Déshoulières, I mean."

Jack winced. He might have known it was futile to try to keep a secret in this household, what with 'Phrina prying and poking about. "Camille never was much of a correspondent, you know. Not really the writing sort."

"All the same, it's been over a month, hasn't it? You must be frantic with worry."

"Not at all," he protested. "Spring is her busiest time of the year."

"I beg your pardon?"

"For—ah—housecleaning," he said quickly. "And—and shopping. Having new gowns made. That sort of thing." He'd forgotten for a moment that Shropley's discretion had extended to obscuring Camille's occupation. And thank God! He could only imagine what his aunt would have made of that news.

"Lucky girl," Agnes said a little tartly. "Perhaps I will have a drink."

"If you hate it here so much," Jack asked, bringing her a snifter, "why do you stay?"

"Where else would I go?" she retorted. "I'm not a man. I haven't the freedom you have, to go where you want and do as you please. I never got a husband. That's what it comes down to, isn't it? I am a failure, a pathetic old spinster."

"Oh, Agnes." Jack wished to hell he hadn't posed the question. "You mustn't think that! You're quick and witty, sensitive—"

"And see where it has got me?" There was a terrible undercurrent of fury in her voice. Then she got hold of her wayward emotions. "I beg your pardon, Cousin Jack. It is, of course, none of your concern what becomes of me. I thank you for the brandy." She set the glass down and fled, her shoulders quivering in their cocoon of mourning black.

Jack sank back into his chair and relit the cigar. It isn't as if *I've* been free, he mused. I've been stuck here in this wretched hellhole for months! But he knew, even as he thought it, that Agnes's lot was far more miserable than his. *God. It must be dreadful to be female.* He sat alone in the study for a long time, wondering how he might ease her sadness, what he could do to make amends. Then a sudden notion struck him, and he rang for Bellows again.

"I have them right here, milord," the butler said reproachfully, thrusting the shipping schedules at him. "I was coming along as fast as I could. I am no longer young, you know."

No. No one in this house was. Except, perhaps, for Agnes, deep in her heart—and 'Phrina. God, who knew what fantasies 'Phrina entertained? "I meant no rebuke," Jack told him mildly. "Another thought overtook me. How long has it been since Avenleigh last hosted a ball?"

"A *ball*, milord?" Jack might have said a boxing bout from the butler's expression. "Really, I could not tell you. Some number of years, though. Before your father's passing."

"Well. It seems time, then—past time—that we hosted another."

"A ball, milord." The poor fellow could not seem to take it in. "You mean—with music? Dancing? I doubt Mrs. Gravesend would approve. She *is* still in mourning for your brother."

"I should say we have all mourned enough for Robert." Jack puffed on his cigar, feeling expansive. How much could a countrified ball set back his departure? And it would please Agnes and Sephrina; he was certain of that. "I want a ball, Bellows. A good, big one. All the countryside invited. Have my cousin Agnes choose the date and make out a guest list." There—that should give her something to occupy her time. Who knows? Perhaps she'd find a beau.

Perhaps 'Phrina would, too. Then he could head off to Castries with his conscience completely clear.

The butler was wagging his head. "Mrs. Gravesend will not be at *all* pleased."

Jack couldn't help himself; his devil-grin slipped into place. "No. She won't be, will she?"

*M*rs. Gravesend was not the only one appalled at Jack's proposal. When he mentioned it to Bennett Shropley on his next visit, the solicitor paled, clearly fearing his new client was meandering down the same primrose path his brother had. "I hardly think, milord, that with the current state of your affairs—"

"Look and see the current state of my affairs," Jack invited, pushing his account book across the desk.

The solicitor examined the most recent pages, paused, and read them over again. Then his face relaxed; he gave a relieved sigh. "Astonishing, milord! Such a complete turnabout in the estate's fortunes! And in so brief a time!"

"It was just as you told me," Jack said modestly. "The trouble never was income—only outgo. Merely a matter of enforcing a few economies."

"That, and playing the 'Change like a veritable devil," Shropley noted with envy. "Why, at this rate, you will be free and clear to return to St. Lucia long before the year's out!"

"My thoughts precisely. And since that's so, I cannot see the harm in putting on a bit of a ball. Surely it cannot set me back more than a few hundred pounds."

"I believe it could be done for that," Shropley allowed. "Nonetheless, I cannot quite see the point in it."

"Have you no sense of fun, Shropley?"

"I've been to any number of Lincolnshire balls, milord. And they are not much fun."

"Mine will be," Jack promised blithely. "Besides, I've hopes this will soften the blow for my cousin Agnes of my leaving. She . . . is not eager to see me depart."

"None of us are," said Shropley. "It has been a distinct pleasure serving you, if you'll pardon my saying so."

"Why, Shropley, you sentimental thing!" The solicitor blushed, and Jack grinned. "But I have every intention that you should go on serving me just as efficiently as you have during my stay here. I thought perhaps you might agree to continue to handle the family's affairs on this end. For a retainer, of course. Shall we say—two hundred pounds a month?"

Shropley gaped. "That is most—*generous*, milord. I would be honored to."

"Splendid. I like to know I am leaving my aunt and cousins in capable hands. In the meantime, let's get to work on that ball."

"Very good, milord." The solicitor took out his notebook, thumbed his quill, then glanced up. "Milord. Might I presume to ask a question that has been troubling me since the day we met?"

"Ask away, by all means!"

"I understood from your brother . . . that is, I was *given* to understand . . . that you were originally sent to St. Lucia on account of a certain . . . unpleasantness at university." The poor fellow was coloring furiously.

Jack took pity on him. "Robert told you I'd cheated on an examination, Mr. Shropley, I presume, and had been caught."

"Quite. That's it precisely. But what I cannot understand—" The solicitor ran a finger under his collar. "Having worked with you both, I mean—your late brother and you—frankly, it's difficult to comprehend why a man of your talents would resort to cheating."

Jack laughed. He truly was in a generous mood. "It

wasn't I who cheated, Shropley. It was Robert. Only he claimed to be me."

Shropley's furrowed brow cleared. "Of course! That would explain it!" Then he blinked. "But no. It wouldn't. How could you possibly allow him to put forth such a falsehood?"

"I didn't. I told the truth to everyone—including our father."

"Ah!" The poor solicitor appeared more perplexed than ever. "But then—why—"

"Was I sent to St. Lucia? Father did not believe me. Robert was his favorite, you see."

"That's terrible!" Shropley burst out.

Jack shrugged, doing his best to keep the bitterness from his voice. "It was the best thing that could have happened to me. I am far happier in Castries than I ever would have been here."

Shropley sat pondering this. "I understand what you mean, I think. The opportunity to carve a place for yourself, away from your brother, when he was so envious of you—"

"Robert? Envious of *me*?" That was a novel notion.

"But he must have been, milord! Why else would he have tried to blame you? Not to mention that whenever I remonstrated with him to curb his spending, remain within the limits of his income, he would remark how he wished it had been *he* who'd been sent abroad in disgrace."

"Imagine that." Jack had never before thought of his brother chafing under the weight of being Avenleigh's heir. He had a brief, fleeting moment of revelation: Perhaps his father hadn't been so sure Jack had cheated. Perhaps, in his disappointment with his firstborn, he'd simply taken the opportunity to put space, a great deal of space, between his sons, see if Robert might be brought up to snuff when Jack wasn't about.

Then he shook off the insight. He wasn't about to discard a decade's worth of resentment just because Robert had once or twice, according to Shropley, expressed jealousy of him. Of *course* Robert would think it easier to run the plantations and the shipping business than the estate here in England. Robert always thought *anything* Jack put his hand to was easier.

Because it was, he realized. *Because I always was more able than he.*

"It isn't any of my concern, of course," Shropley said softly. "And I did not know your father, except by reputation. But according to *on-dit*, he was a formidable man of business. The estate's interests in St. Lucia posed a far greater challenge ten years past than those in England, what with the tangle of war, embargoes, taxes and levies and duties. It hardly seems the atmosphere into which a canny sort would inject a ne'er-do-well son." He paused. "And you know, he had the reports you sent him. So did Robert. They could not help but be aware of how well you had done."

Jack thought of those annual reports, the furious resentment with which he'd signed them and, more, the desperate longing that his father, seeing the ever-spiraling profits, might call him back, revoke his exile, smile at him one time, one time only, and say, "I am proud of you." It never had happened, of course. Distance and death had prevented it. Still, Shropley's words had inspired in him a new, faint hope. *They could not help but be aware . . .*

It was like turning the world upside-down to imagine his father might have sent him away not out of shame at his behavior, but because of confidence in him.

"Well," he said, and cleared his throat; there was something caught in it, hard and tight like a bone, that could not be swallowed. "It is all ancient history. I'll thank you to keep quiet about what I've told you, though. And

now, about that ball. I thought, to start—" Across the
room, one of the windows, open to catch the spring air,
abruptly dropped in its sash, shattering two panes.

"A bit of redding up," Shropley murmured, "of the
ancestral mansion?"

"Quite so. Suppose you consult with the housekeeper
and Bellows, and we'll do what we can to keep the place
from caving in once the music begins."

That night, while he undressed in his rooms, Jack paused,
shirt half off, as his hand touched the love token against his
chest. *Camille* . . . A surge of longing overtook him. As if in
a trance he moved to his bedside table, took out the packet
of Camille's correspondence, read over each letter. Why
had she not written in so long a time?

He wrenched his mind from a clear image of her
clasped in Antoine's brawny arms, lying across her—across
their—white bed. This ball was a terrible mistake. Even
two hundred pounds might mean another week's delay.
Another week of temptation for her, another week of fac-
ing life without him. It was her nature, was it not, to turn
to men in times of trial? It was why she'd taken up with
him. . . .

But the love charm in his fist reassured him. It had
kept him safe so far; hadn't he resisted even Vivienne Harpool's powerful allure? He remembered then, somewhat
guiltily, that he hadn't even seen her since her dinner here;
his aunt had told him she'd gone off to London. And there
had not been much other temptation at hand—nor was
there likely to be.

Still, he could not shake off his sense that Camille
would disapprove of this ball. *It is only a few hundred
pounds*, he argued silently. *You spend that in a fortnight on
gowns. With all that you have—all that* we *have together—*

is it wrong for me to want to give poor Agnes and 'Phrina a spot of pleasure?

The token in his hand was smooth and cold as stone.

He let it slip from his fingers, picked up his brandy glass, took a long, steadying sip. It was his money, dammit. He could do with it as he pleased. She'd wanted an earl? Well, an earl had certain obligations—obligations a carefree, ne'er-do-well younger son didn't. "In for a penny, in for a pound," he whispered. "You *could* have come with me. I asked you to."

He paged through to the last letter she had sent him, read its closing yet again:

> *If you mean this year of absence as punishment to me for urging you to return, know that I am punished each night as I lie in my lonely bed. Now I must go. Esmé reports two sailors—English, naturally—are brawling in the gaming rooms. I shall banish them from the Hôtel forever. Or perhaps just for a month. Esmé says they are very big spenders.*
> *Toujours,*
> *Camille*

Her lonely bed. Well, it would not be lonely much longer. He smiled in anticipation, remembering the homecoming she had promised him. No doubt a letter would arrive from her tomorrow, or the next day.

*P*riscilla Wilcox, on her way out the door with her spade and pail, glanced briefly at the thin sheaf of mail atop the table in the foyer. Her father's usual temperance movement pamphlets in their brown wrappers, an issue of *Christian Ways and Mores*, something from the archbishop of Canterbury—she recognized his secretary's cramped hand—and a large envelope of very fine vellum, addressed to the bishop, but with her own name beneath. Curious, she reached for it, turned it over, saw the Avenleigh seal, and caught her breath. Quickly she ripped it open, then stared in mingled disbelief and dismay at the card within.

His Grace, the Earl of Avenleigh, requests the honor of your presence . . . Pris quickly shut her eyes, kept them shut a long moment, then opened them again. The words were still there. A *ball*. A Midsummer's Eve ball, to be held at Avenleigh on the twenty-third of June.

"Priscilla?" She started at her father's voice from the staircase, clutching the vellum to her chest. He descended slowly, his face stern with disapproval. "Just where do you think you are going at this hour? You haven't even breakfasted, I'll wager."

"The honeysuckle are out, Father. I'd hoped to catch an *Orneodes hexadactylus* before the heat drives them off."

"What's that you've got in your hand?"

"My basket, of course."

"Your *other* hand."

"Oh! Oh, this!" Quickly she held the invitation out to him. "It came from Avenleigh."

He scanned it briefly, then scowled. "A ball, eh? Seems a bit precipitous. But what else could one expect from such a renegade? 'Twill be a drunken debauchery, I'll wager. His aunt tells me he imbibes, you know." The scowl relaxed into a frown of resignation. "Still, we don't dare risk offending His Lordship, do we? Not with the Minster in such dire need of repair."

The Minster—the noble Cathedral of the Blessed Virgin Mary, also known as Lincoln Cathedral—was the apple of her father's eye; he adored every timber of the soaring vault, each stone of its spires. His appointment to the bishopric seven years past had been the culmination of a life-long ambition; to become guardian of its massive glory was all he'd ever longed for. And any threat to its extraordinarily expensive upkeep was a menace he took personally. He showed that now, in his worried expression.

"Do you mean," Pris said in disbelief, "we shall attend?"

"*I* shall. I have no choice. You, however, can plead any excuse you like."

Pris glanced down at her boots. "If you think that is wise, Father, of course I will."

He arched a silver brow. "Have you any reason to think it unwise?"

"No *particular* reason. Only what you said, about the

Minster. The earls of Avenleigh have always been its most generous supporters—except, of course, for you."

His brows knitted. "You think he might perceive it as an insult, Priscilla, for you not to attend?"

"I've no idea what sorts of perceptions a man such as he might have. But I *was* betrothed to his brother."

The bishop sighed again. "So you were. Still, I cannot bear the thought of you exposed to what is certain to be an iniquitous bacchanal."

"Oh, Father." Pris swallowed a giggle. "Surely Mrs. Gravesend would not allow any indecent behavior beneath her own roof."

"It is *his* roof now—and according to her, he has made that quite clear. He smokes *cigars* in the dining room." From his tone, the new earl might have been beheading babies. "But all that aside, Priscilla, I wonder if it might prove too much for you. To revisit that house, which was to have been your own . . . to confront all your memories . . ."

All her memories. Yes. There was that. "I should think I owe it to Robert," she said very quietly, "to make an appearance."

The bishop looked down at her, and his harsh expression softened minutely. "I suppose you do. You *might* serve to remind that heedless cad of what family responsibility means. Very well. I shall send an acceptance for us both. Though I expect you to remember your position. No dancing, young lady! And if I see you sipping so much as a cup of punch, I will have your hide!"

"Yes, Father. May I go now?"

"Go?" he echoed vaguely, paging through the newly arrived temperance pamphlets.

"The *Orneodes hexadactylus* . . ."

"If you must. But I *do* wish you'd give as much thought to catching a husband as you do to those butterflies."

"This one's a moth," she corrected him. He did not

even hear her, he was slitting open a pamphlet. She hesitated, shrugged, and then went out the door.

His mood sanguine again the following morning, Jack set out for a lengthy hike across the estate, intending to take notes for Shropley on what needed repair among the outbuildings and tenants' cottages. The day was fine, uncharacteristically sunny, with wisps of clouds overhead in a sky that palely echoed St. Lucia's brilliant blue.

Toward noon, he found himself near the village. He'd brought along bread and cheese, but the sun had made him thirsty, and he went into the Two Cats for a pint of ale. The barkeep's wife came out and made a great fuss over him, plying him with boiled eggs and pickles and ham, and it was more than an hour before he broke free to resume his walk. He followed the small road over toward the turnpike, to see how the gravel was holding up there.

He'd just reached the gate when he heard hooves pounding in the distance. The tollkeeper's son came sprinting to take the fare. Jack waited, watching the handsome closed coach that was thundering toward him. The horses were in a froth; they had been driven hard. The driver pulled up so abruptly that Jack winced, feeling the bite of iron in the neat bays' gums. "How much?" the fellow demanded carelessly of the boy.

"Ha'pence, sir."

The driver flipped a coin into the dirt; the boy scooped it up and rushed to lift the bar. Jack, scanning the window of the coach, caught a glimpse of a cascade of bright auburn curls. "Give back the money, lad," he told the gatekeeper's son. "This passage is on me." Then he raised his hat to Vivienne Harpool, who banged at the driver's box for him to wait. Jack opened the coach door and caught a whiff of jasmine on the Lincolnshire air.

"Lord Avenleigh! What a delightful surprise!" Lady Harpool said, olive eyes sparkling.

"My sentiments precisely. Returning home from London?"

"Indeed I am."

"And how did you find the *ton*?"

"Much of a muchness. How very bucolic you appear, trudging through the wayside."

"One could not say the same for you. You are the very spirit of civilization, and a sight for sore eyes." He took in the extremely fetching chip hat, trimmed with orange blossoms, that she had tilted over her curls. "Do you know, I've been meaning for the longest time to ask you the name of your milliner."

She dimpled prettily. "Why, Jackie! What a compliment!" Then abruptly her smile dimmed. "But you must already know it. From . . ."

"If I ever did," he said gallantly, "from whatever source, it is long forgotten. Refresh my memory."

"Well, when in Brighton, I generally use Mrs. Glenstone. And in London, of course, Madame Farrell. She is all the rage."

He jotted both names in his notebook. She watched, her head cocked to one side. "Which made that *petit chapeau* you have on now?"

"What, this?" She put a hand on it. "Neither. This is the work of M'amselle Chandaille. A genius. But I do not think your aunt would approve of her."

"And why is that?"

Vivienne dropped her airy voice to a conspiratorial whisper. "M'amselle's clientele includes *actresses*."

While their laughter faded, she looked at him as he stood leaning against the turnstile, in his leather breeches and tweed coat and white shirt open at the throat against the midday heat. "Jackie," she said suddenly, softly. "I never did return to you those . . . those items that we spoke of once."

"I told you to keep them."

"Yes. I know. But they have been preying on my conscience. After all, you have so much to do, haven't you, to repair Robert's damage to the estate? I must give them back."

"Do you know what you might do instead? Wear them for me. At my ball."

Her eyes lit up. "Are you giving a ball?"

"I most certainly am. On Midsummer's Eve."

"What a delightful notion! They say, you know, all sorts of mischievous spirits are about that night."

"More like the demons of hell, if one might judge from my aunt's reaction to the proposal."

Her breathy laughter rang out again. "Poor Mrs. Gravesend. But a ball is such an extravagance! From what you told me when last we spoke, I must confess I am surprised."

"I had a rather good spring," Jack said modestly.

"Did you? I'm so pleased to hear that. But tell me, speaking of spirits—do you propose to serve them?"

"Champagne," he told her in a whisper. "Do you imagine the stones themselves will fall in on my head?"

"I don't much care if they do. I *adore* champagne! Oh, what fun we'll have, Jackie! Just like the old days!"

"Only if you intend to challenge me to a wrestling match."

For a moment, he feared he'd been too forward. But then her bright eyes glinted beneath the chip hat. "I'm still quite good at it, you know."

"Still, I don't think you'd best me."

"We'll find out, shall we, on Midsummer's Eve?" She settled back against the cushions, smiling entrancingly. The carriage shot forward. Jack stood and watched until it drove out of sight.

"Pretty lady, that 'un," said the boy, sliding the bar back into place. "What about that ha'pence, eh?" Jack dug into his pocket, found a shilling, and handed it over. "Oy, sir. I can't make change o' that."

"Keep it," Jack said, and set off back to Avenleigh House, whistling to himself.

$\mathcal{J}$ack stood in his stiff dinner jacket—it was Robert's dinner jacket, actually, borrowed from his wardrobe for the occasion—and surveyed the ballroom with satisfaction. The improvements he and Shropley had effected at the ancestral mansion so far were largely cosmetic, but the difference was surprising. The newly scraped and waxed parquet floor gleamed, and the candles in the chandelier and sconces lent a soft, warm glow to the freshly white-washed walls. The orchestra Agnes had engaged was busy setting up under her watchful eye. He progressed to the dining room, with a tug at his cravat.

'Phrina was at work here, busily directing the laying of the dinner table, ordering the servants about with delightful hauteur. Jack hid a grin as she scolded Bellows for the placement of the name cards. The chimes in the tall clock pealed out six times, and Jack cleared his throat, taking pity on the overburdened butler. "Cousin 'Phrina," he observed, coming forward, "isn't it time you dressed?"

She turned to him, her self-composure wilting. "But I *am* dressed, Cousin Jack."

"In black? For a ball?"

"Mamma says we all must still wear mourning."

"Oh, for heaven's sake!" Then he softened, seeing her crestfallen expression. "It doesn't matter, 'Phrina. Not in the least. You look lovely."

"Do you think so?" She brightened slightly, preening at her hair. "Aggie did my curls and I did hers. I declare, it was just like the old days! I haven't been so excited in— well, I don't know when!"

It was by far the longest coherent speech he'd ever heard her make, and he was suddenly extremely proud of himself for this gesture. Let Camille scold; he owed this to his cousins. "Where is your mother?" he asked gently.

"I couldn't say for certain." But just then they heard her shrill voice from the kitchens. "Oh, dear," 'Phrina murmured, anxiously fluttering her lashes at Jack.

"I'll see to it," he told her, and hurried toward the fuss.

Aunt Bertrice was standing over the cowed cook at the stove. "What seems to be the trouble, Aunt?" Jack inquired.

"The trouble? The *trouble*, Jack Cantrell, is that you seem intent on poisoning us all!"

"You *told* me sherry in the turtle soup, m'lord!" Cook protested faintly.

"So I did."

"Hmph! Work of the devil," declared Aunt Bertrice, and raised another pot lid. "Just what exactly are *these*?"

"Oysters, I believe," Jack responded, bending down to sniff. "Don't they smell delicious! But they're done enough, for Christ's sake. Take them off the fire."

Cook obliged hurriedly. Aunt Bertrice wagged her head. "You may not be aware, Jack, that I cannot tolerate shellfish of any sort."

"Really? I adore shellfish." He scooped out an oyster with his fingers, blew on it, and swallowed it cheerfully.

His aunt's black eyes were glittering. "I don't know what you think you're up to, Jack Cantrell, with your champagne and oysters. Trying to corrupt my girls—"

Agnes, unfortunately, chose that moment to stroll in with a wine flute in her hand. She considered hiding the glass, then decided to present it to Jack instead.

"I only wanted to be certain, Cousin Jack, this met with your approval."

"How very thoughtful, Agnes." He drained the champagne down. "Perfect! A splendid vintage!"

"Hellfire and damnation—that's what's in store for you," Aunt Bertrice muttered darkly. "So help me, Agnes, 'Phrina, if I catch you drinking—" The door knocker sounded, shocking all the women into silence.

"Well!" Jack said heartily—then burped. Aunt Bertrice scowled at him. "Time for the festivities to begin!"

He hadn't expected to enjoy himself, of course—this ball was meant for Agnes and 'Phrina. And his expectations were, alas, fully satisfied. He endured the endless prattling conversation of numerous elderly women, did his best to discuss hounds and horses with their consorts and heirs, danced with a dozen or so simpering misses, and drank as much champagne as was needed to maintain his equanimity.

Bennett Shropley was present, nervous and ill at ease in his formal clothes. Jack hailed him gladly, thinking it a pity the solicitor wasn't old enough to suit either of his cousins as matrimonial material. Of course, Aunt Bertrice never would have allowed any daughter of hers to wed a lowly public servant.

Shropley returned his wave, then made his way through the crowd of chattering ladies to Jack's side. "This may not be the time or place, milord, but I've had troubling news from London."

"Really? And what might that be?" Jack pressed a glass of champagne on him; dammit, the fellow needed loosening up!

"The Crown's agents have set a date for the tax hearing." Shropley dabbed sweat from his brow with his handkerchief. "The twenty-fifth of July."

"And why is that so troubling?"

"Well—you haven't got the money that you owe them, have you, milord?"

"No," Jack acknowledged cheerfully. "But much can happen in a month. Don't fret so, Shropley! You're like a little old maid. I'll go along with you to London if you like, to hold your hand. Here, have a stuffed clam."

"Might as well," the solicitor said glumly. "Not likely to see such fancy stuff in prison."

Jack laughed out loud. "Do try to enjoy yourself, Shropley. Why don't you ask a pretty chit to dance?"

"I would, milord, were there one here."

Jack had to admit, the company was not exactly scintillating. What was it about Lincolnshire, he wondered, that made its women so all-fired dull? "Well, ask a homely one, then," he suggested, having just noticed Bishop Wilcox and his daughter sitting in a corner. He crossed the room, bowed, and gallantly offered his arm to his brother's former fiancée. But before she could even speak, her father cleared his throat. "Miss Wilcox regretfully declines your invitation, milord. I don't hold with dancing. While I have you here, though, perhaps we might discuss the Minster? As you have no doubt noticed in your *occasional* attendances at service, several portions of the building stand in dire need of repair."

"Father," Priscilla Wilcox murmured, shifting in embarrassment. Jack glanced down at her. She was wearing black, too, and the color did not suit her. While he looked at her, the music ended, and the sudden silence gave way to an intense buzz of comment. Glancing over his shoulder, Jack saw the reason for it. Vivienne Harpool had come into the room.

She sported a gown of teal blue, fitted very low and tight across her handsome bosom; its dropped sleeves left her white shoulders bare. Jack could smell her perfume even at that distance, a sweet haze of jasmine that permeated the air. Diamonds glittered at her throat and ears; her shining auburn hair was caught up in a silken net. Jack had taken three steps toward her before realizing he'd never answered the bishop. "I should be glad, of course, to contribute what I can to the cathedral's maintenance. Suppose you speak to my agent. His name is—" Vivienne's bright eyes met his; he forgot for a moment what he was saying. "Shropley!" he finished abruptly, pleased with himself for remembering. "Bennett Shropley!" He scanned the crowd for the solicitor, waved him over. "Mr. Shropley! You know Bishop Wilcox, of course, and his daughter, Miss Wilcox. The bishop has some proposal to make regarding the Minster."

"Miss Wilcox. Reverend Sir. A pleasure to see you." Shropley bowed, but his gaze was anxiously on Jack, who was still staring across the room at Vivienne Harpool. "It's been on my mind, milord, to speak to you regarding the cathedral. As you must know, the house of Avenleigh has always been a devoted supporter of—"

"Yes, yes," Jack said impatiently, waving a hand. "Work it out between you. If you'll excuse me now, I see a new guest has arrived." And he made his way toward Lady Harpool, who was poised beside a potted palm, unfurling a dainty fan.

"Jackie," she said, smiling as he approached her.

"Vivienne. Welcome to Avenleigh."

She gazed about curiously. "I must say, you've done

wonders with the place. You *must* have had a good spring! Did you not tell me the estate's affairs were rather in chaos?"

"A gross exaggeration," he assured her. "Or, rather, nothing that a bit of concentrated effort could not fix." He handed her champagne. "Would you care to dance?"

Three quarters of an hour later, heated and excited, he swiped a bottle and two glasses from the sideboard and invited her to walk in the gardens. She hesitated. "People will talk. . . ."

"Let them," he said brusquely. "Do you really care?"

"Not a whit," she admitted with a charming smile, and let him lead her through the doors onto the verandah. The fresh, soft night air might almost have been Castries. She leaned against the balustrade, dainty tendrils of auburn hair clinging to her throat. He poured them both champagne, then stood beside her, staring down at her.

"Cheers," she said, her eyes nearly golden in the moonlight.

"Cheers." He took a long, deep swallow.

"What is it like," she asked quietly, "in that place you come from?"

"St. Lucia? I don't know where to begin. The sea. The mountains. The sunsets—Christ, the sunsets! They seem to linger forever at this time of year."

"You don't miss Lincolnshire, then? Or the *ton*?"

"God, no! Not for a minute! I'd have been happy never to set foot in England again."

She stirred her drink with the tip of one long, slim finger. "Most folk were surprised you came back. Considering, I mean, how angry you were to be sent there."

"I've been thinking on that, you know. Wondering if Father . . . might have known what he was doing after all."

"Of course he did. He knew Robert."

"What do you mean?"

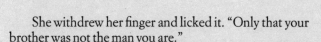

She withdrew her finger and licked it. "Only that your brother was not the man you are."

Jack smiled. "You don't think so?"

Vivienne Harpool shrugged her white shoulders. "He had no head for business, poor soul. He had no head for anything. And he knew it. That was why he hated you."

"Did he hate me, Vivienne?"

"Lord, yes. He couldn't bear to hear your name. When it turned out you were doing so well there in . . . in . . ."

"St. Lucia."

"Yes. He was furious! Said how your father used to taunt him with your success."

"Did he really," Jack murmured, intrigued.

She took a sip of her drink. "But all that's in the past now, isn't it? Tell me, Jackie. What lies ahead for you?"

"I hope to return home within a few months."

She smiled, gazing into her glass. "And so you need the name of my milliner. What's she like, Jackie?"

"Who? Camille? Oh, she is . . ." About to ramble on, he caught himself. "Everything I want in a woman."

"She is to be envied, then." She shifted in a rustle of satin. "Is there any more in that bottle?" He refilled their glasses. "This is excellent champagne," she noted. "But do you know what I would really enjoy? A cool rum fizz."

He laughed. "Do you know how to make a rum fizz?"

"Of course. Doesn't everyone?"

"Not Bellows." He stared up into the night sky. "Camille's maid—Esmé—makes a fine rum fizz."

Vivienne reached up to unbuckle her diamond neckpiece, dropped it into her reticule, then held it out to him. "There you go. It's all in there, Jackie. The jewels he gave me."

"I don't want them. I told you that before."

"But *she* may. You said yourself—ten thousand pounds. It makes me feel so guilty. Soiled."

"Vivienne." Her eyes were downcast; the moonlight sparked against her red-brown hair. "There's no cause for you to feel that way."

"I know." She drew her chin up. "It is the oddest thing, though. I think I would feel better if I had . . . given in to him."

"You mustn't say that. And you must not be sad. You're so young yet, Vivienne. You'll find another true love. I am sure of it."

"I wish I were," she whispered breathlessly.

Behind her back, he saw the draperies part, and 'Phrina, with her eyes wide, staring at them. "Christ," he muttered.

Vivienne peeked over her shoulder, then smiled up at him, edging closer in mock protection. "Poor Jackie, I shall shield you from her, shall I? No wonder you are in such a rush to be off to St. Lucia."

"I begin to think I might be persuaded to stay longer," he said, and tried to take her into his arms.

She yanked free, eyes flashing. "How *dare* you? Are you no different from your brother, seeking to take advantage of a poor widow's misery?"

"For God's sake! We're neither of us children, Vivienne."

"And that gives you the right to—to paw me like some drunken sailor?"

"All I meant by it—"

"I know perfectly well what you meant! You want what all the others want. And to think I dreamed you might be an honorable man." She straightened her slim shoulders, rearranged her mussed gown. "Just because I have been married doesn't mean I have lax morals. I never gave in to Robert, and by God, I'll not give in to you!"

From the garden below, Jack heard a soft scuffling sound—a squirrel, or a fox after a rabbit. He sighed, pushing back his hair with his hands. "Dammit all, Vivienne, when a woman looks and acts the way you do—"

"Oh! So it is *my* fault that you cannot keep rein on your lust?"

"Well, you make it difficult," he said frankly.

"Let me tell you this, Jack Cantrell. I came to Chester a virgin. I was faithful to him. And I intend to remain faithful to his memory. If, by God's grace, I should encounter another man as honorable and kind and good as he was, and if that man asks to marry me, and not merely for a—a tumble in the hay . . ." She raised her chin proudly. "Then I might consider him worthy of the gift of my love."

There was that flurrying again in the gardens. "I'm sorry," Jack said again, cravenly. How could he have been so mistaken as to what she meant with her alluring glances, her flattering words? *I've been too long without it,* he thought, his manhood stiff as a flag.

She gathered in her reticule. "I'd best be going."

"Please, don't leave. I can assure you, I won't repeat my mistake."

"That was what Robert promised, too. Good night, Jackie." She whirled for the doors, the filmy skirts billowing around her. Jack sighed and poured the last of the champagne into his glass.

Cris was just about to make a move with her hairnet when a thick bellow of cigar smoke sent her quarry spinning beyond her reach. "Damn!" she said bad-temperedly, straightening up from the midst of a clump of phlox nearly as tall as she was.

Lord Avenleigh, who had just lit up, leaned on the stone rail, staring down at her in surprise. "Miss Wilcox? Whatever are you doing there?"

"I nearly had my hands on a whole flock of *Adela*

degeerella." She gestured at the tiny winged creatures hovering above them. "But your cigar has chased them away."

He gazed at her with bemused rebuke. "Here I spend hundreds of pounds on food and drink and entertainment, and you have nothing better to do this Midsummer's Eve than poke around in my shrubberies?"

She brushed back her hair, which had come loose since she'd appropriated the net. "Not particularly. I ate all the oysters I could hold, and Father has forbidden me to drink or dance." She paused. "What are you staring at?"

"You," he admitted. "You are not all teary."

"It's a *cyclical* catarrah," she said impatiently. "It only troubles me in the winter and spring. Oh, dammit all to hell!" Brambles had seized hold of her skirts, and she tugged to free them.

"You've a pert mouth on you for a bishop's daughter, haven't you? Just wait. I'll come and help."

"There really isn't any . . . need," Pris finished weakly. But he'd already vaulted over the balcony railing and dropped to the ground. "Really, I am quite capable—no, don't do that!" He'd curled his fists around the offending branches.

"Ouch!" He jerked away at a sudden sharp stinging. "What the devil is that stuff?"

"Seven-minute-itch." He blinked at her. "Well, that's what they call it. It's actually a form of milkweed. *Adela* are very fond of it. Don't worry. The sting goes away."

"Do you often encounter these sorts of occupational hazards?" he demanded, blowing on his hands.

"It adds to the excitement," Pris said dryly.

He laughed, and looked at her more closely. "What exactly is it, Miss Wilcox, that you love about butterflies?"

She returned his gaze, taken aback. "Do you know, in all the time we were betrothed, your brother never once posed me that question."

"If he had, what would you have told him?"

Pris hesitated, pondering how honest to be. But she had nothing to gain by dissembling with this man. "I suppose it is because they start out ugly."

"I beg your pardon?"

"Butterflies. They start out ugly and then turn into something beautiful. It's an option that isn't available to humans, is it?"

He looked embarrassed. "For heaven's sake, Miss Wilcox. You certainly aren't ugly."

"No. I am plain," she said frankly. "Just . . . plain. Your Cousin Agnes told me that there is a—a woman you write to, back in St. Lucia. She is very beautiful, I suppose?"

"That's rather a forward question."

"One of the few benefits of being homely," Pris noted, "is that folk aren't wont to be offended when one is forward. Indeed, at times I feel it is expected of me." He snorted. "So, what does she look like?"

"Camille? She has green eyes and curly black hair. And skin—" Lord Avenleigh stopped abruptly.

"Pale as lilies, I suppose." Pris sighed. "I freckle at the least hint of sun."

"What difference do you think it would have made in your life if you'd been beautiful?"

She glanced at him sidelong, but there was no scorn or pity on his face, simply curiosity "I'd be married by now, I suppose. And have children. I have always wanted children." Her small chin came up, and she gazed at him defiantly. "But you can make a sort of child of your work, I've found."

"Mm. I suppose. God knows I never wanted 'em myself."

"Does she—Camille—know that?" Pris asked, surprised.

"Of course. I've made no secret of it. She is of the same

mind. Did my brother want children?" he asked then, unexpectedly.

Pris flushed in the moonlight. "We never . . . discussed it."

He still had the cigar in his fingers, but it had gone out. He reached for a match, hesitated. "Do you mind if I light up again?"

"Oh, no. You've already chased them all away."

"My apologies. Miss Wilcox. Since you have been so forward, forgive me doing the same. Why did you become betrothed to Robert?"

"He asked for my hand. No one else had."

"Gracious, you are blunt. Did you . . . love him?"

"No fair," Pris noted. "You aren't homely. You don't get to be forward twice."

He sucked on the cigar to ignite it. "I only ask, you know, because you don't seem his type."

Pris's hackles rose. "Because I am so plain? Or because I'm the mere daughter of a bishop?"

"Because you seem far too intelligent for the likes of him."

"Oh, I am intelligent," she agreed. "Unfortunately, that's not a commodity much valued in the marriage mart."

"Even so, I should think you might have done better than Robert."

Suspicious, she searched that handsome face. But his expression, she could have sworn, was honestly perplexed. "Well," she began slowly, "he could be very charming. I wasn't used to charming. And then there was the fact all the local girls were wild over him. When you have lived your life as a—a cipher—"

"A cipher, Miss Wilcox?"

Pris nodded. "Someone who is never noticed. It's extremely annoying. But, do you know, once he'd asked me to marry him, suddenly everyone paid attention to me. A most extraordinary thing."

"You did not mind, then, that it was such a lengthy betrothal?"

Pris busied herself with her hairnet. "It did not seem long."

"Did you have a date set for your wedding?"

"No," she admitted faintly. "I . . . saw no reason to press him."

He blew out a smoke ring, watched it rise to the heavens. "You are welcome, Miss Wilcox, to tell me to mind my own bloody business if you like. But I don't believe you *wanted* to marry him."

"How can you say that?" she countered. "Why, he was Earl of Avenleigh!"

He looked back down at her. "No doubt that influenced your father. I don't think it mattered much to you."

How would the likes of *you* ever know what matters to me? Pris longed to demand. She hadn't missed his little wrestling bout with Lady Harpool on the verandah; she'd been there long before they arrived, driven from the ballroom by the unexpectedly intense discomfort of watching them dance. And her reward had been to serve as unwilling witness while he tried to kiss the sparkling widow. . . . To her chagrin, she felt the sting of tears at her eyelids, sharper than seven-minute-itch.

"Miss Wilcox?" He'd tossed away the cigar and reached his hand toward her face, to touch her cheek. He smelled of leather and smoke, impossibly alluring. "I have made you unhappy, haven't I? Forgive me. If you were satisfied with Robert, it is none of my affair."

If I was satisfied with Robert . . . For a moment she wondered just how blunt homely women could afford to be with extraordinarily handsome men.

"Priscilla?" Her father's voice boomed from the balcony above them. "Priscilla! Are you out here?"

She sniffled, tying up her hair hastily, awkwardly. "Yes, Father!"

He peered down into the shadows. "Who is that with you?"

"Lord Avenleigh, sir," her companion answered.

Pris saw her father's jaw tighten. "I think, Priscilla, it is time we were gone."

"Yes, Father. I was just coming along." She started toward the stairs. "Thank you, Lord Avenleigh, for a most . . . enjoyable evening."

"Sorry about those butterflies," he called after her.

"They were moths," she said sadly as her father tugged her away.

Chapter

9

Pris did her best, over the next week, to drive from her mind the memory of his fingertips caressing her cheek, the scent of his skin, the way his eyes had shone in the moonlight. But she might as well have been trying not to have her heart beat. *You little fool,* she told herself over and over again. One earl of Avenleigh had already made an idiot of her. She would *not*, she swore, let the next do the same.

Still, it was very hard not to daydream about that interlude in the gardens. Brief and offhand though it had been, she'd felt closer to Jack Cantrell in those few moments than she had to Robert in all the years of their betrothal. *Just because they look so much alike,* she thought wistfully, *doesn't mean they are the same at heart.* But then she would recall the way he'd tried to kiss Lady Harpool and realize the ridiculousness of her daydreams. There were magnificent butterflies in this world, and there were lowly closet moths, and it was clear enough which she was by now.

She occupied herself with her collecting, heading out

each morning before breakfast, watching solitary peacocks and mating admirals and swaths of *Urania* hover over wayside weeds but finding nothing she hadn't long since pinned to cork. Still, she made her rounds of the familiar hedgerows and thickets, returning home to her father's increasingly insistent plans to head off to Bath.

And then there was the morning she glimpsed the gadfly hawk moth, bronze and purple and impossibly ethereal, flitting over the corn cockles in Avenleigh's south pasture. "Oh!" she said in a hushed voice, hand clenching on her net. "You lovely thing! *Do* settle!" As if it heard her, the delicate winged creature alighted on a mullein stalk. She crept forward cautiously, taking care not to crunch even a blade of grass. She had the net upraised and was about to make her move when hooves came pounding through the weeds at her back.

"Miss Wilcox!"

That swiftly, the hawk moth was gone. She whirled about in fury. "You great blazing idiot!"

Lord Avenleigh reined in sharply, taken aback. "I beg your pardon!"

Even the sight of his repentant blue eyes could not quell her temper; she stamped her small foot. "What the devil do you want?"

"M-merely to say hallo," he stammered.

"Well, say it and be gone!"

"Are you . . . chasing something?" he inquired belatedly.

"I *was*."

"I'm ever so sorry. I always seem to be blundering in on you, don't I?"

His chagrin softened her a little. "It was a gadfly hawk moth."

"You don't say. Are they rare?"

"Extremely rare. And it was an exceedingly fine specimen."

He dismounted. "Let me go after it for you."

"Oh, you'll never catch it now."

"Why? Where did it go?" he asked, scanning the pasture.

"To North Africa, most likely."

He reached for her net. "Well, I'm not likely to catch it, then. But I shall bloody well try." He started off across the field, the net waving wildly above his head. Pris could not help laughing.

"No, no!" she cried. "Not that way! You must be patient, use stealth!"

He paused in midleap. "Not, alas, qualities I am known for."

"You may be constitutionally unsuited for butterfly-hunting."

"No doubt I am." Something fluttered in the under-growth ahead of him. "Is that it?"

"That's a grouse," she pointed out as it hurtled toward the sky.

He swiped at it anyway, missing by a wide margin. "This is harder than it looks, isn't it?"

"There's a *Notodonta ziczac* to your right, there."

"Really?" He flailed at the wildflowers.

Pris bit her lip. "I think you've smashed it to death."

He contemplated the bit of crushed pulp on the net's wooden edge. "Oh, Lord. It seems I have. Was it rare as well?"

"Not especially. I've several dozen of them."

"Well, thank God for that." He paused to mop his brow. "Thirsty work, isn't it, in this heat?"

Pris reached for her basket, moving toward him. "I have water. Would you like some?"

"Thanks, I would." He took the canteen she held out, popped the cork, and raised it, letting the water stream into his open mouth. Pris watched the muscles in his throat, saw the cool liquid splash over his chin to his shirt front, and felt a pang in her heart.

"God," he said, lowering the canteen at last. "Can't recall the last time I drank water. But it tastes fine." He grinned at her, and that, at least, was not like Robert's proper smile, that devil's grin.

"What brings you out so early in the day, milord? It was my understanding you are wont to stay abed past noon."

"A gross exaggeration, spread no doubt by my aunt, who rises with the sun. I'm on my way to Lincoln. Meeting with Mr. Shropley. He's all abuzz about some dreary interrogation we're to face with the Crown's revenue agents in London next month. I keep telling him not to fret, but it seems to be his nature." He relinquished the net reluctantly. "I'd best be on my way."

"You are going to *London*?" Pris could have kicked herself for the the longing in her voice.

"Mm. You sound envious. Do you enjoy the capital?"

"I've never been," she admitted, shamefaced. "Father considers it a den of iniquity, so he never takes me. Only to Bath, which is full of stuffed shirts and fops and military idiots. We are to go there again in August. There is a second lieutenant he thinks would suit me well."

"And what do you think?"

"I am quite sure he will *not*." She sighed. "And it will take me longer than ever to complete my cataloging."

"You've *never* been to London?" Pris shook her head. "Granted, it's not my cup of tea—or my rum fizz, rather. But it certainly is something everyone should see. Do you think you would like to?"

"Well, I must admit," she said regretfully, "I have a certain scientific curiosity."

He looked at her as she stood dwarfed by the tall weeds. "Perhaps you could come with me."

Pris colored red as the corn cockles. "Lord Avenleigh!"

"Oh, I meant nothing disgraceful. But I was thinking of inviting Cousin Agnes to accompany me anyway. You could go as her companion."

Pris had recovered her breath. "I rather doubt my father would allow it."

"Why not?"

"He seems to think you are the devil incarnate."

He grinned at her again. "Really? He's always been so polite."

"That's only because he is counting on you to shore up the Minster. Robert told dreadful tales about you, you know. Said you were as good as a pirate."

He shrugged. "Well. I like to *think* I am." She giggled; how could she help it? He reached into his waistcoat for a cigar. "I might offer your father a quid pro quo," he mused, striking a match. "Say—two hundred pounds for the Minster in exchange for your company."

"Oh, I am hardly worth that!"

"There's your trouble, Miss Wilcox. You sell yourself too short. I daresay your father wouldn't make the same mistake. I should likely have to offer him a thousand."

She grimaced, with a hint of humor. "Don't feel that you must pay it, though. All Robert did was promise to leave him five times that much in his will."

"Did he really? How odd. There was no such bequest; I'm certain of it."

"Why should there be? Your brother lied the way other folk breathe."

Lord Avenleigh stared at her in amazement. "Why, Miss Wilcox!"

"I—I do beg your pardon. It just slipped out," she murmured in abject embarrassment.

"You don't understand! You are the first soul I've encountered in Lincolnshire who agreed with me! By God, I owe you a trip to London for that alone. I'll speak to your father about it, shall I?"

She shook her head. "I could not dream of imposing on your kindness so."

"My *kindness*? Dear Miss Wilcox, pray remember—I am the devil incarnate."

"Oh, no," Pris murmured, looking up shyly into his enchanting blue eyes. "You are something very different from that."

It took some doing, but in the end Bishop Wilcox consented to agree to allow his daughter to accompany Cousin Agnes to London in exchange for new roofs on the two western towers. Nothing, of course, was ever phrased so baldly, but that was the essence of the agreement. To give the bishop credit, he asked a number of probing questions regarding Jack's mistress—he used the term "fiancée"—back in St. Lucia before granting his permission. Jack, who had still received no correspondence from Camille, was very forthright in saying he intended to sanctify his relationship with Mademoiselle Déshoulières just as soon as he returned to the Caribbean, which must have helped overcome the bishop's qualms.

Any remaining doubts Jack had about the trip were completely dispelled by Cousin Agnes's reaction to the proposed journey. She started up on the ottoman in his bedchamber, sending the brandy bottle tumbling to the floor. "London?" she breathed, her face nearly as luminous as Miss Wilcox's had been. "Me? Go with you to London?"

"I take it the idea is not repulsive to you," Jack drawled.

"*Repul*—oh, dear Lord in heaven!" And she flung herself at his neck and kissed him repeatedly. "Why, I have not been to London in . . ." She paused, retrieved a snag of dignity. "It has been a good many years!" Then the hope fled. "But—it is impossible. Mamma would never allow it."

"You leave Mamma to me," Jack said shortly. The next morning, he invited Aunt Bertrice to his study and showed her his books. She might be a shrew, but she wasn't stupid. Her small black eyes narrowed as she was confronted with hard evidence of how Jack had pulled the family back from the brink.

"I suppose you have some *reason* for tooting your own horn," she concluded after surveying the strings of figures.

He counted to ten. "I do. I have invited Cousin Agnes to come with me to London, as well as Miss Wilcox, who will serve as her companion."

"Bishop Wilcox cannot possibly have consented to such an arrangement!"

"Bishop Wilcox is all in favor of it. Ask him yourself."

"Oh, I shall."

Jack wasn't party to that Tuesday's Bible meeting, but it must have been more interesting than usual. Aunt Bertrice came home with fire in her eye. "I've spoken to the bishop, and he is in total agreement that Agnes is hardly a suitable chaperone for a young lady of Miss Wilcox's tender years. We have concluded that a far more *proper* arrangement will be for all of us—Agnes and 'Phrina and myself—to travel with you. It will be, of course, a *tremendous* imposition on my valuable time—"

Dammit all, thought Jack, and quickly jumped in. "Far too much to ask of you, Aunt Bertrice!"

"I am quite willing to undergo the necessary sacrifices," she intoned, gazing down her pinched nose, "in order to *assure* the young ladies' protection."

Jack bit off a laugh. What the hell! Why not bring all the bats with him? He had taken a leap of faith and booked his passage back to St. Lucia for late August. Four months, and he'd be plying Camille with so many hats, there wouldn't be days enough to wear them. They'd celebrate his homecoming. . . .

Why hadn't she written him? He blinked away that recurrent vision of her lying in Antoine's brawny arms.

"If it pleases you, Aunt," he told her, "you are welcome to come along, of course." His hand went to the token that Camille had given him on the quay. *Keep this with you always . . . never look inside, or the spell will be broken.* I've kept my part of the bargain, he thought angrily. It is *your* love charm. Will it protect you as well as it has me?

Aunt Bertrice was glowering. "I don't know what you have up your sleeve, Jack Cantrell. I do know this, though. I'm not about to send my daughter off alone in the care of such a ne'er-do-well!"

Chapter

10

$\mathcal{J}$ack bespoke a suite of rooms at the Savoy. Bennett Shropley, of course, rolled his eyes at this extravagance. Jack just grinned and assured him the Crown would be more uneasy about the tax payments that were overdue if the earl of Avenleigh's retinue was making obvious economies. "There's the difference between the aristocracy and us poor plebians," Shropley grumbled, surveying the sumptuos rooms he'd been assigned. "If I were being badgered for my unpaid taxes and I put up like this, they'd send me straight off to jail."

Aunt Bertrice, naturally, hadn't a single kind word to say about the accommodations. "Just as I expected," she sniffed, gazing about as the bellboys carried in her baggage. "Dark as your pocket. And it *reeks* of cigars." But Agnes and 'Phrina were like giggling girls, running their hands across the velvet drapes, exclaiming over the polish on the Hepplewhite furniture, walking time and again over the Savonnerie carpets as thick as one's fist. Miss Wilcox scarcely seemed to take any note of her surroundings. When Jack checked in to see that her belongings had been properly bestowed, he found her sitting cross-legged on her bed, her nose buried in a book.

That first night, they dined in the hotel restaurant—without Mr. Shropley, who had engagements of his own. Jack ordered all the dishes he'd been craving for so long back in Lincolnshire: deviled crab, oyster pie, clams d'Orléans, lobster étouffé. Aunt Bertrice turned up her nose. "You know perfectly well shellfish doesn't agree with me," she said curtly, and sent the waiter for a plate of boiled tripe. Agnes and her sister proved game, though, and assayed each new course with such curiosity that 'Phrina actually forgot to polish her silverware. Jack, who'd never shared a meal with Miss Wilcox, observed that she had a remarkably hearty appetite for such a tiny thing. She caught him eyeing her as she accepted a third helping of the crab, and blushed.

"I enjoy seafood ever so much," she murmured. "But Father shares Mrs. Gravesend's digestive troubles, so I rarely have it at home."

"Indulge yourself, by all means," he urged her, only to be rewarded by a withering stare from his aunt.

"A lady never *indulges*," she said sourly. "This tripe is definitely spoiled."

Jack hastened to change the subject. "Well, ladies! What to do tomorrow? I notice Drury Lane is featuring a revival of Sheridan's *School for Scandal*; I imagine we shall want to see that."

"Scandal?" Aunt Bertrice echoed, black eyes gleaming. "I hardly think so."

"It is a classic of the modern theater," Jack felt impelled to tell her.

"It does not *sound* like a classic. If there is any

Shakespeare—any *clean* Shakespeare—perhaps we might go to that."

Jack's heart sank. This had been a terrible idea. Glancing about, he saw more than a few of the elegantly attired habitués of the Savoy surveying the quartet of dowdy females at his table with disdain. And why not? They were as out of place in this fashionable venue, with their antique mourning clothes and frumpish hair and provincial manners, as—as Camille would have been, he realized suddenly. How wise his lover had been to stay far, far clear of all this! His hand jerked up involuntarily to pat the token beneath his waistcoat. With the taste of crab on his tongue, he could almost hear the surf pounding against the white sands of St. Lucia, feel the balmy sea breezes, catch the sweetly provocative scent of jasmine in the air. . . .

"Why, Lord Avenleigh!" The high, breathy voice at his shoulder yanked him back to the present. "What an extraordinary surprise! And Mrs. Gravesend, too!"

Jack turned in his chair to see Vivienne Harpool smiling down at him. He quickly jumped to his feet. "Vivi— Lady Harpool!" He damned near knocked over his wine. "What are you doing here?"

"Just come to the city to visit some friends." He kissed her hand, felt jasmine waft over his soul. She was wearing the most incredibly frothy confection of palest baby-blue swansdown, with a plumed helmet cap to match; her auburn hair was dressed in a sleek chignon. Her ripe mouth pursed in a frown. "And now I find they have unexpectedly gone home to Lancaster. Some trouble with the children. Measles, I think. Or was it the chicken pox? Children are so *impossibly* dreary."

Jack was suddenly unspeakably grateful that this soignée creature had paused at his table, had deigned to grant some imprimatur of *ton* to his humble gathering. "Are you alone, then?" he asked.

"Utterly." She sighed, plying a pristine fan.

Jack took a breath. "Would you be so kind as to join us, since you find yourself at such loose ends? We are well into our third course, but—"

"Oh, that's no matter. I eat like a bird," Vivienne declared, and settled as daintily as one into the chair the waiter hurried to fetch.

It had not occurred to Jack until that moment that his brother's former fiancée might be less than eager to share a table with Robert's obsession. He glanced at Priscilla. She was very busy plying her knife and fork against the crab. Agnes had a most peculiar expression on her face, and 'Phrina was engrossed in eating. Only Aunt Bertrice seemed at all glad to see Lady Harpool again.

"What a very great pleasure," she cooed, if so cold a sort could possibly coo. "No doubt *you* will be able to suggest to us some *proper* forms of amusement here in London. So far my nephew's proposals have been most indecorous."

"Well," said Vivienne, bestowing a smile like flowers on the besotted boy who was laying her place, "*Love's Labours Lost* is at Covent Garden—Bowdler's version, of course. And the Regent is hosting a reception at Carlton House on Thursday." She observed 'Phrina's crestfallen expression. "What? You haven't been invited? Oh, he must simply not have been aware you were in town. I'll write to his secretary, shall I, and see what I can do?"

"I'm sure it's far too late," Jack began, not wanting his relations to suffer the shame of their certain rejection.

"Nonsense!" Vivienne declared. "It is never too late for anything one *truly* wants."

'Phrina gazed at her as though at a star fallen from the heavens. "You don't honestly think . . . to be invited to *Carlton House*—"

"Leave it to me," Vivienne said reassuringly, patting her hand.

Across the table, Priscilla Wilcox folded her napkin neatly. "Would you be so kind as to excuse me?" she said to no one in particular. "I have some reading I must do."

That night, after Aunt Bertrice and her daughters were safe abed, Jack went with Vivienne Harpool to Vauxhall. He hadn't been since he was in school; he was amused anew at the fireworks, the music, the dancing by masked partners that bordered on risqué. They shared champagne, and afterward he led her down a darkened path between the elder trees and kissed her. She was not so resistant as the last time. Her throat was white as a swan's, her skin soft as suede.

"Are you staying at the Savoy?" he murmured into her ear.

"Yes. Yes."

Beneath his hands, he felt the bonds of her stays swelling into the glorious ripeness of her breasts. "I could visit your rooms. . . ."

She drew back a little, searching his eyes in the shadows of the trees. "You did not even come to bid me good-bye."

"I didn't dare," Jack confessed. "Not with the way you tempt me."

"Do I tempt you, Jackie?" She brought her palms up against his chest, paused as her fingers found the love token he wore around his throat. "What is this?"

Jasmine, sweet, sweet jasmine, and her nipples hard beneath his thumbs . . . "Nothing," he told her, dipping his head to her bosom. "Island magic. That's all."

"Magic, eh?" She pulled it free. "Let me see what is in it."

"No!" Startled by his vehemence, she let it fall from

her fingertips. "I'm sorry," Jack said, embarrassed. "Camille gave it to me. She told me—" But that seemed so absurd now, here, in England. He felt a deep wave of shame at his lover's backward superstition, and his own acquiescence. He held it out to Vivienne on his hand. "You may look if you like."

"How do you open it?" Her long fingers pried at the token, searching for its clasp. "Ah, I see! There's a little latch here, and another. . . . How very clever!" She tugged him by the chain toward the nearest gas lamp. "I need a bit more light." But as she took her first step, something in the grass just ahead of her twisted and flickered with an odd green glow.

"Vivienne! Look out!" Jack cried. He threw himself at her, sending her tumbling headlong onto the lawn, just as there came a loud, bright explosion, so near that it rocked them both.

Vivienne screamed, clutching her heart. "My God! I've been shot!"

He pulled himself to his feet, then reached down for her. A little throng of onlookers had collected, drawn by the noise and Vivienne's outburst. "You're all right. But that was close. Must have been an unspent shell from the fireworks."

"You're lucky you weren't killed!" a girl in the crowd marveled with a shiver.

Vivienne clambered to her feet, pushing at her disheveled hair, eyeing her gown in dismay. "Ruined! Absolutely *ruined*!" she declared of the stained, rumpled silk. "It was the first time I wore it, too!"

"First and last," another voice, this one male, murmured, and a few of the onlookers laughed.

Vivienne quelled them with a furious glare. "Take me home, Jackie. Take me home *now*," she hissed. "I've never been so—so *mortified*! I can't imagine what you meant, mashing me about in the dirt like that!"

"I was trying to save your life."

"Well, I'll thank you not to do so again!" She flounced off ahead of him toward the quay. Jack followed, felt the love token bounce against his waistcoat, and started to tuck it back inside his shirt. Then he paused, staring down at the gleaming amulet.

Surely, Camille, he thought, *this couldn't be* your *doing.* Could it?

"Ridiculous," he said aloud, and hurried after Vivienne.

*J*ack sighed, glancing at his watch, tapping his foot as Agnes and Sephrina fussed in front of the looking glass over their black bonnets. "The hack is waiting," he said for the third time.

Agnes turned to him with anxious eyes. "Do forgive us, Cousin Jack. But it is such a challenge, when surrounded by the cream of the *ton*, to try to bring our homespun up to snuff."

"I think, Aggie, a bit more tilt to that will make it more alluring," 'Phrina declared with a giggle. Jack scarcely noticed. He was pondering what Agnes had said.

"I assumed you dressed . . . the way you dress out of choice, Cousin Agnes."

She dropped her gaze. "Oh, I was not complaining!"

"When was the last time you had a new outfit?"

"Why, for Robert's funeral, of course. Mamma had frocks made up for all of us."

"And before that?"

"Really," she said blithely, "I cannot recall."

"For your father's funeral," 'Phrina put in helpfully.

"But that was more than five years past!" Jack noted, aghast. Camille could not go a fortnight without ordering a new gown. He realized suddenly that in taking steps to renovate Avenleigh Hall, he'd been neglectful of its occupants. "Surely your mother has income enough to keep clothes on your back!"

"Papa left us a bit," Sephrina told him, patting her curls beneath the crowlike bonnet. "But Mamma gave it all to Robert, to put into his investment. He was to pay us back out of the profits. I suppose he never got around to it."

"Forget the tour of the Tower of London," Jack announced decisively. "We—you—are going to a mantua-maker's." He searched his memory for the names Vivienne had given him. Why not? He'd have the opportunity to buy his gifts for Camille.

Agnes's handsome face bore warring expressions of wistfulness and shame. "We couldn't *possibly*," she began, just as her sister jumped up and down where she stood, clapping her hands.

"Oh, Aggie, do hush! New clothes!"

"Cousin Jack has already proven far too kind—"

"Aggie, what is *wrong* with you?"

"I simply don't feel it's right—"

"*What's* not right?" Aunt Bertrice demanded, appearing in the doorway to her adjoining room like a figure of doom.

Sephrina stopped hopping. Agnes colored wretchedly. Jack stepped boldly into the breach. "We aren't going to the Tower of London after all, Aunt Bertrice. We are going to Madame Descoux's."

"Who, pray tell, is Madame Descoux?"

"A mantua-maker. She comes highly recommended.

By Lady Harpool," he added, since she and his aunt seemed to be getting along so famously.

"My girls have no need of new frocks."

"Mamma," 'Phrina breathed.

"And even if they did, it would certainly not be *your* place, Jack Cantrell, to provide them! I'll not have my daughters made over into—into Paphians!" Her black eyes bored into his.

Jack bored right back. "You yourself, Aunt Bertrice, could bide a whiff of fashion. You are free to accompany us or not, as you like. But we certainly *will* go."

"Over my dead body," the old lady growled.

" 'Phrina? Agnes?" Jack offered his cousins his arms. Sephrina actually took a step toward him—before abruptly drawing back. Agnes merely stood, head bowed, in her dowdy black bonnet and gown.

Frustration welled up in Jack's soul. Why would they not defy her? Did they enjoy being under her thumb—intend to stay there all their lives? Aunt Bertrice smiled a most satisfied smile. "So, Jack, you are free if you wish to fritter away the estate on *bijoux* for your French mistress. *We* shall visit the Tower."

Damn them all. "Where's Miss Wilcox?" he asked irritably.

"She requested that she be excused from this afternoon's excursion. She isn't feeling well. I could have told her! *Three* helpings of shellfish! 'Phrina! Agnes! Let us go." The cousins picked up their reticules and followed her, moving as though they were scheduled for execution on Tower Green.

For his part, Jack went and asked directions from a hack driver to Madame Farrell's chapeau shop, intending to buy for Camille whatever caught his fancy, pleased his eye or might please hers. Why waste his blunt on those old spinsters anyway? He stood for some minutes staring indecisively at the colorful bonnets and caps in the window display. Perhaps that one there, with the faux pearls and ostrich plumes? Or the tiny, curving frame of blue velvet and veiling studded with sequins and pheasant feathers? He tried to picture Camille in each, but the negligible bits of fluff defied his imagination. He was not accustomed to buying for his lover; back in Castries, when she saw something she wanted, she simply purchased it and handed him the bill. He was still hesitating when a commotion on the street snagged his attention; he heard a shout, then the snorting and stomping of a horse pulled up hard. As he turned, he saw a smart cabriolet wheel wildly to the left to avoid a ragtag child laden with parcels who'd stepped out from the curb. In the instant it took for the child to glance up and see the danger, he recognized the petite figure as that of Miss Wilcox. Then the tip of one shaft struck her shoulder, knocking her to the ground and scattering her paper-wrapped bundles into the air.

"Good God!" he cried, running toward her.

The driver of the cab had got his horse under control and shouted to the onlookers: "Ye saw it all, didn't ye, now? Cut out straight in front o' me, she did! Never once looked where she was goin'!"

Jack had reached her side, and knelt in the dust. "Miss Wilcox! Are you hurt?"

Cris blinked, lying flat on her back. "My packages—"

"Never mind the packages! Are you injured?" Lord Avenleigh demanded.

"Oh, *do* get them for me quickly, before someone runs over them!" she begged.

"For Christ's sake, someone has just run over you!"

"She walked straight out in front o' me, she did!" the sweating driver was insisting.

"Shut up, you bloody fool!" Lord Avenleigh snapped at him.

Pris spoke up then, faintly: "He's quite right, you know. I *wasn't* looking. But my packages—"

An enterprising boy from the growing crowd began to gather them up. Lord Avenleigh put his arm around Pris's shoulders, helping her to sit. "Is there a doctor here?" he barked at the curious faces surrounding them.

"I don't need a doctor," Pris insisted, dreadfully self-conscious. "Only my parcels." The boy came and laid them down beside her. "Oh, you angel, you! Do be careful with that one—it is very rare! Here, let me give you this for your trouble." She reached into her reticule and found a shilling, pressed it on him. "Clever lad, I am so grateful to you!"

" 'T'waren't nothin', miss," he said cheerily, with a tip of his cap.

"*Would* you forget those bloody packages," Lord Avenleigh said with a hint of temper, "and tell me—are any bones broken?"

"Any—" She gazed up at him. "Oh! I don't think so."

"Can you stand?"

"I rather hope I can!" She did, with negligible assistance.

Jack let out a sigh of relief. "I can only imagine what your father would say if I brought you back from London a cripple!" Pris bent down for her parcels. "I'll get those," he told her, and did, staggering at their weight. "Good Lord, what have you been buying?"

"Books. Please do be careful with that one on top; it is—"

"I know. Very rare." He tucked the pile under one arm and offered her his other.

The driver was still highly nervous. "Here, now, sir, I got any number o' witnesses will say I wasn't at fault—"

Lord Avenleigh waved him off. "Never mind. But be more careful next time!"

"Yes, sir. Very good, sir. Gee-up, then!" He slapped the reins and gratefully clattered on down the street.

Blushing, Pris let Lord Avenleigh guide her to the curb.

"What in God's name were you thinking of?" he demanded.

"My luck," she said wryly.

"I'd been given to understand from my aunt that you were feeling unwell."

"Oh, I am!" Pris said guiltily, suddenly recalling how she'd managed to avoid accompanying his aunt and cousins to the Tower that morning. "Or rather—I was. I am much better now."

"You are going to have one hell of a bruise from that stave."

"Nonsense. It barely clipped me." She brushed her tousled hair from her face.

"I'll see you back to the Savoy." He started to signal for a hack, but she tugged down his hand:

"No need for that. I am perfectly fine."

He glanced down at her. "You are extremely dusty."

"Am I?" She brushed her skirts distractedly. "I was likely quite dusty even before I fell."

He grinned at her, that devilish grin that took her breath away. "You gave the boy too much," he chided. "A penny would have been sufficient."

"Oh, no," she protested, cocking her head, the city sun beating down on her drab black bonnet. "He was quite heroic. He did just as I asked."

"I beg your pardon. My concern was more for your person than your parcels."

"I didn't mean—" She blushed again. "I am, of course, most grateful to you as well."

The crowd had drifted off, disappointed by the lack of drama and blood. Pris saw that she and Lord Avenleigh were standing just outside a hat shop. His Lordship gazed down at her thoughtfully, then turned to eye the frippery in the window. "Grateful enough to repay the favor?" he asked.

Her color heightened even more. "H-how, milord?"

"Tell me which of these hats you like best." He guided her to the glass.

"Which *hat*—" Perplexed, she stared at the glittering chapeaux.

"I am looking for a gift for my—for Mademoiselle Déshoulières."

"Oh!" Her confused expression cleared. "I see! But you cannot want *my* opinion. I know nothing of fashion. You ought to ask of Lady Harpool. She is always so exquisitely attired."

For some reason, that suggestion made him frown. "I'd rather not. You must have a preference." Pris surveyed the window display in silence. "Well?"

"Shall I be frank?" she said dubiously.

"I was counting on you to be."

"They are all rather . . . silly, don't you think? Take that one with ostrich plumes. It's so high, you could scarcely fit through a doorway! And that one there, covered in gems—it must weigh ten pounds! It makes my neck ache to look at it."

"What about the one with the pheasant feathers, there in the corner?"

She pursed her mouth up, perusing it. "Looks a bit like a bird after a dog has given it a good shake." Lord Avenleigh burst out laughing. "I told you I was hopeless at this," she apologized again.

"I don't really care for any of them, either, to tell the truth. But I did promise her hats. I'd best go in and get a few. So long as I tell her they are from the most fashionable shop in London, she'll be satisfied. Come along." He started for the door, her arm still tucked through his. Pris held back. "What is wrong?"

"I'm hardly dressed for shopping in such a place."

"Lord, don't be ridiculous. I'm spending money, so what do they care?" He tugged her with him into the shop.

An extremely elegant young woman hurried forward at the tinkling of the bell. "*Oui, m'sieur?* Can I be of service?"

"We need some hats. Three or four should do it."

"*Eh bien,* if m'amselle will just be seated here—" She gestured Pris to a wrought-iron chair before a triple mirror.

"Oh, they're not for *me!*" she cried, highly embarrassed. The saleswoman raised a painted brow.

"No, please, do sit, Miss Wilcox," Lord Avenleigh prompted. "You must be shaken after that close call. And I *would* like to see them on someone, so I can tell Camille which is the front and which the back."

"I simply couldn't—"

But he led her forward and plunked her down. "You said that you were grateful. Kindly repay me this way."

She sat and squirmed in the seat. "We have first to remove *this*," the saleswoman noted, plucking off Pris's sorry bonnet, handling it as if it might bite. Then she stood back a pace and contemplated Pris for a long moment. "Black," she said, "does not suit you."

"I already said, they're not for me," she reiterated.

"What do you think *would* suit her?" Jack asked curiously.

The saleswoman touched Pris's hair, ran a finger along her cheekbone. "Silver-green," she announced definitively.

"Good God!" Pris flinched. "My father would have apoplexy."

"But it would. Here, m'amselle. I will show you." She moved to the display, chose a poke bonnet of wicker with ocean-green ribbands and a cluster of artificial cherry blossoms at one side, and settled it atop Pris's pale straw head. "There! You see?"

Pris, staring at her reflection, was taken aback. The bonnet brought a sheen to her hair, lent a glow to her flushed cheeks that was startling.

"You ought to buy that," Lord Avenleigh said gravely. "You look lovely in it."

"I've more important stuff to spend my money on." Pris tore her gaze from the mirrors. "And anyway, you are shopping for Mademoiselle Déshoulières."

"And m'amselle's hair is . . . ?" The saleswoman prompted.

"Black," Lord Avenleigh told her. "And her eyes green."

"Her complexion?"

"Medium," he said, after a moment's hesitation. Pris was surprised. She could have sworn he'd told her his lover was lily-pale.

She sat still as stone while the woman assayed a whole series of bonnets on her. Lord Avenleigh looked on with narrowed eyes, shaking his head, occasionally grinning his devilish grin. After what seemed *hours*, he finally made his choices. They included the pheasant-feather piece from the window. "I agree with what you said about it," he told Pris with a shrug. "But it will please her, I think."

"That's all that matters, then, isn't it?" She watched as the saleswoman deftly wrapped his purchases in tissue—the cost of them had made her swallow, hard—and laid them in big striped boxes.

"Have them sent to me at the Savoy," Lord Avenleigh directed, taking out his card.

"Very good, m'sieur."

Pris rose gratefully from the chair.

"Sure you can't be persuaded to buy that cherry blossom one?" he asked. "It really is most fetching on you."

"Where would I wear it?"

"To Bath this summer. You'd turn all the men's heads."

"Oh, really," she murmured. But his words had put a glow in her like a red-hot coal.

Back on the street, he whistled, walking beside her. "Satisfied with your purchases?" she couldn't resist asking.

"Sure that Camille will be." They were passing a jeweler's shop—Sadler Brothers, the sign above the door read. His hand tightened on her arm. "I say. What do you think of *that*?" He pointed to a neckpiece of sparkling diamonds, hundreds of them set in bright gold, a brilliant web of refracted rainbow light.

Pris wrinkled her nose. "It's very pretty. But all they are, you know, according to Smithson Tennant and Sir Humphry Davy, is carbon."

"What, pray tell, is carbon?"

"Compressed decomposed vegetable matter."

Lord Avenleigh looked at the neckpiece and then back at her. "Miss Wilcox. May I say that you are sadly lacking in the spirit of romance?"

"I can't help that. I am a scientist."

"You are also a woman. Do you mean to tell me that if someone gifted you with those diamonds, you would view them as rotted vegetables?"

"The supposition, to begin with, is extremely unlikely." She paused. "Of course, it does take eons for material to compress so solidly. There is something to be said for that."

He laughed out loud. "What could a suitor ever give you, then, that you would consider more appealing?"

"You are holding them there in your arm. The books I have bought."

"And you prefer those to diamonds. Do you know, I am beginning to comprehend your father's eagerness to take you to Bath."

"How so?" Pris asked edgily.

"You need to be married off before you acquire any more learning. Otherwise you will daunt General Wellington himself, much less any poor second lieutenant." She started to protest angrily—and then was silent, seeing the unexpected admiration in his sky-blue eyes.

*T*he invitation arrived by a special messenger in the
Regent's own colors. Jack stared at it in disbelief, but there
it was: a summons to Carlton House, addressed to him and
his relatives. For a moment he contemplated crumpling
the thing; it presented the prospect of more problems than
pleasure. Then he thought of Agnes's wounded dignity
and took it to her rooms.

"Something that may interest you," he said blithely,
tossing it onto the dressing table where she sat, having her
hair put up by her sister. She read it with 'Phrina peeking
over her shoulder. There was a moment's pause. Then
'Phrina began to squeal in ecstasy.

"Us, Aggie! Us, at the Regent's reception! Can you
imagine?"

A slow blush climbed right to the roots of Cousin
Agnes's hair. "This is Lady Harpool's doing."

"Well," Jack said, "it is certainly none of mine!"

Agnes spun about on her stool, grasped her sister's wrists. " 'Phrina. Listen to me, love. We cannot possibly go."

"Why not?" Sephrina's blue eyes had taken on a sheen. "Why ever not?"

"Because," Agnes said distinctly, "we haven't proper clothes. Or, for that matter, proper manners."

"We were presented to King George in the year we debuted!"

" 'Phrina, that was twenty years ago!"

Aunt Bertrice, attracted by the hubbub, opened the connecting door, a truly frightful sight in a wrapper and hairpins. "What on earth is all this commotion?"

"Oh, Mamma!" Sephrina danced toward her with astonishing grace, the invitation in hand. "See? We are to visit the Prince Regent!"

Her mother perused the vellum, dark brows knotted. Then she smiled—a horrifying grimace. "We have Lady Harpool to thank for this."

"Or not," Agnes murmured from the dressing table.

"What's that, Agnes?"

"Nothing, Mamma. But, Mamma, you must realize . . ." Her voice trailed away beneath her mother's quelling stare.

"We're as noble as any family there," Bertrice Gravesend said archly. "More noble than most, in point of fact." She scanned the invitation again. "No mention is made of Miss Wilcox."

"Lady Harpool could only do so much," Sephrina said sensibly, "with the notice so brief."

"Still, as her chaperone, I am placed in an awkward position. Of course, we must accept. A royal summons! But what are we to do with Miss Wilcox?"

Jack scratched his chin thoughtfully, glimpsing an opportunity to avoid the sort of evening he most hated: formal clothes, royalty, bad music, and not enough wine. "If it would ease your concern, Aunt Bertrice, I could, I suppose, forgo the invitation in order to take charge of Miss Wilcox."

She eyed him long and hard. Jack was careful to keep his expression crestfallen at the prospect, but was not sure he'd fool the old hag. Fortunately, her greed to attend over-rode any moral qualms. "Kind of you to offer. But we must put it up to Miss Wilcox herself, I suppose."

Miss Wilcox, having it put up to her over breakfast, expressed the deepest regret at not having been included in the invitation and went on humbly to agree to suffer Jack's company on the evening in question.

He wondered, watching her lowered eyes as she spoke this pretty speech, whether his aunt or cousins had noticed the infinite relief on her face.

"*Well!*" Pris glanced up as Lord Avenleigh came into the sitting room she shared with his cousins. "What would amuse you this evening? I have the gazettes; there's surely some opera or play you'd enjoy. Or we could dine out." He snapped his fingers. "I know! I shall take you to Vauxhall Gardens! Music and fireworks, and we can have a boxed supper—"

His forced enthusiasm made her wretchedly self-conscious. "I . . . naturally, milord, whatever pleases you will surely also amuse me."

"But?" he prodded. Pris shook her head, mouth tight shut. "Come, come, Miss Wilcox! Don't disappoint me now; you are one of the few women I have ever known who is wont to speak her mind."

She glanced down at her hands, folded in her lap. "Very well, but only because you urge me. The fact is, I had already made plans."

"You had? You ought to have spoken right up, then! What plans have you made?"

"Professor Eisenroth is presenting a paper this evening at the British Museum. On the lepidoptera of Southern Africa."

"I see," he said after a moment. "And who is Professor Eisenroth?"

She giggled. "Only the world's greatest living lepidopterist!"

"Of course. How foolish of me not to have recognized the name."

"You are jesting at me," she said ruefully.

"No, no! Not at all. I should very much enjoy going to hear his lecture."

"You are very much a liar."

"Well. Let me put it this way. I should very much prefer going to hear Professor Eisenreich—"

"Eisenroth."

"—Speak to accompanying my aunt and her daughters to Carlton House, where they will be the subject of endless sniggers and uplifted eyebrows on account of their manners and dress."

"How cruel you are," she said in a whisper.

"I? Lord, I don't care for *my* sake. As far as I'm concerned, the whole *ton* can go hang. I am thinking of Agnes; she is sure to be mortified, poor soul. Anyway, just yesterday I suggested taking the whole lot of them to the finest mantua-maker in London to remedy the situation. Aunt Bertrice turned me down flat, much to 'Phrina's chagrin. Said she didn't want her girls made over into Paphians."

"Does that mean—Roman Catholics?" Pris asked, wide-eyed.

He quickly stifled a laugh. "It might to your father. It's a term Byron used to describe . . ." Lord, how to put this?

"Fallen women?" Pris suggested.

"Exactly," Jack said gratefully.

"I've never read any Byron," she mused. "Father doesn't approve of any reading but the Bible for young ladies."

"That explains your secretive glee about the books you bought. Confess it, Miss Wilcox! What illicit novels did you purchase yesterday? *The Demon of Sicily? The Romance of the Forest? Castle Rackrent?*"

"Novels?" she echoed, perplexed. "I was fortunate enough to find a number of scientific works on my field of interest—including a first edition of Professor Eisenroth's seminal treatise. Complete with color plates!"

"My felicitations."

"*Must* you always be so ironical?" she asked with a hint of temper that shot green into her gray eyes.

"I wasn't. I was quite sincere. I saw how happy your purchases made you. Really." He reached across to pat her small hand. She jerked away from him as though his touch were fire. The motion was so swift that it surprised them both. "I beg your pardon," he apologized, just as she said:

"You startled me, milord. You must forgive me."

"No, no. The fault was mine. So, tell me! What time is Professor Eisenreich—roth's lecture?"

"Eight o'clock." She was blushing again, and hated herself for it.

"Say half an hour to get there by hack. We'll have to leave at half-past seven." He frowned. "What about dinner?"

"I thought I would just eat here, in my rooms. I've so much reading to do."

Lord Avenleigh nodded, looking relieved. But of course. No doubt he hadn't relished the prospect of dining with her alone in the restaurant downstairs. "I'll come by at half-past seven, then."

"Thank you, milord."

Halfway to the door, he turned. "Miss Wilcox."

"Yes?" she said warily.

"You said you'd already planned to attend this lecture. But you never would have been admitted to the museum without a gentleman to accompany you. May I be so bold as to ask how, if I'd gone to Carlton House, you proposed to gain entrance?"

"Melchior—that's our stableman—very kindly lent me his best clothes, and a hat in which to tuck up my hair. I thought to pass myself off as an impoverished student."

"Dress up as a man, you mean." She nodded. He scratched his chin. "How very enterprising of you."

"You are being ironical again."

"Not at all. I'll see you at half-past seven."

It would be an overstatement to claim Jack enjoyed Professor Eisenroth's lecture. He understood very little of what was said, even with the help of the oversized illustrations set up on easels, to which the good doctor continually referred. He was, however, struck by the excitement running through the fairly large crowd—there must have been several hundred present—and by the spirited give-and-take that went on in the discussion period toward the end. Not since Cambridge, he realized, had he been in the presence of so much intellectual curiosity.

Miss Wilcox took copious notes in an unreadable hand, often muttering to herself as she wrote. During the question-and-answer, she nudged him sharply. "Ask him is he sure the first maxillae are entirely vestigial in the *Bombycidae*," she hissed.

"Ask him *what*? I most certainly will not! *You* go ahead and ask him!"

"I can't. No one will take the question seriously if it comes from me."

"Why not?"

"Because I am a woman."

"There are plenty of women here," he observed, scanning the lecture hall.

"But none who have opened their mouths. Here, I'll write the question out for you."

"I can't read your writing."

"Dammit all!" A few men in the row just ahead glanced back at her, scandalized. Miss Wilcox hesitated for a long moment. Then she jumped to her feet. "Professor Eisenroth!" She waved her hand frantically. Jack scrunched down in his seat. "Excuse me! Professor Eisenroth!" The distinguished gentleman at the lectern searched for the source of the voice—which, Jack noted, was low-pitched enough to be a young man's. The professor pulled up his quizzing glass, blinked, and bestowed on her a bemused smile.

"Ah! I see one of our net-wielding sisters has come forth with a question! What can I answer for you, my dear? No doubt the same query I am always confronted with when I speak to the ladies' societies. Alas, I know of no way to remove grass stains from a linen skirt."

A titter of laughter ran through the assembly. Jack cringed, seeing Miss Wilcox ball her small fists and rise to her full, unimpressive height. "Actually," she called coolly, "I wanted to know if you are sure the first maxillae are entirely vestigial in the *Bombycidae*."

A veil of silence descended in the hall, broken only by a curt, derisive male voice muttering, "Bluestocking!"

"Because," Miss Wilcox went on relentlessly, "my own examinations of the processionary moth indicate clear examples of function still extant, at least during the larval stage."

Jack shot to his feet, propelled by God knew what instinct. "I've made the same observation, sir!"

Professor Eisenroth adjusted his quizzing glass. "Have you really?" he asked, in quite a different tone. "You don't say. That is very interesting indeed. Might I ask your name, sir?"

"Jack Cantrell. Earl of Avenleigh," Jack put in, for good measure.

"Ah! We are honored by your presence here among us, milord."

"Yes, yes. But about the—the first maxillae of the *Bom—Bom—*"

"*Bombycidae!*" Miss Wilcox hissed.

"*Bombycidae . . .*"

"I shall have to examine my notes further on this matter, Lord Avenleigh. Thank you for calling it to my attention."

"Not at all," Jack said, and sat, yanking Miss Wilcox down. "No more questions," he told her sotto voce. "Not one more damned question!"

"That was . . . very good of you," she whispered, and huddled in her chair.

Refreshments were served at the conclusion of the lecture. "Do you want to stay?" Jack asked, taking her arm as they rose in their places.

"Ironical," she said shortly, pushing through the crowd to the doors. Outside, she stood and drank in air. The night was clear, with a host of stars poking through the glow of the gas lamps. Jack hailed a hack.

"Do you suppose we might . . . walk for a bit?" Miss Wilcox proposed uncertainly.

"If you like," he told her, and waved the cab past. "Are you hungry? We could stop someplace—"

"I just feel like walking." And she did, through the darkened streets, her heels making short, sharp clicks.

Jack strode along beside her, wishing he could think of something to say. All that came to mind, though, was, "I am sorry."

"So am I. Had I worn Melchior's clothes, I could have asked any question I pleased."

They were passing a tavern. "Would you like something to drink?"

She paused. "Yes. I would."

They entered, Jack ducking beneath the low lintel. For a moment, he feared he'd made a terrible mistake. The clientele was entirely male, and rough-looking to boot. But then a smiling maidservant toting half a dozen empty mugs beckoned them to a table. "Right 'ere, guv'nor!" she cried cheerily.

Jack held Miss Wilcox's chair, then settled into his own, still gazing warily about him. The drinkers on their stools, the men playing at darts, stared at Miss Wilcox, then at him for a moment, then returned to the business at hand. The girl set down the mugs to be filled by the barkeep and sashayed to their table. She was brunette and buxom, with a pretty, round face, and her eyes never left Jack. "What'll it be for ye, then, guv'nor?"

Jack considered. It was not the sort of spot for ordering brandy. "Claret," he said. "And lemonade for the lady. Or would you prefer orangeade?"

"Claret's a wine, isn't it?" asked Miss Wilcox. He nodded. "I'd like claret, too."

The girl gave Jack a wink and started back to the bar with an amazing amount of movement to her hips. He hardly noticed. "Have you ever had wine before, Miss Wilcox?"

"At communion," she responded. Her eyes were following the maid. "What is it like, to be like—what you are?"

"I beg your pardon?"

"To have women always look at you that way."

"What way?" Jack was busy wondering how much damage a single cup of claret would wreak on a total nondrinker.

"As if they wanted to—to eat you."

He laughed. "I don't know what you mean."

She leaned toward him across the small table. "Oh, come. You must. Lady Harpool looks at you that very same way. And women on the street as well. I have seen them."

Jack ran a finger under his collar. He'd tied his damned cravat too tight. The girl came back with their wine. "Tuppence," she cooed, bending close to his ear, affording him a glimpse inside her bodice. "Or did ye want to run a bill?" He fished for coins, put them into her waiting hand. "Anythin' else ye might be needin', guv'nor—anythin' at *all*— ye snap yer fingers for Bessie," she whispered, and left with her hips a-swish.

Priscilla Wilcox stared after her the way she might contemplate a particularly exotic moth. Jack took a long, deep draft of wine. His companion tore her attention from the barmaid and raised up her cup. She took a sip, made a face, and then tried it again.

"It isn't very *good* claret," Jack apologized.

"I like it well enough. I think."

"Your father would hog-tie me if he knew I'd brought you here."

"He wouldn't know how to. All he knows is how to preach." Her gaze glanced off his and over to Bessie, who was chatting with some customers but keeping one eye on Jack. "You could have any woman you pleased, I imagine."

"You exaggerate."

She cocked her head at him. "It is because you are so handsome. And tall. It helps, I think, being tall."

"When you are reaching for something on a high shelf, it certainly does."

She tasted the wine once more, scrunching her nose. "That's rather what life is, isn't it? Reaching for something on a high shelf. And never quite getting there, no matter how you pile up the boxes and chairs."

Jack laughed. "I suppose one could say that. What are you reaching for?"

"My catalog. But I'll never finish it now."

"What if you went to your father, told him how important your work is to you?"

"Do you imagine I *haven't* told him? But he doesn't understand. He *can't* understand. Nothing like that has ever been on his shelf. He knows what ought to be on mine: marriage and children."

"You once told me it was," he reminded her gently.

"And that it wasn't anymore."

"You speak as though you were a spinster of sixty! You are only twenty-two years old!"

"Twenty-three. Yesterday was my anniversary."

"You ought to have said something," Jack chided. "We'd have celebrated."

"I did. I bought myself books."

"That's no proper celebration for a birthday."

"A woman of my age," she said wryly, "sees no great cause to celebrate."

"Finish your wine," Jack told her. "I am taking you dancing."

"I don't know how to dance. I'm not *allowed* to dance. And besides, where would we go at this hour?"

"You're not allowed to drink, either, as I recall." She started guiltily, hand on her wine cup, and he smiled winningly. "I know the perfect place. Drink up, Miss Wilcox."

"I'm not dressed for dancing," she protested. "And what if I am seen by someone who knows Father?"

"I can guarantee you—I stake my *life* on it—that no one will recognize you."

"I don't see how you can promise that," she said dubiously. But she swallowed what was left in her glass. The hefty tip Jack left for Bessie did not seem to appease her;

she glowered as she came to collect it, and sniffed audibly
as Miss Wilcox gathered up her drab skirts.

He took her to Vauxhall after all. He bought two black
dominoes from a vendor on the riverbank and helped her
settle hers over her fashionless bonnet. Then they took a
scull across to the watergate, with a rowdy crowd of drunken
young blades. "Are you sure," she whispered nervously,
"this is a good idea?"

"You'll enjoy it. Stop worrying!" He gave her his arm
to help her onto shore.

Beneath the cover of the mask, her eyes widened as
she took in the groves and colonnades illuminated by thousands of lamps. The orchestra was playing across the lawn,
in its kiosk glittering with colored lights. Jack made for the
pavilion. All the tables in the mirror-lined supper room
were taken, but he scared a foppish gentleman away from
one simply by towering over him until he muttered and
left. He helped Miss Wilcox into her seat, gestured to a
waiter, and ordered champagne and oysters. His companion could not stop staring at the parade of people going
past. "What is *she*?" she asked of a heavily painted woman
clad in a filmy gauze gown, with an eager young tulip of
fashion clinging to each of her arms.

"A Paphian," Jack told her, and laughed at her startled
gray eyes.

He showed her how to roll back the domino so she
could eat and drink. She declared the champagne more to
her liking than claret, and had two glasses. She refused the
oysters, but watched, giggling, as Jack sucked them down.
"I thought you liked shellfish," he said.

"I'm not hungry. There is too much to see! Could I
have a bit more champagne?"

"I think you had better go easy."

"I feel perfectly fine," she insisted. Not without misgivings, he filled her glass halfway.

After that, he took her to dance. But the floor was so impossibly crowded that they could barely move, and the gang of rowdies who'd come over in the scull with them was dashing about, doing its best to cause havoc. So they went instead to see the Grand Cascade, the Fountain of Neptune, and finally the fireworks, with their great Catherine wheels of sparkling flame shooting into the sky. She was enchanted; she stood staring upward, hands clasped together, and caught her breath as each fireburst unfurled. When the last spark faded, she let out a sigh. "Is that all?"

"All the fireworks. But we could walk through the groves, if you like."

"Oh, let's do."

So they strolled along the darkened walkways of the gardens, the distant music drifting on the air, its sweetness pierced now and again by a feminine gasp or murmured words of masculine passion from beneath the shadowy trees.

"What are they doing?" Priscilla Wilcox whispered of a couple hopelessly entangled on an arbor bench.

"Kissing," Jack said, and tried to lead her away.

"Is that what they *all* are doing? Kissing?" She stopped where she stood to scan the shades half hidden by the night and the shrubs.

"Mostly."

"Why? Is it amusing?"

He paused as well, staring down at her. "Don't tell me, Miss Wilcox, you have never been kissed!"

"Not like that I haven't."

He thrust her pointing arm to her side. "Didn't Robert ever . . ."

"Just—you know. Like this." She lifted her chin and pecked at the air. The night breeze fluttered the silk hard against her profile; he saw her puckered mouth, her straight nose, the clean sweep of her throat, all outlined in black.

"Would you like to be kissed that way?" he asked.

She shrugged. "I have a certain scientific curiosity."

"Come here," Jack said, and pulled her under the sheltering branches of a willow tree. The darkness there was absolute; even the music could not get in.

She stood very still as his fingers found the edge of the mask she wore and raised it up. "Birthday wishes should come true," he murmured, stuffing his own domino into his coat. He bent down to find her—bent very low.

His mouth brushed her hair first. He was surprised by the smooth feel of it against his lips, and by its scent, so faint and elusive that for a moment he pressed his cheek to that blond weight, inhaling, trying to determine it. Castile soap, he finally realized. He hadn't smelled that since his childhood, when Nurse would scrub him and Robert in their bath. Pleased that he'd placed the fragrance, he moved his mouth to her forehead. Her skin was cool as ivory; it even *felt* pale. He kissed her cheek, discovered she was turning her head, and gently drew it back. "What's wrong?" he murmured. "I won't hurt you." He found the line of her lips with his fingertip, traced it. She quivered in his grasp like a frightened bird. Jack was momentarily overcome with awe. Had he ever before kissed a girl—a woman—who had never been kissed? A virgin . . . he quickly thrust that thought from his mind. His manhood, however, neglected for so long, seemed to have developed a mind of its own. It rose to stiffness in an instant, bulging his breeches in an alarming way.

Her hand at his throat bumped Camille's love token. Jack flinched, half expecting an exploding shell, but nothing like that occurred. He brushed her mouth with his; it was cool as well, and dry. Too dry for kissing. He touched it gingerly with his tongue. She stiffened in his arms, and for a moment he thought that she would bolt from him, flutter off into the darkness. But as he pressed his lips to hers, she leaned up to him, standing on tiptoe. The tightening of her back, her buttocks, the rise of her small breasts beneath their black-damask cocoon, made the blood pound in his head.

She put her arms around his neck. He straightened, pulling her off the ground. She clung to him, mouth parting in a sigh. His manhood thrust at her waist, rigidly unruly. He quickly scooped her up, holding her cradled above it. But he went on kissing her, while she melted to him.

She weighed no more than a butterfly's wings; he felt that to press against her was to crush her. His one hand was curled beneath her knees; the other encompassed her slight shoulders with room to spare. Experimenting, he found that allowed him ample leeway to caress her breast. It was small but perfect, hardly filling his cupped palm, and its tip beneath the layers of damask was as firm as his cock. He rolled it gently between his forefinger and thumb, heard her breath quicken, knew his own had, too.

A kiss, he reminded himself brusquely. That was all of their bargain. But her mouth was so impossibly sweet; the Castile scent of her hair made him think of holidays from school and the old copper tub in the nursery. He thrust his tongue between her lips, hoping that might frighten her, give him some excuse to stop. But she only held to him, her own tongue meeting his, hesitant and yet willing, in the most arousing way.

He came up for air. "Miss Wilcox. You have not been frank with me. Either you've been kissed quite thoroughly before, or you're a prodigy."

"I've always been a quick study."

That made him laugh despite himself and renew his caresses, planting his mouth against her breast through the wool of her gown. She caught her breath; he played his tongue against the small bud of her nipple, felt her arms tighten around him. His hand stroked her tiny waist, slipped downward, smoothed her thigh. His own state of excitement—his throbbing manhood, the fire in his loins— was shocking. Her responses were so unlike Camille's, or Vivienne's; he had the sense he was a navigator, an explorer on the threshold of uncharted lands, and he wanted desperately to be their discoverer, set his seal and name to them forever. But the very intensity of his desire sobered him. He forced his head from her breast. "We have two choices now," he announced.

"And what are those?" she murmured, her low voice dreamy.

"We can return to the pavilion, have another glass of champagne to toast the evening and then hie ourselves back to the Savoy, or—"

"Or?"

"Or," he said, dipping his mouth to hers, "we can go on to finish what we've begun."

"I have—" Miss Wilcox started to say.

"And don't you dare tell me again about scientific curiosity!"

"No, no," she assured him. "I was going to say . . . I have a feeling it is best we stop."

"You're sure?" He was amazed at how disappointed he sounded.

"Yes. You see, one of the unfortunate aspects of scientific inquiry is that it leads one to understand . . . well, the birds and the bees."

"And butterflies," Jack noted dryly.

"Those, too."

"If Robert ever had kissed you—really kissed you," Jack observed, setting her back on the ground, "he never would have gone near Vivienne Harpool again."

She toed the earth beneath her slipper. "Do you know, that is the nicest compliment anyone has ever paid me."

"I mean it," Jack said, and stood for a moment staring

down at her. "You're a remarkable girl—*woman*—Priscilla Wilcox."

She raised her small face. It caught a glint of starlight, and Jack saw the tracks of tears on her cheeks. "Perhaps someday a man who isn't in love with someone else will feel that," she mumbled. Then she yanked on her hood and squared her shoulders. "We should just go home, I suppose. I don't think it wise that I drink any more champagne."

The meeting with the Crown's revenue agents was highly entertaining. Jack entered the examination chamber trailed by Bennett Shropley, who staggered beneath a tower of records and receipt books. "You won't need those," Jack had told him as they left the Savoy.

The solicitor looked startled. "Of course I will! How else are they to know we have the wherewithal to pay the taxes and fines?"

Jack had straightened his coat, gave a final tug to the cravat he'd arranged in the latest Cascade. "Wait and see," he'd said.

Shropley saw soon enough. There were four agents ranged against them, and a grimmer set of men could not have been plucked from a cell at Newgate. Without waiting for an invitation, Jack dropped easily into a chair, sprawling, crossing his legs, his Hessians immaculate. The solicitor hesitated in the doorway. Jack waved him in impatiently. "Come, my good man!" he said, his voice booming in the

small, dank chamber. "Let's have this over and done with.
I've an engagement with the Regent in a quarter of an hour."

The leader of the quartet of vultures spoke up. "I'm
afraid, Lord Avenleigh, you will miss that engagement."

Jack looked shocked. "Dash it all, I hope not! Prinnie
would be ever so cross." Then he grinned his devil's grin.
"And not, I assure you, with me!"

"We'd best get down to it, Hitchens," the smallest vulture quavered.

Head vulture Hitchens paged through a stack of papers. "You do understand, milord, that your debt to the
Crown currently stands at nearly twenty thousand pounds."

"Quite." Jack reached into his coat. "Will you take a
bank check?"

The quartet exchanged glances. "A . . . check, milord?"
Hitchens echoed uncertainly. "In what amount?"

"Shall we say a third of the amount I owe you? Which
would be six thousand, four hundred and fifty-three
pounds. Have I got that right, Shropley?"

"Uh—absolutely, Lord Avenleigh."

"A third of the amount," Hitchens said.

"That is, if I am not mistaken, twice what the Crown
customarily obtains through prosecution for outstanding
debts."

"He's right about that," the little vulture put in.

"I'm sure accommodation could be reached for the
total you mention. But don't you wish to—to make out a
schedule of repayment?" Hitchens asked, his voice cracking slightly.

"Why? Let's get it over and done with; that's what I
say." He handed Shropley the check, and the solicitor
crossed the room with it.

The vultures huddled their heads together at their table.
Jack took out a cigar, rolled it between his fingers, cut it, lit
it, then blew a great puff of smoke in the agents' direction.

The little one raised his nose. "I say, Lord Avenleigh. Might I ask what brand it is you are smoking?"

"This?" Jack peered at his cigar. "My own, my good man. I import them from the islands. Care to try one? Shropley! Set down that pile of nonsense and take these over there." Shropley did as he was bade. There was a brief pause while the vultures also lit up. The chamber filled with fragrant haze.

"Very nice indeed," Hitchens acknowledged grudgingly.

"If you like, I'd be more than happy to arrange for each of you to receive a box."

"That would hardly be prop—"

"At my special discounted rate," Jack continued smoothly. "The one I reserve for my friends."

"Best damned cigar I ever smoked," another vulture, a portly one, murmured happily.

"Extraordinary," the fourth one agreed.

"Shropley! See you find out these good gentlemen's directions, and arrange to have two dozen cigars shipped to each posthaste."

"Very good, milord," Shropley said nervously.

Hitchens made one last stab at business. "I take it, milord, you intend to keep up with your payment of taxes on the estate? From this point forward, I mean."

"Absolutely," Jack said from within a cloud of tobacco smoke. "Shropley here is my agent. Payments will be quarterly, punctual—and accompanied by another box of cigars for each of you."

"I really don't see what else we have to ask him," the little vulture noted.

"Nor do I, Mr. Hitchens," the fat fellow agreed.

"Excellent!" Jack declared, rising from his chair. "I'll be in time for Prinnie after all! Shropley! Pick up that mess of books and come along!"

"Very good, milord."

Hitchens offered his hand. "A pleasure doing business with you, Lord Avenleigh."

After the merest hesitation, Jack took it. "And with you, Mr. Higgins."

"That's Hitchens."

"Of course. Hitchens. You made a note of that, Shropley?"

"Yes, milord."

"Well! We're off then! Tallyho, gentlemen!" Jack gave them a vague salute, stubbed his cigar out on the table, and left.

In the corridor, Shropley was sweating profusely. "How *could* you get his name wrong there at the end?" he demanded in a hiss.

Jack waved a hand. "That, dear Bennett, was the crowning touch. Men such as he expect to be beneath my notice. I simply played to his hand."

"You *bribed* them," Shropley said, sounding scandalized.

"They expected that as well. Cigars, at least, are less crass than money."

"Do you really have a meeting with Prinnie?"

"Of course I don't! Can't stand the man."

Shropley glanced up at him. "Will that check clear?"

"If it doesn't," said Jack, "that will be your concern. I'll be in St. Lucia." Then he laughed, seeing the solicitor's horrified expression. "It will. Here, give me some of those." He took half the burden of documents from the redhead's arms. They walked in silence down the long hall.

Then Shropley spoke up again. "You just made yourself twelve thousand, nine hundred and six pounds, milord. By having them agree to settle, I mean, for a third."

"So I have. Well, you know what they say, Shropley—you must *have* money to *make* money."

"Christ! To have been born a lord!" the solicitor said in envy.

"It's not all beer and skittles," Jack noted modestly.

"The hell it's not!"

*B*ut it wasn't. There was, for example, the guest awaiting Jack upon his return to the hotel: Vivienne Harpool, who'd settled in the sitting room clad in a fanciful gown of blue-green jaconet muslin with a treble ruff of pointed lace at the throat. Her expression, beneath an extremely becoming chip hat of peacock-blue silk tied with yellow ribbands, was mutinous.

"Jackie," she said as he entered.

"Vivienne! What a delightful surprise!"

"I wish I could say as much about the surprise you gave me last evening."

Jack headed for the sideboard for a celebratory brandy. "Would you like something to drink?"

"I'd *like* an explanation!"

He turned to her, snifter in hand. "Explain your conundrum, pray do, and I'll attempt to appease you."

Something about her reminded him of an engraving he had in an old schoolbook of Mt. Vesuvius about to explode. "I went to an *unimaginable* amount of trouble—*and* expense—to secure that invitation to Prinnie's reception last evening," she said, her fine mouth very tight.

"It was most kind of you to do so. I had an early meeting with the Crown's agents, so I haven't yet spoken to Aunt Bertrice. But I have no doubt she enjoyed herself immensely."

"The invitation," Vivienne said pointedly, "included *you*."

"Yes. I know. But it did not include Miss Wilcox. Since it did not, suitable arrangements had to be made. I could not, in good conscience, deprive my aunt or cousins of an experience so sure to enthrall them. And so I volunteered as chaperon."

"I did not think Miss Wilcox's father would approve of her presence at such a gathering."

Jack pondered that, sipping brandy. "You are probably right there. Nonetheless, arrangements had to be made."

"You were out with her until nearly one o'clock!"

"Was it so late as that?"

Vivienne Harpool made a visible attempt to get a grip on her wrath. "Your Cousin Agnes mentioned it in passing this morning. I hardly think, Jackie, that keeping a child such as that out to all hours is appropriate!"

"Miss Wilcox is not a child." Jack hid his nose in his snifter, fighting the memory of her breast in his hand.

"Don't diddle with me, Jackie! You know what I mean! She may not be in years, but she certainly is in experience!"

He raised his blue eyes to her. "How would you know that, Vivienne?"

"Why—I know what Robert said of her."

"And what did Robert say?"

"Just—that she had been so sheltered. By her father. That he'd never allowed her any freedom, any liberties. He kept her at tight rein." Her impatience broke. "Lord, Jackie, you have only to look at the girl to realize it! She has no more sense of fashion than—than a cow!"

"She knows a great deal about *Bombycidae*," Jack said thoughtfully.

Vivienne glared at him with deep suspicion. "Where did you go with her last night?"

"To a lecture on butterflies. At the British Museum."

The suspicion vanished abruptly; she burst out in high, breathy laughter. "Oh, God! You poor dear!" She doubled over on the sofa. Jack watched, not joining in her mirth. "A lecture on butterflies! You must have been bored to tears!"

"Actually, it was most instructive."

"Pish," she said knowingly, plying her fan. "You really are too good for words. Squiring her to such a dreary thing—why, I believe I owe you an apology! I scarcely see how a lecture on butterflies could compare to an evening in the presence of the *crème de la ton*!"

"Nor do I," Jack said, and swallowed brandy. "How did Aunt Bertrice and the cousins fare, by the by?"

"About as you'd imagine. I just kept whispering to everyone that they were in quaint Lincolnshire mourning outfits." Her olive eyes took on a hint of rebuke. "Had you been there, they'd have had an easier time of it. So would I. But it was tolerable—except when Sephrina took it into her head to ask Prinnie to dance with her. I wonder sometimes, Jackie, if she is—well, *compos mentis*."

"I very much appreciate, Vivienne, your hard work on behalf of my family. You must allow me, naturally, to recompense you for whatever . . . ah, expenditures you stood."

She fluttered a graceful hand. "It was not so much as that. Only a bribe to Prinnie's secretary and another to his valet. I suppose one could say I owe it to your family, in light of what Robert spent on me."

"Nonetheless," Jack said gravely. "I'll feel better if I repay you. Will a hundred pounds cover it?"

Her jaw dropped open. Just as quickly, she pulled it up again. "Didn't you meet with the Crown's agents this morning about the taxes on the estate?"

"So I did. We came to terms. You haven't answered my question."

"A hundred pounds," she said smiling enchantingly, "is just exactly right."

Jack was rather chipper as he went to gather the ladies for dinner that evening. He'd made plans to take them to

Gaillard's—devil take the expense; it would be a treat. He was a trifle uncertain what Miss Wilcox's reaction upon seeing him again might be, but was relying on her discretion. She wasn't the type to turn simpering or clingy, he was sure, simply on account of their scientific explorations the night before.

Cousin Agnes and Cousin Sephrina were, as usual, parked before the pier glass, jockeying for position as they arranged their bonnets. Aunt Bertrice was glowering at them, invoking Scripture against the sin of vanity. Miss Wilcox was not in evidence. He felt a flash of disappointment in her. So she *was* intending to play coy. "Ready to go, ladies?" he said, falsely hearty. "You all look most elegant."

"We can't go," Aunt Bertrice snapped. "Miss Wilcox has run off."

Jack paled. "Run off?"

"To the Egyptian Hall," 'Phrina put in. "To see the curiosities."

"She said," Cousin Agnes noted, "there were bound to be butterflies."

The tension flowed out of Jack's broad shoulders. "Egyptian Hall, eh? She should be safe enough. It's right in Piccadilly Square. A simple matter for her to hail a hack home."

"The bishop would never forgive me," Aunt Bertrice intoned, "for allowing her to go alone."

"Well, the bishop is in Lincoln and hardly likely to learn of it unless you tell him. Meantime, I've reservations at Gaillard's. The finest eating place in London."

"Shellfish, I suppose," Aunt Bertrice said dourly.

"Actually, they specialize in beef and lamb."

"I was at Gaillard's once," Agnes said unexpectedly. "With Lord Cowper. It was one of the most . . . most enjoyable meals I've ever had in my life."

Lord Cowper? Jack wanted to ask who the devil he

was. But the distant glow of memory on his cousin's face
stayed his tongue.

"I wonder if it has changed," she went on dreamily.
"They had, as I recall, the most *incredible* velouté of veal."
Her eyes were positively aglow. Women certainly are pecu-
liar when it comes to food, Jack mused.

"I think," her mother said, sharp chin jutting, "Jack
had better go and find Miss Wilcox immediately."

"Suppose I do that," he proposed, "and bring her
along with me to Gaillard's. Meanwhile, you can go ahead.
I should hate to miss the reservation. They are quite difficult to procure." His aunt hesitated.

"And raspberry charlotte," Agnes murmured, still enthralled, "to kill for."

Aunt Bertrice hesitated. "With whipped cream?"

"*Oceans* of whipped cream."

The old lady snatched up her reticule. "Hail us a hack,
Jack. But mind you hurry that willful little chit along."

At this hour of the evening, the Egyptian Hall museum
was cool and silent and nearly deserted. Jack paid his shilling admission and wandered through the high-ceilinged
rooms. A little group of schoolboys was gawking at the tall
statues of pharaohs and their consorts; two elderly women
accompanied by a young man had their monocles up to
peer at an immense slab of carved hieroglyphs. Jack strode
through each of the exhibits but saw no sign of Miss
Wilcox. Finally he asked of a guard at the exit, "Are there
any butterflies on display?"

"Third gallery, guv'nor," the man said wearily. "But
we close in ten minutes."

"I'm just looking for a friend." He followed the fellow's languid wave back into the dim rooms.

He found the butterflies—one sizeable glass-covered

display of them—but no one was in evidence except a thin young student busily taking notes, his nose pressed up against the case so avidly that he never noticed Jack. She must have gone back to the Savoy, he concluded, turning again for the exit. Then something about the student's ill-fitting trousers and countrified hat made him swing back. He approached the lad with more caution than was necessary—an earthquake likely could not have diverted him—and peered over his shoulder at the notebook. The illegible scrawl made him swallow a laugh. He leaned down close to the hat. "Miss Wilcox, I presume?"

She started so abruptly that the notebook flew from her hands. Her eyes met his, and the guilty fear in them tugged at his heart. He bent down for the notebook. "I beg your pardon. I didn't mean to frighten you," he apologized.

She was blushing above the rough-spun man's shirt. "Are you going to tell my father?"

"Tell him what?"

She glanced down at her absurd outfit. "About . . . this. You know."

"I'm no tattletale, Miss Wilcox. Though I admit I am puzzled. You certainly would have been admitted here in your own clothes."

"Perhaps," she admitted. "But I would not have been allowed to behave as I pleased. To stand here for as long as I like without someone calling me a bluestocking, or mentioning that brains and beauty rarely go hand in hand."

Jack smiled. "So. Is the display worth the risks of your deception?"

"Oh, my, yes. Do look here." She tapped her pen on the glass, drawing a rebuking stare from the guard at the gallery doors. Jack obliged, bending low. "It's an *Endromidae*. I've never seen one before, only sketches—they are native to North Africa. But Professor Eisenroth writes that a single captive female will cause *hundreds* of males of the species to flock to her."

"I've known females like that myself," Jack said wryly. "What else is there?"

She pointed again. The guard at the doors cleared his throat: "Closin' in five minutes."

She spoke more quickly. "*Bombyx mori*. The silk-worm. There at the left is the cocoon."

Dubiously Jack eyed the dull brown mass. "Do you mean to tell me that's what all the silkcloth in the world is made from? You are going to make an unromantic out of me, Miss Wilcox. First insisting diamonds are no more than rotten vegetables and now showing me this—"

"Here. Look here. A *Lasiocampidae*."

"And what distinguishes it?"

"It's one of several families in which the larval and imaginal stages show a complete differentiation in function."

"I beg your pardon?"

"When it's a caterpillar," she clarified, "it does nothing but feed. But once it gains its wings, it never eats at all. It can't; its jaws no longer work."

"What does it do, then?"

"Nothing but reproduce."

"Mate, you mean." She nodded. "For how *long*?"

"Months, Professor Eisenroth says."

Jack looked more closely at the fanciful butterfly pinned beneath the glass. "I'm not sure if I pity him or envy him."

She glanced up suspiciously. "If I am boring you to tears, you needn't be polite, you know."

"I like hearing you talk about them."

"Three minutes," the guard put in dauntingly.

"Here's a death's head moth. We have the pupae in England—I've found them myself in potato fields—but they never survive the winter to mature at this latitude.

Butterflies migrate, you know. Some species fly thousands and thousands of miles every autumn to their wintering grounds. They move in great swarms, millions at a time together, across oceans, across continents. I imagine some of your sailors have seen such clouds. Wouldn't that be a sight to behold? Oh, my lands, there's a *Rothia*, from Madagascar!"

"What distinguishes it?" Jack asked, following her avid gaze.

"Nothing I know of," she admitted. "Just its beauty. But I suppose that's enough."

"Two minutes," said the guard.

"*Parnassius apollo,*" she said reverently, pointing to another specimen.

"A highfalutin name for such a wisp of a creature."

"*Nymphalis jason.*"

"Heroes and gods . . . I really had no idea."

"I've got to close up now, sirs," the guard said with a yawn.

Jack came to his senses, pulled away from the soft scent of her hair. "Good Lord. I sent the hag—I mean, I sent Aunt Bertrice and my cousins ahead to Gaillard's, to hold the reservation. Are you finished?"

"No," she said wistfully. "But I don't think they'll let me stay the night, even in these clothes."

"I've got to get you back to the Savoy to change."

"Oh, no. I've got my stuff right here." She picked up a small carpetbag from the floor. "I can pop into the lavatory and be changed in a dash."

"How very adept you are at deception," Jack murmured.

"Ironical," she threw back over her shoulder, vanishing past the guard.

Jack trailed after her, hoping that stalwart fellow wouldn't notice that she'd gone into the women's stalls. Fortunately, the man busied himself with polishing the butterfly case that Miss Wilcox's eager nose had left smudged. By the time she emerged, in her usual drab garments, Jack himself would have made no connection between the demure, downcast-eyed bishop's daughter and the excited scholar who had stood at the glass only moments before.

*H*e arrived with Miss Wilcox at Gaillard's just as his aunt and cousins were digging into the raspberry charlotte. There was a visitor at the table, too, he noted: Vivienne Harpool, her handsome mouth tight. "We'd given up on you, Jackie," she declared, stirring her coffee.

"What a pleasant surprise, Lady Harpool." It occurred to Jack that he'd been saying those words to her quite frequently of late.

"Lady Harpool was outside the hotel as we were leaving, and Mamma invited her along," Sephrina burbled happily. "You really *must* taste this charlotte, Cousin Jack."

"You've missed supper completely," Aunt Bertrice noted.

"That is my fault," Priscilla Wilcox told her. "I simply could not tear myself away from the Egyptian Hall."

"Those dusty dead things," Vivienne said with distaste.

"I found my visit quite . . . illuminating." Jack flashed a grin at Miss Wilcox. Vivienne's olive eyes narrowed minutely.

"I don't know *what* you're to do about dinner," Aunt Bertrice said balefully.

"I needn't eat. I'm not especially hungry," Miss Wilcox murmured.

"Well, I am," said Jack. He waved to the waiter. "Beefsteak, rare, with au gratin potatoes. And the lamb ragout for the lady. Will that suit, Miss Wilcox? It's a specialty of the house." She nodded bashfully.

"Surely, Jackie," Vivienne Harpool began, her voice uncharacteristically tart, "you don't intend for us to sit here while you eat an entire meal!"

"Certainly not. I'll be more than happy to have the maître d' hail a cab for you."

"I'd thought we might go on to Lord and Lady Somerleigh's reception," she said in a dangerous tone.

'Phrina perked up, but her mother shook her head. "Impossible. We don't even *know* them."

"Neither do I. It won't matter in the crush," Vivienne assured her.

'Phrina still looked eager, but Jack declined. "We're to make an early start back to Lincolnshire tomorrow. I think it best we go to our beds."

Vivienne seemed about to argue it more when a party of young, stylish lords and ladies appeared in the doorway, their voices bright and gay. She glanced toward them for a moment; then she stood up, nodding quickly. "As you wish. I'll be on my way, though. Have a safe journey home."

"We're ever so grateful," Aunt Bertrice said in what for her was a gush, "for your attentions to us here in London."

"I'll say," Sephrina put in.

"Any time. Any time at all," Vivienne said distractedly, waving a hand at them. *"Au revoir!"* She hurried off with her head ducked low.

"Where are your manners, Jack?" Aunt Bertrice demanded. "Go and get a cab for her, for heaven's sake!" He got up to do so, observing that Vivienne had chosen a most roundabout route to the exit. He took a more direct one, past the well-dressed newcomers still waiting for their table. As he excused himself and went by, one of the ladies caught her breath.

"Why, Edwin!" She grabbed her companion's arm and pointed to Vivienne's retreating back. "Isn't that your stepmamma?"

"Where?" he asked. "By God, so it is! I wonder what poor fool she's got her hooks into now."

Another of the gentlemen chuckled. "I take it, Eddie, there was little love between you?"

"She hounded the old man to death, so help me," Edwin muttered angrily. "Between frittering his money and whoring with his friends, she led him to an early grave."

"Edwin told me," the first lady who had spoken hissed, "his father found her in bed with Lord Trayputtle—on their *honeymoon*!"

"She has had her comeuppance," Edwin declared with satisfaction. "No one of note receives her anymore."

"Really?" One of the ladies glanced after Vivienne. "I could have sworn I saw her just the other evening at the Regent's reception."

"Anyone of note *and* taste," Edwin amended, making his companions laugh.

Ears burning, Jack went out to the street. Vivienne had vanished. He stood for a moment in the glow of the gas lamps, pondering what he'd heard.

The doorman tipped his hat to him. "Can I do somewhat for you, sir?"

"No," Jack said shortly. Then he reconsidered. "Perhaps. The party that just came in. Would you happen to know who they are?"

"Why, that would be Lord and Lady Harpool, sir, with their friends. And a nicer young couple you never will find. *Excellent* tippers." He winked.

"Thank you," Jack told him, and returned inside. On the way back to the table, he considered that the grown son of a widower who had taken a new young wife might have any number of reasons for resenting her. On the other hand . . .

His aunt was still rhapsodizing over their departed companion. "Delightful woman, Lady Harpool," she de-

clared with approval. "Truly delightful. So kind of her to
go out of her way for us as she did."

Jack took his seat and stared over at the table where
Lord Harpool and his party were now installed.

"Jack?" Agnes said tentatively.

He roused himself. "Yes?"

"Your beefsteak is here."

He glanced down at the platter before him. "So it is,"
he murmured, taking up his knife and fork, chewing very
thoughtfully.

*L*ate that night, Pris sat atop her bed with Professor Eisenroth's treatise open on her lap, never turning the page. She kept remembering the way Jack Cantrell had looked as he leaned down beside her to gaze at the butterflies in the Eygptian Hall, so patient and attentive. Then later, at the restaurant, he'd been ever so gallant—ordering for her, insisting that she have a glass of wine over his aunt's objections, arranging with the waiter that a serving of the renowned mousse be reserved for her. The way he'd behaved had made her feel nearly as elegant and worldly as Lady Harpool And when he'd left her at the doors to her room, he had kissed her hand.

"Oh, I *am* being silly," she murmured aloud, contemplating the same engraving of an imperator moth she'd been staring at for the past hour. He'd only shown her common politeness. Still, when she was with him she felt alive in ways she never had before. And every time he grinned at her, excitement played along her spine like a set of invisible wings waiting to unfurl.

She knew, of course, that he was in love with his mistress back in St. Lucia. Still, she was grateful to him for showing her what all the . . . well, what all the *fuss* between women and men was about. Her brief attraction to his brother, in the earliest days of their acquaintance, was as close as she had ever come to love—and that paled before this maelstrom of emotion like a flour moth beside the glorious specimen engraved on the page. She'd liked Robert the way a child appreciates a gaudy new toy, for the envy and attention their betrothal gained her. What she felt toward his brother was altogether different, deep and mysterious; it flowed in her blood, seemed buried in her bone, and she was awed by it.

He would be returning to Mademoiselle Déshoulières all too soon, she knew. But at least he'd taught her she was capable of womanly desire. That was more than his brother ever did.

Sighing, she set the book aside at last and reached to turn off the lamp beside the bed. But before she could, she froze, her eye catching on the slow, silent raising of the latch at her door. Her heart swelled, its beating furiously fast. *He is coming,* she thought, watching in stunned fascination as the door swung open slowly. *He is coming to me.* A lifetime of lessons from the pulpit guttered to nothingness in that instant; she could not wait to damn her soul.

"Expecting someone else?" Vivienne Harpool inquired sweetly, entering the room with a taunting smile.

Somehow Pris swallowed the knot of disappointment in her throat. "I wasn't . . . expecting anyone at all. Why should I be, at this hour?"

"Oh, of course not. Butter wouldn't melt in your mouth, would it, mousy Miss Wilcox?" She closed the door behind her, took a step toward the bed. "I don't know what game you think you are playing. But I'll thank you to keep your sly little hands off Jack Cantrell. He's mine."

"He isn't," Pris said bravely. "He's in love with a woman—his mistress—back on St. Lucia."

"She's a long way off," Lady Harpool said complacently. "I'm here. Unfortunately, so are you."

Looking at her in her gorgeous cape and hat and gown and jewels, Pris was nearly tempted to laughter. How could Lady Harpool honestly think her a threat? "Lord Avenleigh has been very chivalrous toward me. That is all."

"You don't fool me, mouse. You know damned well you wish he would be something more. But he's far beyond *your* grasp." Her red mouth curved in scorn. "You couldn't even get Robert to wed you."

"What makes you think I wanted him to?"

That gave Her Ladyship pause. Then she laughed, and it was not at all breathy. "Come, come, Miss Wilcox. Let's not pretend. An earl and a bishop's daughter?"

"He may have been an earl, but he was also an ass. I had no intention of going through with any marriage."

Those painted eyebrows arched. "You're awfully high and mighty, aren't you, for a girl with no looks and no fortune?"

Pris stared straight into those cold eyes. "He did not marry you, either."

Lady Harpool's laugh was a little tardy once again. "Marry *me*? Poor child, you are deluded! Robert meant nothing to me."

"I believe that. But you told Lord Avenleigh you never lay with him. And that's a lie."

The golden gaze had narrowed. "Foolish girl. What would you know of such things?"

"I saw you," Pris said evenly. "More than once. When I was out with my nets."

"Saw me?" Lady Harpool fluttered her lashes in innocence. "Whatever do you mean?"

"Saw you copulating with him."

Vivienne Harpool drew in her breath. "Why, you filthy little—how dare you make such accusations? I've a good mind to tell your father you've been spreading vile rumors about me!"

"I haven't spread them—yet." Pris got up from the bed, stood tall and straight as she could. "Robert *was* an ass, but he wasn't a bad man. Just a weak one. You played on his weaknesses. What you did to him—not to mention his aunt and cousins—was unconscionable."

"I haven't the least notion what you're talking about!"

Pris looked her up and down. "There's nothing more despicable in a female than using the wiles of sex to lure a male to disaster. You ought to be ashamed."

"To lure him to—listen to you! What would *you* know about such matters, you pathetic old maid?"

"Humans and moths are not so very different," Pris said shortly. "They both tend to flutter toward flame. Now, pray, *do* listen to me. I haven't said a word to Lord Avenleigh regarding my . . . field observations. And I won't—"

"Who's to say he'd believe you if you did?" Lady Harpool demanded.

"Frankly, I'm astonished he took *your* word on the substance of your relationship with Robert, after his brother ran the estate into the ground buying baubles for you." Lady Harpool opened her mouth to protest. "If you're wondering how I know that, his solicitor, Mr. Shropley, called on me a month or so before Robert died. He wondered if I might care to press a suit for alienation of affection." The mouth widened into an O. "I declined. But he showed me the receipts."

"That flame-haired *bastard*!"

Pris cocked her head. "It was really a very decent gesture on his part. But I was able to reassure him that since I didn't want to marry Robert, it made no difference to me."

"To think I believed you such an innocent," Lady Harpool murmured in astonishment.

"As I was saying, though, I've told Lord Avenleigh none of this. And I'll continue to keep silent on one condition. He is scheduled to return to St. Lucia in a month or two. If you keep your distance from him until then—"

"Oh, I see! So that *you* can seduce him!"

"So that he can return safely to the woman he loves, I'll go on holding my tongue."

Lady Harpool was silent for a moment. Then her fine mouth tightened. "I don't grasp it. What's the advantage to you?"

"His happiness," Pris said simply. "He's not a fool. But he's a man, with a man's . . . vulnerabilities. And you are extraordinarily adept, Lady Harpool, at taking advantage of those."

"You don't want him for yourself?"

God. The thought of it . . . But she smiled. "A mousy little thing like me? What chance would I have? Come, Lady Harpool! There are plenty of fish in the sea. And the damage you wreaked to the Avenleigh fortune will not be wiped away easily."

Lady Harpool gave a tug to her glove. "That's what I thought as well. But if he has settled with the Crown, he must be faring well indeed." She paused. "What makes you imagine knowing about me and Robert would make any difference to him?"

"It would mean you'd lied. He's not a man to hold with lies."

"You think you know him so very well, don't you?" Lady Harpool sneered. "He's just a man. They're all alike at the core. Only after one thing."

"You'd be a better judge than I."

Lady Harpool touched the jewels at her throat. "For your information, I have every intention of staying on in London. It just so happens there is a noble gentleman very desirous of marrying me."

"How old is this one?"

Lady Harpool shot her a look of true hatred. "Snippy little mouse. Let me tell you this. If I stay in London, it will be because my prospects here are far superior to Jack Cantrell in every way—and *not* because of anything you might threaten to do. But I'll offer you this bit of advice, out of the goodness of my heart. There's no sense being generous when it comes to men. The world's a lonely place. You had best look out for yourself." She straightened her hat, swept her cloak around her, and sashayed out.

Pris managed to stay upright until the door had closed behind her. Then she collapsed in a quaking heap, hardly believing she had been so strong. Only the admiration and—and affection she harbored for Lord Avenleigh had emboldened her. A verse from First Corinthians was running through her head: *Love suffereth long, and is kind; love envieth not . . . love bears all things, believes all things, hopeth all things, endureth all things.*

Oh, it must be love, true love, she thought, that makes me so willing he should return to his lover.

Then the impossible irony of it all made her burst into tears.

Jack raised his cup in a toast. "Ladies. I wish to thank you all for a most—ah—most *remarkable* visit to Lincolnshire." It was late August; rain was pouring down, and he was departing for London, to take ship to St. Lucia the following week.

"And we must thank you for all you have done for us," Agnes said bravely. "As well as for our journey to the capital."

"We shall never go there again." 'Phrina sighed and began playing with the salt.

"I don't see why anyone would *want* to," Aunt Bertrice said squelchingly. "Dirty, filthy city! I count my lucky stars I won't ever have to return there so long as I live."

Jack raised his glass again. "And we all hope, Aunt Bertrice, that you live for a very long time."

There was a moment's pause. Then Agnes clinked her orangeade to her sister's. "Hear, hear!"

"Where?" 'Phrina queried, looking nonplussed.

Agnes sighed. "It's a pity, isn't it, Jack, that you won't

have the chance to bid farewell to Miss Wilcox? I thought it ever so odd of her to rush off to visit her cousins in Sleaford when we'd only just returned from London."

Jack's hand came up to touch the love token that dangled at his chest. "It is a pity," he agreed. "She is a most unusual young woman. Very . . . very learned. I enjoyed her company."

"She'd best take care to hide that learning if she ever hopes to marry," Aunt Bertrice intoned, staring down her nose. "Men don't cotton to that sort of girl."

Just then they raised their heads at the crunch of carriage wheels on the drive.

"Who in the *world* do you suppose that might be?" 'Phrina asked, brightening.

Aunt Bertrice glared at the clock. "Devil of a time for anyone to come calling"—she sniffed—"in the midst of the luncheon hour!"

They waited, while the door knocker sang out and Bellows went to answer it. A murmur of voices drifted up the stairs, one too soft to tell even its sex and the other the butler's, brusque and sharp. More murmuring. Bellows, even more vehement. A thump. Bellows in outrage, and that soft whispering again . . .

'Phrina's blue eyes were like saucers. Agnes had moved forward to the edge of her chair. Lord, Jack thought in bemusement, it doesn't take much to upset a household of spinsters! He pushed back his seat. "No doubt it's some unfortunate traveler caught in the storm, seeking refuge," he assured them. "Suppose I go and—" He was interrupted by the sudden arrival of Bellows in the doorway.

"Forgive me, madame," he told Aunt Bertrice with a bow. "But a situation has arisen that requires your attention."

"Oh, for heaven's sake," she snapped. "Can't it wait until we've finished dining?"

"I'm afraid, madame, it cannot."

She threw down her napkin and swept past him through the door. Bellows trailed along in her wake. Jack speared a slice of Cook's pasty nutcake. He'd just crunched down on what was unmistakably a shell when Aunt Bertrice's shrill voice stopped him in midchew. "Leave my house *immediately*," she was barking, "or I shall summon the authorities and have you clapped into jail!"

'Phrina looked about to faint with excitement. Jack fished the bit of shell out with his fingernail and got to his feet. "I'd best go see," he began. There was the sound of a scuffle below them, and then the whispering voice at last raised itself enough to be heard.

"M'sieur!" it cried. "Oh, M'sieur Jack!"

"Esmé?" Jack said in wonder.

He leaped up and ran, taking the stairs three at a time.

It was Esmé, bedraggled and wild-eyed, standing in the foyer. Bellows had her by the elbow and was doing his best to push her out the door. Another woman, fat and black-skinned, was peeking past the threshold, looking scared out of her wits.

"Be gone with you, I say!" Aunt Bertrice screeched, just as Jack landed at the foot of the stairway.

"Take your bloody hands off her, Bellows!" he roared at the butler.

"Toss her out, Bellows!" Aunt Bertrice countered.

Jack thrust past her and punched the butler hard as he could in the face. The man fell to the floor with a thump. Esmé straightened her skewed shawl with dignity. Jack's eyes narrowed as his aunt stepped toward her. "How *dare* you?" he thundered, with such fire in his eyes that she backed away uncertainly. He hurried to Esmé's side. "Did he hurt you, *chérie*?" he asked anxiously.

She shook her head. *"Ce n'est rien."*

Aunt Bertrice had regained her composure—or, rather, her voice. "This—this *disgusting* bit of trash had the *audacity* to demand an interview with you!"

"Shut up," Jack told her levelly, "or you'll be the next one on the floor."

"But she's a—"

He brought his fist up, hoping she would faint, but apparently she wasn't the type. "Come, Esmé," he said gently, leading her toward his study. She paused to beckon to the woman in the doorway, who shuffled in cautiously, swathed in a mountain of bright cotton shawls.

Once they were in the study, Jack closed the door and ushered both women into chairs. They sank down gratefully, and he realized how weary Esmé looked. He brought her brandy and offered some to the stranger in the shawls, but she shook her head. "God! It is good to see you!" Jack exclaimed. "But what brings you all the way to Lincolnshire? Don't tell me Camille sent you here to check up on me!"

Slowly Esmé raised her dark eyes. "Camille is dead."

"Dead?" Jack couldn't help it. He laughed. "*Dead?* Don't be absurd! She couldn't die!"

"God forgive me, she is dead!" Esmé wailed, bursting into tears. The woman in the shawls joined in with her, keening, high and tight.

Jack staggered to a chair. "Dead . . . when?"

"Two months past," Esmé blubbered miserably.

Two months . . . "Of what?" he demanded incredulously.

"Of a fever. Oh, m'sieur, forgive me coming here! I just did not know what else to do!"

Dead. The word had fallen into Jack's brain and was rattling around there meaninglessly. Dead. What did that signify? He tried his best to recall, but all he could think of were her lithe arms, her rich black hair, her wide green eyes. Beauty like that could not *die*. He put a hand to his throat, felt for the love token she had given him. It was still in place. So must she be.

Esmé was sobbing helplessly, fists digging into her face. "I just did not know what else to do," she cried again.

Jack put that word *dead* aside. "You did right, of course, to come here! You will always have a place with me, Esmé. Always, no matter what." He stole a glance at the fat woman swaddled in shawls. "And your friend as well." He noted, with some wonder, that the woman had unbundled her wrappings and was holding a baby—suckling it, in fact, from her huge brown teat. "Along with her child, of course."

"It is not her child," Esmé whispered.

He stared at her. "You have become a mother? My congratulations! I had no idea! Who is the lucky—"

"*Mon Dieu,* the child's not mine!" she interrupted, and let loose another torrent of tears. "He is yours, m'sieur! Yours and Camille's!"

Esmé's story came out in dribs and drabs, between sips of brandy and fits of grief. Jack knelt beside her, holding tight to her hand. Camille had discovered she was *enceinte* only shortly after Jack's departure. Esmé had urged her to write to Jack with the news, but Camille proudly refused. "He will think it is a trick," she'd argued, "a womanish wile to bring him back." There would be time enough to tell him when he returned, she had insisted. "I could not understand," Esmé whispered, "why she would hesitate to share such news with you. It was as though she was hoping something would happen. That she would never have to tell you about it at all. But everything went perfectly, right up through the delivery. It was only *after* that the sickness hit her. Puerperal fever, the English doctor called it." She pronounced the name carefully, with dread. "M'sieur, I swear to you, I had the best doctors for her—English, French, native, everyone I thought might help!"

"I'm sure you did," Jack said vaguely, dazedly, from the great gaping hole where his heart used to be.

"They could do nothing." Esmé wrung her handkerchief. "She died three weeks later. It was the twenty-third of July."

The twenty-third of July. What, Jack wondered, was I doing on that day? He had no recollection at all, which seemed impossible. Surely he must have felt it, sensed it, when she'd drawn her last breath. . . .

"If I hadn't stayed here," he said. "If I'd gone back. If I had been there—"

"*Non, non,* m'sieur! What could you do? What could *anyone* do?" She hesitated, then wiped her eyes. "I will tell you the truth. I think—*vraiment*, I do—that she preferred it this way. She said to me, just at the last—"

"What?" Jack demanded.

The maid dropped her gaze. "She pleaded with me to raise the child as my own. Never to tell you of its birth. And I gave her my word." She raised her tear-streaked face to him. "But I could not do it. That is—I will be more than happy to keep him if you like, m'sieur. I love him as my own. But it seemed to me—a son! A man ought to make up his own mind about such things."

Tentatively Jack stole a glance at the suckling baby. He had Camille's thick, curling black hair, and her cream-in-coffee skin. "He is—how old?"

"Three months," Esmé said softly.

"What's his name?" Jack asked, his voice low and gruff.

"Camille never named him," her maid confessed. "But I took the liberty—we—the nurse, Jamalla, and I—we call him John. Johnnie. After you."

"Johnnie," Jack muttered. The baby heard, twisting

from the nurse's breast, staring at him. His eyes were blue, bright blue, as blue as St. Lucia's sky.

Jack hid his face in his hands.

Esmé stood up, nodding to her companion. "We will go away," she declared. "I never meant to impose him on you, m'sieur. I only thought . . . a man's own son . . ."

The nursemaid heaved herself to her feet, winding her shawls over the baby. They moved slowly past him. Reluctantly Jack looked up and saw the child still staring at him.

Oh, God. To have him here, to keep him, a constant reminder of all he had lost . . .

But to let him go, pass out of his life . . . This was all he had left now of Camille, of the years they had shared . . . *Dead.* The word had meaning to him suddenly. It was awful and final, grim-gray as gravestones. Camille. *Dead.* He'd never see her again.

The baby cooed suddenly, happily, a brave, bright, joyous sound.

"Pretty boy," Esmé said fondly, tousling his black curls.

"Wait." Jack put his hand out, touched him. Touched his smooth brown cheek, let his fingers wander toward that curly head . . . "Johnnie," he whispered again. And the baby smiled.

"Would you like to hold him?" Esmé asked. "Just this once?" Before he could say no, she had nodded to the nursemaid, who pressed the infant into his arms.

So small. So soft. Unwillingly he let his cheek rest against the baby's forehead. He smelled of jasmine, by God!

"Take him back, Jamalla," Esmé said quickly.

"No," Jack told her. "No." And he clung to his namesake, gripped him so tightly that the baby squealed and fought to wriggle free. Jack looked down in amazement. "God. He's strong."

"A fine, strong boy," Esmé noted, her voice faint with hope.

How tongues would wag! Jack thought vaguely, as his son blew a bubble of spittle at him. But there was no reason, he reminded himself, why he must stay in England. He could take the child back to St. Lucia . . . although without Camille, that paradise suddenly seemed bleak. Well, he need not depart right away. It would hardly be fair to Esmé and the wetnurse, not to mention the baby, to make them undertake that long journey again so soon. For now—

"He's—he's leaking," Jack said, thrusting him back into Jamalla's arms. Her broad face split as she laughed.

The sound rang through the gloomy house like a breath of Caribbean sunshine. Jack went to the door, yanked it open, and called up the stairs: "Cousin Agnes?"

She came, tiptoeing and fearful. "Cousin Agnes," he said again, when she stood on the threshold. "This is my son, John, and the women who have brought him to me. Would you be so kind as to make arrangements for their accommodation, please?"

$\mathcal{I}$t seemed impossible that the arrival of one very small child and two servants could cause so much uproar. It had been two months now since Esmé had landed on Jack's doorstep, and still the furor had not died down. Aunt Bertrice, of course, was at the heart of the trouble. When Jack announced the visitors were staying, she'd taken one look at the baby and suggested he be raised as a post-boy.

Jack had stared at her. "He's my *son*," he managed to growl out.

"He's naught but a half-breed bastard."

How Jack kept from striking her, he never would know.

Agnes, on the other hand, was positively enthralled to have an infant in residence, to the point that she fought with Jamalla over who would get to change his nappies. And 'Phrina—well, 'Phrina was 'Phrina. She could not seem to comprehend how this cocoa-colored child could be Jack's. He left it to Agnes to explain as best as she could.

He was still trying to come to terms with the loss of

Camille, to imagine her cold and dead when she was still so very much alive in his memory. He could not decide whether he was glad Esmé had come or not. He had the most outlandish notion that if she'd stayed in St. Lucia, if she hadn't thrust that world into this one, matters might have been different. He could have fallen off his horse on his ride to London and broken his neck; highwaymen could have shot and killed him; his ship to Castries might have sunk in a storm. And he'd be dead, yes, but at least he'd be spared the haunting vision of Camille dying in their clean white bed. He was tormented with guilt for the way he'd imagined her betraying him when all the time she was waxing great with his child in proud, lonely silence. And he was angry with her, too, for not having realized he would have forgiven her for this unexpected heir.

The baby—he didn't know what to make of the baby. Agnes said the boy looked like him. To Jack, Johnnie was all Camille. He had her dimples, her long, lean body. His feet were even big. To be in his presence was the strangest commingling of curiosity and distress. The prospect of being a father—how did one *be* a father?—was chilling, daunting. He watched Esmé and Jamalla and Agnes cooing over their charge, celebrating each minute milestone—first time rolling from front to back, first night slept through without waking—and wished he could *connect*, share their womanly pleasure. But he felt distant and useless, unable to tell when his own son was crying whether the cause was a pin or the colic or a draft from the nursery door.

"You will learn, m'sieur," the nurse would assure him, smiling her wide grin as he'd push the bawling child back at her. Jack knew, though, that he never would.

Priscilla Wilcox, returned from Sleaford, came to call on a Tuesday, when his aunt and cousins were at Bible study. He received her in the parlor distractedly, neglecting to offer tea. She sat on the sofa in an ill-fitting gown of dull serge, her blond hair stuffed up in a bad poke bonnet, and offered her condolences on his mistress's death. Jack nodded numbly and thanked her, then asked, "Does your father know you have come here?"

"No," she admitted. "He—is quite horrified by this revelation."

"You had best be gone," he said heavily. "Aren't you afraid of what people might say?"

"I'm more surprised by what they *do* say, when a man does no more than take responsibility for what's his," she retorted in a burst of spirit. Esmé bustled in just then with Johnnie in her arms, eager to show his father the merest stump of tooth. Priscilla Wilcox looked down at the baby while he laughed and cooed. "God, she must have been lovely indeed," she said wistfully, and swiftly took her leave.

"I did not mean to interrupt," Esmé apologized, staring after Jack's visitor. "I did not know you had a guest."

"Miss Wilcox? She was my brother's betrothed."

"Ah! So that is Miss Wilcox!" He raised a brow. "M'amselle shared some of your letters with me," she said in explanation. "She chases butterflies, *non*? M'amselle asked me why I thought anyone would want to do so."

"I posed that same question to Miss Wilcox once. She told me it is because they start out ugly and turn into something beautiful. Said it was something human beings couldn't do."

"I see," Esmé said thoughtfully. "She seems *très gentille*. But—*phui!* Such an outfit!"

"Lincolnshire, as you must have noticed, is where fashion comes to die." Jack chucked Johnnie's chin, earning a delighted gurgle.

"What mother would allow her daughter to go about in such *outré* clothes?" Esmé demanded.

"Her mother's long dead," Jack told her. "And her father's a bishop. Church of England."

"Ah." The maid nodded. "That, then, explains *that*."

Somehow Jack made it through that winter, managed to dress and eat and sleep—and work like the devil himself. Bennett Shropley came to see him every few days, with updates on the estate's affairs, problems that needed solving, questions about the Caribbean holdings Jack was doing his best to manage from afar—so many updates and problems and questions that Jack suspected the solicitor was attempting to keep him occupied. He even suggested Jack buy himself a hunter that Lord Ashton had up for sale—an extravagance he never would have proposed before Camille's death.

"What do I want with a hunter?" Jack asked idly.

"Exercise, milord. Fresh air. I could arrange for a brace of hounds as well. One of Lord Canterling's bitches has just whelped."

"I didn't know you for such a sporting sort, Shropley."

"Oh, I'm not. But I'm fond of animals."

"I'm not, especially."

Esmé appeared in the doorway with Johnnie in her arms. "M'sieur! Oh, m'sieur, he just now pulled himself up on the chair in the nursery—pulled himself up to a stand!"

"Did he?" said Jack. "Mr. Shropley. Have you met my son's—my son's—" He broke off, bewildered as always by how to explain Esmé.

"I assist the nurse," she said easily, pleasantly.

Shropley bowed. "Delighted to make your acquaintance, Miss . . ."

"Oh, I am called Esmé. Everyone calls me Esmé." She had taken Johnnie to his father, who smiled at him absently.

"New tooth, you say, Esmé?"

"No, no. He was standing!"

"Standing. Imagine that."

Bennett Shropley gave Esmé a pointed glance. "I was just suggesting to Lord Avenleigh that he purchase a horse. A hunter. Ride about a bit, get some exercise. Good fresh air."

"Ooh, m'sieur, I think that is a splendid idea!"

"And a couple of pups as well."

"Ooh, baby dogs! Johnnie would love that! Wouldn't you, *chéri*?"

Jack knew they meant well, but he was annoyed by their obviousness. "I've got enough to take care of without a passel of critters," he said brusquely. "Shropley, how about that accounting on the *Alice Fair*? Has she reached Lisbon yet?"

"Two weeks past." Shropley reached into his omnipresent stack of papers.

"I—I had best go," Esmé offered. "Time for his bath."

Shropley bowed once more. "A pleasure, M'amselle Esmé." Over Jack's head, bowed to study the report, their eyes met once again, Esmé's bright and desperate. Shropley paused, glanced at Jack, then mouthed at her: "Ten minutes?" She nodded furtively and left with the child.

"Eight hundred casks of rum?" Jack was asking, leafing through the pages. "I thought we sent her out with a full thousand."

"Two hundred were seized, milord, as an assize upon docking."

"Bloody Portuguese taxes," Jack growled.

"Quite so, milord." Shropley took out his pocketwatch. "Forgive me, but I have a meeting in Lincoln at four."

"What's that?"

"I said, I have an engagement in the city at four."

"Oh! Well, go ahead, then, by all means. Leave this stuff here, though. I want to look it over."

Shropley hesitated. "Shall I have Lord Ashton's man bring that hunter 'round for your inspection?"

"Hell, no," Jack said, and buried himself in the papers strewn across his desk.

"Something must be *done*," Esmé hissed as Shropley appeared at the door to the nursery. It was their third meeting since she had approached him privately a month before, to ask for his assistance in reengaging Johnnie's father's interest in life.

The solicitor nodded a greeting to Jamalla, who had the baby pressed to her breast. "You know I agree. But I've tried all I can think of! He cares for nothing except business."

"Business," Esmé said darkly, "is no reason for living. I learned that well enough from Camille." And she sighed. "I believe desperate measures are called for."

"What would you suggest?"

"A lover."

Shropley flushed but kept his voice under control. "Have you anyone in particular in mind?"

"You know better than I what is available."

"Were you thinking of . . . something permanent? Or merely a distraction?"

"*Mon Dieu,* what does it matter? Anyone who will give him a reason to live!"

"There is Lady Harpool," the solicitor said thoughtfully. "She certainly showed much interest in him in London."

"What is she like?"

"Beautiful. Very beautiful."

"Beautiful is good," Esmé noted, encouraged. "He never mentioned her in his letters to m'amselle."

"No?" Shropley pondered that. "She was his brother

Robert's—well, his *something*. The late earl spent considerable sums of money on her, for jewels and gowns and such."

"Then she was his mistress."

"Lord Avenleigh thinks not."

"Men are fools," Esmé decreed with a dismissive wave. "Would she suit him?"

"I'm not sure."

Esmé went and stared out of the window. "*Sacrebleu*, more snow. Always more and more snow—little wonder the man is half out of his mind! Never in all my life have I been in such a wretched place!" Abruptly she turned back. "What about *la petite*? The little girl with the butterflies?"

"Priscilla Wilcox?" Shropley stifled a laugh. "I don't think so. From what you've said of Camille, I cannot imagine—that is to say, she is extremely *nice*, but—"

"Not the sort to hold his attention." Esmé nodded briskly. "*Je comprends.* Still . . . where is this Lady Harpoon now?"

"Har*pool*," Shropley corrected with a smile. "In London, I believe."

"Would she have heard about my m'amselle's death?"

"I don't know from whom she would have."

"*Eh bien.* See you take care of that. *Moi*, I will give some more thought to the girl with the butterflies."

Chapter
17

"I don't really see how *I* can be of any use to you," Priscilla said nervously, staring down at the infant Esmé held. The nursemaid's note, in mangled English, had arrived at Wilcox Hall out of the blue. "I know nothing of babies."

"You are a scientist, *non?* M'sieur wrote to my mistress that."

"A seeker of science, yes, but not a physician. What you need is a physician. My father uses a very good man. Dr. Allison. I'm sure he'd be only too happy—"

"Just look and see what you think," Esmé coaxed, unraveling Johnnie's blanket. "Is that a rash or *non?*"

Priscilla hastily averted her eyes from the baby's nether regions. "It certainly *appears* to be a rash."

"And what would you suggest?"

"Perhaps some—some calamine?"

Esmé's worried brow cleared. "There! You see? What do I need with a doctor?"

"That is what Dr. Allison always prescribes for me,"

Priscilla explained, "when my skin is red." She sniffled self-consciously into her handkerchief.

"I have noticed," Esmé said, "that your complexion is not *de rigueur*."

"Far from it," Pris laughed ruefully. "I have a cyclical catarrah. Something in the air, in the winter and spring, makes me sneezy and teary."

"Really? I knew a girl in Castries who suffered that same problem. Madame Gris-Gris remedied it, though, for her."

"Who is Madame Gris-Gris?"

"A witch," Esmé said.

Pris recoiled from her. "Oh! Not really!"

"But yes. She makes the potions, you know, for this and that. Broken hearts. Evil spells. Red noses."

"Lord Avenleigh mentioned to me once," Pris said hesitantly, "a love potion made from moths' wings."

"*Oui, oui.* That is Madame Gris-Gris's."

Pris's gray eyes widened. "You don't actually *believe* in such stuff!"

Esmé shrugged. "Nothing I ever saw on St. Lucia taught me *not* to."

"It is the work of the devil!" Pris said, scandalized.

The maid cocked her dark, curly head. "To make the nose less red?"

"Well, not that, perhaps. But the other things you mentioned—broken hearts. Evil spells."

"A broken heart is less important than a red nose?"

"Oh, I don't mean that! I only mean—well! I'm not certain *what* I mean."

Esmé moved to the hutch near Jamalla. "Calamine. Moths' wings. What is the difference between them?" She took a small jar from a shelf, held it out to Pris. "Here is Madame Gris-Gris's *baume* for the nose that is red."

"What is in it?" Pris asked, suspicious.

"*Je ne sais pas.* I only know the girl in Castries swore by it." She pressed it into Pris's hand. "Try it! What have you to lose?"

"What indeed?" Pris echoed a little wistfully. She squared her small shoulders. "Very well. I will. Thank you, Esmé. And I'll see that Johnnie gets his calamine, shall I?"

Jamalla waited until their visitor's footsteps had faded before she grunted, "Hard going."

"*Oui.* Hard going," Esmé acknowledged. "But not, surely, a hopeless task."

"Oh, Jackie." Vivienne Harpool's olive eyes were bright with tears. "I am so ashamed! To think that I was thoroughly enjoying myself in London while all the time you were here, mired in misery—" She caught her breath in a sob. "My poor dear Jackie! How bravely you've borne up!"

"Not much else to do," Jack said briefly.

She came toward him, reaching for his cravat. "You look like bloody hell, if you'll excuse an old friend saying so. I'll wager you haven't been eating."

"I hate English food."

"You would not hate *mine*," she told him, settling the neckcloth. "You must come to supper. Tomorrow night?"

"I'm afraid, Vivienne, I'll not prove good company." He was vaguely astonished at how her intimate ministrations evoked no response whatsoever from his body or blood.

"Then I'll send something over. What would you like? Crab? Prawns? Lobster? Or shall I surprise you? Oh, it's little wonder you are lost in grief, is it, in such winter drear? It took me six days to journey up from London."

Jack was aware, dimly, that some polite response was required. "You ought not to have gone to so much trouble."

"Now, Jackie, no more talk like that! How could you imagine I wouldn't come running the moment I—" She broke off. Esmé had appeared in the doorway to the parlor with a bundle in her arms.

"*Pardon*, m'sieur, but I really did think you would want to know this straightaway. He stood up! By himself, without any support!"

"Did he really?" Jack said. "Good boy." He stared down at his boots for a moment. Then his sense of duty prevailed. "I beg your pardon. Vivienne, this is the—the nurse's assistant, Esmé."

Esmé dropped an elegant curtsy. Vivienne Harpool was staring at Johnnie, who'd raised his curly black head at the sound of his father's voice. "And . . . this?" Vivienne asked faintly.

"This," Esmé announced with pride, "is m'sieur's son."

"His son?" Vivienne took a step toward the baby. "His *son*?" Esmé dutifully unwrapped Johnnie, so as better to present him in all his glory. Vivienne staggered on her feet. "His *son* . . . oh, my heavens, Jackie! You must be so—so—so—" Words failed her. She stared down at Johnnie.

"Yes," Jack said from within his web of sorrow. "Yes, I am."

"A darling boy," Vivienne decreed, and reached her hand out gingerly to pat his wiry curls. "I don't believe in all my life I've ever seen such a *darling* boy!"

*C*ris looked in disbelief into her bedchamber mirror, then down at the jar in her hand. *Whatever* Madame Gris-Gris put into her salve, there was no question the stuff worked. For the first February she could remember, her skin was smooth and creamy pale, with no hint of those wretched red blotches. She put her hand to her cheek, let her fingers wander down to her mouth. That was where he had kissed her—there, and there, and *here* . . .

Her father's heavy footsteps thudded in the hallway.

Swiftly Pris let her hand fall from her breast and spun away from the looking glass.

Bishop Wilcox entered her room without knocking, as usual. "The coach is waiting," he intoned, rifling through the cards that held the notes for his sermon. "St. Paul today. First Corinthians. I think it should go over well."

" 'When I was a child,' " Pris muttered mutinously.

"How's that, dear?"

She said it again, loudly: " 'When I was a child, I spake as a child. But when I became a man, I put away childish things.' "

"Quite so. You need a hat, I believe?"

Pris jammed one onto her head. "Have I got marmalade on my chin, Father?"

He blinked at her. "Not that I can see."

Pris sighed. *I've been kissed, you know,* she longed to tell him. *Kissed and—and touched by the most glorious man in the world. My life was turned completely upside-down, and you never even noticed any difference in me! How could you be so blind?*

The bishop offered her his arm. They went down the stairs and out the doors into a burst of early-spring sunlight so bright that Pris blinked and nearly stumbled. Her father patted her hand, helping her into the coach. As he bent to enter beside her, he glanced at her curiously. Then his voice turned as thunderous as it could from the pulpit. "Priscilla Margaret Anne Wilcox! What have you got on your face?"

"On my—nothing! Nothing at all, Father!"

"You're not painted?" he demanded in outrage.

"No! Of course I am not!"

He peered more closely. "Then what's become of your splotches?"

"I don't know," she murmured guiltily. "They just have . . . disappeared."

"Hmph!" And then he had the audacity to wet his handkerchief with his tongue and press it to her nose, just as though she were five again!

"Father!" She jerked away from him in fury. "What do you think you are *doing*?"

"Merely checking, my dear. Can't have folk whispering that Bishop Wilcox's daughter is painted like a common harlot!"

"Honestly!" Pris muttered, and sank back in the seat.

She sat up, though, as they neared the Minster, eyes scanning the carriages lined up along Broad Street, searching for the bays and the coach bearing the Avenleigh blazon. When she glimpsed it, her heart seemed to catch in her throat. Then she remembered: He would not be inside. Only Mrs. Gravesend and Agnes and 'Phrina. The earl himself had not attended services since he'd gotten word Camille had died.

The bishop no longer called at Avenleigh House, not since Mrs. Gravesend, at a Tuesday Bible meeting, had blurted out Jack's dreadful secret. "Not only has he got himself a *bastard*," she'd hissed to her host and the goggling ladies, "but the boy's black as sin!" A most unfair metaphor, Pris thought dreamily, remembering Johnnie's beautiful skin. And those curls! Those blue eyes! She'd never in her life seen anything so exotic as that baby. Johnnie's smile spoke of flowers and oceans and butterflies in colors beyond her imagining.

Their coach had drawn up beside Lady Harpool's elegant curricle. Pris watched as Robert's former mistress alighted with smooth, sure grace, her auburn curls in a cunning cascade beneath a brilliant yellow poke bonnet trimmed with ribbons and roses. Her hand came up to feel the sorry bit of wickery crowning her own head. How did women learn to be so stylish and elegant? From their mothers, no doubt. But she could barely recall her own mother, and was certain her dour father would have ground out every breath of fashion that poor soul might have had. In the posthumous portrait that hung in his bedchamber, Margaret Wilcox stood unsmiling, clad all in gray, a bleak, blank chrysalis.

Pris did not, of course, remember her that way. She remembered, vaguely, the scent of roses, and thick blond hair that she had grabbed her fists in, and a laugh so rich and full that it could charm any nightmare away.

Charm . . . The servants of Avenleigh House, she noted, had arrived, and were filtering into the Minster. Esmé was among them, as stylish in her own way—her long skirts of bright, rich cotton and a neat sapphire turban covering her black curls—as Lady Harpool was in hers. Have *I* a fashion? Pris considered, gazing down at her sturdy brown serge gown. If I could, what would I want to look like?

But she knew the answer to that, had seen it in Johnnie's face. Like the mysterious brown-skinned, green-eyed woman who'd won Lord Avenleigh's heart and had broken it with her death.

Desirable. That was what he'd made her feel as he'd held her and kissed her. That sensation, that appreciation, was what she once had thought she'd found in Robert. He had asked for her hand; surely he'd found her appealing! But she never sensed he did. Once, when, puzzled and confused, she'd mentioned to her father that her fiancé's behavior toward her was a trifle cold, he'd colored and cleared his throat and told her that respect was the crucial foundation for a successful marriage. *Respect!* What about love? What about *passion*? she had wanted to demand.

The years wound on, and Robert's infrequent visits to Lincolnshire brought no increase in emotion, no sense of connection, none of the intimacy she had anticipated. It had been, in an odd way, a relief that first time she stumbled across him in the bushes with Lady Harpool, his breeches down, her skirts hiked up, both of them panting in ecstasy. At least then Pris had known it wasn't her expectations that had failed her. Clearly, Lady Harpool could arouse Robert to passion. The trouble was with Pris.

She ought to have broken off their engagement then and there. But being betrothed had brought valuable dividends. Her father finally stopped harping at her to find a husband and dragging her off to Bath to endure the company of bored, disinterested second lieutenants. And she'd had immense stretches of time on which to work at her catalog. Besides, had she cried off at that point, the gossiping and whispers would have been unbearable. Who did Priscilla Wilcox think she was, to spurn an earl? every biddy in Lincolnshire would have demanded. How could a homely thing like her ever aspire to better? And so she'd just let matters stand.

Her father left her at the doors, hurrying to don his cassock. Pris let the usher take her arm, guide her to her pew. On the way they passed Lady Harpool, kneeling devoutly in prayer. Pris fought off a sudden urge to spit at her. Agnes had whispered to Pris at last Tuesday's Bible study that Lady Harpool was forever coming by the house on one excuse or another, sending His Lordship notes, having her maidservant bring him dainties and delicacies. And then Agnes had looked at her oddly and murmured, "*You* ought to come by more often, Priscilla. You've made yourself such a stranger. Jack needs his friends."

Friends. What a dreadful word. She didn't want to be Jack Cantrell's *friend.* She longed to be his lover, to fulfill the promise of that kiss at Vauxhall, to take back that moment when he'd stared down at her and said, *We have two choices now. . . .*

For if she could have, she'd have made him a very different answer indeed.

Chapter
18

On the following Monday, Pris was just headed out of
the house with her pail and gloves when the door knocker
sounded. Vaguely, from the back hall, she heard the butler,
Sheffler, making some pompous speech to the visitor. He
would not have dared speak that way to the earl of Avenleigh, who was the only guest Pris would have wanted to
see. Quietly she let herself out through the garden, antici-
pating a peaceable morning of questing for chrysalises and
caterpillars in the light, drizzling rain. She bade Melchior
saddle her little roan, Maggie, and rode westward, making
for a thicket of heath bushes on Avenleigh land; two years
past, she'd found a rare *Ilalias* cocoon there. She hadn't
spent ten minutes searching the tangled roots now before
there came, from the road, a snatch of French song that
made her raise her head and stare.

It was M'amselle Esmé, trudging on foot along the
muddy gravel. Her voice sounded unspeakably lovely,
floating over the fields. *I ought to thank her for that salve,*

Pris thought, and caught up her gear, sloshing through a ditch and across the bank. "Esmé!" she called, and the song broke off abruptly; the maid looked to her, dark face creasing in a smile.

"*Quelle coincidence,* M'amselle Wilcox! I have just now been to call on you!"

So it was she to whom Sheffler had been so haughty. "We must only just have missed each other," Pris said, embarrassed by the butler's behavior.

"*Oui.* But we are well met now! I saw you in the church on Sunday. The baume—it is working?" Pris had come close enough for Esmé to see, but she nodded anyway.

"Remarkably well. I ought to have thanked you before now. My father actually accused me of painting myself!"

The maid's dark eyes considered her so closely that Pris flushed. "I will send an order for more to Madame Gris-Gris, then, shall I?"

"Oh . . . I don't know. I don't see much purpose to it."

Esmé's shoulders drew together beneath her shawl. "No purpose in a woman seeking to look her best?"

"I'm afraid it will cause trouble with Father."

"How could he possibly object to having his daughter look more lovely?"

"You don't know my father," Pris said ruefully. "He insists appearances don't matter. Only what is in the soul."

Esmé considered her. "And what is in your soul, m'amselle, pray tell?"

Pris laughed. "Oh—nothing much. Nothing at all."

"What *I* was taught," Esmé said thoughtfully, "was that the body is the soul's mirror. What is outside must match what is inside, or there will be unhappiness." Abruptly she reached out to stroke a bit of Pris's hair that had worked loose of its braid. "With what do you wash this?"

"With—with Castile soap."

"Soap?" Esmé echoed in horror. "Soap on the *hair*? Oh, *mon Dieu!* Soap on the hair—did your mother never tell you it will leave a scum?"

"My mother's long dead," Pris confessed.

"I should hope so!" the maid announced righteously. "There would be no other excuse!"

"What would you suggest?"

Esmé reached into her reticule. "*Eh bien*, it so happens I have here a special wash for the hair. Only a bit of it made up, but the recipe is simple enough. Chamomile and lavender—you know of lavender? And oil of roses. With a *soupçon* of potash and vinegar."

Pris took the small vial she was handed. "Is this also Madame Gris-Gris's?" she asked dubiously.

"Still worried about witchcraft?" Esmé asked, with a teasing smile.

"More than ever," Pris admitted, fingers clenched around the glass. "My skin—it seems a miracle."

"And this miracle—you like it?"

"I'm not certain."

Esmé gave a cheery wave. "Go home, m'amselle. Wash your hair."

Pris did. She ordered up a bath and sank below the water's edge to soak her head, then gingerly opened the vial and poured the contents into her palm. She sniffed at them suspiciously. The stuff smelled only faintly of roses. Good. Couldn't have her father shouting at her for using perfume. Rubbing her hands together, she spread the pale, foaming liquid onto her damp tresses and worked it through. The scent seemed to intensify, spreading to fill the room. Quickly, guiltily, she washed it out. It left a froth of bubbles atop the water in the tub.

Silly, she knew, to think so small a thing could make any difference. But as she sat on her bed and combed out her hair, she found herself glancing in the mirror. Surely there was a sheen to the waving blond mass that had not been there before. She turned her head this way and that, admiring the play of the candlelight against it. Why, her hair looked almost like silk—and felt like silk as well, she thought, running her fingers through.

Tentatively she took up her brush. How did Lady Harpool make that sleek chignon that bared her throat so enticingly? Pris tried for a good hour, fussing with pins and combs, to mimic the effect, to no avail. It must be something you are born with, she decided. Or born without.

Still, there was no denying that silken shine. Instead of looking colorless, her hair seemed bright and alive. She ripped out the mess of pins and tossed her head, trying a small, gay laugh. The face that laughed back at her—smooth skinned, framed in gleaming pale gold—looked almost like a stranger's. Looked almost . . . "Lovely," she whispered. "Imagine that. Lovely. Me!"

Her gaze traveled downward to her well-worn, practical cotton robe. What had Camille worn for dressing? Satin—no. That would have been too heavy for the tropical heat. A thin wrap of gauze, transparent in the sunlight. Or perhaps, with Jack standing at her shoulder, nothing at all.

Picturing them together that way, private and intimate, flooded her with embarrassment. She turned from the looking glass abruptly, braided up her locks, donned a gown, and went down to supper. Her father barely glanced up from the temperance pamphlet he was engrossed in. But over the potted hen, Pris noticed one of the maids, Constance, sneaking peeks at her from her post at the sideboard. When she came to clear the plates, she took Pris's, hesitated, and then said gaily, "Beggin' yer pardon, miss, but yer hair—it looks so sparkly and pretty!"

"What's that, Constance?" the bishop demanded.

"Why, sir, I was just sayin'—" Pris was frantically

shaking her head, trying to warn her off the subject without being noticed. But the maid rushed on: "How pretty miss's hair looks tonight."

Bishop Wilcox stared hard at Pris over the edge of his pamphlet. She sat trembling beneath his cold gaze. "Trick of the candles," he barked then. "Unless—have you done something to it?"

"I washed it," Pris said softly.

"Hmph. Vanity. 'All is vanity, saith the Preacher.' Get to your work, Constance."

"Sorry, sir," the maid murmured, and hurried off to the kitchens with her load.

"What's this?" Jack inquired, lifting the cover off a platter at dinner.

"Deviled ham," his aunt said with complacence. "Lady Harpool sent it. *And* leek bisque."

"And for dessert, petits fours," declared 'Phrina, who was too busy eating to even contemplate the salt cellar.

"Very kind of her, I must say," Aunt Bertrice noted. "It all came with another very gracious note. How she hoped you were feeling more yourself, Jack."

"I feel as much myself as I ever did." He scooped some ham, stared at it on his plate.

"She is concerned for you," Agnes said softly from across the table. "All of us are."

"No cause for you to be." He flaked the food with his fork, lifted it to his mouth, chewed. It might as well have been sawdust. And I shall have to thank her for it, he thought vaguely. What a bother.

He set his fork down. "Try the bisque," Agnes urged, nodding to Tupper to bring him the tureen.

"No, thank you," he told the maid.

"Perhaps," 'Phrina proposed, "some nice buttered bread?"

Jack took a long draft of claret, wishing them all far away.

"Did Esmé tell you what Johnnie did today?" Agnes asked brightly. "Clever boy, he managed to get himself straight out of his nappie! I went to get him in his crib, and there he was, buck na—"

"Agnes!" her mother said in horror. "Hardly fodder for the dinner table!"

"He was so pleased with himself," Agnes said wistfully.

Her words actually pierced Jack's fog. "I don't believe I've thanked you, Agnes, for your attentions to him. You've been . . . very kind. Very kind indeed."

She blushed furiously. "No cause for thanks, Cousin Jack. I adore him. How could anyone not adore such a winsome child? Can you believe it? Esmé says he is nearly ready to walk."

Aunt Bertrice had her mulish look on. "If you ask me, both those foreign creatures ought to be sent away from here for good!"

"Mamma," Agnes said in gentle rebuke. "I hardly think it is your place to interfere with Jack's choice of nursemaids to his son."

Her mother's black brows nearly climbed off her forehead. "How *dare* you answer back to me?"

Jack closed his eyes, drained the last of the claret. "If you'll excuse me, ladies—"

"Oh, but what about the petits fours?" 'Phrina cried in dismay.

He rose to his feet and smiled at her absently. "You may have my share, 'Phrina." He lumbered toward the doors. Bellows rushed to open them—and even the butler, Jack noted curiously, had a worried look on his jowly face.

"Shall I bring up brandy, milord?"

"Please."

He stood in the corridor with the strangest sense of having no idea where he was going. Then he recollected, and started up the stairs.

He paused as he passed the stairway up to Johnnie's room. From above he heard Jamalla's rich Caribbean laughter, and Esmé, speaking French, coaxing his son on to some new feat. Then there came another voice, one it took a moment for him to place: low and soothing and sweet. Priscilla Wilcox, he realized. Whatever was she doing there? He climbed the stairs, went to the door, raised the latch. At the sight of him, the three women froze.

Esmé was first to come to her senses; she came and took him by the elbow, drawing him into the circle of firelight where Johnnie was playing. "See what your son has done!" she cried gaily. "Torn apart the little toy Miss Wilcox made him—ripped it all to shreds!"

"You must use stronger thread next time, m'amselle!" Jamalla exclaimed, wiping tears from her eyes.

"Yes," Miss Wilcox agreed, laughing, "yes, I certainly shall!"

"So strong. Just like his papa, *non*?" Esmé noted fondly.

Priscilla Wilcox was on her knees on the hearth rug, holding Johnnie's hands as he fought to stand. There was something . . . different about her, though he could not have said what. "Surely my aunt is not aware you are here, Miss Wilcox, or she would have invited you to dinner."

"Oh, no! I didn't tell her I'd come. I'm here to see Esmé. She—she is writing down a recipe for me. For washing one's hair."

Her *hair*. That was what had changed. He remembered it a mousy dull blond, and here it was glistening in the firelight, rippling like Scottish gold in its thick, chaste braids. While he stood there staring down at her, Johnnie moved abruptly and yanked one of those glorious plaits, using it to haul himself to his feet.

Jamalla doubled over, gasping with merriment. "*Voici!* He does it again!"

"Your son has taken a liking to M'amselle Wilcox's plaits," Esmé said unneccessarily.

Jack had a sudden urgent wish to touch that plait himself. It looked so silken and fine. . . . He dredged up decency, for the last time that night, he hoped. "You must not let him hurt you, Miss Wilcox."

She smiled at him, her arm around his son. "He isn't hurting me at all."

"I am glad of it." He crossed the room, bent down a long, long way, and kissed Johnnie's forehead. "I only came to say good night."

"Say good night to your papa," Esmé urged the infant. Johnnie burbled, seeming very pleased with himself as he hung from Miss Wilcox's braid.

Very gently, Jack reached to untangle the boy's fist. "Mind your manners, John," he grunted. It was as soft as it had looked, her hair. "Good night to you, ladies," he said abruptly, and went out to their chorused echoes. There was a thump, and then the baby's high-pitched giggle, followed by a muffled yowl from Miss Wilcox.

"You little devil!" Jack heard her cry.

"*Et puis*, again!" Jamalla hooted. "Johnnie, did you not hear your father? Mind your manners!"

Miss Wilcox's low, delighted laugh trailed Jack all the way down to his rooms.

"M'amselle Wilcox," Esmé began as Pris knelt in front of Johnnie.

"Call me Pris, please. I am more at home with it."

"M'amselle Priscilla," the abigail countered. Her deep-brown eyes swept over Pris's dreary serge gown. "You will forgive me this impertinence, please. But your clothes—"

"Oh, they are hopeless, I know," Pris offered willingly.

"Who makes them for you?"

"Mrs. Sheffler. My father's butler's wife. She is reputed to have a fine hand with a needle."

"She is a *butcher*," Esmé said with disdain.

Pris glanced down at her skirts. "Well. Perhaps she is. But you must consider, my father's dictates regarding clothing are rather stern. He will not allow me the Empire style, for example, or any colors other than black, brown, and gray."

Esmé shuddered. "And why not, please?"

"Something in St. Paul about the dangers of feminine adornment. So you see, Mrs. Sheffler hasn't much latitude."

"Even within such constraints, there is much might be done."

"Such as what?" Pris's voice was cautious.

"You take brown," said the maid. "There is brown, and there is brown. Gray and gray."

"What do you mean?"

Esmé glanced around the room, then reached to seize the hearth brush. "Here. What color would you say the straws are?"

"Brown," Pris acknowledged. "With black at the ends."

Esmé pointed to Johnnie's plump cheek. "And this?"

"Oh! That is brown, also. But such a beautiful color!"

"*Précisément.* You look at Jamalla's skirt, there." The nurse obligingly stood, hoisting Johnnie in her arms. "What color is that?"

"Copper," Pris said promptly. "The exact shade of a twenty-four-plume moth's wings."

"But *non*, m'amselle. That is brown also."

Pris cocked her head. "I wouldn't say so. Too much gold and orange in it to be brown."

"Jamalla," Esmé said, "once was a seamstress at the finest *couturière* in Castries."

"Were you really, Jamalla?" Pris's eyes were wide.

"*Bien sûr,* before the births of my children."

"Where are your children now?"

"The oldest—my son—is a cabin boy on one of M'sieur Jack's ships. The youngest two died of yellow fever."

Pris gasped. "Oh, Jamalla! I'm so sorry!"

The nursemaid shrugged. "Life is hard, *n'est-ce pas?* We make of it what we can."

Esmé's fine brown eyes had narrowed. "On that subject, m'amselle—Jamalla has told me of her wish to keep her hand up with the needle. I thought perhaps she might make you a gown."

"I could not *dream* of putting her to such trouble! Not when she is so busy with Johnnie."

"Johnnie needs me less and less. He grows up," the nurse said complacently.

Pris shot another glance at the glorious plume-moth skirts encircling Jamalla's wide hips. "It would not be . . . risqué? I mean, it would be suitable for a bishop's daughter?"

Jamalla tittered, and Esmé joined her laughter. "Not every woman in St. Lucia has the same profession my mistress did."

"What—what profession was that, exactly?"

"She owned a—what is the English, Jamalla?"

"Brothel," the nurse said cheerily.

Pris blanched. "Oh, dear God!" And then a thought occurred to her. "Who owns it now?"

"Why, M'sieur Jack, of course. Naturally," Esmé went on with pride, "it is a house of great distinction. The finest in the Caribbean."

"Naturally," Pris said weakly.

Jamalla set the baby on the rug, and he crawled off eagerly in search of his toys. "I could take your measurements now, m'amselle, if it is convenient."

"Oh, no! That is, I'm very—very honored by your kind offer. But I truly don't think—"

"M'amselle," Esmé said softly. "It is possible you have no interest in attracting a husband. If that is so, by all means, go on dressing as you do. But if you harbor any hopes of ever catching the eye of a man of discernment—" Pris went straight scarlet—"then you must seize your destiny. I can promise you, your papa will find no fault in the creation Jamalla makes you."

"You don't know my father."

"Perhaps not." Esmé smiled. "But I do know men."

"I—I'll think it over," Pris promised, knowing in her heart that she never would be brave enough.

*B*ishop Wilcox reached over the edge of his pamphlet to stab another slice of boiled beef. "Sauce," he said shortly, and Constance scurried to bring the boat and ladle to him. Priscilla sat picking at her own meal, hoping she did not look as guilty as she felt after her visit to Avenleigh the evening before. The bishop scooped a healthy helping of horseradish cream. "According to this report, the Prince Regent has got another of his hussies with child." He scowled at his daughter. "How anyone can expect common folk to hold to any sort of decency when the aristocracy behaves so disgracefully is beyond my ken! Take that Lord Avenleigh!" He waited, obviously expecting some response.

Oh, how I wish I could!

His pale eyes considered her more closely. "You missed the Temperance Society meeting last night."

Priscilla considered lying. But some incipient germ

of insurgency prodded her to truth. "I was at Avenleigh House."

The bishop's eyebrows arched. "Were you? I cannot imagine on what business. I saw Mrs. Gravesend at Bible study this morning, and she mentioned no such visit to me."

"The—the maidservant from St. Lucia. Esmé. She had asked me to procure some calamine ointment for the baby. This damp weather has given him a dreadful rash."

"That bastard's needs are no concern of yours."

"Father!" She was shocked to her soul. "He is only a little child! Didn't Jesus say—"

He lowered a stern finger at her. "Don't you spout Scripture at me! 'The sins of the father shall be visited upon the son.' "

Pris set down her fork. "How can you be so harsh? He is a *baby*, a poor motherless child!"

"*And* upon the mother as well. You see how God works."

"What if it had been *I*?"

"What's that?" he demanded, startled.

It had suddenly become breathtakingly clear to Pris why Johnnie tugged at her heart. "I said, what if it had been I, denied my mother's comfort and presence, and my father so—so engrossed in his own cares that he paid me no mind?"

A flash of shadow crossed the bishop's stern face—but then was gone so quickly that Pris wasn't sure it had been there. "I don't believe, Priscilla, you have ever had cause to complain of any lack of attention on my part."

Lack of attention—no. Lack of *affection*, however . . . "Do you love me, Father? Did you ever love Mother? Do you love anything in this world besides that great Gothic heap of stones?"

"Did I—what sort of question is that?" he huffed, and heaped more sauce atop the helping he'd already poured.

"A fairly simple one, I'd say," Priscilla noted, and stood in her place. "Excuse me, Father."

The following Tuesday, at eleven o'clock, she presented herself in the Avenleigh nursery. "Jamalla. If you are still agreeable," she told the nurse very nervously, "I would like that gown."

Chapter

19

"Voilà!" Esmé declared in triumph, turning Pris toward the looking glass. "What do you think?"

Pris stared at her reflection, took a cautious step forward. "Oh! Oh, my!"

"It would be better with the neckline lowered," Jamalla observed modestly.

"If it were any lower, I would never dare wear it!" Pris heaved a sigh. "I don't know that I will dare as is."

"Pourquoi pas?" Esmé demanded.

"Because it is so . . . so . . . so . . ."

"Lovely?" the maid asked shrewdly.

Pris ran her fingers over the skirts of rich silver-gray sateen, reached up to the tight, tailored bodice, plucked at the full, cuffed sleeves. "I don't look like myself in it," she said hesitantly.

"Au contraire, m'amselle. At long last, you do."

Johnnie had crawled to her and was tugging at those

skirts, pulling himself up, stretching for her braids. Pris caressed his curls. "Pretty boy! You seem to like it!"

"Ma," he mouthed, making all three women stare.

"What did you say, Johnnie?" Esmé demanded.

"Ma," he repeated as Pris dropped to her knees, put her arms around him. He smiled up at her, hauled at her braid, and laughed.

"I must go tell m'sieur!" Esmé announced. "His first word!"

"It wasn't a word," Pris protested. "It was only a sound."

"Nonsense! It was a word!"

"Ma," Johnnie said again, his blue eyes alight as he held Pris's hair.

"Don't—don't bring him," Pris begged, suddenly self-conscious.

"You would deprive a father of such a moment?" Esmé sounded appalled.

"Well—go on and tell him. But let me change into my old dress first."

Jamalla threw up her hands and burst into a long string of French. "She *says*," Esmé noted darkly, "she knew you would not care for the gown."

"Oh, it isn't that, Jamalla! The dress is beautiful—more beautiful than I deserve!" Pris blushed, meeting their reproachful dark eyes. "And I *will* wear it. When—when there is a proper occasion."

"Such as what?" Esmé asked shrewdly.

Pris faltered. "I don't know. When Father takes me to Bath this summer."

"Is there someone special in Bath that you hope to impress?"

"No," Pris confessed faintly.

"I am going for the master. Do as you please," the maid declared, her gaze flashing as she strode toward the door.

"Ma," Johnnie said once more, with a miniature devil-ish grin.

"Jamalla," Pris hissed. "Do help me out of this."

"*Pardon,* m'amselle. But I must fetch a clean *couche.*" She hurried off into the changing room.

Pris sighed in exasperation, then tried to unfasten the gown herself. Unlike her old, shapeless dresses, however, this one was far too snug to allow her to reach. Besides, Johnnie was still pulling at her skirts. "Monster," she told him fondly, and raised him into her arms. "So much trouble you cause everyone!" He grabbed for her eyelashes. "Ouch! You need those fingernails trimmed! I don't suppose you'll sit still and be a good boy while we do that." He caught her earlobe in his fist. "No. I didn't think so. I could nibble them off for you, though." She took his plump finger in her mouth, and he stared at her with those deep-blue eyes.

That was how Jack found them. He stopped on the threshold, taken aback. "I beg your pardon, Miss Wilcox. Esmé did not mention you were here."

She turned to him, disengaged the finger gently. "Milord. I only stopped by to . . . to . . . ." Then her voice faded as she stared at him. He looked so thin. And that dullness in his gaze was wrenching.

"You ought not to pick him up," he said gruffly. "A tiny thing like you—he has gotten too big." He moved toward her, and for one heady instant she thought he meant to embrace her. Then she realized he was only reaching for his son. Hurriedly she relinquished the child to him, blushing as their hands brushed. They stood for a moment in silence. Then, "Esmé told me," he began, just as she said,

"Well! I really should be—"

Both stopped. "Go on," he urged, at the precise second *she* said,

"I beg your pardon; do finish."

Pris's sense of the absurd bubbled up. She dutifully repressed it. "What did Esmé tell you?" she asked politely.

"Just that Johnnie spoke."

"I don't think he really was speaking," she demurred. "It was more of a sound than a word."

"What sound?"

"Da," Pris proclaimed without hesitation, looking up at his wounded eyes. "He said, 'Da.' "

Jack arched a brow, considering his son. "Did you, clever boy?"

Johnnie, alas, had no patience with white lies. He twisted in his father's grasp, stretching his arms out for Pris, and pronounced very clearly, "Ma! Ma!"

"Two words in one day," Jack observed. "How precocious."

"He must want Jamalla," Pris said hastily, glancing over her shoulder. How long could it take to fetch a nappie, anyway?

"I would say he wants you." Jack handed him over, and Johnnie smiled beatifically, gathering in her braids.

"Ma." He laid his curly head against her shoulder, snuggling in.

Pris felt horribly embarrassed. "It's only baby babble, milord. Just sounds with no meaning."

"Aye. No doubt," he agreed. "Still, Esmé seemed to think it a milestone."

"Well. She's so fond of the boy."

"Do I sense rebuke in that remark, Miss Wilcox? Have I been neglectful in my parental duties, do you think?"

"No! Oh, dear God, no! I didn't meant that at all!" Pris cried, the color rising in her cheeks. "I think it is *wonderful* what you have done for him—taken him in, given him a home."

"Wonderful?" he echoed. "Why? Because of his color?"

"Of course not!" she said, impatience making her forget her awkwardness. "Because of what you have lost!"

"What I have lost." He pondered that. "But surely, Miss Wilcox, you must partake of the local sentiment regarding the Negro race."

"Esmé and Jamalla have been kinder to me than any women I have ever known in my lifetime," Pris said hotly. "Any decent human being would be honored to be counted among their friends." At the tone of her voice, Johnnie raised his head anxiously. She soothed him with a stroke of her palm to his cheek.

Jack observed them for a moment without speaking. Then he said, "I forget. You are a scientist."

"What has that to do with anything?"

He shook his head. "Nothing, perhaps. And now you must excuse me. I have work to do."

Esmé bustled in from the hallway. Pris had a sudden suspicion she'd been listening outside. "*Pardon,* m'sieur! I stopped to consult with Cook about Johnnie's porridge. Did you hear him? Did he speak?"

"Very prettily," Jack assured her.

"*C'est remarquable, n'est-ce pas?*"

"Remarkable," he agreed, heading for the door. "Good evening, Miss Wilcox."

"Good evening, Lord Avenleigh," she said miserably, from within the flattering new gown. He had not even remarked it. . . .

When he had gone, Esmé came and patted her shoulder. "Never mind, *ma petite.* You must give him time."

Pris gathered her tattered dignity. "I'm sure I don't know at *all* what you mean, Esmé."

"Why, for him to come to love the baby," the maid assured her, dark eyes wide. "What else?"

What else, indeed. Pris turned about to hide her

shameful blush. "Would you be so kind as to undo me *now*, please?"

"*I* won't take no for an answer this time, Jackie," Vivienne Harpool said gaily, setting her gloved palms flat on the desk in his study. "No more excuses! It's a gorgeous day outside, the curricle awaits us, and the hamper is packed."

Jack sighed, leaning back in his chair. "I would like to, Vivienne, honestly. But I—"

She tossed her auburn ringlets, clapping her hands over her ears. "I won't listen! I *mean* it! You are coming with me!" She perched on the desk and leaned toward him, with a rustle of her blue-and-white-striped skirts. "Ham sandwiches with Cheshire cheese and mustard. Deviled eggs. Pickles. Shrimp salad. Compote of peaches." She winked. "And *three* kinds of cakes!"

"I only just had breakfast," Jack protested, though it was nearly eleven o'clock.

"We'll have a good long drive first. I thought to head up to Lampley Lake."

"It's too cold out to picnic."

"It's the finest April morning I ever have seen."

But he shook his head. "I am sorry. I just don't—"

"Jackie." She reached across for his hand, took it between her lacy gloves. "It's been *months* and *months*. Why, I'll wager you are still wearing that—that hoodoo charm she gave you."

He managed to keep his hand from going to the amulet. "What if I am?"

"Perhaps that's why you're still wallowing in mourning,"

"I'm not wallowing in mourning. I'm working."

"All work and no play," Vivienne sang, in her high,

breathy voice, "makes Jack a *very* dull boy. Come with me on my picnic."

"I wish I could. But I can't."

She brought her lovely chin up. "Can't come on my picnic. Can't come to supper with me. Can't accompany me to London. I am worried for you, Jackie! I see how you closet yourself away here, with no visitors, no company, no one but these dre—but your cousins and your aunt. Lord in heaven, little wonder you're morose!"

"Shropley stops by often enough."

"And for what?" She grabbed a handful of papers from the desk. "For this! Business! Nothing but business!" She moved as if to tear them. Jack lunged toward her, but she danced daintily away, keeping the desk between them. "Come with me."

"Some other time."

"You've turned me down too often." She began to rip.

"Vivienne! For God's sake! Those are my latest reports on the ships!"

"Come with me," she taunted as he came around toward her, "or I'll shred them to pieces."

He hesitated. She stood, red-brown head cocked, her hands poised on the papers. He took another step. The reports suffered slightly. "Oh, very well!" he burst out. "I'll come along on your bloody picnic! Just give those papers back!"

She did, instantly. "Another day," Jack amended. "When I am not so—"

She grabbed another fistful. "Now," she said, her olive eyes filled with daring.

Jack felt too tired to argue. "All right, Vivienne. Now."

He fetched his coat and a walking stick from his bedroom. In the corridor they encountered Esmé, with Johnnie in her arms. "Oh, m'sieur! Are you going out?"

"Lady Harpool has wrung my acquiescence to a pic-nic," Jack admitted.

"A picnic? What a splendid idea! Give me only five minutes, and I will have Johnnie ready."

"Here, now," Vivienne declared abruptly. "I didn't—"

"Jamalla has a touch of the—how you say—indigestion? So I will come with you instead."

"I don't see how that's possible," Vivienne noted, brightening. "We are going all the way up to Lampley Lake. Surely dear little Johnnie cannot be away from his nurse for so long as that will take."

"You will simply have to choose another destination, m'amselle," Esmé said with a shrug. "Something closer to home."

"Not to mention that I have the curricle, and only two seats."

"We'll follow along behind you," Esmé said with com-placence. "An outing is just what Johnnie is needing."

Vivienne Harpool hesitated. "Oh, very well," she fi-nally said, none too graciously. Then she recovered herself and chucked Johnnie's chin. He promptly burst out crying. "I'm sure," Vivienne said above the howls, "he'll prove a most delightful companion! The darling little boy!"

𝒥ack drove the curricle; Esmé and Johnnie followed be-hind in the Avenleigh carriage, the stableboy handling the worn blacks. Vivienne leaned contentedly against Jack's shoulder on every turn, murmuring compliments on his mastery of her spirited team. The early-spring sun was daz-zling, and the countryside was alive with flushes of new green. Fritillary bobbed beneath the budding hedgerows; the fields were carpeted with buttercups and violets. De-spite his misgivings, Jack felt his heart thawing, just a bit, at the sight of two larks hurtling skyward from a stand of weeds. *Life goes on,* he thought, and glanced back at the carriage in which his son rode. *The world does go on.*

"Where are we headed?" Vivienne cried above the breeze, the ribbons of her bonnet flapping wildly.

"I scarcely know." He forced himself to think back, recall the expeditions of their youth. "How about to the abbey?"

"Perfect!" Vivienne declared, and laughed, clinging to his arm, as he took a turn at reckless speed.

Burnton Abbey, some three miles from Avenleigh House, was the shell of a medieval monastery. Years before, when they'd managed to escape their tutors, Robert and Jack had often ridden there to pick through the rubble and sun themselves on the fallen gravestones in its cemetery. Once or twice, Jack thought, Vivienne might have come with them; he had a vague memory of chasing her along the stones. As they cleared the Wold and reached the foothills of Lincoln Edge, he saw the ruined towers in the distance and slowed the team. "What are we waiting for?" Vivienne asked impatiently.

"Esmé and the coach."

"They'll follow easily enough. There is only the one road."

"I suppose you are right." He spurred on with a jolt that made her clap her bonnet to her head.

They drew up alongside the ruin a quarter hour later. "Eat first, or explore?" Vivienne inquired as he helped her down, his hands about her waist.

"Explore," he told her gruffly.

"I was hoping you'd say that."

They walked among the tumbled walls and jumbled tombstones in the graveyard, her arm tucked within his. "You won't remember, I suppose, but you kissed me once here," Vivienne said suddenly.

"Did I?"

"Mm-hmm. On a dare from Robert. We were ten. It was my very first kiss. They say one never forgets that."

"It must have been mine as well." He cast his mind back, shrugged. "Sorry."

"Oh, don't you recall? I can see it all so clearly. You had on a white shirt and those blue cambric breeches you were forever tearing in the knees. Robert was teasing you mercilessly. I didn't think that you would have the nerve. But finally you did. Right here." She pressed her fingertip to her lips. "It made me hungry for more."

Jack flushed, ill at ease. "Speaking of hungry," he noted, "we'd best go back and see if the coach has caught up to us yet, so we can have our picnic."

"If you like." She stooped suddenly to pluck up a violet and hold it to her nose. "Oh, Jackie. Smell how sweet." She offered it to him in her gloved fingers. He bent his head, then shook it.

"All I can smell is you, Vivienne. You—and jasmine."

"You never have remarked my scent before," she said coyly, her eyes alight.

"Every time I am with you, I think of St. Lucia," he confessed. "It grows there in masses. It grew—"

"Where, Jackie?" she whispered.

"Outside her room . . ."

"Oh, my poor Jackie." She twined her arms around his neck. "If you only knew how I have mourned with you, felt for you . . ."

"Don't," he warned, trying to push her away.

"Don't what?"

He caught his breath. She was standing on tiptoe, her body very close to his. "Vivienne—"

"Aren't we both," she whispered, pressing even closer, "enough acquainted with grief? Oh, Jackie, if there is solace for us anywhere, isn't it right that we take it?"

"No!" he said, but his loins, hard against hers, were at

odds with the word. He had long since stopped counting the months since he had been with Camille; he only knew that something in his body, something in his *soul*, was aching for release. He gazed down at her, saw her wide eyes, her beguiling smile of invitation, and his self-control snapped, quick and clean, like a stepped-on twig. He grabbed her by the shoulders, pulled her to him, crushed her mouth beneath his.

"Why, Jackie!" she gasped in surprise. He silenced her with another kiss, then tumbled down with her into the long graveyard grass.

He was yanking at the bodice of her gown before they even landed. Her breasts popped free of their scant containment, and he buried his head against her lush white flesh. She let out a breathy little sigh, writhing beneath him. "Oh, Jackie!" she murmured as he grasped her nipple in his mouth, pulled at it long and hard.

"You like that, do you?" He tugged at her again, hand sliding down over her waist and thigh, seeking the edges of her skirts.

"Yes, Jackie, yes!" Vivienne whispered. "Go on. . . ."

"I thought you said you never would—"

"Take me," she moaned, gloved fingers tugged at his breeches. "I cannot help myself. . . ."

He got his hand beneath her pettiskirts, flung them upward, scrabbled to unbutton his breeches. She was clinging to him, holding him by his hair, by the shirt, by anything she could grasp. He felt the smooth sheen of her drawers beneath his fingertips, wondered if they were silk, and red. She arched, rubbing against his manhood, which was taut and hard and felt to be on fire. He pulled the drawers away, slid his hand between her thighs. They were swift to part. She was slick and wet and warm, open to him like an unfurling trumpet of jasmine. He knelt above her, thrust into that willing sheath, and ejaculated instantly, in a burst like a pistol shot.

He grunted, low in his throat. She was still coiled beneath him, twisting and moaning, and he recognized, dimly, that he'd not been quite fair. Accordingly he went through the motions, bringing her along, teasing her with his hands and tongue, his slack rod still within her, until her small sighs reached a crescendo. It seemed to take forever. But at long last she went limp in his embrace, with a pretty little whimper of satisfaction.

He opened his eyes then, saw her stretched in the long, cool grass, smiling up at him. "Oh, Jackie," she whispered. "I've never, ever, *ever* . . . not with Chester . . ." She drifted away on a sigh.

From beyond his shoulder he heard carriage wheels. He straightened her bodice, buttoned up his breeches, already regretting what he'd done. He raised her to her feet, and she ran her fingers through her tumbled ringlets, adjusted the trim bonnet. "Lord, I must look a sight!" she said, and giggled, tucking her arm through his.

The carriage had reached the abbey; he could see Esmé peering anxiously from the window, searching for him. He felt he had to say something. "That was—that was—" He could not find a proper word. "Indescribable," he said at last.

"It was, wasn't it?" And she skipped along beside him happily, back to the curricle.

Esmé alighted from the coach, took one look at Jack, and frowned like thunder. He could not meet her gaze; he felt cheapened, like the worst sort of cad. His son—Camille's son—clambered from Esmé's arms into the warm grass, crawling across the open ground to his boots.

"Whatever took you so long?" Vivienne cried to the maid. "We have been waiting and waiting!"

"One cannot safely drive an infant at such speeds," the maid said darkly, "as you two seem to crave."

"Well, it makes no difference. We managed to entertain ourselves." Vivienne took Jack's hand with blithe familiarity. "But by now, Jackie, you must be *powerfully* hungry. Come, let's have our picnic! Do fetch the hampers, Esmé. What do you think the perfect spot, Jackie? Beneath the trees, for the shade? Or shall we wallow in this delectable sunshine?"

"Whatever you think best," Jack told her, sounding very subdued.

The remainder of that afternoon was the worst sort of nightmare. Besides avoiding Esmé's angry glare, Jack was also occupied with keeping Vivienne's possessiveness within reins. She could not seem to keep her hands from him; if she wasn't dabbing mustard from his mouth with her napkin, she was patting his cheek or his shoulder or, worse, laying a cozy arm around his waist. She cooed, she simpered; she played up to him more shamelessly than did Johnnie, who seemed to sense his father's tension and cried throughout most of the meal.

"I *told* you this outing would prove too arduous for him," Vivienne observed to Esmé in triumph. Esmé scowled at her and fed the baby a nibble of bread.

Jack had never in his life been so glad to see the skies cloud over. "Looks as if rain is coming," he noted. "We had best head home."

Vivienne, about to argue, reconsidered. "If you think so, Jackie," she said sweetly. They gathered up the remnants of the feast she'd prepared, bundled them into the hampers, then ran for their vehicles as the first heavy raindrops pattered onto the grass.

"You'll be soaked, madame," Esmé said, with a dangerous edge to her voice, "in that open cab."

"Who minds a bit of wet?" Vivienne declared with a laugh.

"I think it safer that you ride in the closed coach with us. There could be lightning."

"There already has been," Lady Harpool murmured into Jack's ear. "Go on and lift me in."

He took the drive home at a considerably saner pace, and the carriage had no trouble following. "Spur 'em!" Vivienne urged, curled close to him on the seat.

He shook his head. "The road is too slick."

"I am getting cold," she told him, nudging even closer.

"Would you care to move to the carriage?"

"Oh, no! But you might put an arm around me." She snuggled even more tightly.

"I need them free to drive."

Her gaze slanted up at him. "So very cautious, Jackie! I did not find you so earlier this afternoon!"

It would have made a perfect opportunity for him to speak up, express his regrets. But he hadn't the heart. He'd been a heel. He had used her shamelessly to gratify his body's needs. And yet he could not bear to admit as much.

At the gate to her cottage, he helped her down and delivered the curricle to her boy. "Stay for dinner?" she purred, holding tight to his soaked sleeve.

"I must see Esmé and Johnnie safely home."

"You could come back after that."

Christ. What a tangle. Goddamn his unruly rod and that scent of jasmine! He kissed her gently on the cheek. It was the first time in all his life that he'd felt worse *after* sexual gratification than before. "Let me see how it goes," he equivocated.

"I'll be waiting up for you," she promised, rain-drenched gown clinging to the luscious curves of her figure.

"I'll come. If I can," Jack said, because it was easier that way.

Chapter

20

*H*e didn't go. He sent a note, with the excuse of the storm still raging, adding that Johnnie seemed to have picked up a touch of chill. It took him half an hour to decide how to sign the damned thing. "Sincerely"? "Truly yours"? Hell, no. "Fondly"? Ugh. He settled at last on "Your servant." Then he made himself a tall rum toddy and sat before the fire in his rooms, staring into the flames.

Esmé brought Johnnie in to say good night. She was aloof and formal. He wanted nothing more than to throw himself at her feet, confess and beg forgiveness. Johnnie, on his lap, somehow found the chain around Jack's neck that held the love charm Camille had given him and tugged it from beneath his shirt. "You wear that still, m'sieur?" Esmé asked in exaggerated surprise.

"Yes, I wear it," he snapped, yanking it from Johnnie's grasp and tucking it back. "Why shouldn't I?"

"No reason that I know . . . for certain." She sniffed and took the baby from him, striding out with her skirts swinging furiously. He'd just settled back in his chair when Agnes knocked timidly:

"I brought your brandy, Jack."

"Forgive me, Agnes," he mumbled. "But tonight I'd like to be alone."

"Oh! Oh, of course! Very well. Do forgive my presumption!" She closed the door, her face flushed with embarrassment.

To hell with her. To hell with them all. So what if he'd given rein to his lust? He didn't even *like* Vivienne Harpool. It was another girl—another *woman*—altogether who occupied his thoughts, one whose respect for his grief had made her keep her distance even while he ached to talk with her, laugh with her, lose himself in her wry, droll sense of the absurdity of life. But to admit that, even to himself, was to insult Camille's memory insufferably. Look at how offended Esmé was over what she suspected—hell, *knew*—had gone on with Vivienne that afternoon. Priscilla Wilcox was the most honest, decent soul he'd ever met. She'd be repulsed if she learned he'd been harboring secret longings for her since even before he'd learned Camille had died. Since . . . when? That night they'd gone to the lecture and then on to Vauxhall. When had that been? Late July. The evening before his meeting with the Crown's agents. The twenty-fourth of July, it must have been.

The twenty-fourth of—Christ! Only the day after Camille had died. How unspeakably strange.

The realization made him uneasy. He recalled perfectly the sensation he'd had, holding her in his arms, that he stood on the brink of a new world, a new beginning, as if she had the power to wipe out the past . . .

Jack was not a man given to mysticism, but the coincidence in dates shook him. He downed the toddy, then had another, and another, and fell asleep in his chair, hand clasped over the receptacle of guilt and magic beneath his shirt.

*B*ennett Shropley, dripping wet from the storm, took the stairs to the nursery two at a time and arrived, out of breath, just as Esmé was tiptoeing away from the door. "*Dieu merci!* You have come!" she hissed, beckoning him toward her rooms.

"Your note . . . emergency . . . you wrote . . . is His Lordship all right?" He leaned against the lintel, panting with exertion.

"*Non!*" the maid declared dramatically. "The worst—it has happened!"

"My God! He's *dead*?"

She drew him inside, shut the door behind him. "The *worst*, I said!"

"What could be worse than that?"

She whispered into his ear. His pale, freckled face reddened considerably. "You don't say! The devil he did!"

"And then—" She whispered again. Shropley could not help grinning. Then, abruptly, he laughed. She pulled away from him, outraged. "You find this a matter for humor?"

"Well—" He spread his hands in deprecation. "It is hardly on a level with mortality, is it? Besides, I thought you intended all along for him to take a lover!"

"Not *that* lover," Esmé said grimly.

"You had me arrange to get word to her in London—"

"I had not met her then." Her dark gaze slanted toward him. "You—you like her? Find her attractive?"

"Like a snake," he said promptly. "And I don't believe even Robert Cantrell would have been fool enough to bestow more than ten thousand pounds in gifts on her without something in return. No matter what His Lordship says."

Esmé relented, a little. "Did you not tell me yourself, if

m'sieur has a fault, it is that he always sees the best in anyone? I do not blame him. Oh, *non*. This was all her doing.
She—" Shropley sneezed enormously, and she suddenly
became aware of his greatcoat leaking rivulets onto the
carpet. "But forgive me, m'sieur! Here I am going on, and
you suffering of chill!"

"I'm perfectly—" Shropley sneezed again. Esmé hurried him out of the coat, sat him down by the fire, knelt to
pull off his boots. "I say. That's really not necessary." He
tried to draw his foot back.

"You are my only ally," Esmé announced, reclaiming
it in her hands. "I will not have you dying." She brought
him shawls and a lap robe and set the boots by the fire to
dry. Then she fetched a bottle of brandy and a snifter and
rolled the glass between her palms.

"What are you doing?" he asked curiously.

"Warming the glass. M'sieur likes it that way."

Shropley laughed. "I haven't had anyone look after
me this way since—well, since never, come to think of it."

"Haven't you servants?"

"A housekeeper who cooks. And her son, who helps
her. But she isn't the coddling type."

"Coddling?" Esmé crinkled her nose.

"Ah—pampering. Spoiling."

"It is not spoiling for the servant to take proper care of
the master."

"Mrs. Henderson, I'm afraid, does not agree."

"You must teach her to," Esmé said simply. "It is the
master's job to train."

"To tell you the honest truth, I'd as soon not have servants. Devilishly awkward, I find, telling other folk what
to do."

"Good servants," she noted, "anticipate the master's
needs." She brought him the brandy. He took a sip and
then a long, appreciative swallow.

"It *is* better this way. Thank you very much. Won't you—won't you sit down?" She perched on a stool. "Would you care for a drink?"

"I do not drink. I have seen it ruin too many servants."

"Perhaps that's Mrs. Henderson's trouble," Shropley mused. "But to get back to the matter at hand, what precisely do you find unacceptable about Lady Harpool?"

"*Everything.*"

"You can't deny she is attractive."

"Handsome is as handsome does."

He let out a sigh. "The trouble is, the other options available to us here are so slim. Were we in London, now—"

"No London," Esmé announced decisively. "Too many forces at work. Too difficult to control."

A corner of Shropley's mouth tugged up. "You make me wonder, m'amselle, who is the true master and who the servant!"

She waved an impatient hand. "I think only of his own good. He is too distraught still to act logically. This afternoon was proof of that!"

"And how did he seem . . . after the fact?"

She stared at him. "I do not know what you mean."

"Was he—cheerful? Gratified?"

"*Non, non.* He was miserable, the poor man. And all the time she was clinging to him, cooing at him, making the eyes at him."

"Ah-hah! So perhaps this is all for the best."

"How can you say that?"

"Think, Esmé. Think of his sense of duty. He is certain to see this as a betrayal of your mistress, of her memory. And it is highly dubious he will form any lasting attachment to the woman who seduced him into that betrayal." She did not look convinced. "Tell me this, then. How far behind their carriage was yours?"

"Oh, not far at all. Five, perhaps ten minutes."

"'Five minutes? Christ! You call that lovemaking?'"

"It is on the average . . . for an Englishman." Her dark eyes were sly, and he laughed.

"As a matter of national pride, I am tempted to disprove that. But mark my words, this is a step forward. Lord Avenleigh has . . . relieved himself of tension. And he will be ready now to contemplate new love. Speaking of which, how have your efforts with Miss Wilcox fared?"

Esmé stood, pacing the room. "She is difficult, that one. Very difficult. And yet . . . I have made progress, I think. She let Jamalla make her a new gown."

"That's a blessing," Shropley said frankly. "Her clothes are appalling. And did His Lordship see her in it?"

"But of course! Do you think me an idiot?"

"Very far from it," Bennett Shropley said, with an odd gleam in his gaze. "What was the result?"

"Not . . . what I had hoped. Not what she hoped, either."

"You mean she cares for him?"

"Oh, *mon Dieu!* She is so in love with him, poor child!"

"Poor child indeed." Shropley sipped his brandy contemplatively. "Still, it is something to work with. If only Lady Harpool weren't so overwhelming."

"She invited him to her house tonight." Esmé grimaced. "He wrote back with his regrets. Told her that Johnnie was unwell. He signed it, 'Your servant.'"

"He sent *you* with it? In this rain?"

"*Non, non.* He sent the stablehand. But I . . . intercepted it first and opened it with the cloud from the kettle."

"You steamed open the *seal*?"

She shrugged. "Why not? It is in his best interest."

"It is also against the law!"

"Is it? I did not know." She almost managed to look contrite.

"Remind me never to make an enemy of you, Esmé," Shropley said with a laugh.

"You need not worry on that account. Not so long as you serve m'sieur faithfully."

"He is one of the most remarkable men I've ever met, you know. I feel—*honored*—to serve him. It is quite strange, really. I imagine it's the same way soldiers feel about their general, going into battle. As though they would lay down their lives for him."

Esmé gave him a dazzling smile. "You do understand. *Eh bien*, we must work like good soldiers. We must have a plan of battle against the enemy."

"Against Vivienne Harpool, you mean. Very well! I'm all for it! But for the life of me, I cannot think how to stymie her."

"An idea has occurred to me," Esmé said, so nonchalantly that Shropley raised his head.

"Is it illegal?" he demanded.

"Not in St. Lucia. Here—" She made a face. "Probably."

"I ought to warn you, Esmé, it is against my oath as a solicitor to break any English laws."

She waved toward the door. "It is best that you leave, then. I can carry on without you, M'sieur Shropley."

"Call me Bennett. Please." She smiled; his own use of her first name had not gone unremarked. "And you'll notice—I'm not going anywhere."

"In that case . . ." She drew her stool closer to his chair and leaned her curly head toward him, murmuring softly. Shropley listened, turned pale, turned red, turned pale again. She finished. There was a pause. Then he laughed.

"M'amselle Esmé, you astonish me! I thought you a practical woman!"

"I *am*," she told him, greatly affronted.

"Why, you sound like the worst sort of superstitious peasant, spouting such mumbo jumbo!"

"It is *not* mumbo jumbo! It is magic—and it works," she said stubbornly.

"It's utter stuff and nonsense."

"Who are you to say?"

"If such things *did* work, wouldn't everyone use them?"

"Only those who know about them," she noted complacently. "Not everyone does."

"It is ridiculous."

Esmé rose to her feet, gesturing toward the door again, very grandly. "Then I will proceed without you, M'sieur Shropley."

"It is Bennett. I already told you that." He hesitated, staring at her stony face. "Well. What the devil. Anything is worth a try, I suppose. If Vivienne Harpool gets her claws into the Avenleigh fortune again, I'll be looking for a new master soon enough anyway."

"And so you see, m'sieur, I thought it might be helpful if you were to invite the two of them for dinner," Esmé concluded, bouncing Johnnie in her arms.

"Shropley and Priscilla Wilcox? They'd make rather an odd couple."

"I do not see why you say that. She is perfectly charming. And he is very much a gentleman."

"Well, that's true, of course. But still . . ."

Esmé came closer to his desk. "M'amselle Wilcox tells me her father is determined to take her to Bath this summer. I do not know what this 'Bath' is, but from the way she speaks of it, she would sooner go to hell."

"Ah, yes. Those second lieutenants . . . But tell me, Esmé. Has Mr. Shropley expressed any—sentiments for Miss Wilcox?"

"M'amselle Agnes mentioned just the other day he'd told her he finds Miss Wilcox most delightful."

"Why, that sly devil!" But beneath Jack's bemusement lurked a certain discomfiture.

"Since that is so—" Esmé shrugged. "I thought to play the part of Cupid, with your assistance. If you could just invite them both to dinner tomorrow evening—"

"By all means!" he assured her, ignoring the small pang in his heart. "I'll send a messenger straightaway."

"The meal will have to be late, though. I happen to know M'sieur Shropley will be busy in the city until six o'clock."

"I'll say seven. That should give him time enough to ride here."

"It is good of you, m'sieur," Esmé told him, "to try to make others happy when you are still so unhappy yourself."

"Nonsense," Jack said gruffly. She curtsied and started from the room, then stopped as he called her name. "Esmé. I say. Have you any reason to believe Miss Wilcox reciprocates Mr. Shropley's affection?"

"I have no reason *not* to." She smiled, taking Johnnie's hand in hers. "Wave bye-bye to your papa!"

When she was gone, Jack dutifully wrote out invitation cards for dinner on the following evening. His head was still clouded from too much brandy, not to mention his muddled sentiments about the picnic and Vivienne yesterday. God. Vivienne. He was going to have to deal with her, nip the thing in the bud before she started imagining whatever it was that women imagined in such circumstances. He rang for Bellows. "There will be two guests at dinner tomorrow," he informed the butler. "Mr. Shropley and Miss Wilcox. At seven o'clock. I have cards. Have them delivered, if you will."

"Very good, milord."

"Oh, and Bellows. Set the table for wine, would you? The St. Émilion. The '98."

"Special occasion, milord?"

"What's that?" Jack tore his mind from the memory of the slight, sweet weight of Priscilla Wilcox in his arms.

"I only wondered—is it a special occasion?"

"It could be, I suppose." Would she let Shropley kiss her? In his own gardens, perhaps?

"Very good, milord." But instead of leaving, the butler took the invitations and then stood shifting from foot to foot in a most un–Bellows-like way.

"Was there something else?" Jack demanded in irritation. He was more out of sorts suddenly than his headache could account for.

"Forgive me, milord. I only wanted to say . . . the new liveries."

Jack glanced at him again, saw that his usual thread-bare coat and breeches had been replaced by a rather splen-did outfit of hunter green, with shining brass buttons. Jack had forgotten he'd ordered the old coats be replaced.

"I suppose they displease you," he said wearily.

"Quite the contrary, milord! I intended to express my deepest satisfaction! I have no doubt they will contribute to the improved morale of all the staff as much as they have to mine!" And he puffed out his pigeon chest.

"Glad to hear it, Bellows. You look most . . . dignified."

"Just what I thought, milord." The butler clicked his heels with military precision, executed a sharp turn, and strode toward the door with his head held high. Jack man-aged not to laugh until the butler closed the portal behind him with a clean, brusque *click*. Once he'd started, though, he could not stop laughing. He went on until he had to bury his face in his arms on the desk.

"I still don't understand what you are doing here," Priscilla said wildly, as Esmé plunked her down in front of the dressing table in her rooms at Wilcox Hall.

"I have come to dress you for dinner," the maid said

with great calm, picking up a brush. "Did you not receive your invitation from Lord Avenleigh?"

"I did—but Father would not let me accept. Besides, I've already *had* dinner! Father and I always dine at five o'clock on Thursday evenings, so he can attend the Temperance Society meeting!"

"I know," Esmé said with a smile. "And he is gone until at least eleven o'clock."

Pris stared at the maid in the mirror. "How would you know such a thing?"

"I have my ways. Now, for your hair. I thought a chignon—*comme ça*." She twisted the thick blond mass deftly into place, fastened it with pins she pulled from her reticule. "A few loose tendrils here, and here—*mon Dieu*, your hair is thick!" She reached into the reticule again and took out a curling iron, setting it on the fire to heat. "While we wait for that, I will help you into your gown. The one Jamalla made you." At Pris's blank expression, she muttered a French curse. "You have it still, don't you?"

"Of course I have. But I scarcely see the point in wearing it to Avenleigh House."

Esmé let out a heartfelt sigh. "*Ma chère* m'amselle. Have we not discussed how if you wish to capture a husband, you must learn to pay more attention to your dress and hair?"

"Yes, but—"

"And have we not also discussed the necessity of learning how to flirt, to attract the members of the opposite sex?"

"I wish you would not use that—"

"And we have also spoken, have we not, of the art of making conversation, of how to make a man feel he is the most intriguing, the most desirable creature you have ever known?"

"We talked of all this in passing!" Pris burst out, her

color heightened. "It was idle badinage, nothing more! And I certainly do not intend to begin such lessons at Avenleigh House!"

Esmé arched a brow. "And why not?"

"Because—because—" But Pris could not bring herself to say, *Because he is there.* "Because I thought to put your teachings to purpose in Bath. There is no one at Avenleigh House who is at *all* a likely prospect."

"True," Esmé acknowledged. "Which makes it the perfect starting point. You have nothing to lose." She tested the iron with a wetted thumb. "This is ready. Hold still." Pris was too cowed to do anything else. She watched, eyes wide, as the maid spun perfect loose, luxurious ringlets from her wayward locks.

"Oh!" she cried in amazement. "Constance never effects anything like that!"

"Of course not. Constance is a kitchen maid."

"Only half the time," Pris demurred.

"Half a kitchen maid, always a kitchen maid." Esmé twirled the last wispy ringlet. "Now, into that gown."

Against Pris's protests, she managed to get her into the rich silvery garment and button up the back.

"Nearly perfect," Esmé observed, and reached into her reticule one last time. Pris was staring, transfixed, at the image in the mirror. Esmé drew out a pair of ear-drops, gold and pearl, and fastened them carefully onto Pris's lobes. "And, I think, a neckpiece." That was of pearls as well, a simple graded strand. The rich, burnished gems glowed against Pris's throat, catching the candlelight.

"Whose are these?" she whispered, touching them gingerly.

"My late mistress's."

Pris jerked her hand away. "Oh, I could not possibly wear them! Not ever in the world!"

"And why not?"

"Why, he *gave* them to her! It would be such—such audacity!"

"But he did not, m'amselle. Someone before him did."

"Someone before . . ." Pris raised wondering eyes to the maid's reflection. "There was . . . someone before him?"

"Many, many someones," Esmé acknowledged with a hint of a smile. "He has never seen the pearls or the ear-drops. They were other admirers' gifts."

"What sort of woman *was* she?" Pris asked in bewilderment.

"The sort who did what she had to, to get what she wanted out of life."

"How brave," Pris breathed after a moment.

Esmé laughed. "*Brave?* That is a most charitable ob-servation for a bishop's daughter!" She picked up Pris's cloak, settling it over her shoulders and head to hide her handiwork from the bishop's servants. "Shall we go, m'am-selle? It is nearly seven o'clock."

$\mathcal{P}$ris entered the drawing room very nervously, joining Mrs. Gravesend and Agnes and Sephrina, who was detuft-ing the sofa back. Her hostess's jaw dropped as Pris came closer to make her curtsy. "Good God, child!" she cried in shock. "What have you done to yourself?"

'Phrina, torn by her mother's tone from her attentions to the sofa, turned to stare. Her pale blue eyes went wide with wonder, and she skipped across the room. "Ooh, you look so beautiful! So very beautiful!" Enchanted, she reached out to touch Pris's gown and hair. "Such gorgeous jewels! Were they your mamma's?"

"They belonged to a . . . a friend of the family." Pris was squirming with embarrassment.

Agnes had come forward, too, her worn face alight.

"You look just like a princess, Priscilla. What an utterly becoming gown! Did you buy it in London?"

"I—" Pris was spared further untruths by the sudden entrance of Lord Avenleigh and his solicitor, Mr. Shropley.

"Aunt Bertrice, Cousins." Jack nodded to them, then glanced at Pris. She fought not to tremble as he came to kiss her hand. "Miss Wilcox, I'm so glad you could come."

"Mi-milord," she managed to stammer.

He stared down at her for a moment, still holding to her fingertips. Her flesh burned where he had pressed his lips. He was on the verge, she was sure, of saying something more when 'Phrina danced over, bubbling with excitement.

"Doesn't Miss Wilcox look dazzling this evening, Cousin Jack?" she demanded.

"Miss Wilcox always looks dazzling," he replied politely.

Pris could have kicked silly 'Phrina. How she longed to know what he might have said without her putting words in his mouth!

"Miss Wilcox, a pleasure to see you again." That was Mr. Shropley, who seemed rather edgy. "How is your father?"

"Very well, thank you." Her host had drifted off toward the sideboard.

"May I add my compliments to those already swirling about you?"

Pris wrenched her attention from Lord Avenleigh's broad, strong shoulders and back. "May you what?"

"I merely wished to say how radiant you are looking this evening."

"Oh! Oh, thank you kindly."

Mrs. Gravesend rose from her chair with a thump of her walking stick. "*If* you don't mind, Jack, we've already put dinner back to an unconscionable hour."

"All my fault," Shropley said in apology. "A late meeting in the city, don't you know."

"You might at least make up for the inconvenience by offering me your arm, young man."

"Certainly! I'm honored to, madame!" He hurried toward her, nearly stumbling on the edge of the rug and barely catching himself. He is such an anxious fellow, Pris thought, recalling how uneasy he had been when he'd called on her to propose she file suit against Vivienne Harpool for stealing Robert's heart away. Then she froze as Lord Avenleigh appeared at her side, offering his elbow.

"Shall we, Miss Wilcox?"

She found she was seated at Lord Avenleigh's left, with Shropley beside her and then Mrs. Gravesend at the foot of the table; the two sisters were across from Pris and Shropley. Mrs. Gravesend's bushy brows rose as Esmé, of all people, came forward with the soup tureen. She scanned the row of servants, scowling, then fixed the scowl on Bellows. "Where is Tupper?" she demanded.

"Gone to visit her ailing mother, madame," the butler told her.

"Why wasn't I informed?"

"It all came up very suddenly, madame."

"Hmph!" she said.

Esmé approached with perfect aplomb. "Cream of asparagus soup, madame?"

"Very well. But see you don't slosh it all over my lap." Her expression placid, Esmé expertly ladled the steaming soup into the bowl, then went around the table.

Something, Pris noticed, was odd about the settings. Then it dawned on her: There were wineglasses at every place.

Bellows had stepped toward Lord Avenleigh with a bottle, wrapped in a napkin. He proffered the cork. "The St. Émilion you requested, milord. The '98."

"Excellent," His Lordship declared. His aunt put her hand over her glass most emphatically. Her nephew raised his brows at her. "Aunt Bertrice, it is a remarkable vintage."

"It is the devil's work," she snapped. " 'Phrina, Agnes, don't you dare!"

Agnes's arm wavered toward her glass. Then she tucked it firmly back down. "I'd like to try some, Bellows, thank you."

" 'Sharper than a serpent's tooth,' " Mrs. Gravesend moaned, " 'is an ungrateful child.' "

"You may fill mine right up, Bellows," 'Phrina said gaily, and Shropley accepted some as well. That left Pris. Dreadfully self-conscious, she said nothing as Bellows poured wine into her glass. That doesn't mean I have to drink it, she reassured herself—then squirmed as Lord Avenleigh raised his in a toast.

"To our honored guests." His eyes met hers. He smiled. She melted, bringing her glass up to his.

"Our honored guests!" 'Phrina chortled, echoed in a more subdued manner by her sister. Mrs. Gravesend glowered at the lot of them.

Pris tasted the pale straw-colored wine, just barely, with the tip of her tongue. "Oh, my!" she exclaimed before she could stop herself.

Lord Avenleigh smiled at her again, with approval. " 'Oh, my' indeed! I am glad you appreciate it. It is one of my favorites."

"Your father," Mrs. Gravesend began witheringly, "will be *furious* when he hears about—"

"Do you know," Shropley broke in, to a sort of general astonishment at his audacity, "I've often wondered where the temperance folk find support in the Scriptures for their position. There's absolutely no doubt whatsoever, is there, that the Savior imbibed? I mean, take the miracle at Cana. Take the Last Supper. If we are to truly attempt to emulate

Christ in our lives, I cannot see the harm in an occasional drink."

"Hear, hear!" cried 'Phrina, raising her glass to him. "Very prettily spoken, Mr. Shropley!"

And Agnes gazed at him with renewed respect. "I don't believe, Mr. Shropley, I've ever heard the antitemperance argument put any more eloquently!"

"I'll drink to that," Lord Avenleigh announced, grinning, and did so.

Pris found herself emboldened to take one more minute sip. God. That wine was amazing. It tasted of summer itself, of sweet willow and fireworks and green grass. Like Jack Cantrell's kiss . . .

"Is something wrong, Miss Wilcox?" Lord Avenleigh inquired, having noticed her rush of color.

"The—the wine. It put me in mind of a memory."

"The best wines, I've heard it said, hold within themselves the entire history of mankind," Shropley said helpfully.

"You've a touch of the poet about you, haven't you, Mr. Shropley?" 'Phrina cried in delight.

"Not at all," he assured her with great modesty.

It had only been a birthday kiss, Pris told herself sternly, prolonged by her own shameless yearning and his great kindness. Still, there was what he'd said: *If Robert had ever kissed you, really kissed you* . . . Would Jack Cantrell ever kiss her again? She glanced at him from beneath the cover of her lashes, the pearls—Camille's pearls—lying heavy against her throat, the ear-drops hanging unfamiliarly beneath the ringlets Esmé had pressed. To her chagrin, he met her eyes and shot her a quick, small smile that riveted her heart in her chest.

She stared back down at her soup plate, unable to eat, scarcely able to breathe. It was the most exquisite torture to be in his presence, knowing she could never have him, that his love belonged forever to the exotic foreigner who had borne him his child. Lost in thought, she did not hear Esmé, at her elbow, inquiring whether she would care for crab *Caribe*. When the maid repeated the question, Pris bobbed her bowed head.

"Crab?" Mrs. Gravesend echoed peevishly. "Why are we having crab? Cook knows perfectly well that shellfish does not agree with me!"

Mr. Shropley refused the crab as well, but 'Phrina and Agnes accepted hearty helpings. And Lord Avenleigh, no less surprised than his aunt, let Esmé fill his plate. He took one taste, and his face abruptly contorted.

"Bit of shell, Jack?" 'Phrina asked with concern.

His clear blue gaze was on Esmé. "You made this," he stated flatly.

"*Oui*, m'sieur. Is it not to your liking?"

"It's terribly . . . spicy, isn't it?" 'Phrina observed dubiously, having taken a huge bite and apparently regretting it.

"Delicious," Agnes murmured, chewing thoughtfully. "I believe, I'll have a wee bit more."

Pris, already full from the meal she had shared with her father, nibbled at a crispy edge of the crab. If the wine had tasted of English summer, this dish bore the unmistakable imprint of the Caribbean. It burst on her tongue in a hot explosion of mysterious herbs and dark spices, an intense reminder of a world she'd never know.

Jack had pushed his helping way. "I—it is exquisite, Esmé. As always."

"I taste thyme," Agnes said thoughtfully, "and I believe a touch of curry. But what else is in it, Esmé?"

"A mixture of spice I brought with me from St. Lucia."

Pris took another bite. She thought the taste very odd. The spice made her thirsty, and she finished the wine that was left in her glass.

Agnes was positively devouring the crab. Pris glanced

at Mr. Shropley, thinking to initiate some conversation, and saw he was staring at Agnes with dismay.

"You'll make yourself ill, gobbling like a pig," Mrs. Gravesend told her daughter in disgust.

"Do be quiet, Mamma," Agnes said, in such a quelling tone that even 'Phrina blinked.

"I beg your pardon?" Her mother looked at her, astonished.

"You heard me. If you haven't anything nice to say, then be quiet." And she scooped another spoonful of crab into her mouth.

Mrs. Gravesend leaned back in her chair. "Well! Of all the insolent—"

"Or have some wine," Agnes suggested with a giggle, draining her own glass. "It could only improve your temperance—I mean, your temperament."

Her mother lowered a finger at her. "If you think I intend to sit idly by while you—"

"Door's over there," Agnes said, pointing. "Feel free to leave. I say, Bellows. A bit more of that St. Whatever, eh?"

"Cousin Agnes." Jack's voice was half amazed, half amused. "You cannot mean what you're saying."

Her brown eyes met his blue ones, utterly unashamed. "I mean *exactly* what I said. If she doesn't care for the company or for the repast, let her hie herself off to her rooms, where she has only herself and the maid to make miserable. Why should she spoil *our* fun?"

Mrs. Gravesend was seething. "You see now, Jack Cantrell, what comes of demon drink! You have made her intoxicated!"

"Nonsense!" Jack retorted, laughing. "Why, I've seen her down an entire snifter of brandy without any such effects."

"You've *what?*" her mother screeched.

"I'm *not* drunk," Agnes insisted—and Pris had to admit, she didn't sound it. "I'm merely speaking the truth." She reached for 'Phrina's plate. "I say. If you're not eating that crab . . ."

Esmé, Pris suddenly noted, was trying to catch Mr. Shropley's eye, her brows raised in alarm. Agnes finished off her sister's helping, then turned to the sideboard. "More of that crab, Esmé, if you've got it."

"It—it is all gone, m'amselle."

"Don't be absurd! I saw how much you made. Bring it here." Dragging her feet, the maid did so. Agnes heaped another helping onto her plate.

"Agnes!" Mrs. Gravesend gasped. "I've never in my *life* seen such appalling behavior!"

"No?" Agnes abruptly stopped eating. "What about what you did to Lord Cowper?"

"Oh, Aggie!" 'Phrina cried in alarm.

"Who the devil," Lord Avenleigh interjected, "is Lord Cowper?"

"The man I love," Agnes declared with great drama. "*And* the man who loved me."

"A roughneck ne-'er-do-well," her mother said dismissively.

"He was a *good* man!" Agnes cried bitterly. "He was my last chance at happiness! And *you* made me give him up!"

"Really, Ag," her sister whispered in a soothing tone, "I do believe that's all water under—over—the dam."

"It wouldn't be," Agnes shouted at her, "if Mamma hadn't interfered!"

Bellows was observing the scene with his broad chest heaving; Pris began to fear he'd have an apoplectic fit. "Shall I—shall I bring the next course, milord?" he asked Lord Avenleigh.

"Don't you dare!" was his master's response. "Agnes. Who is Lord Cowper?"

Her mother answered instead: "Some obscure Irish lord who once had aspirations toward her hand."

"He *isn't* obscure! He has a seat in the Parliament," Agnes appealed to Lord Avenleigh, "and he has done a good deal of hard work on behalf of the nation. But he is Irish! That's what you couldn't stand about him, isn't it, Mamma?"

"No," 'Phrina observed suddenly. "That wasn't it at all, Ag. It was that he might take you away."

"Take me away—oh, God! I wish he had! I wish I had married him when he asked me!"

"You have no *right*," Mrs. Gravesend said furiously, "to say such things!"

Mr. Shropley was red as boiled lobster at this airing of the family linen. Pris was watching Agnes Gravesend in fascination. She seemed to be on fire, alight from within. Her voice when she spoke again was a stranger's voice, tight and low and bitter. "You've put a finger on it there, 'Phrina. And you know I'd never, ever leave you to be her only victim. I could not live with myself if I did."

"I have no notion *at all* what has come over you girls!" their mother said archly.

"You see there, 'Phrina? 'Girls,' she calls us. And I am—what? Thirty-eight. You are thirty-six. What do you suppose makes her think us still girls?"

Lord Avenleigh cleared his throat. "Agnes. I gather this Lord Cowper asked for your hand?"

"No. He tumbled me in the rose hedge," Agnes said curtly. Her mother blanched. "Of *course* he asked for my hand!"

"How long ago?"

"Four years, two months, and ten days." The precision of the answer made Pris gasp.

Lord Avenleigh arched a brow. "And your mother refused to permit the marriage?"

Agnes faltered a little. "Not—not exactly."

"Then why did you not wed him?"

Agnes fell silent. It was left to 'Phrina to explain: "Papa made sure we had dowries, you know. Quite considerable dowries. I suppose it speaks volumes about our social failings that even so, we remained unwed. But by the time Lord Cowper offered for Agnes, all the money was gone."

"Gone? Where did it go?"

Mrs. Gravesend gathered her dignity. "Your dear late brother had need of it for an investment he was making. He came to visit and asked if he might borrow against the trusts. He brought us lovely gifts," she reminded her daughters accusingly. "That Turkish delight, and my Norwich shawl—"

Lord Avenleigh rolled his eyes. "I see. You let him have the money. And as for you, Agnes, your precious Lord Cowper refused to wed you once he knew it was gone."

"No!" Agnes cried angrily. "That wasn't it at all! I refused *him*. I never told him the reason. I could not bear to. We had spoken so many times, you see, about how we would use the dowry. We meant to set up a school for unwed gentlewomen, to teach them how to secure posts as governesses or as schoolteachers. Anything, so long as they would not be subject for the rest of their lives to their parents' domination. Anything that would teach them how to make their own way in the world."

"A ridiculous notion," Mrs. Gravesend huffed. "Their place is in their homes. And had Robert only lived, he would have repaid the money."

"Would he have?" Agnes demanded dangerously. "If you were so sure of that, why did you agree to allow him to have it only if he became betrothed?"

Pris drew in her breath.

"It was high time he settled down," her mother said complacently.

"You *made* him get engaged. You forced him, and he chose Miss Wilcox, even though they were utterly unsuited and he didn't give a fig about her! And you knew it, and you didn't care!"

Pris blushed wholly at this unwelcome revelation.

"Bloody Christ," Lord Avenleigh said, and at the open blasphemy, all the women at the table stared at him in shock. "How many female lives did my brother destroy?"

"I'm sure I've no idea whatsoever," Mrs. Gravesend declared, "what you could *possibly* mean."

Pris had her hands clenched in her lap, aghast at the sorrow in his tone. So that was what he thought of her—that Robert had ruined her life. That she was as helpless and pathetic as his cousins . . . but Agnes did not seem, at that moment, either helpless or pathetic. She was glowing like some Old Testament prophet in the throes of testifying. Pris had never heard a woman speak that way, the way her father did from the pulpit, with such an absolute ring of truth to her words.

"Mamma let Robert have the money," Agnes said evenly. "She set the condition. It was her fault more than his that he made Miss Wilcox so unhappy."

"Whatever became of Lord Cowper?" Lord Avenleigh asked, his own voice gentle.

"He . . . has never married, to the best of my knowledge," Agnes confessed. "I honestly think he was in love with me."

"You are making a mountain out of a molehill, Agnes," her mother announced. "I'm sure if you had asked Robert, he would have returned your dowry."

"How could he, when he'd frittered it all away on—"

"Agnes," His Lordship said warningly.

She gave no sign of having heard him. "His own sinful

pleasures? How dare you hold him up to us as some—some paragon of virtue, when the real paragon is sitting right across from you? Haven't you noticed that the roof no longer leaks here, that the windows aren't falling in on us every time we open them? What about the new liveries, the improvements to the tenants' homes? If you love Avenleigh as much as you profess, you ought to show a jot of gratitude to the man who has saved it for you!"

"Jack Cantrell a paragon?" Mrs. Gravesend snorted loudly. "We've proof enough of the sort *he* is in the nursery upstairs!"

"Oh! You stupid, self-centered, stubborn—"

"Agnes, that's enough," Lord Avenleigh said emphatically.

"I need no defense from you," Mrs. Gravesend snarled at him. "I can look to my daughters myself. Agnes, go to your rooms!"

For a moment, Pris thought Agnes meant to cry, "Go ahead and make me!" like a furious five-year-old. But instead she flounced from her chair and started for the door. "So I shall! I'd sooner do anything than listen to you babble about how splendid Robert was!" At the threshold, she whirled back. "*He* drank a whole bloody bottle of brandy a night—*every* night! If you don't believe me, you can just ask Bellows! A dry house indeed!" With that, she stomped out.

"Well!" 'Phrina exclaimed in the sudden silence. "I wonder what has got into Aggie! I'd better go after her." She paused, as if hoping someone might dissuade her. No one did, though, so she trailed off uncertainly in her sister's wake.

Mrs. Gravesend folded her napkin with cold dignity. "Excuse me," she announced, "but I shall withdraw."

Mr. Shropley, silent all this time, also rose to his feet. "Gracious, the time! I had best be headed back to the city." Pris, looking up from her lap, saw him shoot a quick, meaningful glance at Esmé, of all people, who reacted with a very slight nod. Pris was so distracted by wondering what on earth might be going on between them, it took her a moment to notice that their hurried departure left her alone at the table with Lord Avenleigh.

When she realized it, of course, she, too, stood at her place. "It seems, milord, that the meal is to be cut short."

"Yes. What a pity," he noted. "Just when everyone was getting along so swimmingly."

Pris could not help herself; she let out a wisp of a giggle. Once that escaped, it seemed impossible to hold in another. His blue eyes met hers. "For-forgive me, milord!" she gasped. "I mean no disrespect . . ."

He glared at her sternly. Then a corner of that hard mouth twitched. And the next thing she knew, he was laughing more heartily than she was, letting out enormous gusts of deep, rich laughter that rolled through the room and seemed to clear every hint of dejectedness from the air. She joined in, giving rein to the ridiculousness of it all, and they laughed together beneath the outraged glare of Bellows until tears streamed down their cheeks and they had to grip the arms of their chairs.

Jack, coming up for breath, noticed the butler's haughtily affronted expression. "Oh, get out of here, you sour old goat," he commanded, and hurled a spoon at his head.

"May I say, milord—"

"No! You may not! Get out! But leave that wine," Jack added hastily, seeing him about to abscond with the bottle. "All of you, get out!" he told the goggling servants, who scurried off in the butler's wake. "Now, then, Miss Wilcox. Allow me to top off your glass."

"I don't know that I ought to. I've never witnessed such an exhibition at Wilcox Hall, under the influence of orangeade!"

"Don't you start with me, too," he growled, and filled

her glass and his own. Then he leaned back in his chair, took a cigar from his pocket, and lit it.

Pris bit her lip. "Just rife with vices, aren't you?"

"Absolutely. But never a dull moment, you'll admit."

She sobered slightly. "I should not jest. Poor Agnes . . ."

"*Poor* Agnes? Why, she was splendid! She said everything I've been thinking about her mother for the past year. *And* she's finally explained what I've been wondering ever since I returned here—why on earth my brother got engaged to you."

"How very flattering," Pris murmured.

"Oh, for Christ's sake, don't be coy. You understand what I mean. He needed someone who would fulfill Aunt Bertrice's perverted sense of what was proper for the lord of Avenleigh. Who better than the bishop's daughter? Clearly he never intended to wed you, but only wanted the money she promised him if he became betrothed."

"I might have insisted," Pris countered. "I could have demanded—"

He snorted. "Why should you have? How long was it before you saw through him? You must have realized the sort of man he was."

"I . . . yes. I did."

"And yet you did not break off the betrothal."

Pris brought her chin up. "Since he did *not* intend to marry me, I saw no reason not to take advantage of the situation. To play it out for as long as I could, for the sake of my catalog."

"No wonder you were so distressed when he died."

"I *was* distressed. What future had I to look for, when the only man who'd ever professed interest in me had revealed himself as such an unspeakable cad?"

"Oh, Priscilla. The *only* man?"

"The only one who wasn't some sniveling second lieutenant, or grotesquely unattractive, or a devout teetotaler!"

"*Now* we are getting down to it! Face the truth, Priscilla! You are too demanding!"

"Damn you, anyway," she muttered. "How would you know what it is like to be . . . undesirable? When all you have to do is stride into a room to have every female head turn?"

"You could walk into Carlton House tonight," he said softly, fingertips sliding over the curve of his wineglass, "and every eye would look to you."

She flushed beneath his steady gaze. "But you are right about Mrs. Gravesend," she noted, quickly changing the subject. "She *is* rather like a mantis."

"What's a mantis?"

"A *Manteodea.* An insect," she clarified, at his puzzled expression. "They eat their young."

"A most apt analogy," he said with approval. "Whoever said science was useless?"

"Whoever did?" Pris inquired pertly.

"Well, your father, for one."

"What a shame he couldn't join us this evening."

He looked at her, his glass raised—then laughed so hard that wine spurted from his mouth. "I do beg your pardon!" He mopped the table with his napkin.

"Not at all. Just part of the aura of the aristocracy."

"Precisely," he agreed, and reached into his coat again. "Would you care for a cigar?"

"There are limits," Pris informed him, "to my willingness to learn."

"Does it offend you if I smoke?"

How could anything you do offend me? "Oh, no! Not at all!"

"Still," he mused, sucking on his own cigar gratefully, "you are right. It isn't amusing. For Robert to have asked you to marry him without any intention whatsoever of going through with it—"

"Oh, the harm to me was negligible enough."

"Far less than actually marrying him, certainly!"

"It is Agnes I feel sorry for. I cannot help but wonder—"

"What?"

"Well—if Lord Cowper truly did love her, and if it was only her pride that kept her from admitting to him that her dowry was gone . . ."

"What if he were told the truth?" Lord Avenleigh said, completing her thought.

"She never would allow it," Pris concluded sorrowfully. "Her pride again."

"There's no reason, is there, why she would have to know?" He seemed to be relishing the notion. "I could go to London, explain the situation to him man to man. If he's at all the sort of fellow I'll wager he is—judging from Aunt Bertrice's disapproval of him—I bet he'd hightail it here in a minute! And even if he doesn't, if his circumstances or his heart have changed, Agnes would never know." Very pleased with this notion, he sank back in his seat and blew an enormous smoke ring, watched it drift toward the chandelier. When the ring dissipated, he glanced back at Pris. "What? What is it?"

"None of them realizes, do they," she said slowly, "what an extraordinary treasure they have in you."

He looked at her. Her thick blond hair was shining; her throat gleamed like precious ivory above the cunning bodice of her gown. He recalled perfectly the first time he'd seen her in it, when she'd been holding Johnnie in the nursery, his finger caught in her lip. He felt a sudden nigh-overwhelming urge to put his own finger there. The pearls at her neck and ears gleamed in the light from the candles, and her eyes were luminous, huge and lovely. He remembered that celebration of her birthday at Vauxhall, how small she'd felt in his arms, the longing she'd unleashed in him with her tentative response to his kisses. A virgin . . . so pure she was, so *clean*.

That made him think suddenly of Vivienne and what he'd done to her—with her—so recently. *I'm no more worthy than Robert was*, he thought miserably. *Not worthy to touch her, hold her, ever again.*

Oh, but his body ached to! He had again that strange sensation that in making love to Priscilla Wilcox he could absolve all his sins, become as pure as she was, begin life anew. Look at how she had affected him already! How long had it been since he had laughed without bitterness, since he'd glimpsed even the possibility of a future, for Johnnie, for him? "Priscilla," he said quietly. "I am only a man. What I do—I do for the most selfish of reasons."

"I cannot believe that," she whispered. "You are too good."

He laughed—ironically this time. "You don't know me very well."

" 'By your works shall you know them,' " she quoted quietly. "How better to judge a soul?"

"If I did go to see Lord Cowper, it would only be to assuage my own conscience. I could not bear to leave here with Agnes so unhappy."

"Robert never cared if she—if any of them—was unhappy." *Nor if I was.* She left that unsaid.

He found he wanted desperately to tell her what had happened with Vivienne, attempt to explain it. She would understand—wouldn't she? It had been no more than animal need. And she *was* a scientist. Then he looked into her shining eyes, and the impulse died abruptly. A scientist, but a woman, too.

Just then, the door opened to Bellows.

"I thought I told you—" Jack began angrily.

"Beg pardon, milord. You have a visitor."

"Jackie!"

Vivienne Harpool, devastating in a diaphanous sapphire-blue gown, pushed past the butler to embrace Jack, kissing both his cheeks. The air suddenly reeked of jasmine. "I was on my way home from Lord and Lady Battleston's—supper and cards, very elegant; you would have enjoyed it. A Lord Antrim was there as well. He recalls you from Cambridge, very clearly, and wishes you would call on him soon! Anyway, as I said, I was passing by, and thought I'd stop in and ask if dear little Johnnie is better."

"Is something wrong with Johnnie?" Pris inquired, alarmed.

Vivienne turned, seeming to notice her for the first time. "Why, Miss Wilcox." Her olive eyes raked over the new dress, the chignon and curls Esmé had fashioned, the pearls that hung at Pris's ears and throat. "How very . . . *unusual* you look this evening." Pris felt her newfound confidence wither completely. The gown was all wrong on her; one had only to look at Lady Harpool's exquisite attire, her coiffure, her hat, to know as much. Meanwhile, Vivienne had curled her arm through Jack's cozily. "The poor boy took a chill yesterday," she purred, "while Jackie and I had him out on a picnic. We were caught in the rain. Soaked straight through to the *skin*, weren't we, Jackie, by the time we got home?"

Pris flushed at her intimate tone, the possessive way she gazed up at the man beside her. She'd slept with him; that was clear as day. That he had fallen for her at last ought not to have been so surprising. Still, she had thought him stronger, better than that. Her disappointment was nigh unbearable. She wanted nothing more than to be gone from that room.

As for Jack, he was standing immobile as stone. Lady Harpool settled daintily into Agnes's vacant chair in a rustle of silk. "Do get me a brandy, Jackie, pet, would you?" she drawled, pulling off her gloves.

Jack roused himself. "You must forgive me, Vivienne. I was about to see Miss Wilcox home."

"Send the stableboy," she suggested airily. "After all, you and I have much we must talk about—*don't* we?"

"Please," Pris put in wryly, decisively, "you must not trouble yourself on my account."

"Pris," he began. But whatever Lord Avenleigh intended to say, she did not want to hear it. She bolted for the door and let it close behind her before he could move from his place.

𝒰pstairs, in Esmé's bedchamber, Bennett Shropley had confessed just minutes before that he would never again doubt the efficacy of magic. "Truth potion—you have made me a believer! To see timid Agnes turn so rebellious and defiant!"

Esmé shrugged. "What a pity Lord Avenleigh did not partake as liberally of the crab as she did. Or Miss Wilcox, either."

"And thank the Lord I didn't!" Shropley said gratefully.

"Why, m'sieur." Esmé arched her brow at him. "What secrets could Maman Gris-Gris's truth potion possibly unlock from your most gallant bosom?"

"I shudder to think," he told her. "What the devil is in that stuff?"

"Herbs and roots and seeds. The parts of flowers—"

"Eye of newt? Toe of frog?"

Esmé shrugged. "It could be. Maman never gives her best secrets away."

"It failed, though. At least, in the effect we intended."

"Did it?" Esmé moved to the window, threw it open. From the dining room below, they heard the unexpected sounds of laughter, Jack's deep and rich, Priscilla Wilcox's more delicate but no less delighted. "Perhaps not," the maid noted with satisfaction. "The magic, sometimes it works in unexpected ways."

"I can see that for myself," said the solicitor, and took a step toward her. She smiled at him. It was just at that instant they heard wheels rattling up the drive.

Esmé turned back to the window, murmuring foreign curses. "Who the bloody devil!" Shropley exclaimed, more vehemently than the circumstances warranted, perhaps. But he'd been feeling a touch of magic in his own soul at the sight of her smile.

"Lady Harpool," Esmé hissed. "That cat!" And she gathered her skirts, hurrying toward the door. "I must go to the rescue. I shall say Johnnie is ill, that he has the nightmares. I shall—"

"Esmé." Shropley captured her hand as she brushed past. "Do you believe in magic, or no?"

"Of course I do! But that one has magic of her own— *bad* magic."

"In the stories I read to my nieces and nephews, good magic always conquers bad."

"I did not know you had nieces and nephews." Then Esmé caught herself. "But those are only stories. In real life—"

"Or it does," he went on thoughtfully, "so long as one has faith."

"What do you propose I should do?" she asked dubiously.

"Nothing. Nothing at all. Let the magic take its course." He tugged her toward a chair by the fire. "Let me tell you about my nieces and nephews. I have four of them." She hesitated, still troubled. "Or you might pour me a smidgen of brandy. No need to warm the glass with your hands. Your smile will do it as well."

"Oh, m'sieur." She giggled, nearly distracted from Jack's plight. "What a *gredin* you are!"

"Is that good?"

"It can be."

He sat in the chair and patted his knee. "Come. Let me tell *you* a story."

"What sort of story?" Esmé demanded as he drew her down onto his lap.

"One as old as Adam and Eve," he murmured, and put his mouth to hers tentatively.

Chapter
22

"*Y*ou see what you have done?" Esmé raged as Bennett Shropley rounded the turn of the stairs the following evening.

"What? What have I done?" he demanded in puzzlement, while she pulled him into her rooms and slammed shut the door.

"Only this! While you were making love to me last night, our cause was lost!"

"How so?"

"Why, m'sieur sent Miss Wilcox home with the stable-hand! And that—that Harpool creature was alone with him in the dining room for the better part of an hour! But you have not heard the worst of it! He is gone!"

"Lord Avenleigh?"

"*Non*—the king of France," Esmé exclaimed in disgust. "Of course Lord Avenleigh!"

"Gone *where*?"

"No one knows," she told him dramatically. "He left without a word to anyone."

Bennett Shropley, very pale indeed, flopped down into a chair. "My God. You don't suppose he's headed back to St. Lucia?"

She stared at him. "Without Johnnie? *Non!* But . . . it is possible, I suppose. Oh, if only you had let me take the baby to him when I wanted to! 'Have faith in the magic,' you told me. And now look what has happened!"

"We don't know yet what *has* happened," Bennett told her reasonably. Then he stood up, just as abruptly as he had sat down. "Where is Lady Harpool?"

Esmé shrugged. "*Phui!* That one! Why should I know or care?"

"Because," he said darkly, "if she should be gone as well—"

Esmé's hand flew to her mouth. "Oh, *mon Dieu!* You cannot mean—"

"It's rather an obvious inference, isn't it?" He grabbed his hat from where he'd flung it and strode toward the door.

"What are you going to do?" Esmé asked fearfully.

"Go on to Lady Harpool's, of course. If I find her ensconced in her parlor, sharpening her claws, at least we can be sure he hasn't run off with her."

"And—if you don't find her there?"

"Then," he said very grimly, "I'll never again be able to read a fairy story to a child. Because I'll know for certain that good magic doesn't always triumph over bad."

Pris heard the news on Saturday from Mrs. Blathersby, by way of Lady Battleston, by way of Lord Ashton, who'd heard it from Lady Chesterfield, who got it from one of the deacons at the cathedral, who learned of it from his valet, who'd been stepping out nights with Avenleigh House's belowstairs maid. The bishop had invited Mrs. Blathersby to tea because several of the stained-glass windows in the narthex were in desperate need of releading, and Lord Avenleigh's abrupt departure had left him in some doubt as to the resources to be had at that hand. Mrs. Blathersby's late husband had left his widow in possession of a fortune large enough to make most of the surrounding countryside forget that he had earned it from the textile trade.

The bishop, therefore, was at his most ingratiating as he handed round the berry tarts and ginger biscuits. He deftly led the conversation through the glories of the Minster to the dreadfully high cost of renovations to the duty any devoted servant of Christ had to ensure that all aspects of this sublime example of God's glorious handiwork be perpetuated for future generations to revere. It was at this point, just as Pris was engaged in refilling Mrs. Blathersby's teacup, that that august lady leaned toward her host and said, "Speaking of future generations, I suppose you've heard—it looks as if Avenleigh House will be welcoming a new heir."

"New heir!" The bishop straightened on his seat. "If you mean that heathen half-breed bastard, I can assure you the Church has no intention of recognizing—"

Mrs. Blathersby interrupted with a laugh and a wave of her napkin. "Oh, good heavens, no! As though there were any question!"

"I should say not!" Bishop Wilcox harrumphed. Then he paused. "What exactly did you mean?"

"Only that His Lordship's eloped with Vivienne Harpool."

Very carefully, using both hands, Pris managed to set Mrs. Blathersby's teacup on the tray again.

"Eloped?" the bishop barked.

"Absolutely. Last Thursday evening. I have it on *irrefutable* authority." She proceeded to give, in great detail, the entire provenance of the story as she'd had it. And Pris, her heart as leaden as Cook's crumpets, listened and had to admit that the chain of gossip seemed without a single weak link.

The bishop evidently concurred. "I can only say," he intoned, when his guest's recitation was finished, "that I am grateful to God for this unlikely news. Had His Lordship applied to me to perform a marriage service, I should of course have been forced to refuse, on the grounds that—Priscilla!" She'd risen from her chair. "Where do you think you are going?"

"Forgive me, Father, Mrs. Blathersby." She dropped what was undoubtedly the worst curtsy of her life. "I just remembered that I—that I—" Desperately she searched the room for inspiration, seized upon the mothbitten plumes atop their guest's bonnet. "That I promised Cook to gather eggs."

She stumbled upstairs to her bedchamber, only to be greeted by an image in the pier glass of her mousy hair, her dull eyes, the fashionless brown serge gown she wore. "What else did you expect?" she raged at the dowdy figure in the mirror. She felt a nigh-Biblical urge to rend her garments, tear her hair from her head.

Instead she turned away, hot and miserable at the recollection of the way her flesh had seemed to catch on fire from his merest touch, how his briefest smile could ignite that same flame. Be sensible! she told herself in fury. What did he ever do for you that was not out of guilt or pity? Even his wondrous birthday kiss had been no more than a sop thrown from a very rich table to an unworthy dog.

She thought of gilded, glittering Lady Harpool and wished to hell she could hate her. But her scientific bent, that damnable instinct to observe and draw conclusions, left her with only this one: Jack Cantrell had the chance to choose between them, and he'd made his choice.

Perhaps it wasn't true.

But of course it was. Hadn't she known it the moment Lady Harpool had arrived to interrupt the aftermath of that uneasy dinner, in a swirl of scent and silk and savoir-faire? She pictured again the easy intimacy of Vivienne's hand curling around his arm, the casual order she'd given: *Do get me a brandy, Jackie, pet, would you?* They'd been two creatures speaking the same language, and she the interloper, desperate to unlock the key to the code they shared.

Desperate . . . that word made her think of how very near she'd come to giving herself to him beneath the willow trees at Vauxhall. I suppose I should be grateful, she mused, that I preserved my honor. And yet at the core of her being, she was not. She had no hope now of escaping her father's plans to drag her to Bath, no future to imagine but a life tied to some passably acceptable husband, whomever among the crowd of not-quite-*ton* she might conceivably attract. And if that was so, if that was all she had to look to, she wished to bloody hell she hadn't stopped Jack Cantrell's wandering hands when she did.

Even if it were only out of pity, she would have liked, just once, to have been made love to by him.

Chapter
23

$\mathcal{M}$ore than a month passed without a soul in Lincolnshire hearing from Jack Cantrell or Vivienne Harpool—which, of course, did not quell the gossip. There were second- and third- and fourth-hand reports that they'd been married at St. Paul's in London, that they were honeymooning in Italy, that they hadn't married at all but were living in luxurious sin together in Brighton, where someone's cousin's friend had seen them dancing in utter bliss at one of the Regent's balls. Though she despised herself for it, Pris found herself listening cravenly to every sighting and tale; she even took to attending Tuesday Bible studies again, for the snippets of information she might glean afterward, when the ladies lingered over tea and cakes.

Mrs. Gravesend seemed to harbor a certain satisfaction in this outcome; she kept mentioning Lady Harpool's kindnesses to her and her daughters in London. Agnes had the look of a damp rag, as though her explosion to her mother on the night of Jack's departure had wrung every drop of spirit from her soul. 'Phrina's already odd behavior took a twist toward the truly bizarre; at one Bible study, Pris sat and watched in horror as the spinster methodically unwound the wool of her left stocking from knee to heel. Pris would have liked very much to go and visit Johnnie. But she didn't dare; the scandal swirling around Avenleigh House was too dense.

Her father's plan to visit Bath had been taken up again, with a vengeance. Pris let his talk of all the "suitable young men" with "upstanding moral judgment" to be found there wash over her like the harmless spring rains that drenched her when she went out into the fields with her pail and net.

Even her collecting had turned desultory. Somehow, chasing butterflies had come to seem like nothing more than chasing a dream. And since she'd learned well enough the uselessness of *that*, her excursions to the pastures became little more than opportunities to escape the bishop's pompous assurances that on this trip to Bath, she would at last find a worthy man.

Then, early in May, something truly remarkable happened. Pris was wandering along the thickets of juniper bushes that ran beside the toll road north of the village when a man came thundering past on a gorgeous black stallion whose hooves churned wildly through the mud left by the spring rains. "What on earth?" she murmured, staring as he flew on down the road. He hadn't even got a hat on—and little wonder, moving so fast as that! She shrugged, with the fleeting thought that she hoped it wasn't bad news for someone, and went on meandering. Not half an hour later, the same hatless fellow blew by her again. Only this time, riding sidesaddle on the horse with him, clinging madly to the pommel, was Agnes Gravesend, her gray-streaked curls streaming back on the wind, a smile of ineffable happiness illuminating her face.

"Miss Wilcox!" she shouted, waving to Pris so excitedly that she nearly fell off. "Congratulate me! I'm off to be—" That was all Pris heard, for the rest of her words were swept away by the horse's momentum and the brisk spring breeze. Pris returned the wave, then stood and stared as the black grew smaller and smaller in the distance. "Married"—that was what it had sounded like Agnes had said.

That evening, Bishop Wilcox had a visit from Mrs. Gravesend. For the first time in her life that she could recall, Pris deliberately eavesdropped, creeping down the staircase to huddle outside the closed door. What she heard made her smile in the darkened hall.

"Disown her?" the bishop was inquiring of his guest in astonishment. "Why on earth would you disown her?"

"For eloping without my permission!" Mrs. Gravesend snapped, and Pris could picture the wrath in her beady eyes.

The bishop cleared his throat. "You'll forgive me, Mrs. Gravesend, but your daughter is—how old?"

"That has no bearing on the situation!"

"Legally, I'm afraid it does. Most mammas of a woman her age surely would rejoice to see her settled."

"*Settled!* He abducted her from my house, right beneath my nose!"

"Now, that is quite a different charge, my dear Mrs. Gravesend. If you are alleging a kidnapping, we must send at once for Constable Martin."

A long pause. Then: "It wasn't a kidnapping," Pris heard the old crone admit with great reluctance. "She accompanied him willingly."

"And who do you say the fellow is?"

"Lord Henry Cowper." Pris, crouched in the corridor, raised her fist in a silent cheer. *Hooray for you, Agnes!*

"Lord Cowper?" Pris could picture her father's

uplifted brows. "The same Lord Cowper who put forth the bill in Parliament last session to close down the London gin mills?"

"You know of him?" Mrs. Gravesend said uncertainly.

"Naturally I do! He is one of the movement's staunchest defenders—really quite surprising, don't you know, in an Irishman. I have followed his career with great interest. Made quite a name for himself, he has, with progressive social legislation. Several sessions past, I recall, he introduced a bill providing funding for a series of schools for impoverished, unwed gentlewomen to be trained as governesses. Splendid notion, I thought." And he laughed a little. "Particularly since I sometimes fear my own daughter will someday join their company. Alas, it went nowhere, as such innovative ideas so often do."

"Am I to understand that you *condone* Agnes's behavior?" Mrs. Gravesend demanded in outrage.

"Oh, I would not go so far as to say I condone it. I'd have been far more pleased had she seen fit to ask me to marry them, at the Minster. Still, it seems to me this Cowper is a godsend. Yesterday you had two daughters dependent on you for their happiness; today you have only one. Your troubles, so to speak, have been sliced in half."

Pris heard the harsh scrape of Mrs. Gravesend's chair. "I don't see how you have the nerve to call yourself a man of God!"

"Here, now." Bishop Wilcox sounded somewhat alarmed. "No need to work yourself into a tizzy, my dear Mrs.—"

"Don't you dear Mrs. Gravesend me! I don't know what's become of this parish! First that bastard son of Jack's shows up on my doorstep, then Jack goes running off, and now Agnes—there must be something mightily amiss in your delivery of the word of God to your flock, sir, to inspire such goings-on!" Pris bit down hard on her lip to keep from laughing, imagining her father's chagrin at this charge. Her impulse to mirth died abruptly, however, as Agnes's mother continued to rage: "And while we're on that subject, what about *your* daughter?"

"What about her?" Bishop Wilcox inquired anxiously.

"Well! If you ask me, all my 'troubles,' as you call them, only began when you acquiesced to permitting Priscilla to travel to London with that rogue nephew of mine!"

The bishop had regained his equilibrium. "I will confess to you, Mrs. Gravesend, that for some months I harbored fears my Priscilla might be growing fond of your nephew. Certain changes in her aspect, her countenance, even her behavior—"

"That's precisely what I mean! Agnes showed the same signs of rebellion. Why, only a month past, at dinner, she had the nerve to accuse me of conspiring with Robert Cantrell to spoil her betrothal to this Cowper fellow!"

"So he'd asked for her hand before." The bishop's voice was very thoughtful.

"Years and years ago. But she hadn't seen the man in nearly half a decade! And this afternoon he comes boiling up to the doorstep, without even a portmanteau—without so much as a hat!—and two minutes after Bellows admits him, he and Agnes are riding off together. Just like that!"

"Mm. One wonders, doesn't one, what might have impelled his abrupt reappearance on the scene?"

Pris stifled a gasp. She'd just then recollected the conversation she and Jack Cantrell had on the night before *his* disappearance, the way he'd mused over what Lord Cowper might do if told the true circumstances of Agnes's refusal to marry him so many years ago. Could Jack have made good his intention to visit Agnes's erstwhile fiancé? It seemed a very odd act of mercy for a man freshly eloped with Vivienne Harpool to perform.

Guilt, she decided. He'd only acted out of guilt. Hadn't he told her himself? *What I do, I do for the most selfish of reasons. . . .*

Still, it warmed her heart just slightly, as she tiptoed back up the staircase, to think what Lady Harpool must have made of her new husband's inclination toward charity.

Chapter
24

The next morning brought one of those brilliant blue skies so rare and thus so deeply treasured in an English springtime. Pris woke with a smile, feeling the sun on her face and her whole bedchamber suffused with warmth. For a moment, as she washed her cheeks and plaited her hair, her sense of satisfaction faltered; she wondered whether, wherever Jack Cantrell was with his wife, the day was equally glorious. Then she resolutely put that thought from her mind. It was ridiculous to mourn over what couldn't be changed. Life was full of surprises—didn't Agnes Gravesend's miraculous escape from Avenleigh prove so? This was precisely the sort of weather that brought out butterflies. And though it wasn't likely she would encounter any specimens she had not already got pinned to her corkboard, science was, like life, a matter of serendipity.

She went downstairs to breakfast in better spirits than in quite some time and found her father sitting, staring at a soft-boiled egg. "Pondering the universe?" she inquired, slipping into her chair. She nodded to Constance, who hurried to pour her tea.

"Perhaps I am." He raised his leonine head and looked at her across the table. "You'll no doubt hear it from some garbling gossip, so you may as well have the truth from me. Miss Agnes Gravesend has eloped. With Lord Henry Cowper."

"No!" Pris stirred cream into her cup, saw the tea turn the color of Johnnie's cheeks. "What an extraordinary turn of events!"

"Isn't it?" the bishop said glumly, and swung his spoon against the egg, shattering its shell. "Tell me, Priscilla. Have you remarked anything in my preaching of late that could be construed as encouraging . . . moral laxness?"

"Let me think a moment." She did, for quite a long moment, for she needed to gain control of her facial muscles. "No, Father. I can honestly say I cannot recollect any such thing."

"Neither can I. And yet Mrs. Gravesend accused me yesterday of having done so. Perhaps I was wrong to dwell on Sodom and Gomorrah at such length last Lent."

"I hardly think Lincolnshire has sunk to those depths," Pris observed, buttering toast.

"Still, it does make one ponder . . . such a string of unhappy incidents."

She peeked at him beneath her lashes. "Father, Christ Jesus himself could not keep his flock from wandering. And what do you mean, 'unhappy'? What is so unhappy about Agnes finding a husband at long last?"

"Mrs. Gravesend does not find him suitable."

"Mrs. Gravesend wouldn't find any man in England suitable. She only wanted to have Agnes under her control. That is what makes her so bitter and angry—that Agnes has defied her."

"'Honor thy father and thy mother,'" he quoted defensively.

"To what point? To the point where one subsumes one's life to theirs?"

"There is a *hierarchy*," Bishop Wilcox said in quiet anguish. "God, then man, then woman. Parents and then children. King and noble and then commoner. If folk feel free to go about subverting the natural order, who's to say where it might end?"

"It *might* end," Pris muttered, "in a better world all around."

Fortunately, her father hadn't heard her. He was already musing on the sermonic possibilities of his train of thought. "There's quite a good bit on that in Ephesians. Perhaps I'll work something up. 'Wives, submit yourself unto your own husbands, as unto the Lord. For the husband is the head of the wife. . . .'"

"Egg, miss?" Constance asked at Pris's elbow.

"I've lost my appetite," she responded tautly, and left the bishop plotting out his message to the faithful for Sunday next.

Her good humor was restored the moment she stepped out into the sunshine with her net and pail. It was impossible to be cross on a day such as this, she reflected, heading for the stables.

Melchior, who was burnishing tack, greeted her with a grin. "Fine weather for a ride, miss!" he called cheerily, setting aside his work to fetch her saddle.

"Fine weather for anything at all," she agreed. "I'm headed to the Wold. Care to come with me?"

"Ach—" He hesitated, torn between duty and pleasure. "I ought not to."

"Come along!" she urged. "We'll have a race."

But he shook his head. "Nah. I've this to finish, 'n' then Cook bade me ride to town."

"Melchior, don't you ever get an urge to subvert the natural order?"

"All the time, miss. All the bleedin' time. But I leave such luxuries to 'em what can afford 'em. Me, I'm more concerned with holdin' onto my post."

"I'll give you a start on me. Clear to the end of the drive," she offered temptingly.

He laughed and threw the saddle onto Maggie. "Get thee behind me, Satan. Now be off with ye!"

She was sorry he had turned her down. A day like this was meant to be shared, she thought wistfully as she rode out, scattering a flock of starlings pecking along the drive. Refusing to allow regrets to spoil her mood, she spurred fast enough to send her bonnet flying back off her head, so it flapped by its ribbon tips.

She finally drew to a halt at the edge of the Wold, her attention snagged by a fluttering shape above a stand of eglantine. "I'll be damned," she whispered, slipping down from her saddle and tossing the reins around an elder tree. "I could *swear* that is a gadfly hawk moth." She fetched her gear from the saddlebag and advanced slowly, ever so slowly, on the wisp of gold and orange and blue. "And so it is. Oh, you're a beauty, you are! And once I've got you, only five more species to go in the whole of Lincolnshire!" The fluttering creature alighted for an instant on a flower. Tempted to swipe at it, Pris forced herself to wait, held her breath, stared longingly at the brilliant stripes on those delicate wings. . . .

A clatter of hooves on the road at her back made her turn and swear: "Damn! You stupid bloody idiot!" The moth quivered atop the bud, then skittered away, toward a high clump of dame's rocket. "Farther from the road," Pris grunted in satisfaction, trailing after it through the underbrush. Her boot caught in a rabbit burrow, and she stumbled, falling on her face in the dirt. But she recovered quickly, never losing sight of the prize she sought. "Good boy. Good boy. Now stop and have some nectar. . . ." Just as if it had heard her, the moth came to rest with tentative grace atop the pink flowers. A swarm of gnats arose from the grass along the forest edge; she raised a hand to shoo them away. Eyes trained on the wisp of beauty before her, she brought her net up over her head, creeping forward by inches. The hoofbeats on the road, she noted happily, had vanished. She was about to make her move when the moth unfolded its wings and sailed skyward again.

"Oh, you bloody thing!" But Pris wasn't cross, not really. She was sure she would catch this one, so sure that already she was picturing it pinned to her corkboard, those intricately striped wings spread beneath the protection of glass. She watched as it fluttered from the phlox toward a single pale stem of wood lily that had opened its trumpet in the shade from the tall trees of the Wold.

"Settle down," she whispered, edging through the weeds all around her. "Settle down, my lovely." She raised her net once more, bending low, stalking expertly, soundlessly, forward. The moth obligingly alighted on the tip of one lily petal. "Sweet, sweet nectar," Pris breathed, so focused on the object of her longing that the footsteps behind her barely crossed her consciousness. "Drink deep," she murmured—and then started as a hand seized her waist.

"What the bloody hell—" Furious, she jammed the handle of the net backward against the figure standing behind her. "Dammit, Melchior! You know better than that!" She heard the stableman's breath escape in a sickening rush. "Well, it serves you right! You've cost me a gadfly hawk moth!" She plunged through the weeds toward the lily, but her quarry, alerted by the fuss, had flitted far beyond her reach. She watched helplessly as it soared into the cloudless blue sky. Shading her eyes with her hand, she stared after the beautiful, insubstantial thing for as long as she could bear to. Then she whirled on Melchior in a frightful wrath. "You stupid, stupid idiot!"

"I—I beg your pardon." Jack Cantrell was bent over, clutching his groin where the net handle had jabbed him. "You can rest assured . . . I will never make *that* mistake again."

Chapter

25

ris stared at him in stupefaction. "What in *hell*," she demanded, finally coming to her senses, "were you doing skulking through the woods after me?"

"What—in hell—were you doing—trying to make me a eunuch?" he gasped out, still holding to his privates.

"I didn't know you were you! I thought you were Melchior!"

"Are you always so harsh with your stableman? I thought you said he was your friend!"

"He is. And he knows better than to interrupt when I am on the verge of a capture!" But she relented, watching him cringe in pain. Some sort of apology seemed in order. "I am sorry," she said curtly.

"So am I." He made a grimace. "Far more sorry than you."

"Melchior's much shorter," she explained. "I only would have hit his gut."

"Lucky Melchior. He might have mentioned that when he told me where to find you."

She reached into her bag of gear. "Would water help?" He shook his head queasily. "Well, that's all I have to offer. No doubt your wife will know how to tend the injury."

"My *wife*?"

"Or is she only your lover still? Some folk did claim that."

"I have no idea whatsoever," he said brazenly, "what you are talking about."

Pris laughed. "God. You're a cool one."

"And you truly are crazy. What makes you think I am married?"

"Oh, now that I reflect on it, I am certain you're not. You're not the marrying kind, are you? You'll let a woman bear your baby, let another ruin her reputation for you, leave another believing that you cared for—" She broke off abruptly; his hand was reaching for her hair.

"Pris. Where do you fall in that litany of evils? Has your reputation suffered?"

"Of course not! No one knows. . . ." She found she was blushing, and hated herself for it.

For his part, he was smiling with great satisfaction. "And unless the laws of science have all been upended, you cannot possibly have borne my child. Which leaves only . . . that you believe I care for you."

"Believed!" She reemphasized the past tense. "Before you went running off with Lady Harpool!"

"I haven't seen Lady Harpool," he responded evenly, "since the night you dined at Avenleigh. When I told her that I was in love with you."

"And while we are on that subject," Pris went on, gathering steam, "what sort of father would desert his—" She faltered. "What is that you say?"

"I said, I have not laid eyes on Lady Harpool since the night you dined at Avenleigh."

She blinked. "No, no. The other part. I—I must have misheard you."

"When I told her that I was in love with you? Is that the part you mean?"

"In love with . . ."

"You," he repeated patiently, and then grinned. "You, Priscilla Wilcox."

She stared up at him with the sort of expression she might have worn had a lunar moth appeared in Lincolnshire. "With *me*?"

"I'll keep on saying it for as long as you like. I love you, Priscilla Wilcox. I love you, Priscilla Wilcox. I love you, Priscilla—"

"How can you be in love with *me*?"

He shrugged, those impossibly blue eyes shining. "Just lucky, I guess."

Pris took a breath and rubbed a smudge of leaves and dirt from her cheek. Her skirts were muddied and studded with briar prickles; her hair had blown free of its pins and was hanging all to the left in a tangled mass. She had never felt so disheveled and unattractive in all her life—yet here was Jack Cantrell saying . . .

"I love you, Priscilla Wilcox."

There, he had done it again! "Stop *teasing*!" she cried out, and burst into tears.

He wiped their muddy tracks with his handkerchief and put his arm around her quaking shoulders. She fought the urge to collapse against him, clung instead to reason, to her scientific knowledge of the world. "Men such as you," she insisted, sniffling, "do *not* fall in love with girls such as me!"

"And why not?"

"It would be like—like a peacock butterfly mating with a clothes moth!"

"I don't know much about lepidoptera, but I have seen clothes moths," he said after a moment. "And they are fairly plain. Unlike you."

Her mouth curved with resentment. "Now I know that you are jesting with me."

"Never," he swore, in a voice that swept her breath away again. "Not about this, anyway."

He was still holding her, and the expression on his face was most remarkable. He looks, Pris thought, as though he means to kiss me. Then he did, hard and sweet and very thoroughly. His mouth against hers tasted like the best of that fine day—the blue sky, the clear sun, the clean wind—bundled up into one. Pris let out her long-held breath in a slow sigh. He took advantage of the parting of her lips to push his tongue between them, his hand clasping the back of her head, tilting her face up to him. Her knees went weak, but his arm held her firmly, crushing her to his chest. After quite a long time, he came up for air, and to push her wayward hair from her face.

"If you love me," Pris began, taking advantage of the momentary interval.

"Ah, I am making progress! You admit the possibility!"

"Oh, be still. Then why did you disappear so abruptly, without a word to me?"

"You knew where I was going. I told you that night at supper."

"You most certainly did not!"

"I most certainly did. We discussed it at length—how I would go to Lord Cowper and tell him about my Cousin Agnes, and find out if he was still in love with her."

"I didn't think you meant it! That is—" She broke off. She had to. He was kissing her again. She struggled to pull free, but he clearly had no intention of letting her go until he was ready. And by the time he was ready; she was no longer so eager to be released. "You are *very* good at that," she told him breathlessly.

"Well. I had all those years of practice. My question is how *you* became so adept."

She dropped her gaze. "I don't imagine I am."

He caught her lowered chin in his fingertips. "Pris. Don't. You are what I love. More than that, you are what I want." His hand slid down to her breast, making her shiver. "See how I want you?" he whispered, and held her to him once more, so that she felt the hard bulge in his breeches.

"If you love me so much, where have you *been* all this time?" she demanded.

"I told you. I had to go and see Lord Cowper."

"It is only a four-day ride to London. You have been gone six weeks!"

"Parliament was in recess. I had to go all the way to Ireland. Lovely country, Ireland. Or it would be, if the sun ever shone."

"You went to *Ireland* to see him?"

"I did. It was rather a remarkable interview. After all the time I'd spent in tracking him down, I'd stammered out no more than half of what I came to say when he flew out the door, ran to the stable, and leaped onto his horse. I don't believe he even had a hat."

"He didn't," Pris confirmed. "Oh, I wish you could have been there! He rode past me on the toll road, headed hell-for-leather for Avenleigh House—though of course I didn't know that at the time—and then, not half an hour later, he and Agnes came thundering back. . . . Your aunt is thoroughly scandalized, by the way. As is most of the parish. Though not, I might note, as scandalized as they are by your having eloped with Lady Harpool."

He frowned. "What made anyone imagine I'd eloped with Lady Harpool?"

"She disappeared the same night that you did. And there were various sightings—in London, in Brighton. Even in Italy, I believe."

"*You* ought to have known better," he said with reproach.

"Did you really tell her . . . you were in love with me?" He nodded. "And was she—very angry?"

He grinned. "Let's say she was not pleased."

"Where do you think she has gone?"

"I neither know nor care. Christ, Pris. Let's not speak of her."

She sensed tension in his tone but was willing to ignore it, with his arms around her, his mouth brushing her hair. "Then let me ask you this. Lord Cowper came by yesterday. How am I to explain your tardiness, except to postulate that his affection for Agnes is twenty-four hours stronger than yours for me?"

"I had to stop in London."

"Ah. Business, no doubt."

"Very important business." He reached into his waist-coat. "I needed to fetch this."

The small, square box he presented her was of dove-gray velvet. She glanced up at him, saw him smile and nod, and opened it gingerly. Inside, within a nest of stark white satin, was a golden ring set with an enormous stone. "I know it is only compressed vegetative matter," he apologized.

She stared at the diamond. "Yes, but so *much* of it!"

That made him laugh. "God, how I have missed you!" He took the box from her and slipped the ring onto her finger, smiling in satisfaction. "A perfect fit. Just like you and me." He drew her into his arms again and bent to kiss her. "Though you *could* be a tad taller."

"*You* could be a tad shorter." But she raised herself on her tiptoes.

"How accommodating of you," he murmured, holding her close, his body tight to hers. "You haven't said yet if you'll marry me."

"You haven't yet asked."

He was quiet, looking down at her. "The truth is, I'm afraid to," he told her at last. "Pris. I know I am asking a great deal of you. Too much, perhaps. Another woman's child—"

"I love Johnnie!"

"Even his color?"

"He is a beautiful color," she said stoutly, and he laughed and kissed her. "What? He is!"

"But he will always remind you of the past."

"And remind you as well."

He had turned sober. "I don't know, Pris, if this will make any sense. I have contemplated it all the way from Ireland, and this is what I've come up with. I was young and angry when I met Camille. I—desired her greatly. She took me under her wing. She taught me certain things. How to be a man. But—damn! This is hard to explain. Camille . . . made a business of loving."

"I know. Esmé told me."

He arched a brow. "You must have been shocked."

"I was. For a bit. And then I thought—well. She found a way, didn't she? A way to earn her own living, break free of the constraints of being female. And I admired her instead."

"So did I," he admitted. "She was a remarkable woman. But the fact remained—I came into her life when I could provide what she needed: money. And I think, to her, that was inseparable from affection. The love . . . and the money. I would have preferred it . . . had there been only love." To her complete astonishment, he dropped to his knees at her feet. "Pris. If I could, if I only *could*—you don't know what I would give to come to you the way you come to me. I won't say I regret the past, except for that. I am what I am. All I can tell you is that in you I see, I *feel*, a new beginning. You can save me. I know that you can."

"You aren't such a sinner," she scoffed, "as to need salvation."

"You don't know," he whispered. "You don't know what I am."

She began to unbutton her jacket. When she had it unfastened, she reached for her bodice buttons. He realized what she was doing and clasped her small hands in his. "No. There's no need for that."

"I think there is." Defiantly she went on unbuttoning. The bodice fell open, revealing the batiste shift she wore beneath. He gazed hungrily, then averted his eyes.

"Christ, Pris!" he said, his voice strangled. She reached for his hand, held it to her breast. He let his fingers brush her taut nipple through the sheer cotton, then jerked away abruptly. "No," he told her emphatically.

"Listen to me. I won't have you imagining . . . that I'm something I'm not."

"I want to marry you. I want you for my wife."

"And I want to be sure that you do," she told him evenly, settling into the nest of underbrush beside where he knelt. "Think of it as satisfying my scientific curiosity."

He pushed back his hair. "No. It is much more than that. You know that it is. It's something sacred, holy. A gift that, once given, cannot be taken back."

"You sound like my father," she said in surprise.

"I told you. I've had a deal of time for thinking. And this isn't in my plans. For once in my life I intend to do right—and for the right reasons. And that does not include tumbling you in broad daylight by the side of the Lincoln Road." He straightened, holding out his arm to pull her to her feet.

Pris hesitated a moment, clinging to his fingertips. Then she cocked her blond head. "Very well. I shall be frank. How can I be sure that you will satisfy *me*?"

He stared down at her, disconcerted. "I . . . Jesus, Pris!"

"I'm not the sort to buy a horse unridden."

"What a thing to say!" A flush of color had risen on his cheekbones.

"Why so? How much misery has been made in this world by husbands and wives who find too late they are unsuited to one another? Why, wars have been fought, whole kingdoms lost, over this very matter. Look at Eleanor of Aquitaine! Look at Henry the Eighth!"

"I thought you were a scientist, not a historian. And anyway, I should rather look at you." He stroked her smooth white throat, smiling despite himself at her vehemence. "Listen, love. I shall have a difficult enough time convincing your father that I am sincere in my intentions without the guilty secret of having deflowered his daughter."

"What makes you so certain you *will* be deflowering me?"

His hand abruptly stopped stroking; he sucked in a deep breath. "Was it Robert?" Then he squared his shoulders. "No. I won't ask. I'd be a hell of a one, wouldn't I, to balk at such a revelation? It makes no difference to me."

"Liar," she whispered, watching him closely.

"It's God's truth. Though I won't deny wishing I could be your first." He smiled again, crookedly. "It would make the matter of comparisons less daunting all around."

With wonder she realized that Jack Cantrell, beautiful, splendid Jack Cantrell, who had women on two continents swooning over his every move, harbored the exact same fears she did. Love for him swelled up, threatened to overwhelm her. She twined her arms around his neck, kissed his mouth, still tilted in that uncertain smile. "Oh,

Jack. You goose, You *are* the first. I've never wanted anyone but you."

He was relieved beyond words—and tried to hide it with mock anger. "How *dare* you toy with my affections that way? Come along now, and I'll see you home." He put his hands on her waist to raise her from the forest floor.

"Not yet."

"Pris—" She brought her hand around to his groin, pressed the bulge beneath his breeches and heard him gasp. "Don't . . ."

She scarcely heard him. There was magic in her touch, strong magic in the way his blood had surged to meet her hesitant fingers, his entire body shuddering. He let his tongue graze her ear, tracing its shell-like curves. Then he put his mouth to hers, and she returned the kiss ardently, giving rein to all the love for him she had hidden in her heart for so long.

He raised his head after quite some time, dazed but pleased. "Why, Priscilla!"

"Shut up and kiss me again," she said impatiently.

He did, and this time his lips ranged lower, over her chin and throat to her shoulder blade. When he moved lower still, his fingers pushing aside the edges of her jacket and bodice, and set his mouth to her breast through the scrim of her shift, she felt her nipples tight as dew-flushed rosebuds. His tongue rimmed against first one and then the other, circling their sweetness, plucking at them hungrily. He was stretched out beside her; she turned to him, her thighs molding hard against him.

He let out a desperate groan. "Pris. I can't . . . don't tempt me." For answer, she clutched the smooth swell of his buttocks in both her hands. "Oh, Jesus!" he burst out, rigid with desire, certain he would come against her then and there. "I want you. God, how I want you!"

"Take me," she whispered.

He raised his head. Her eyes were dove gray, soft as a dove's wings, wide as the sky. "Love. Are you certain?"

"As certain as I will ever be of anything in this world."

He bent and kissed her once more, infinitely tender. Then he tore the shift away. She smelled of Castile soap and roses, of innocence and beauty, and he could not get enough of her skin. Her naked shoulders were carved ivory, her breasts . . . " 'Like two young roes that are twins,' " he whispered, " 'that feed among the lilies.' "

She looked up at him through her lashes. "Father would be impressed."

"Oh, I doubt that!" But his heart was singing with the words of the Song of Solomon: *Behold, thou art fair, my love; thou hast doves' eyes within thy locks. . . .*

" 'I rose up to open to my beloved,' " Pris said very softly, and did, arching toward him.

Jack threw off all hope of resistance and let desire run wild.

He drew her gown over her head, while she obligingly sat up to allow it. He eased off her boots and stockings, planting kisses along her thighs. When the moment came to take off her drawers, he could not manage to undo the knot. She did it for him, staring steadily into his eyes, that were like blue fire.

He was still fully clothed, he recognized impatiently, and cursed, fumbling with his cravat and waistcoat and shirt, flinging them into the brambles. She reached up to touch the golden amulet that hung by its chain at his chest. "What is this?"

He flushed. "From Camille. A love token. I'd forgotten I had it on still."

"What is in it?" she asked curiously.

"I haven't the slightest idea. I never looked. She told me I must not open it. Here. I'll have it off." He started to raise it over his head, but she stayed his hand:

"Leave it."

"Not now. Not anymore. There's no purpose."

But the thought of his lost lover did not haunt Pris any longer; the fire in his eyes, that burned only for her, had laid her fears to rest. "Leave it on. Please. It may be our love token now; who is to say?" He hesitated. "If she loved you as I do," she went on gently, "she would be glad to see you made happy."

"You didn't know Camille," he said dubiously. But he let the love charm fall against his chest, because she asked him to.

His boots—God, he could not get out of his boots! He had to sit back among the leaves and let her remove them; she eased his breeches down, too, after she had unfastened the buttons with a delicate touch that made his manhood surge. His linens he ripped off himself, while she waited, kneeling beside him. When at long last they faced one another, Adam and Eve in a Lincolnshire Eden, he was so desperate for her that he was trembling. He put out his hand, touched her cheek, then her gold hair and her breast. She lay back onto the matted leaves and roots beneath them. Above him, the branching weeds made a vault more glorious than that of the Minster. Pris closed her eyes.

She felt his palm slide over her breast to her belly, and then lower still, to her mound of Venus. It slipped to her thigh, caressing her, relishing her soft, smooth skin. And then it drew upward; his fingers teased, probed, explored with amazing gentleness. He stroked her, soothed her, found what he was seeking: the sweet bud of her desire.

Pris caught her breath as he touched her there. "Oh. God," she whispered.

His touch intensified, awakening the most amazing flood of sensation. She felt as though her very soul were being stroked, as if he'd somehow reached past her body and into her being, and if he stopped, she would die. He did not stop. She felt him bring his manhood up against her, felt its smooth, broad head replace his palm and fingers. Then, very gently, he pushed toward her—and went on pushing, until he had sunk himself inside her, straight to her core.

He gave a sigh of intense satisfaction, his mouth reaching for hers. "Love," he murmured. "Oh. My love." And Pris did not think any feeling in all of creation could match what she felt at that moment: the pride, the pleasure, the fulfillment. She was wrong. He withdrew, drew all that great length of hard rod out of her, then thrust in again, more forcefully this time. She gasped, clutching his shoulders, nails raking his skin.

"Did I hurt you?" he asked anxiously, pulling free once more. She shook her head, not trusting herself to speak. "Are you certain?" For answer she smoothed her hands down his back and over his buttocks, drawing him to her. He sank in with desperate eagerness.

Something was happening inside Pris, something beyond the sensation of his manhood piercing her. Heat was coiling in her belly, a raging red heat that threatened to consume her, swallow her entirely. He started to withdraw again, and she would not allow it; she clung to him, holding him to her, against her. "Pris," he said in that strangled voice.

"What?" she demanded, impatient.

"I can't hold back any longer."

Her eyes opened at last, bright, like Eve's, with knowledge. "Why should you?" she asked.

He laughed and plunged into her. She laughed, thighs parted in welcome. The laughter died in his throat; he thrust in and out and in again with desperate force. The fire in her belly raged and flared and became blinding, spreading out to the tips of her hair, to the ends of her toes, until she thought she would die of ecstasy, until she feared only that it would never subside.

And just when she thought she understood, she *knew*, another wave of sensation flowed through her, so infinite and profound that it left her shuddering helplessly, with tears rolling down her cheeks. Deep in her belly, she felt his seed burst forth. His heavy head sagged against her breast; he was panting, fighting for breath, while the world around them slid very slowly back into place.

"Oh, Christ. Oh, Pris," he said when he could speak. He smoothed her hair from her face, looked down at her tear-streaked cheeks and kissed the wetness away. In all the times he'd made love to Camille, he'd never seen her cry. "I am sorry. Forgive me. Please say you forgive me." She regretted it now, he was certain; she wept for her lost innocence.

She looked up at him, and he caught his breath. Her eyes, her lovely soft dove's eyes, were all the colors of sunset; they seemed on fire from within, the way a cloud looks when the last rays of the day break through. Far from regret, they blazed with a newfound knowledge of love, of its remarkable power to heal and restore. The knowledge made her so impossibly beautiful that tears sprang to his own eyes and spilled down. "I love you, Pris," he whispered, and then sobbed wildly, without embarrassment, while she cradled him in her small white arms. He cried for Camille, for Johnnie, for his father, even for poor damned Robert, the bloody fool, who'd had all this in his grasp and hadn't the sense to recognize it. By the end, he was crying the way those who've witnessed miracles cry, soundlessly, out of wonder and awe.

Slowly the storm passed. He held her tight to him, whispered against her ear: "You see how you've changed me? I can't think when I last cried. Certainly never like that. Not even when I heard Camille had died." He was astonished at how easily the name came forth, how comfortable he felt confessing that to her.

"Healing takes time," she whispered back. "We must do it each in our own way."

He smiled down at her. "How did you ever get to be so wise?"

"My father's sermons, I suppose."

Jack laughed, nuzzling her breast. Then he sobered slightly. "Speaking of your father—what do you suppose he will say to all this?"

"I neither know nor care."

He wound a strand of her long, bright hair around his finger. "Don't be too hard on him, Pris. He wants what is best for you, you know."

"You are what's best for me."

"I can't imagine he will see it that way. There are any number of strikes against me, you realize, from his point of view. From *anyone's* point of view."

"Not from mine." She let her viewpoint linger over his broad shoulders, his slim waist and hips. "Tell me something, would you?"

"Anything. Anything at all."

"I know a great deal about butterflies' mating habits. What I don't know is how long it takes a man to recover from lovemaking."

Jack thought it over. "That depends. Sometimes a week. Sometimes a month. I believe that's the average."

"A *month*?" She stared at him. "And a woman—how long is proper for her to wait before wanting it again?"

"Oh, much longer. Most decent women are satisfied to have sexual congress two or three times a year."

"Two or three times a year . . ." She averted her gaze, and he grinned.

"Of course, *indecent* women—"

"Yes?" she asked tentatively.

"Cannot go without it for ten minutes at a time." He would have gone on teasing her, but his manhood betrayed him; it had straightened up hard and stiff as a flagpole. She noticed and settled her hand around it, making him gasp.

"Liar. I ought to make you wait a month," she muttered. "Perhaps I shall."

"I can stand it," he said, not especially convincingly. "Of course, no one ever has suspected *me* of being average."

"And I have just discovered I am indecent," she noted. "How appalling."

"How *wonderful*," he corrected, attacking her ravenously. "I am sorry about the gadfly hawk moth, though."

"So am I," she whispered, as his mouth closed over hers. "But it's my only regret."

Chapter
26

On Sunday next, Bishop Wilcox delivered what he thought was a truly outstanding sermon on the vital importance of preserving the natural order, based on Ephesians and with subtexts from Isaiah, First Romans, and the prophet Joel. Replete with satisfaction, secure in the knowledge he had done his utmost to prevent any further social upheavel in the bishopric, he returned home to find Jack Cantrell waiting in his parlor, asking for his daughter's hand.

"Is this some sort of bad jest?" the bishop demanded, thoroughly annoyed.

"Not at all, sir. I assure you, I am all too aware of my unworthiness," Jack told him with conviction. "She deserves far, far better than me."

"I should say she does! What do you have to recommend you, eh? A bastard son, a checkered past, all manner of gossip surrounding you—and what's become of Lady Harpool, that you eloped with?"

"I can at least plead innocent to that, sir. I never eloped with the lady in question."

"Then where the devil have you been?"

"To Ireland. You see, there had been a sort of misunderstanding between my cousin Agnes and Lord Harry Cowper, who'd once asked her to marry him. When the circumstances of the misunderstanding came to my attention, I thought it only my duty to do what I could to clear the air."

"So *you* were behind that entire affair!"

"I hope you won't hold it against me, sir." Jack grinned winningly. "If you only could have seen Lord Cowper's eagerness to reinstate his claim to Agnes's hand, once he had been informed of her true feelings for him—"

"I've heard as much. The whole county has. Didn't even wear a hat!" The bishop tsked in disapproval.

"Well, I brought mine this afternoon," Jack assured him. "Your butler took it from me."

Bishop Wilcox heaved himself down onto a horsehair chair. "You seem mightily cocksure, Lord Avenleigh."

"Giddy, rather. My love for your daughter has done that."

The bishop plucked at the nailheads on the arm of his chair. "I had plans, you know, to take her to Bath."

"Yes, sir. So she told me."

"Some nice, steady military sort, I thought, would prove just the thing for her."

"Begging your pardon, sir, I'm very sure it would *not*."

Bishop Wilcox sighed and ran a hand through his silver hair. "She's always been an utter enigma to me. Women! Who can understand what they long for in life?"

"I think," Jack said, very gently, "what most of them long for is to be cherished. And I do cherish Pris."

"Do you?" The bishop had his pulpit voice on, and

had lowered a finger at him. "What about this mistress you had back in the Caribbean? Did you cherish her as well?"

"It would be ignoble of me to claim anything else. She died giving me my son."

"Hmph!" said the bishop, and then seemingly could not think of any more to say.

"Sir." Jack took a step forward, which made the old man glance up nervously. "Having a child of my own has made me all too aware of the—the expectations we place on our offspring. I know I'm not the son-in-law you always dreamed of. You're not the sort to put undue emphasis on my social standing. After all, you are a vicar of God. You realize there are deeper, more vital aspects to a man than mere wealth and a title. There is a matter of *character*."

"Mm. Quite."

"Simply knowing that your daughter would always be extremely well provided for and would become a countess cannot sway your opinion. Of that I am sure."

"*How* well provided for?" the bishop asked astutely. "There has been talk your brother ran through most of the family fortune."

"Robert did make some unfortunate financial decisions. But I have applied myself, to the best of my ability, to putting the house back in order. The current income of the Avenleigh estates stands at forty thousand a year." The bishop's mouth made an O. "That does not include, of course, proceeds from the Caribbean holdings, which as of the last quarter stood at some twenty-eight thousand."

The bishop was visibly adding in his head. "So, some sixty-eight altogether . . ."

"My solicitor and I expect those numbers to increase considerably in the future, since we have invested heavily in improvements to the estate. But as I said, sir, these considerations hold no influence over a man such as yourself."

"Would you make your home here in Lincolnshire,

Lord Avenleigh? And would you *tithe*?" Bishop Wilcox had a sudden vision of renovations to the cathedral on a hitherto unimagined scale.

"The earls of Avenleigh have always donated generously to the Minster, sir, as you know. I fully intend to keep up that tradition. But to return to the question of character—"

"Ten percent of sixty-eight thousand a *year*," the bishop murmured audibly. "Why, we could replace the whole narthex, shore up those flying buttresses . . ."

"I won't deny my life to this point has been less than unspotted. But let me *assure* you, sir, that my respect and love for your daughter are such that I have turned over an entire new leaf. If you can only find it in your heart to take pity on a sincerely repentant sinner—"

"And the rose window! No more teas with Mrs. Blathersby . . ." He paused. Jack managed to hold his tongue. At last the bishop stood up and took Jack's hand, pumping it with great enthusiasm. "Jesus himself spoke of the Prodigal Son and how God rejoices a hundredfold at his return. Welcome to the family, my dear boy! Welcome indeed!"

The first of the banns proclaiming Lord Avenleigh's betrothal to Priscilla Wilcox was read out at Lincoln Cathedral the following Sunday. A ripple of disbelief ran through the congregation at the news. Aunt Bertrice bowed her head in her pew, but 'Phrina stood and started applauding wildly, until her mother yanked her down again.

Pris was far beyond happiness, moved into a realm of bliss so utter and entire that she moved dazedly, going through the myriad duties of a soon-to-be-bride with her head in the clouds. Jamalla was engaged to create the wedding gown. Mr. Shropley took charge of the invitations and announcements. Esmé was pressed into service in a thousand ways, planning the wedding supper, overseeing the

flowers and wines, and ordering, at Jack's behest, a trousseau
from London that would have done one of the princesses
proud. 'Phrina occupied herself with a thorough spring
cleaning of Avenleigh House. Aunt Bertrice kept muttering direly to anyone who would listen about marrying in
haste and regretting at leisure, but even she could not dis-
pel the general joy.

Agnes and her new husband came north from London
well in advance of the wedding date, and Lord Cowper
raised a lovely toast on their first dinner with Priscilla and
Jack. "I only hope," he said, with a meaningful glance at his
own bride, "you'll prove as happy as we are."

"No one could ask any more," Jack responded. And it
was true: Lord and Lady Cowper were clearly, radiantly, in
love. "I have to laugh every time I see them together and
then glimpse Aunt Bertrice's pickled expression," he told
Pris one evening in the nursery as she played with Johnnie.

"It must be wretched, don't you think, to be so completely incapable of contentment?" she responded, while
Johnnie gleefully yanked her hair free from its pins.

"Positively. And speaking of contentment, isn't it his
bedtime?"

"No!" Johnnie said with great force, making both of
them laugh.

"He has that word down pat, at least," Jack noted ruefully, and watched, his heart brimming, as Pris kissed his
son's soft cheek. "Come and kiss me that way." But she
tossed her head, sending slivers of candlelight shooting
through the room.

"Later," she promised. "Show Daddy how you can
walk, my big boy." Johnnie agreeably toddled toward
Jack, who caught him in his arms and nuzzled his black hair.

"Very good, Johnnie!"

"Mamma," Johnnie said distinctly, and headed back
to Pris again.

"Already he prefers you to me," Jack said, frowning. "Do you know how lucky you are, Johnnie boy, to be getting a mamma such as she?" Tumbling into Pris's lap, Johnnie blazed out a grin that left little doubt he did.

From the corner of the nursery, Jamalla, taking neat stitches in the hem of Pris's wedding gown, beamed at them benignly. "I will be ready for you to try this on, m'amselle, in another minute."

"After he's asleep," Pris told her.

"I had other plans for then," Jack noted.

Jamalla's rich laugh echoed through the upper story, making Esmé poke her curly head through the connecting door to her rooms.

"Is it not Johnnie's bedtime?" she demanded.

"What's the matter, Esmé? Is the noise disturbing Bennett?" Jack asked with such innocence that Pris had to giggle.

"M'sieur Shropley," the maid said archly, "is assisting me with the wedding preparations." And she shut the door.

"I should very much enjoy assisting *you* with the wedding preparations in that same way," Jack murmured to Pris, who blushed becomingly.

Jamalla took the hint. "Let me put him to bed," she offered.

"I'll do that, Jamalla." And Jack watched as she did, changing his nappie and shirt very deftly despite Johnnie's wriggling resistance. Seeing her with his son—her patience, her devotion—raised a lump in his throat. He swallowed it and went and kissed her, enveloping them both in his arms. "Beautiful boy," he murmured. "Won't you *ever* be ready to sleep?"

"He is waiting for you to sing to him, m'amselle," Jamalla noted.

Pris lifted him up, moving to the rocking chair, and began a lullaby in her sweet, low voice:

I gave my love a cherry that had no stone,
I gave my love a chicken that had no bone,
I gave my love a story that had no end,
I gave my love a baby with no crying.

Jack stood and listened, his heart on fire with longing and love.

Later, when Johnnie had been laid abed, Jack took Pris to his own bed, to the room that had once seemed his sole refuge in a house that was lonely and grim. Now, he reflected, coming toward her as she lay naked and smiling, her blond hair loose and wild, everything was changed— and all on account of her. "Does your father expect you back tonight?" he murmured, bending to kiss her.

"Of course he does."

"Let's disappoint him again."

He began the soft, slow caresses that drove her wild with desire. She answered, clinging to him, stroking his shoulders and back. Her mouth brushed his; he seized on it, kissed her with an intensity made stronger by knowing she would soon be his for all time. She caught her hands in the golden chain of Camille's love token, drawing him downward, her legs parting beneath him in eager anticipation. But he dawdled, teasing her, lips playing at her breasts until her sighs grew frantic, until she dug her nails into his buttocks, pleading with him: "Now, love. Oh, my love. Now . . ."

Still he waited a little longer, wanting to extend the miraculous sensation of being wanted so wholly, so desperately. Then he could stave off his own raging desire no longer; he plunged inside her, felt her smooth walls close around him. God! Had he ever truly made love before he made love to her? She had none of Camille's arousing tricks, that was true. But neither did she ever pout, or turn the conversation to business, or withhold herself from him for reasons of her own. Every time he took her—and he took her recklessly, at each conceivable opportunity—he was amazed and humbled anew by her longing for him.

Now, for example, she was twisting in the bed beneath him, pulling free her long, pale hair—"What are you doing?" he whispered.

"I want to be on top."

Biting his lip, he asked, "Why?"

"Because I never have been," she told him, shrugging. And she clambered onto him, hands flat against his chest. He arched his head and caught the very tip of her nipple in his mouth, pulling at it hungrily. She gasped and leaned back; he cupped her buttocks in his palms and thrust inside her, unable to keep from groaning as his rod slid home. She rode him tentatively at first, and then with abandon, until they climaxed within seconds of one another and dissolved together in a heap on the disheveled linens, limp with fulfillment.

"Ah," Jack murmured when he'd caught his breath, when his heart had stopped thumping. "The pleasures of experimental inquiry! I really had no idea how fascinating science could be."

"It all depends," Pris noted primly, "on the worthiness of the subject under study."

"How do I stack up against butterflies, pray tell?"

"It's far too soon to say. I know so much more about them still than I do about you."

She was learning, though, day by day—learning his likes and dislikes, what repelled and intrigued him, bored him, made his clear blue eyes come to life. He had no patience for the details of the wedding, for example—the minutiae of guest lists and responses and where to hire extra chairs for the supper—yet he'd memorized his portion of the vows long before she knew hers. Questions of rank and courtesy, such as whether Lady Chesterton should be

seated higher than Lady Ashton, made him hoot with derision. He despised his butler, Bellows, openly, yet was as
kind as could be to be the understairs maid when she
scorched his best shirts ironing them. He hadn't even got a
valet. "All gentlemen have a valet," Pris objected when she
realized this. "Don't they?"

"What for? To dress me? I'm not Johnnie, thank you
kindly; I can get myself into my breeches. And I have you
now to get me out of them."

"Who blacks your boots for you?"

"I do. It takes five minutes, twice a week. I've got a
polish some old woman back in Castries makes up. Maman
something-or-other. Esmé gets it for me."

The mention of the witch, Maman Gris-Gris, made
Pris think of the token he still wore around his neck. He'd
tried again to remove it, the first time he'd made love to her
here in the house, and again she would not let him. She'd
come to think of it as a talisman, proof that Camille did not
object to his marrying her. He'd fallen in love with her
while he was wearing it; to remove it now, she argued,
might jinx everything. Jack laughed and called her an odd
sort of scientist, to trust in hocus-pocus. But after that, he
left it in place.

Sometimes, when he was meeting with Bennett Shropley over business, Pris brought Johnnie into his study and
played with the boy while the two men hunched over his
desk, talking tariffs and taxes and restrictions of trade. He
may not have cared whether Lady Chesterton's pedigree
took precedence over Lady Ashton's, but no detail of his
business practice was beneath his notice. She began to listen with one ear while she built block towers for Johnnie to
knock over, and gradually the morass of unfamiliar language and terms began to make some sense. One afternoon, when Shropley proposed rerouting a ship through
Aberdeen to pick up a cargo of loomed fustian, she spoke

up from where she knelt on the carpet without thinking: "You'd do better to send it by way of Berwick."

Both men turned to stare at her. Johnnie swatted her latest tower with a gurgle of glee.

"I beg your pardon?" Shropley said politely.

Pris blushed. "I only meant . . . you did say last week, did you not, that the burgesses of Aberdeen had tacked on a new cotton-good excise?"

"She's right, by Christ!" Jack burst out laughing, while Shropley paged through his notebooks with some embarrassment.

"Here it is," he acknowledged, pointing to an entry. "Five shillings the hundredweight. You owe the lady"—he calculated with his quill—"Forty-six pounds, milord, for the savings."

"Or you do," Jack said with mock fierceness. "I'll have it out of your stipend. Any other words of wisdom, my love, for us hapless men of business?"

"Well . . . since you ask, I must admit I cannot see why you are shipping cotton cloth to St. Lucia in May. Assuming two months in transit, it should arrive in Castries by July. Distribution from there to Boston and Philadelphia takes—what, another month and a half?"

Jack nodded, bemused. "More or less."

"And then one must allow still more time for it to reach the wholesalers, and the retailers after. As I understand it," she added hastily.

"Seems to me you understand it quite well," Shropley said with a grin.

"So, with another month for that, your fustian ought to reach the shelves of shops in America by the first week in September."

"My calculation exactly," Jack agreed. "Is there a problem with that?"

"Wouldn't the ladies in Boston and Philadelphia more likely be shopping for woolcloth than cotton in autumn?"

"Jesus." Now Jack's face had turned red. "She's absolutely right, Bennett. Cancel the fustian and see if you can pick up woolcloth. As for you, Priscilla Wilcox—" She held her breath, fearing her boldness in speaking out had displeased him; even Johnnie froze, clutching a block in each fist. But he smiled at them both, his eyes bright with pride. "Why don't you come and have a look at the rest of the autumn schedules for us, to see what other blunders we poor benighted males might have made?"

Far from resenting her interest in his business, he took great pleasure in recounting that tale to Lord Cowper and everyone who visited. Pris glowed under the beaming sun of his approval, grew more sure each day of his regard for her. His work was so much a part of his life that she could not have borne to be shut off from it; that he welcomed her interest and advice surprised and then delighted her. But perhaps, she thought, with less assurance, Camille had taken part in his affairs of business, too. She broached the subject to him, hesitantly, when they went out walking one day.

"I wanted to ask you, Jack . . ."

"Anything at all," he responded, taking the opportunity to pause and kiss her in the shade of a linden tree.

"You and Camille were partners, were you not? Business partners?" she went on, when he drew away at last.

"Not exactly. I was an investor in her business. In the Hôtel de l'Isle." He glanced at her. "You know about that?"

She nodded. "Esmé told me. Well, actually, Jamalla had to. Esmé did not know the English word for 'brothel.' "

"And what do you think of my investment?"

She toed the new grass beneath her slipper. "I think it was very kind of you to assist Camille. And that it was most—most *courageous* of her to do so well in the world."

He tilted his hat down to shield the sun, so he could

see her eyes. "But as a bishop's daughter, what do you think of the moral side of my investment?"

"I—I don't know. It bothers me a bit. I'm aware that men have needs their marriages don't always fulfill—"

"Camille had women among her clientele as well."

"No!"

"Oh, yes. She kept a stable of strapping young men to accommodate them."

"Imagine that!" Pris thought it over. "I suppose what is good for the goose is good for the gander. Or do I mean the other way around?"

"Though the foundation of the Hôtel was always gambling."

"I don't hold with gambling," Pris said firmly. "It seems to me it is always those least able to afford it who are drawn to it."

A corner of Jack's mouth twitched. "So the gambling offends you more than the other."

"Neither of them really makes me comfortable," she admitted.

"Nor did they ever me. I sold the place in February."

"Did you? Oh, Jack. I am glad." She stood on tiptoe to kiss him, but even then he had to bend his head to reach her mouth.

"If it troubled you, you ought to have asked about it before now."

"Did you get a good price?" she asked anxiously, and he erupted in laughter. "What?" she demanded in bewilderment.

"I really cannot credit sometimes that you are your father's daughter. No. I did not get a *good* price. I got a fair one. The place is now in the hands of an eager young man named Antoine. Have you any more questions?"

She recalled what had initiated the entire discussion.

"As it happens, I have. Did Camille take an interest in your business holdings?"

"Only insofar as they assured her a constant stream of gowns and hats. But she never had the slightest inclination toward memorizing the excise tax rates of the world's major ports, as you have. And on that subject, have you finally learned your wedding vows?"

"I'll know them when the time comes," Pris promised.

"It is coming quickly." He held her tight against him, his head buried in her thick gold hair. "Shall we practice again? 'I, Priscilla Margaret Anne Wilcox, take thee, John David Howard Cantrell, to be my wedded husband . . .'"

"To have and to hold," Pris whispered breathlessly, "from this day forth. For better, for worser." She scrunched her nose. "What sort of word is 'worser'? Whoever says 'worser'?"

"Don't get distracted," he chided. "'For richer, for poorer—'" His hand had slid beneath her cloak to cup her breast.

"Who is getting distracted?" she demanded. "No wonder I haven't learned them yet! We never finish reciting them without you starting in on me!"

"'In sickness and in health,'" he went on calmly.

She giggled, feeling the press of his manhood. "You seem very healthy this afternoon, milord. Very healthy *indeed.*"

"'Until we are par'—oh, Priscilla!" She'd reached for his breeches buttons.

"I don't like that end much anyway," she concluded, and drew him down with her beneath the shelter of the linden branches that quivered in the wind.

*L*ater, strolling back toward Avenleigh House hand in hand, their passion very temporarily sated, they passed the toll house along the highway. The boy who kept the gate called out a cheery greeting. "Looking to what he'll make in fees on the day of our wedding," Jack noted cynically. "All that to-and-fro of the gentry, and plenty of champagne to impel them to tip . . ."

"We *could* have eloped, like Agnes and Harry."

"How could I do that to your father?"

"It would serve him right. Imagine trading your daughter to the devil for the sake of new leading on the rose window!" Jack had told her, at her insistence, the entire context of his interview with the bishop, requesting her hand.

Jack shrugged. "He must not truly think me such a devil."

Pris let out an inelegant snort. "That's the crux, though. He does."

"You don't give him credit enough," he said gently.

"And you give him too much."

"Would you prefer he'd refused me?"

She cocked her head, in the new poke bonnet Esmé had ordered from London. It was of basket willow, with striped grosgrain ribbons the dove-gray of her eyes, and was impossibly becoming. "No, silly. It's his hypocrisy I detest."

He tucked her hand more firmly against him. "I think he simply realized he had no chance of prevailing, since you'd made up your mind to have me."

"Still, to be swayed by your *income*—"

"He wants you to be well provided for. Any father would want that."

She paused along the path. "You really *do* have the most infuriating tendency to see the best in everyone, don't you?"

"My greatest fault," he said gravely. "Bennett always tells me so."

They both glanced up at a sudden clatter of hooves

and wheels in the distance. "Someone's in a frightful rush," Pris noted curiously, as a post-chaise hurtled toward them down the road.

"The driver ought not to be permitted to goad horses that way." Jack frowned, watching him ply on the whip. Something, some vague memory, tugged at his mind as the blue-liveried fellow thundered past, driving two perfect matched bays. The window of the coach was drawn back; he caught the merest glimpse of a pale cheek beneath cascading auburn curls. . . . "Christ," he murmured before he could stop himself.

Pris's wide gray gaze met his with alarm. "What is the matter?"

"Stone on my heel," he lied, and ducked his head swiftly, fiddling with his boot until the coach had rushed on out of sight.

It did not take long for the news of Vivienne Harpool's return to Lincolnshire to reach Avenleigh House. Aunt Bertrice made the announcement herself that very evening, at dinner. Pris had stayed on, as she usually did, to see Johnnie to sleep. "I was going over the guest list Mr. Shropley finally provided me," the old woman announced, her black eyes agleam, "and I could not help but note one fairly major omission. Our neighbor, Lady Harpool."

"No one knows where she is, Mamma," Agnes said blithely.

"I know exactly where she is," her mother countered. "She's in residence at the cottage. She sent a most polite note this afternoon informing me, along with a strawberry shortcake."

"Strawberry shortcake?" 'Phrina echoed in delight, not noticing how the information had reduced the rest of the table to silence. "I must make sure to leave room!"

Jack glanced at Pris, whose shining head was lowered

over her soup plate. He cleared his throat. "Aunt Bertrice. Under the circumstances, I hardly think it necessary Lady Harpool be included. She is not, after all, a close friend of the family."

"How can you say that, Jack, after all she has done for us? Why, it was solely thanks to her that we had the honor of being presented to the Regent in London last autumn! It would be the *height* of rudeness not to issue her an invitation at once. Indeed, I find it very odd she was not on the guest list initially."

Bennett Shropley, who was also present—he seemed to be spending all his time at Avenleigh these days—cleared his throat discreetly. "I believe, Mrs. Gravesend, to proffer a belated invitation could be perceived as an affront. She is certain to conclude she is an afterthought."

"I'm inclined to agree with Mr. Shropley," Agnes said, stealing a glance at her husband. "Wouldn't you say so, dear?"

Lord Cowper met her gaze and then nodded emphatically. "Absolutely! Best to let sleeping dogs lie, eh?"

Jack was profoundly uncomfortable with this discussion. He wished Pris would look up from her soup.

"It was *lovely* being presented to the Regent, though, wasn't it, Ag?" 'Phrina said dreamily, and then started. "What? Why did you kick me?"

"I didn't *kick* you," Agnes retorted crossly. "I was stretching my leg."

"And she was so agreeable about squiring us to the theater, seeking out amusements that were *appropriate*," Aunt Bertrice went on smoothly. "Indeed, Jack, I recall that you seemed very grateful she had appeared on the scene."

Bitch, Jack thought, not missing Pris's involuntary cringe. And Pris didn't even know the extent of his guilt. . . .

It was time to take a stand—past time, by God. Vivienne Harpool had done enough damage to the Cantrells. He wasn't about to watch her ruin Pris's bliss. "I really—" he began, only to be interrupted by Pris's voice, very soft, very small, as she set aside her soup spoon.

"I really do think, Jack, she ought to be invited." She swallowed hard, but gathered strength as she went on: "And I'm quite sure, my love, that is just what *you* were about to say."

"*A*nd you tell me *I* think the best of everyone," Jack growled, pacing across his bedroom. "What in God's name made you give in to the old shrew on this?"

"I just don't see why there should be so much fuss," Priss said steadily. "She *was* very kind to your aunt and cousins in London." She watched as he strode to the sideboard and poured another drink. "That's your fourth brandy, is it not?"

"I wasn't aware you were counting," Jack snapped, then bit his tongue as she stared at him with wounded dove's eyes. He set the glass down abruptly. "Forgive me, love. But that woman has caused naught but mischief to this family."

"Oh, I would not say that."

He glanced at her. "No? If not for her, you'd have married Robert."

She shook her head. "No I wouldn't."

"Well, then, what about the ten thousand–some pounds he spent on her red silk unmentionables?"

That made her gaze go wide. "How do you know she has red silk unmentionables, pray tell?"

"Robert was an idiot, but he hired excellent agents. They had it all laid out in his account books—every penny he threw away on her. He was showering her with jewels

and gowns while he was swindling Agnes out of her dowry."
He paced across the room again. "And the really peculiar
thing is, she wasn't even his mistress!"

She looked up at him. "Are you sure of that, Jack?"

"She swore it to me up and down. And Bennett didn't
naysay her. Agnes and Aunt Bertrice and Sephrina didn't
know anything about what was going on between them. If
she *had* been his lover, *someone* would have known of it,
don't you think?"

*The two of them entwined in the shrubberies. Robert
grunting in satisfaction, thrusting into her again and again . . .*

"I suppose so," Pris acknowledged quietly. *What
could it matter now? Why should I tell him? He loves me,
not Vivienne Harpool.* It offended Pris's sense of fair play,
to contemplate making such a revelation. "But if it means
so much to your aunt, I don't see why we should not invite
her."

"Because," Jack began, and then bit his tongue. He
never could explain the true reason, confess to her about
that much-rued afternoon in the long graveyard grass at
the abbey. Her newfound self-worth was too fragile; she'd
have been crushed to learn he had betrayed her. It would be
a blow from which her love for him might never recover—
and that he would *not* risk. She meant too much to him now.
Just to remember how bleak and barren his heart had been
before she brought it back to life made him shudder and
reach for his brandy glass.

"It might even seem peculiar if we do not invite her,"
Pris mused, taking up the pillow cover she was embroider-
ing with their entwined initials.

"How so?"

"Well. There *were* rumors about the two of you, even
before you were supposed to have eloped with her. Of
course, I knew it was never more than *on-dit*."

He dropped to his knees at her feet, grasped her small

hand in both of his. "It never was," he said fiercely. And in a sense, it was true. Vivienne had touched his body, but not his soul. It was a Scholastic distinction, yet one he clung to as tightly as he gripped her hand.

"I would not blame you," she went on with that same forced brightness. "She surely is handsome, and elegant, and worldly—all the things I am not."

"Stop it, Pris!" That had been the perfect opportunity for him to confess, to clear his conscience—and he might have taken it, if there had not been that little hitch in her voice at the end of her speech. "I told you once, and I meant it—no man who'd ever kissed you could bear to go near Vivienne Harpool again."

Her lower lip was trembling; a tear like a small perfect pearl hung on the cusp of her eyelid and then slid downward. "I am sorry to be such a ninny," she whispered. "But if I ever lost you, I don't know how I would go on living."

He kissed that salt pearl away and crushed her in his arms. "Don't you know I feel that same way?" he murmured into the soft nest of her hair. She was still crying quietly against his chest; he could feel the swift beating of her heart, frail as a butterfly's wings. "I never would do anything to hurt you." And he meant that, too. If he could have erased that reckless quarter hour in Vivienne Harpool's embrace, he'd have done it at the cost of his life.

Gently he pried the 'broidery hoop from her grasp, laid it down on the carpet, lifted her up in his arms, and carried her to his bed. "I promised Father I'd be home," she began.

"To hell with your father. To hell with all of them," he said angrily, and undressed her with such desperate haste that he ruined her bodice and her sash. He went on to prove to her the best way he knew, wordlessly, with his mouth and hands and manhood, that she was all he wanted in a woman, and always would be.

Afterward, when she was smiling again, lying lazy and sated in the curve of his arm, he felt a prickle of conscience. *Tell her and be done with it,* his heart urged. The woman who had just shivered and shuddered beneath him, begging for release, crying his name as she climaxed with such wondrous joy, surely was beyond doubting him. He opened his mouth—and was forestalled by her voice, low and soft and dreamy:

"Love?"

"Mm?"

"I—I would rather, honestly, that we did not invite her."

Damn. He smoothed her hair, twisted to kiss her. "That's what I said all along," he reminded her.

"Aye. So you did." She fell asleep then, leaving him to stare up at the ceiling in uneasiness.

*A*top his mail the next day, Jack found a slim ecru
envelope addressed in a sloping hand that was unmistakably feminine. A response to the wedding, unintercepted
by Shropley, he thought, and shifted it to the side. As he
did, a very faint whiff of jasmine wafted over his desk.
Christ, he thought, and lunged for the envelope, stuffing it
into a drawer just as Pris came into his study bearing a tray
of coffee and biscuits, with Johnnie toddling in her wake.
"I slept through breakfast, Bellows informed me," she announced, looking bewitchingly rumpled, her hair in loose
braids, one of Esmé's cotton blousons thrown atop her
torn gown. Something in his expression halted her in midstep; Johnnie stumbled against her, nearly making her
drop the tray. "I beg your pardon," she said uncertainly.
"Am I interrupting?"

"Not at all," he assured her, clearing space for the coffee on his desk. "Johnnie, step off of Mamma's skirt, before you send her crashing to the floor."

"Give Daddy the sugar, Johnnie." He presented it proudly, the silver bowl clasped in his fists.

"Good boy! You didn't spill even a grain, did you?" Jack smiled, ruffling the baby's black curls. "No, no! You can't eat it that way! Pris, take the spoon from him!" Johnnie, having made his delivery, had taken the top off the sugar bowl and dipped in with glee. There was a brief struggle for the utensil in question, which Pris finally won by bribery and biscuits. Johnnie circled the desk and sat against his father's chair, nibbling happily.

"If you want breakfast, say the word and I'll have Bellows bring you up anything you like," Jack offered. "Eggs in cream sauce. Champagne and strawberries. Hell, I'll have him shoot a deer and roast it, cure a side of bacon."

"I'm not hungry." She perched on the desk's edge to stir his sugar into the coffee she'd poured.

"You ought to be," he said, grinning, "after last night."

"Hush! Do you want to corrupt your son?"

Jack laughed and glanced down. Johnnie, having finished his treat, was gazing avidly about for new distractions. He reached for the pull on the drawer into which Jack had thrust the letter. "No!" Jack burst out, so sharply that the baby and Pris both stared at him in surprise. Then Johnnie let out a whimper. Jack hurried to soothe him, pulling him onto his lap. "I'm sorry, my big boy. But I can't have you mucking about with my business papers. Your future depends on all of this, you know."

"It's just the shiny brass that tempted him," Pris said in anxious expiation. "He won't do it again. Will you, Johnnie?"

The baby stared straight at her, smiled, and grabbed for the drawer pull.

"You little devil!" Jack exclaimed, lunging for his chubby hand. "Didn't you hear me say no?"

"No," Johnnie said proudly.

"You need to expand your vocabulary, son. Try saying 'yes.' "

"No," Johnnie said, bending down and going for the drawer again.

"Let me take him," Pris offered. "We didn't mean to disturb you while you were working." On any other day, Jack would have laughed and insisted she stay. But that jasmine-scented missive in his drawer loomed between them, a guilty secret.

"I should be finished in a little while," Jack said instead. "I was just . . . going through my mail."

Pris blinked, having expected the usual disclaimer. "Well! We'll hie ourselves back to the nursery then, shall we, Johnnie? You can join us there when you are through."

"I will. I'll do that. Just the moment I'm done." Christ, he was jabbering.

She hesitated, just for a moment, then scooped the baby up in her arms. He made one last wild grab for the shiny lion's head on the drawer as she pulled him away. "Johnnie! Naughty! Daddy said no!" Quickly she pried his fingers from the handle. "I am sorry, Jack."

"No harm done," he assured her, his voice strangely stuffy, almost like the bishop's. She blew him a kiss and went out, her steps noticeably less carefree than when she came in.

"Damn it all," Jack muttered as the door closed behind them. He yanked open the drawer and stared at the offending envelope, then turned it over with his letter opener, as if touching it again would contaminate him. He hadn't been wrong. The back bore Vivienne's seal. Distastefully he picked it up in his fingertips and slit it open, shaking the single sheet of folded vellum out onto his desk.

He sat staring at it for a moment, astonished by the strength of his repugnance. One might almost think she had the power to corrupt him simply by penning a letter.

But she had no hold on him now. Defiantly he unfolded the page and read the message inside:

> My dear Jackie:
>
> I read of your betrothal in the Gazette. My most sincere felicitations! Under the circumstances, there is no longer any question in my mind that I must return those certain items given me by your brother. Sell them, and buy your bride the most wondrous trousseau! I have a number of suggestions for milliners and mantua-makers beyond those I've already mentioned. Please come by anytime you like. I really do insist. As you begin your new life, I intend to do the same. I trust you'll share my happiness at learning I've accepted Lord Chomundley's proposal of marriage. So it's to be a season of rejoicing all around!
>
> Very truly yours,
> Vivienne Harpool

Jack laughed out loud, crumpling the letter in his fist. God, what a fool he'd been, imagining all sorts of danger! And she was getting married! What infinite relief! Heaven help you, Chomundley, he thought bemusedly; you've a tiger by the tail! He leaned back in his chair and tossed the letter onto the fire that guttered in the grate, wishing now that he'd agreed to invite her to the wedding. Perhaps it wasn't too late.

He drained his coffee. An hour, he'd told Pris. Time enough for him to ride to Vivienne's cottage, offer his congratulations, and fetch back the jewels. Though once he told Pris who they were from, she likely wouldn't want any part of the proceeds. I'll put them in a trust, then, for 'Phrina, he decided abruptly. It should be enough for her to buy a little house of her own, if she wants to. She can unravel the drapery ropes anytime she chooses, have a mess of cats—be a true eccentric English spinster, free of Aunt Bertrice's unholy meddling.

The notion pleased him greatly. He grabbed his cloak, hurried downstairs, and went out to the stables, whistling happily.

*H*is exuberance diminished slightly as he dismounted in front of the cottage. There was a hitching post right by the front gate, but he was disinclined to leave his horse where it might be seen by any passerby with a wagging tongue. While he hesitated, Vivienne herself appeared in an upstairs window, waving gaily. "Put him in the back," she suggested, almost as if she had read his mind. "Plenty of new grass to crop there. I'll come open the kitchen door."

He led the black around the cottage and then left him crunching contentedly. Vivienne was dressed in a saffron-colored gown and dainty matching sandals; her hair was tied back at the nape of her neck in a ribbon, like a girl's. "You've caught me in the midst of spring cleaning," she apologized, taking off the apron she wore and dusting her hands. He started to stammer an apology, but she waved it off, beckoning him inside. "We are old enough friends that you won't take offense at the state of the place. I have to get it ready for sale, you know."

Jack had to duck to fit beneath the low lintel to the kitchen. "Sale?" he echoed, blinking in the sudden cool dimness.

"No need to hold onto it. Nick—Lord Chomundley— has more than enough houses already."

"Of course! Naturally!" Jack said, feeling stupid. "I haven't offered you congratulations yet. My very best wishes to you and Lord Chomundley."

"Thank you." She giggled, laying the apron on the table. "Though if he could see me now, I daresay he would reconsider his offer."

"You look lovely," Jack told her, and meant it.

She brushed a loose auburn curl from her throat. "Well. No surprise. I am happy!"

"Is this where you made that remarkable strawberry shortcake?" Jack asked, gazing about. The kitchen was small but tidy, the flagstone floor gleaming, copper pots and utensils hanging on hooks all along the white walls.

"I'm so glad you enjoyed it!" she exclaimed, dimpling becomingly. "I remembered, you see, how you do like sweets."

Jack turned, sniffing the air as he did. Not a hint of jasmine—just the clean scent of beeswax, and something else, herbal, dark and unfamiliar. "Where's your girl?"

"Gone to the city for silver polish. I thought to offer the place furnished. I won't need any of this now." She sank into a chair at the table. "Lord, I'm glad I wasn't born a servant! Do you mind if we just sit here?"

"Not at all." Jack slid into the seat across from her, smiling as she fanned herself with her hand. Seeing her in the midst of preparing to leave Lincolnshire for good was most reassuring.

She smiled back at him as a breeze from the open window brushed over them. "You look tired, Jackie."

"Wedding plans," he said with a grimace. "You cannot imagine the to-do—yes, I suppose you can."

"Absolutely. Isn't it odd how what ought to concern only the two folk being married grows into a sort of monster?"

He laughed and nodded. "Exactly. Whom to invite, whom to seat beside whom—" Suddenly he colored. "That reminds me. For some inexplicable reason, you were left off the guest list. But I've brought an invitation along—"

"Keep it in your pocket," she said calmly, as he reached

for it. "June twelfth, isn't that what the *Gazette* said? I'll be in Brighton by then, submerged in my own conundrums over whom to seat beside whom."

"You're . . . being very decent, Vivienne, considering . . . everything."

She shrugged airily. "Jackie. We're both adults, aren't we? I won't deny that I enjoyed what we shared together—enjoyed it immensely. But I knew from the start that I wasn't your sort. Let's not have any regrets. It would only spoil what's turned out best all around."

He felt a flush of shame at all the nasty thoughts he'd harbored about her. "I haven't seen a notice as to the date of your wedding," he said, to fill the space. "Will it be in June as well?"

"The last of the month," she confirmed, "at St. David's. You know the spot? Charming little church. We're not making a fuss. After all, it's the second go-around for both of us."

"You mentioned to me once before that Chomundley'd asked for your hand and you'd refused him. What made you change your mind?" he asked curiously.

She crinkled her nose. "It's rather hard to explain. But have you ever been in a situation where you knew someone for a long time and then one day suddenly saw him differently?"

"Absolutely. That's how it was with Pris. Miss Wilcox, I mean. She—she always was *there*, but it was as though I woke up one morning and found myself in love with her."

"She's a lucky girl."

"No," Jack said truthfully. "She's a remarkably forbearing one. I don't imagine I'm every proper English bishop's daughter's notion of an ideal catch."

"How has her father taken the news?"

"Not too badly. Though he wanted to know if I intend to tithe."

Vivienne laughed in delight, then started up from her chair. "All this washing and scrubbing has made me thirsty. Can I get you something to drink?"

"Oh, I don't—"

"I have limes, and seltzer. And rum."

He grinned. "You've won me over. Bellows seems constitutionally incapable of concocting a decent fizz."

He watched admiringly as she prepared the drinks. "Betrothal suits you, Vivienne. Or house-cleaning does. You have a glow to you."

"You think so? Just the sheen of perspiration, no doubt." She handed him a brimming glass, touched hers to it. "Cheers. Here's to our futures."

"To the future," Jack repeated, and took a sip. "God, that's good!"

"Speaking of the future—" She jumped up again and vanished down the corridor, then reappeared with a lacquered casket, setting it on the table before him. "These are yours, I believe, Lord Avenleigh?"

"I don't want them back," he protested, as he had before.

"But I want you to have them," she responded firmly. "I never wanted them in the first place. I have told you that."

The rum had started a faint buzzing in Jack's brain. All that brandy last night, he thought ruefully. So much worry for naught . . . she really was being incredibly decent. If only Pris could be counted on to prove so philosophical, he might have cleared his conscience about what had happened at the abbey. But Vivienne, alas, was a woman of the world, and Pris certainly was not.

"How dreadfully serious you look," Vivienne said in her breathy girl's voice.

"I was only thinking . . . how splendidly things have turned out for both of us."

"Yes. They have, haven't they?" she agreed, and sipped her drink, her olive eyes staring into his from over its rim. Jack raised his own glass and took a slow, deep swallow.

The next thing he knew, Vivienne was standing over him, shaking his shoulder and laughing. "Good Lord, Jackie! Wake up!"

"Wha—" Dazed, he pulled his head up from the table, where it was inexplicably resting.

"This is one for the record books," Vivienne announced, the words rippling with mirth. "I can honestly say no man has ever fallen asleep in my company before!"

"God! I do beg your pardon!" Jack shook his head to clear it. "I was up late last night. I drank too much brandy. And the rum on top . . ."

"You ought to go straight home to your bed," she chided him. "And *without* Miss Wilcox."

"Vivienne!" he said, scandalized.

"Never you mind. You forget, I've known you since we were children." She patted his head, as a mother might. "Go on. Get off with you. Rest up for her. She deserves it."

Still befogged, he reached into his coat again. "I do wish you'd take this invitation."

"I already told you, I won't be here." She bent and brushed his forehead with her lips. "You've got a treasure in her, you know. Take good care of her. Treat her as she deserves."

"And you—be good to Chomundley."

"I'll be as good as I can." She winked coquettishly.

Jack laughed, staggering a bit as he stood and headed for the door. "You're a treasure yourself, Vivienne. I'm glad you've found a man who deserves you."

"I am lucky, aren't I?" she said with a contented sigh. Then she ran after him with the casket. "You mustn't forget this! It will buy a lot of butterfly nets!"

"Are you certain?"

"Lord, yes. Nick is rich as Croesus. I've no need for them."

"Well, in that case, I accept. I thought to sell the jewels and set up a trust for 'Phrina. Give her the chance to break free of Aunt Bertrice, get herself a house a long way off from her mother, and a few servants. Do you think she would like that?"

Vivienne was silent for the space of a heartbeat. Then her smile blazed out at him. "Oh, Jackie. You must be the most thoughtful man in all the world. I am sure she'd *adore* it!"

He contemplated offering his hand but decided to kiss her instead—on the mouth, not the cheek. It only seemed fitting. "Good-bye, Vivienne."

"Au revoir!" she said gaily. "Now get along, and get some rest! And if you know anyone who'd like to buy a small, bucolic cottage in Lincolnshire, do direct him my way!"

Jack headed home with a frightful headache but with his soul at ease. A very *decent* young lady, he told himself again, and wondered what he might purchase as a wedding gift for her and Chomundley. A silver-seated siphon, perhaps, in memory of that rum fizz. He ought to get her recipe for Bellows before she decamped for London. Or maybe not, he decided, noting how the trees along the road were all blurred. That had been *demon* rum! He managed to steer back to Avenleigh House, but maneuvering up that extra set of stairs to the nursery was too much for him. He made it as far as his chambers and collapsed there, fully clothed, on his bed.

The sun was low in the sky when Pris tiptoed in. "Jack?" she whispered. "It is time for dinner."

"I didn't hear the bell."

"Have you been in here all *day*?"

"Afraid so. You were right to try and stop me from drinking that fourth brandy last night."

"I didn't mean to—" She stopped, staring as he drew himself up on his elbows. "You are wearing your cloak."

"So I am. Very nice and cozy it is, too."

"You said you'd been here all day. So why would you be wearing your cloak?"

"I don't know. Must have started to go out somewhere. Never made it, I guess."

"And there is mud on your boots!" She started to brush it from the coverlet. "How would you get mud on your boots if you hadn't been out?"

"Ought to get myself a valet," he said apologetically. The dinner bell rang out again impatiently. "Christ. Back to the lair of wolves," Jack murmured, swinging his legs off the bed and nearly sending Pris sprawling in the process. "So sorry." He put out a hand to steady her.

She had the strangest expression on her face. "I am going home," she announced. "I've been waiting for you with Johnnie since eleven o'clock. I *thought* you were occupied with business. Now I am not sure at all what you have been doing all this time."

"You'll pardon me, I trust." He unbuttoned his pants and headed for the chamber pot, misjudged the distance, and sent the thing spinning with the toe of his boot. "Damn!"

"You're cockeyed," she said tartly.

He glanced at her, eyes swimming. "Am not. Couldn't be."

She shook her head worriedly. "I'm no advocate of temperance, but I do think, Jack, you might reconsider your attitude toward liquor."

"Spoken like your father's daughter," he mumbled.

Her gray eyes blazed at him. "I *am* my father's daughter. And drunks disgust me. They always have."

"You did not find me so disgusting," Jack said thickly, "that evening at Vauxhall. Or many evenings since."

"Oh, Jack." She sighed. "Let's not quarrel. It is just that Johnnie was so looking forward to your visit to the nursery. I should think you'd be more careful, considering your responsibilities toward your son."

"I know my responsibilities toward my son!" he shouted, seized with sudden anger. What right did she have to be so aloof, so supercilious, after all they had shared? She wasn't even very pretty, he realized, staring at her worried face. Vivienne was a much better-looking woman, by any standard. Priscilla Wilcox ought to be *damned grateful* he had offered for her.

She looked back at him, her expression stricken, as if she knew exactly what he was thinking. "You are sorry," she whispered. "Sorry that you are to marry me. I ought to have known."

"Pris. Don't be a damned bloody fool. Of course I'm not sorry." He meant the words as he said them, but they came out lame, lacking all conviction. What was wrong with him?

" 'Phrina went into the village today," she said, with a wretched sort of resignation. "She took the back path. She told me she saw your horse tethered behind Vivienne Harpool's cottage."

" 'Phrina's a goddamned busybody," Jack snapped, infuriated at having been spied on.

"The visit does explain your languor." Pris's mouth drew tight as pins. She looked, Jack thought suddenly, like a grim old maid.

"What if I did go see her?" he burst out. "What does that have to do with anything?" He would have gone on to say that she was marrying Lord Chomundley, and explaining about the jewels, and the cottage for 'Phrina, and the rum fizz. But he never had the chance.

"You jest at my father," Pris said curtly. "He may be wrong-headed in all sorts of matters. But I begin to think his assessment of you was entirely correct. You are an utter bastard."

"For Christ's sake, Pris!" But she had spun on her heel and left him there alone.

Chapter
29

"*B*ad magic," Esmé announced as Bennett Shropley ducked his red head to kiss her. "There is bad magic in this house, and I know why."

"Esmé. Love. Every couple has its falling-outs. Haven't we?" he demanded, trying to meet her mouth. She'd twisted from him, though, and was drumming her fingertips along the headboard of her bed.

"This is more than that. This is witchcraft."

"For heaven's sake, pet! Who in Lincolnshire would be working witchcraft?"

"I am," she noted implacably.

"Besides you, I mean. And why should this someone's magic prove stronger than yours?"

"I do not know," she admitted. "But I can feel it. I feel the force of it, struggling against me. Struggling against my m'amselle."

"Against Camille?" he said in surprise. "You told Lord

Avenleigh that Camille wished for you to bring Johnnie up as your own, never let him learn of the child's existence."

"I lied," she said with complacence. "That was not what m'amselle said."

"You frighten me sometimes," Bennett observed, leaning back with his head against the pillows. "What *did* she say, pray tell?"

"That I should bring the boy to Lord Avenleigh in Lincolnshire and see that he was brought up as a proper lord. *And* that I should do my best to have m'sieur marry. But only to a woman who would love Johnnie as her own."

"She asked a lot of you."

"You do not know the half of it. She laid a curse on me if I should fail. That I never would find happiness for myself."

"We've been happy, Esmé," he said softly, his fingertips running through her curls.

"So were m'sieur and Miss Wilcox—until today. He was at *her* house, you know. That Harpool creature. That is where the bad magic is coming from." She paused, thinking, while he stroked her dark skin. "I will need for you to get me a chicken and a goat."

"You know I'll give you the moon and the stars, love." He realized what she'd said. "But—a chicken and a goat?"

"For the magic. To break the evil spell."

"What exactly will you do with this goat and this chicken?"

"Carve them up. Burn the entrails. Scatter the ashes around her house at the new moon."

He recoiled from her. "You aren't serious."

"Oh, but I am."

Bennett sat up in the bed. "Now, see here. This is Lincolnshire, not St. Lucia. You can't go about butchering animals and burning them and scattering ashes about people's houses!"

"Better I should suffer under m'amselle's curse for the rest of my days?"

"Esmé. Love. That stuff—witches and hexes and spells—only ignorant folk believe in it."

"Do you call me ignorant?" she asked, eyes suddenly blazing.

"That isn't what I meant, and you know it. You're as clever a woman as I ever met. It isn't your fault you were brought up with such foolish superstitions."

"Watch what you call foolish," she warned him. "Do you not remember the truth potion?"

"Any number of things could have accounted for that. Agnes was ready to break free. The more I think on it, the more certain I am that crab you concocted had nothing to do with it."

"Does not England have witches?" she demanded.

"Not anymore. The last English trial for witchcraft was more than a hundred years past. We've moved beyond all that, into an age of enlightenment and reason."

"How fortunate for you. Will you get me the chicken and goat?"

"I will not. I'll not be party to such absurdity."

Esmé knelt beside him with her arm outstretched, pointing to the door. "Go, then. Get out."

"Oh, for God's sake, love—"

"Go!" she cried, dark eyes flashing. "You say you love me. How can you love me when you will not help me fight against m'amselle's curse? When you mock at me?"

"I'm not mocking you," he began miserably. "I only—" He broke off; she had lowered her head and was muttering in some language, neither English nor French, that he did not understand. "Esmé. What are you doing?"

"You don't believe in curses? See what happens to you on your ride home tonight."

"I'm not going home tonight. I'm staying here. With you." He reached for her, but she slapped his hand away.

"Go," she ordered again. "Go, and do not come back until you are prepared to apologize to me."

"I'll apologize now."

"Will you get me the goat and the chicken?"

He stared at her hands, imagining them clenched around a dagger, slitting the throat of a helpless animal. "No."

"Then I have no use for your apology. Leave me."

"Esmé! For God's sake—" She turned away, stone-faced. After a moment, he got up from the bed, found his breeches and shirt, and yanked them on. "Very well. I *will* go." She was muttering again, infuriating him. "And I'm not afraid of your mumbo jumbo, either! Go ahead! Do your worst! Put your blackest spell on me!"

For a moment she glanced up, and her expression, the hard glint of her gaze, rattled him badly. He was so accustomed to seeing those eyes wide with love. . . .

"Mind you ride carefully," she said quietly.

"I'll ride as I always do," Bennett snapped at her, and stomped out the door.

Jack couldn't sleep. That wasn't surprising, considering he had snored away most of the day. He paced his room, back and forth, until his own movements got on his nerves and he sat down at his desk. He tried to go over his books, read the correspondence he'd neglected earlier, but was far too restless. Getting up again, he went to the window, staring out over the dark gardens and fields.

She had no right to be so angry with him. If she'd only behaved in a civilized way, he would have explained about his visit to Vivienne. But she'd assumed the worst, pro-pelled by jealousy. God! Was she to rebuke him for the rest of their lives each time he spoke to another woman, or one spoke to him? He recalled, with a pang, her words to him on that long-ago night in London, at the tawdry tavern: *What is it like . . . to have women always look at you that way? As if they wanted to—to eat you.* It's not my fault the ladies find me attractive, he reflected, staring at his image in the window glass. I'm not some sort of Lothario. I was true to Camille. I would be true to Pris, too.

A woman with more knowledge, more experience—someone, for example, like Vivienne—would know better than to carp at him as Pris had. But her innocence, that quality of purity and chasteness, was what had drawn him to her in the first place. She'd offered him salvation. He distinctly remembered thinking that.

But what if salvation was a lot like temperance—something that seemed like a good idea until you came right up to it?

What had he ever done that was so awful, anyway, that he needed to be saved? Look at how Vivienne had dealt with their brief fling! That was the adult way of behaving—you shrugged and kissed and parted gracefully, without regrets. Why, I wager if I were to go to her cottage now, tonight, he thought, despite the fact we both are betrothed to others, we'd have a jolly good time together, with no one worse off in the end.

The notion, once he'd put it into words, was extremely enticing. One of those fine rum fizzes, with a cigar. Her auburn curls sweeping across his face, and jasmine filling the air . . .

He stopped, contemplating the reflection of his devilish grin. God! What was he thinking of? He ought to be seeking ways to reconcile with Pris, not hankering after Vivienne! He closed his eyes tight, trying to picture Pris holding Johnnie, with the baby's fingers curled inside her lip. The only image that formed, though, was of Vivienne sprawled in the long grass of the graveyard, and her quick, high cries as he thrust into her.

Instinctively his hand came up to find the love charm beneath his shirt, touch it for strength and reassurance. Pris was the woman he wanted. Pris, and no other. Pris, with her hair like gold and her warm dove's eyes . . .

Vivienne's hair was, in point of fact, more lovely. She had a better figure, too—more curvaceous, with those heavy white breasts.

No. Pris's breasts were perfect—smaller, perhaps, but perfect. Christ, why had she insisted on going home, leaving him to such ignoble longings? If she'd been here, he never would have been thinking of Vivienne.

Jasmine, and a sea breeze wafting. Camille. Pris. Vivienne. His mind was a tortured tangle of all three women, their features changing and shifting, melting from one to the other, until he clenched his fists to his face to block them out, fade them all to black.

Slowly he opened his eyes. Beyond the window, the night sky studded with stars stretched all the way to Lincoln. Somewhere far in the distance, lights flickered in another window. Whose? It could be Vivienne's. Still at her spring cleaning with her apron and duster, her hair in a ribbon, just like when they were children. *I've known you since we were children, Jackie.* She knew him better than anyone, better even than Pris. She'd known Robert and his father, recognized all they had done to him, the unfairness of it. She understood. She would know what to say, to do, to quiet the demons and let him sleep.

He slung his cloak over his shoulders and strode toward the door. In the hallway he paused, listening. No sounds from the nursery, nor any from the wing where Agnes, her nightly visits having ceased since her marriage to Lord Cowper, was no doubt worn out by bliss. Nothing at all to stop him. . . .

Then he jerked his head up, hearing the opening of a door farther along the hallway, and slow, shuffling footsteps. 'Phrina, damn her, wandering about . . . he ducked back into his bedchamber, waiting impatiently, waiting forever, while she moved down the corridor on whatever daft mission propelled her this way. When, after a lifetime, he heard her start to shuffle up the stairs, he counted to thirty and then slipped out of his room again.

The stables were deserted. He saddled the black in flat darkness. The horse was spooked, unaccustomed to such interruptions of sleep. She steadied, though, as he rode her out through the gates and down the lane toward Vivienne's cottage, toward comfort and quiet and acceptance and—he was not so bad, really, was he? He'd done all that was required of him, and more—a sparkling rum fizz.

He was halfway there, riding hard, when the black jerked her head up abruptly. "Get on with you," Jack cried impatiently, and then reined in, hearing what the horse had: faint moans coming from the ditch at the side of the road. "Who's there?" he called out, somewhat spooked himself. The groans were almost ghostly.

"Oh, thank God! Is that you, milord?"

Jack scrambled down from his saddle. "Bennett? Bennett Shropley?" He pushed through the weeds. "Where are you? What the devil's happened?"

The solicitor was lying sprawled on his back in the ditch-water. "H-horse threw me," he managed to stammer. "Shied at a rabbit. Maybe. Think I've broken . . . my spine."

"Can you move your fingers? Can you move your toes?"

"Got to move 'em." The man in the ditch-water groaned. "Got to get Esmé . . . a chicken. And a goat. The new moon is three nights hence."

*J*ack never did find out what that nonsense about the chicken and the goat and the moon meant. He put it down to Bennett's delirium and pain. The results of the fall *were* excruciatingly painful—Dr. Allison said the solicitor was damned lucky he hadn't been killed. In the end, though, no bones were broken, only severely bruised. Jack left him in the hands of the doctor and an oddly gratified Esmé. Then he went to bed, *almost* glad his expedition to Vivienne's cottage had been interrupted in such an unpredictable way.

He fully expected Pris to appear on his doorstep the next morning to apologize to him. She didn't. By luncheon, then, he thought, and when that passed without a visit, by tea. Surely by the dinner hour! He found himself watching the clock, waiting for the door knocker and Bellows's announcement of His Lordship's fiancée's arrival. But six o'clock came and went, and he descended to the dining room in a black mood indeed.

The entire household seemed strange, unsettled. "Miss Wilcox does not join us tonight?" Aunt Bertrice asked him as they sat down to table, her black eyes agleam.

"No," Jack said shortly. 'Phrina was singing under her breath, letting the salt trickle from its spoon. Agnes did her best to fill the gaps in conversation, but naturally enough her questions mostly concerned the upcoming wedding, and when Jack's sullen responses put an end to that topic, she had little to say. Only Lord Cowper appeared unaffected by his host's rudeness. He ate the overcooked rump of beef and starchy roasted potatoes with a gusto that made Jack wonder what in hell *Irish* food must be like.

"Dreadful what happened to Mr. Shropley, isn't it?" Agnes queried nervously. "I do hope he is feeling better. Is he, Cousin Jack?"

"Mm. Suppose so."

"You haven't been to visit him?" That was Aunt Bertrice, perched at the table's head like a black-gowned vulture.

"Not since last night." He glanced up from the gristle-studded beef, found them all looking at him. "What? I have had Dr. Allison in. And he has Esmé."

"*That* woman," Aunt Bertrice said with a disapproving sniff, "is strange. *Very* strange. Just this afternoon, she demanded that Cook procure for her a chicken and a goat."

Christ! The chicken and the goat again! "She has a hankering for the tastes of home, no doubt," Jack told his aunt. "Goat is a very popular foodstuff in Castries."

"But if she meant to eat it, why would she have been so particular about what it looked like?" 'Phrina piped up unexpectedly, setting the salt cellar aside. "A pure-white ewe, she said, unmarked and unspotted, and one that never—never—one that hadn't—" She lapsed into embarrassed silence.

"Hadn't been mated?" Agnes proposed, and her sister blushed, nodding. "Perhaps that makes the meat tougher."

Lord Cowper laughed, and hid it with his napkin and a covering cough.

"Bit of bone," he explained. "Beg your pardon. Could be, my love, I suppose."

Jack had had just about enough of 'Phrina's wandering and eavesdropping. "Did Esmé apply to you for the animals in question before going to Cook?" he demanded of her.

"Apply to—why, no." She giggled. "Apply to me for a goat? Why in heaven's name would she?"

"Just what I was wondering. But you were in the kitchens when she asked it of Cook?"

"Well . . ." 'Phrina's pale-blue eyes circled the table with some apprehension. "Very *near* the kitchens, certainly." She looked back down at her plate. "I don't suppose Lady Harpool has sent a sweet to us again?"

"Where precisely were you, Cousin 'Phrina, when you heard this conversation between Esmé and Cook?"

"Precisely? I could not say for sure. Somewhere very close by."

"Jack," Agnes began in a nervous tone.

"Oh, Jack yourself! I'm growing sick and tired of running across your sister in the dead of night, tiptoeing down the corridors, peeking into rooms, listening to other folks' private speech."

"It's what she does," Agnes explained, embarrassed. "It's what she always has."

"Well, I want it to stop! I don't like being spied on!"

"I'm sorry," 'Phrina said, wringing her napkin. "I have trouble sleeping. It soothes me to walk the halls."

"And it gives me the bloody creeps to hear you doing so!"

"Jack, really!" Agnes chided, reaching across the table

to pat her sister's hand. "I should think by now you'd have realized 'Phrina is not—is not—"

"Not sane?"

That roused Lord Cowper. "Now, see here, my good man," he began. "I hardly think it's cricket to attack poor 'Phrina for what she can't help."

"I don't need any lessons in etiquette from a bloody Irishman!" Jack roared, shoving back his chair. In the silence that followed, while he stomped toward the doors, he heard 'Phrina sobbing quietly, and then Aunt Bertrice, her voice cool and venomous:

"Do you know, the most peculiar aspect to *me* of Mr. Shropley's unfortunate injury is how Jack should have come upon him there in the hedges in the middle of the night." He whirled to her, saw her crone's face settle into a taunting smile. "Of course, we're all most *grateful* that you happened along. I just can't help wondering where you might have been headed. It *was* past midnight when you brought him back here."

Jack took a deep breath. "I rode out for fresh air—something I find scarce in this household. For any further information, you shall have to rely on 'Phrina's clandestine reports."

That made 'Phrina burst out wailing. "Jack!" Agnes cried, appalled. "How can you possibly imply—"

"Oh, do shut up," Jack exploded. "All of you, just shut up and give me some peace!" He stormed out, slamming the doors shut, and headed straight for the stables, goaded beyond caring what they thought of him.

He started out for Wilcox Hall, intending to confront Pris, demand to know what she meant by staying away from him, defying him. If she'd been there at dinner tonight, he thought in fury, things never would have gotten so out of hand. She knew how to handle 'Phrina and Aunt Bertrice; she would have known just how to defend Esmé's sudden hunger for goat. She was so good at soothing ruffled feathers. Instead she'd been absent, and he had made a fool—no, worse, a boor—of himself. *I'm not myself without her,* he realized, pulling up on the reins. He sat astride the black in the darkness, breathing hard, remembering the impossible sweetness of her smile.

The trouble was that she was too good for him. She was a creature of sunlight, a butterfly, and he was all darkness. He was Devil Jack. By God, I haven't any right to want her, he realized. I'll only taint her, corrupt her. Look how he already had! She slept with him without benefit of any marriage blessing; she drank claret; she wore the rotted vegetative matter he had bought for her. I've turned her into a Paphian, he thought with a pang of regret. *My* Paphian.

But how much worse it would be if he abandoned her now, after he'd taken her maidenhood, her innocence. What would be left for her? What would she turn to? She was too honest not to tell any suitor about her past. What decent man would want her, corrupted as she was?

Lost in misery, he bowed his head until it touched the black's mane. He was all wrong for her, true. Yet it was too late to turn back. He clenched his eyes shut against a vision of her struggling, always struggling, to become what he wanted, lowering the bodices of those gowns, dyeing her hair as it faded, taking to patches and paint. Surely it was better to break off their engagement now, spare her such humiliation—and him the pain of watching as all her remarkable brightness was subsumed, swallowed by the darkness in his soul. Devil Jack. He was the devil, by Christ. He'd led her into temptation, and far beyond. Now it was up to him to allow her to break free.

He did not want to hurt her. Still, he was certain that marrying him would only lead to far greater grief on her part. She knew it, too, didn't she? That was why she'd left him last night, and why she'd stayed away all this day. She wanted to be rid of him. She would be happier left to her butterflies. She was just too good to tell him so.

The black was growing impatient; she pawed the road, flicked her tail, eager to be headed *somewhere*. Jack raised his head at last and stared up into the skies. The stars shimmered like Pris's eyes in the absence of the moon.

It was too late to go to Wilcox Hall; the bishop was more than likely asleep and would not take kindly to a nocturnal visitor. Tomorrow, Jack decided, turning the black around. Tomorrow he would visit, ask her to release him from the betrothal. As the horse wheeled about, he caught a glimpse of light in the distance. Vivienne's cottage. Still at her cleaning, he thought bemusedly. A creature of the night. Just like him.

Just like him. She was, really, when you came right down to it. Taking the easy way always, picking up the pieces, going on, forging through. His throat itched, as though it could feel the pleasure of a rum fizz and a cigar. Resolutely he yanked the black back toward Avenleigh— and then, to the horse's perplexity, turned her about once more, toward the cottage, unable to bear the prospect of encountering 'Phrina on her night rounds, or being called by Jamalla to soothe Johnnie's nightmare, or having to think of Bennett Shropley flat on his back in agony. Who did they all think he was—their savior? Didn't they recognize him for the Prodigal Son?

Chances were the father in that story ended up bailing the boy out of whatever the contemporary equivalent of prison was within a month. Jack spurred toward the beckoning windows of Vivienne's cottage with sudden haste. Leopards didn't change their spots, and neither did people. Better to know and accept, once and for all, exactly what one was.

Chapter

31

Tuesday's Bible study class was extremely well attended. Pris had noticed that since her betrothal to Jack, women who ordinarily were no more than polite took an unnatural interest in her—or, rather, in the wedding plans. Mrs. Blathersby, Lady Ashton, Lady Battleston, all fussed and cooed over her in a way they hadn't since—well, since her previous engagement to Robert. There'd been the same sort of intense flurry then, which had faded to nothingness as the months and then years crawled on without any setting of a wedding date.

But her marriage to Jack was to take place in a few scant weeks—wasn't it? She replied as politely as she could to the ladies' questions about her gown and trousseau, forcing a smile onto her frozen face. And all the time they buzzed around her, Mrs. Gravesend sat on her chair between Agnes and 'Phrina with the oddest expression. *I know something you don't,* her small, beady eyes seemed to say.

It was three days—and three nights—since she'd seen

him. At first she had felt guilty for her show of temper when she found him in those mudstained boots in his bed-chamber. But 'Phrina's report of having seen his horse tethered behind Lady Harpool's cottage had unleashed all her latent fears. He was too fine for her. Everyone thought so—certainly the dubious ladies demanding to know how she would dress her hair, what flowers she would carry, whether the new gown she had on was a gift from her fi-ancé. She glanced down nervously at her pearl-gray satin skirts, the bodice that, while not nearly so revealing as any-thing worn by Lady Harpool—or, for that matter, Mrs. Blathersby—had nonetheless earned a rebuke from her fa-ther for its indecency.

The ring Jack had given her sparkled on her finger. It had evoked ecstatic comment from the ladies. She twisted it absently, listening while her father droned on, quoting St. Mark: " 'But the days will come when the bridegroom shall be taken away from them, and then shall they fast in those days.' "

She'd had no appetite since she'd left him. She could not concentrate on the slightest task—and so many tasks faced her—without him by her side. Why did he not come and apologize? What kept him away?

" 'And no man putteth new wine into old bottles,' " her father intoned, staring down his nose at the ladies be-fore him.

Was that the trouble? Had he compared her to Lady Harpool and found her lacking—in passion, in expertise, in beauty? Had he—God forbid!—got from Pris what he'd wanted, and now was content to let their engagement lapse? Oh, he could not be so debauched as that!

"Let us pray," the bishop declared. Pris quickly bowed her head, to hide the tears that were forming. "Our Father, which art in heaven, hallowed be thy name. Thy kingdom come, thy will be done . . ."

Perhaps this present misery was her penance for not having properly honored *her* father. He'd warned her, hadn't he, that Jack Cantrell was not to be trusted? A small, desperate sob escaped her. Horrified, she glanced up and found Mrs. Gravesend staring steadily at her, with that air of extreme satisfaction stamped on her haggish face.

When the prayer was finished and the company withdrew to the parlor for tea and cakes, Jack's aunt sidled toward her, trailed by Sephrina. "My dear Miss Wilcox! Those of us in residence at Avenleigh have remarked your absence from the house these past few days. Nothing, I trust, is amiss between yourself and my nephew?"

"No, no, not at all!" Pris flinched, hearing how hollow her voice sounded. "I simply find myself . . . overwhelmed with preparations for the wedding. There is so much to do yet, and so little time."

"What a pity," the old crone purred, "Jack does not share your sense of dutifulness."

"Whatever do you mean? He's been *extremely* helpful in all of our plans," Pris declared, springing to his defense.

Mrs. Gravesend raised her bony, black-clad shoulders and shrugged. "I only thought—since he has not come home to Avenleigh House for the past two days—and nights—he showed some lack of—shall we say, conviction?"

"I seem to recall," Pris said airily, "he mentioned going into Lincoln on business."

"Lincoln?" 'Phrina giggled. "He's not in Lincoln! He's holed up with Vivienne Harpool! I heard Cook and Bellows talking of it just last night!"

The ladies with their teacups and plates paused in their conversations. Pris summoned up the tattered shreds of her dignity. "Lady Harpool and Lord Avenleigh have been friends from childhood," she said as steadily as she could. "Her advice has been invaluable to *both* of us in making the host of decisions necessary at this time."

Mrs. Gravesend smiled in an extremely nasty way. "As you say. All the same, I should not want *my* betrothed loitering about with another eligible—and, I might add, most attractive—woman."

"I have perfect faith in Jack!" Pris snapped. The ladies faded back from them, murmuring among themselves, raising eyebrows. "I do!" she insisted, and thought she'd conquered the demons until she glimpsed Agnes's troubled face.

That night, after supper, Pris waited until she heard her father pass her door on the way to his bedroom. Then she crept downstairs and out to the stables, where Melchior was waiting, forewarned. "I still think I ought to come with ye," he told his mistress. "Ridin' about in the dead o' night—"

"I am only going out to the south pasture, to see if the cocoons on the lindens there have opened. I'll be back in less than an hour."

Still the stableman hesitated. "No matter what your mission, miss, better to have company about ye." She looked at him in the flickering torchlight and wondered: *What did he know? What did everyone know that she didn't?* "I'll go alone," she said coldly, and he saddled the roan for her without another word.

She started out slowly in case he was watching, heading to the south. Once the road turned, though, and she was hidden from his sight, she spurred across the open fields, making for Lady Harpool's cottage. She did not believe what 'Phrina had said, of course. But she needed to see for herself.

It was the night of the new moon; only stars lit her way as she rode through the underbrush. She felt Jack's ring heavy on her finger, remembered his sweet kisses, the marvelous sensations his lovemaking evoked in her. He *did* love her. He *had* to. But as she neared Vivienne Harpool's cottage, she was not so sure.

Lights glowed in the downstairs windows. Ashamed and yet unable to stop herself, she hitched Maggie to a pine tree and crept forward on foot, through the gate and into the yard. A sudden burst of laughter from within the house made her duck low among the snaky hollyhocks and roses in the garden. She crept to the nearest window and peeped inside.

God. He *was* there, seated in an elegant armchair, ashtray and brandy snifter on a table at his elbow. He looked like bloody hell, she thought, staring at him. His hair was tangled and unkempt; he was coatless, and his shirt hung open at his throat. His eyes were bleary red from smoke and wine.

Lady Harpool, reclining on a chaise across from him, seemed fresh as a flower in contrast. She was clad in a gorgeous paisley dressing gown, tied negligently at the waist in such a manner as to reveal the deep cleft between her heavy breasts. They were playing cards. I did not even know he *liked* cards, Pris thought wistfully.

She tore her gaze from the cozy couple to glance around the parlor; she'd never been inside the cottage. The appointments were like nothing she had ever seen before: very luxe and foreign and exotic, the fabrics rich and glowing, the wood polished to a gleam. Little candles in glass dishes flickered everywhere, and vases of heavy-headed flowers lent a hothouse aura to the room. As she watched, Jack drained his glass and stumbled to the sideboard to refill it. He passed close by Lady Harpool, and the intimate way in which she stretched her long white arm up to stroke his cheek made Pris's heart constrict.

For a moment, crouched there in the darkness, she was sorry she'd come. So long as she hadn't seen the proof with her own eyes, she could go on pretending this was all

some misunderstanding, that he was simply too proud and
stubborn to apologize, that the future they had planned together would yet come to pass. Now, though—well, there
was no sense in pretending when reality was perfectly clear.

He came back from the sideboard and bent down to
Lady Harpool, his hand sliding inside her dressing gown to
caress her breast. Pris could not stand any more. She turned,
creeping silently away—and promptly blundered into some
black bulk moving in the dark.

She started to scream but felt a firm hand clamped
over her mouth. *"Chut!"* a woman's voice whispered: *Hush!*
French. She'd heard that word often enough, in Johnnie's
nursery.

"Esmé?" she said in disbelief. "What are *you* doing
here?"

Esmé wagged her dark head, finger to her lips. She had
a basket over her arm, and as Pris watched, she reached inside, cupped something in her palm, and shook it out over
the ground in a careful line. "Are you fertilizing?" Pris asked,
perplexed, following as Esmé moved on, circling the cottage. "What on earth *are* you doing?"

Esmé said nothing, just kept walking and reaching and
sprinkling until she'd reached the front gate. She paused
then, straightening up, staring back at the house with a
frightful expression on her face. She mumbled something
under her breath, flung the last of the basket's contents
into the air, and ducked out of the garden through a break
in the hedges, tugging Pris along.

"Pardonnez-moi. I could not say any more while I was
working the spell," she said at last, when they'd reached
the safety of the road.

"Working the *spell?*"

Esmé nodded. *"Oui.* The spell against the spell that
witch in there has worked on him."

"On Lord Avenleigh?"

"*Bien sûr.* How else to explain why he is in there with her, instead of home with you?"

"Oh, Esmé." Pris didn't know whether she felt more like laughing or crying. "It isn't a magic spell. He has just—just decided that he wants her more than he wants me."

"That is my point. What man not bewitched could possibly prefer her to you?"

Pris did laugh, with a strong hint of irony. "He could, obviously,"

"Because she has worked magic on him," Esmé said stubbornly.

"There's no such thing as magic." Pris had never been so certain of that. "Only passion, and charm, and beauty." All the qualities she lacked, that Lady Harpool possessed in such abundance.

"You looked in there? You saw him?" Esmé hissed. Pris nodded. "How can you say, then, that she has not bewitched him? He is not himself, not at all!"

"But perhaps he is."

"*Non.* That is *not* m'sieur." She patted the basket she held. "You wait. You will see, when this has had its effect. I will teach that amateur to make magic against me!"

"What was in there, anyway?"

"The burnt entrails of a chicken and a goat. Mixed with herbs." Her teeth flashed in the darkness. "I cannot say more."

Pris didn't want her to. "I'm sure you mean well, Esmé. But if Jack has made up his mind he prefers her to me, there is nothing to be done about it. I am going home now. I'm tired."

The maid clutched her arm as she turned away. "M'amselle, you cannot give in without a fight!"

Pris thought of how she'd cried after glimpsing Robert and Vivienne Harpool together that first time. And she'd never even loved Robert, not the way she loved Jack. The prospect of making such a—such a *damned fool* of herself all over again was simply too daunting. "I've no fight left," she told Esmé, and shook off her imploring arm to go and unhitch her horse.

"No matter!" the maid called after her, almost gaily. "This spell will do the trick. You will see. Tomorrow, he comes crawling back to you for forgiveness!"

"Don't hold your breath waiting for that," Pris said, and rode off into the night.

Chapter

32

$\mathcal{H}$e didn't come back to her the next day. Nor did he the day after, or the next, or the next. On the one-week anniversary of the last time she saw him, she put his ring back into the gray velvet box and sent it to Avenleigh House, with a brief, formal note ending their betrothal that she very much doubted he would even read.

In His Lordship's absence, the ring was delivered to Bennett Shropley, still abed in the guest room. He groaned when he opened it, and not only from the pain that still wracked his back.

"What is it?" Esmé asked anxiously, coming toward him with a hot compress.

"Miss Wilcox has broken the engagement. She's returned his ring."

"There is a note, is there not?" Esmé reached to grab it from the nest of brown paper. "What does it say?"

"I'm not about to *read* it! It's private correspondence!" He snatched it back.

"You are his solicitor, *non*? You have his power of attorney?"

He glanced at her admiringly. "You are picking up quite a smattering of legal jargon. Yes, I have his power of attorney. But this hardly falls within the purview of business."

"How can you say that? You told me that ring is worth two thousand pounds. If m'sieur's estate has been enriched by two thousand pounds, is it not his solicitor's business to discover why?"

He laughed. "You are incorrigible, Esmé."

"Is incorrigible good?"

"I am not at all certain." But he reached to the bedside table for his letter opener.

"Well?" she demanded as he scanned the few lines Pris had set down.

"Just what one would expect of Miss Wilcox. Humble and self-effacing. 'Lord Avenleigh. In consideration of my belief that neither of us can expect to be made happy by the marriage we lately contemplated, I hereby return your ring and relinquish any claim to your heart or your hand. Yours,' etc., etc."

"La pauvre petite," Esmé murmured. "How she must be aching!"

"Four nights past, when you returned from having encountered her outside Lady Harpool's cottage, you seemed quite convinced she had no reason to be. What became, pray tell, of that spell you worked with the chicken and goat guts?"

"Something is working against me—something very hard and strong."

"Perhaps Lady Harpool is a better witch than you."

Esmé snorted. *"C'est impossible.* I tell you, I came here to England fully armed, with every weapon in Maman Gris-Gris's arsenal. Do not forget, part of Camille's charge to me was to find m'sieur a wife who would love Johnnie as her own. I knew how hard that would be." She paced away from the bed. "If only I had Maman here . . . no one knows better how to make a love charm." Suddenly she stopped pacing. "*Dieu en ciel!* The love charm!"

"What love charm?" Bennett demanded.

"The one Maman made up for Camille to give to Jack! To bind him to her . . ."

"You think that is keeping Lord Avenleigh from marrying Pris?"

Esmé frowned in concentration. "It cannot be that. Death releases the spell. Maman told me so herself. But the charm—he wears it still. Or he did. I wonder . . ." Then she shook her head. "But—*non*. How could Lady Harpool know what to do to turn the magic to her?"

"What is in the charm?" Bennett asked curiously.

"I do not know," she admitted.

"But you said—you came armed with every weapon—"

"No witch in her right mind would give away *all* her secrets," Esmé said irritably.

"I beg your pardon. How foolish of me."

She turned on him. "When it comes to that, I thought you did not believe in witchcraft!"

"Let's just say I have . . . an open mind now. To go with my bruised limbs. At any rate, *something* has got to be done. His Lordship's over there wallowing in dissoluteness while his business suffers—not to mention his son. He hasn't paid the least attention to my repeated requests that he return home and go through his correspondence. If he's not careful, he'll end up in exactly the same hole Robert did." Esmé shuddered. "Oh, I didn't mean 'hole' literally. But you're the witch. Have you any ideas?"

"One," she told him slowly. "But it requires the assistance of Miss Wilcox."

Bennett looked down at the letter she had written. "Somehow I doubt you'll get that."

"Still," Esmé said, brightening slightly, "she loves him—did love him. Would you not agree?"

He pulled her to him, kissed her lovely dark cheek. "As much as I love you."

"Then there is hope," she decided. "I will call on her tomorrow. Explain what must be done."

"Will she listen, do you think?"

"*Qui sais?* If she does not love him, though, enough to fight against that woman's magic, then all is lost." Bennett crossed the fingers on both his hands. "Why do you do that?"

"No reason." He uncrossed them quickly. "Just an old superstition."

"Magic, you mean." Esmé sniffed. "You see? You *do* believe."

"*N*o," Pris said very calmly, stuffing a pair of butterfly nets and a pile of corkboard into a valise. "I won't do it."

"But, m'amselle," Esmé said in despair. "You saw him. He suffers, suffers under a spell!"

"Lord Avenleigh's *suffering*—if one could call it that— is no longer my concern." Pris fit her strongest boots into the valise. "Indeed, I find myself extremely grateful to him. His caddishness has made Father agree to allow me to travel to Scotland to visit my Uncle Abner. It's an opportunity to capture species I would never otherwise have seen."

"How can you even *think* of butterflies, with all that is at stake?" Esmé reached for her hand. "Do you love him?"

"No. Yes. Oh, I don't know!" She gave the recalcitrant boots a furious shove. "And it doesn't matter anyway. The point is that he no longer loves me."

"Because he is bewitched," Esmé said patiently.

"Because he is what he is, and I am what I am! Oh, Esmé. I know that you mean well." Pris plumped down amid the clutter of packing on her bed. "And maybe on St. Lucia, there is magic. But here in Lincolnshire, there is only reality. And the reality is that Jack wants her instead of me."

"You would give him up so easily as that, after all that you have shared together? After he took from you *votre innocence*?"

"If that means what it does in English," Pris said wryly, "I don't blame him for it. I surrendered it—more than willingly." She clenched her eyes shut for a moment, remembering that afternoon on the edge of the Wold. There had been magic then, all around them: in the sky above her head, the earth beneath her, the vaulted weeds. And on all those nights afterward, when she had shared his bed . . . "How is Johnnie?" she asked abruptly, to tear her mind from the memory.

"Not happy. He asks for his papa. He asks for you."

"I ought to go and see him. To say good-bye."

"You *ought* to be his *maman*."

"I still love *him*, at least." She reached for a box of pins. "What will happen to him, do you suppose, when Jack weds Lady Harpool?"

"What becomes of any child whose stepmother does not want him about? Boarding school, in a few years. Until then, governesses. He will need *someone* to look after him."

"You won't be staying?" Pris asked in surprise.

"With her as mistress of the house? *Non*. Nor will Jamalla. We will return to St. Lucia."

"That seems so cruel. You have been . . . the only constants in his life."

"But perhaps," Esmé mused, "Mrs. Gravesend will prevail on m'sieur to have him turned into a post-boy at last. I imagine the new Lady Avenleigh will only favor the plan."

"Jack never would allow that!"

Esmé shrugged. "Can you envision that one agreeing to grant Johnnie equality with her own sons?"

Pris stood and walked across the room toward the pier glass. "I never thought of what would happen to Johnnie."

"But why should you?" Esmé said softly. "He *is* only a half-breed bastard."

Pris whirled on her visitor. "How dare you say such a thing about Lord Avenleigh's son?"

The maid was chuckling to herself. "So you *do* still care."

"I don't—I'm not—it's just so terribly unfair that Johnnie should have to suffer!"

"That is in your power to prevent."

"How?"

"Witchcraft."

"I don't *believe* in sorcery. I already told you! Anyway, you swore Jack would come back to me, begging for forgiveness, after you sprinkled that—that whatever around Lady Harpool's cottage."

"Her magic fights mine," Esmé said simply.

"Aye—the magic of her hair and her smooth white skin and her . . . her . . . those breasts!"

"*Non.* That is not magic, m'amselle. That is only what draws the male dog to the bitch."

"It has certainly drawn Jack to her."

"M'amselle." Esmé went to her, turned her to the pier glass, smoothing back Pris's hair. "Look at yourself! See how lovely you are!"

Unwillingly Pris studied her reflection. "I am not lovely like her."

"*Non.* You are lovely like you. Look! See! See the woman you have become."

Pris stared into the mirror. The vision she saw there—gleaming hair, clear skin, wide mouth that Jack had once longed to kiss, dove-gray gaze deepened by her knowledge of what went on between a man and a woman—was one she would have ached to claim only a few months past. "But—I cannot compete with her," she said with a sigh.

"You mean that you *will* not."

"I mean that I cannot!"

"You could if you chose to."

Pris flounced away from the pier glass. "Oh, what is the use?"

"If it meant Johnnie not being made into a post-boy?"

"I would do *anything* for Johnnie."

"Do you mean that?" Esmé demanded.

"You know that I do!" Then she reconsidered, seeing the gleam in the maid's dark eyes. "Well—anything that would not damn my immortal soul."

"Even if it might save m'sieur's?"

"You honestly believe—it is so serious as that?"

"More so," Esmé pronounced with unmistakable conviction. "More lives, more souls, hang in the balance than I have even said." She paused. "But beyond lives and souls, more happiness. Oh, m'amselle." To Pris's astonishment, she saw tears in the depths of the maid's dark eyes. "Will you not at least try to end the evil magic?"

Pris hesitated, her heart in her throat. Then, "What would I have to do?" she whispered uncertainly.

Chapter

33

Christ. What a bother, Jack thought, wincing against the sunlight. His head was throbbing—the usual state of affairs now, anytime before the dinner hour—and his coat stank of cigars and the brandy he'd spilled across it . . . had that been last night? The night before last? Time was blurring for him into one long smudge of smoking and drinking and making love to Vivienne. He'd thought Camille was adept, but Lady Harpool put his former mistress to shame. His mouth curled as he recalled the leavetaking she'd given him not half an hour before: naked on the Oriental carpet in her boudoir, the draperies drawn, candles setting her pale skin aglow. She was magnificent, glorious, the most satisfying lover he had ever known.

He'd been inclined—*deeply* inclined—to ignore Priscilla Wilcox's note when it arrived at the cottage, forwarded by Shropley. Vivienne, though, had taken it from him and perused it, while he'd nibbled her breasts. "She says she has returned a ring to you. What sort of ring?"

"I don't know. The ring I gave her." Vivienne's hand slipped across his naked buttock, found his manhood, limp still from too much wine. But she had ways. She had ways. . . .

"How much is it worth?"

"I think I paid two thousand pounds."

She'd pulled her fingers away abruptly. "*Two thousand pounds?* It must be the size of a mountain! Where did you buy it?"

"Sadler Brothers. What do you care?"

"What do I *care?* It took your dear late brother *years* to spend ten thousand pounds on me! And you spend a fifth of that in one visit to Sadler Brothers—for *her!* For that insipid little bishop's daughter!"

Jack had stared at her, bemused. "It's a simple stone. I don't think you would wear such a ring."

"I wouldn't, as it happens. But there is a gold-and-diamond necklace at that very shop I've been hankering after for ages. Like a spider's web, it is."

"I think I know the piece. I thought of buying it. For Camille."

Her hand found his manhood once more. "You must go and fetch the ring," she purred, "and get the necklace for me." Her fingers quickened their strokes.

Gratefully Jack felt his manhood stiffening at last. "You don't mind my going to see her?"

"You must be jesting." She'd lowered her head, tracing the vee of black curls down his chest to his groin. Jack had groaned as her expert mouth encircled him, coaxing him to hardness, to the ecstasy that blotted out every trace of regret. Pris, he thought as she caressed him, had done this, too, but differently, with an air of scientific curiosity. Vivienne was far past exploration; her motions were as practiced and polished as a court musician's. She played him as adroitly as Camille had. Odd, that, if she'd truly had only old Chester Harpool to practice upon.

"Go," she whispered, raising her head. "Go. Go. Go. . . ."

Something in the words, the insistent tone of her voice, made Jack's manhood wither. Then he realized: That was what Camille had said to him about journeying to England.

"What is wrong?" Vivienne had her fist closed around the love charm at his throat. "I cannot . . . convince you?"

Jack yanked his mind back to the present. The past, after all, was long over and done.

"Go," Vivienne urged him again. "Get the ring. And then return to me."

It had been positively spooky, the way she echoed Camille. But then Jack's thoughts had blanked as his body responded to her siren call, the prowess of her fingers and mouth. "You'll go?" she'd asked again, when he fell back against the carpet in satisfied exhaustion.

"I'd do anything for you," he'd whispered cravenly.

So there he was, riding to Avenleigh House on a painfully bright May morning. What day was it? he wondered, as his horse scattered a covey of ringdoves that took to the air with wild, soft gray wings. How long had it been since he'd gone home? He thought for an instant of the sheaf of correspondence that must await him, and then of Shropley—God, he'd forgotten all about poor injured Shropley. Was he still at Avenleigh? That cargo of hemp—had it arrived at Castries? And what about the ship that was bringing wool to Philadelphia, at Pris's suggestion? I've let a great deal go, he realized, and felt a small, swift pang at the irony. The truth was, though, that he and Pris were never suited to each other. Her behavior since he'd tumbled into Vivienne's—God, he had almost thought "clutches," when what he meant was arms!—certainly proved that. If Robert's former fiancée truly cared about him, if she was suffering from his ill treatment of her, surely she would have done more than send that brusque note along with his ring. *She deserves better than me.* He repeated the comforting litany and brought the black up short as he reached the stable gate.

"Yer Lordship!" The boy who ran to catch the bridle seemed bewildered at his sudden appearance. "Does Mrs. Gravesend know ye're comin'?"

"She will soon enough," Jack said curtly, spotting 'Phrina staring down at him from an upstairs window. Bellows opened the door to him, looking extremely subdued. "Is Shropley hanging about, Bellows?"

"In the south chamber, milord. Would you care for some liquid refreshment?" the butler called hopefully as Jack stalked up the stairway. "Brandy, perhaps? Or a rum fizz?"

"I'll ring if I do," Jack told him, then knocked at Shropley's door.

"Come in." The solicitor's voice was distracted. He was sitting in bed, the coverlet strewn with piles of account books and receipts and bills and letters, and his freckled face lit up when Jack came in. "Your Lordship! How good to see you! There are a number of matters here that require your immediate attention. This report from the captain of the *Beauty of the Isles*, for example. And the overseer of the western plantation on Castries has written to say a fire wiped out fifty acres of cane. Not to mention these bills, all of which need signatures."

"Later," Jack said with a wince. "I came for the ring."

"Begging your pardon, milord, but—later when? Several of these are already past due."

"I talked you out of debtor's prison once. I can do it again. What about that ring?"

"I believe Esmé has it at the moment. I thought she might as well return it to Sadler Brothers on her way back to Castries."

"Esmé is going back to Castries?" Jack was shocked for a moment, then shook it off. "Never mind. Glad to hear you're feeling better." He left the solicitor sputtering in his wake, and only then realized he'd never even asked the fellow how he *was* feeling.

It didn't make any difference. Another few minutes, just enough to get Vivienne that damned ring, and he'd be quit of them all—and quit of this wretched house as well. He'd be back at the cottage, where Vivienne would be waiting for him, clad in those red silk unmentionables that took his breath away. He rushed up the extra flight to the nursery, then paused, hearing through the open door Johnnie's laughter, sparkling as the chatter of the parrots in St. Lucia's palm trees. The sound, with the rush of memories it evoked, nearly sent him spinning on his heel. But he pressed on, to stand at the threshold looking in.

Jamalla was sitting in her rocking chair, chuckling, watching Johnnie scoot back and forth across the room chasing a stuffed dog that Pris and Esmé were tossing to one another above his head. Jamalla saw him first. She brought the chair to a stop, the smile dying on her face, and shot a pointed look at Esmé, who let the dog drop and stared at her master. Johnnie whirled around, following her gaze, saw his daddy, and ran to Pris to hide behind her skirts. The room was full of sunlight and smelled of Castile soap and calamine and fresh laundry. Pris looked up last of all.

"Go and greet your father, Johnnie," she urged gently, pulling his fists from her gown. It was one he hadn't seen before—or had he? There was something familiar in the tucked bodice, those full, wide skirts of silvery green. Her hair was in a loose chignon; her exertions with Johnnie had left blond tendrils floating over her bare shoulders and throat in the breeze from the wide-open windows. Her cheeks were flushed with rose; her eyes were wide and clear gray shot with green, like the underside of willow leaves. She looked radiant. *Clean . . .*

He glanced away to his son, who still cowered against her. "What's wrong, Johnnie?"

"I imagine he does not recognize you," Esmé said tartly.

"I haven't been away so long as that."

"Long enough to let your beard grow." She sniffed as only Esmé could sniff, taking in his neglected chin and hair and clothes.

Jack knelt on the polished oak floor, holding out his arms. "Come and let me hug you, son."

"No," the child retorted, ducking behind Pris again.

By God, Jack wasn't about to beg! "The devil take you, then," he said shortly, making Jamalla gasp and mark the sign of the cross against her broad bosom. Jack got to his feet, scowling at the women. "Teaching him to hate me, are you? All of you?"

"He does not need us for that," Esmé retorted with fire in her gaze.

Pris, of all people, came to his defense. "That's enough, Esmé. You and Jamalla take Johnnie for a walk in the gardens." Her hand caressed the boy's tight-curled hair. "Pick a rose for me, will you, pet?" He nodded. Jamalla grasped him by the wrist, and he skirted his father uncertainly. Esmé followed them out, still glowering.

Jack kicked shut the door. "I got your note," he grunted.

"Esmé has your ring," Pris said simply, willing her voice not to shake. Even though she'd reluctantly acquiesced to the maid's wild scheme, she'd been sure that once she saw him again, she'd despise him so thoroughly that she wouldn't even care to carry it out. What was soaring through her heart and soul now, though, wasn't hatred, but a pity so deep that she wanted to cry. *Oh, Jack. What has she done to you?* she wondered, taking in his besmirched clothes, the dark shadows on his cheekbones, the awful hollowness in his eyes.

Seeing her compassionate expression, he laughed. It was a bleak, harsh sound. "Thinking I look like the devil, I suppose. Well, that's what they called me in Castries, wasn't it? Devil Jack . . . and now you know why."

"Esmé told me it was for your smile." *Do you ever smile anymore? Does she make you smile?* "How is . . . Lady Harpool?"

"I'll tell her you asked after her." *There* was a smile, but one so cold and foreboding that it would have frightened Lucifer himself away.

Pris fought off a desperate urge to go to him, take him in her arms, soothe him as if he were a babe like Johnnie, so lost and bewildered and helpless. But he wasn't a child; he was a man. And men made their own choices, didn't they? Her back went up. Men *got* to make choices. Women such as she didn't, could only react to what the males in their lives—fathers, brothers, husbands, uncles, lovers—did to them and for them. Jack was free to squander all his talent and money and goodness away on that auburn-haired vixen if he wanted to.

"I need that ring," he reminded her, trying not to notice the way the sunlight pouring through the windows ignited her hair, turned it to a soft nest of gold. And that impossibly becoming gown— "Have I seen that dress before?"

"I was to have worn it for our wedding." Pris was proud of her steadiness.

He arched a black brow. "And you wear it now to play catch with Johnnie?"

"It was here at the house. He spilled jam across the one I had on. Esmé said the stain would set if I didn't have it laundered immediately." He would see through the lie; she was sure of it. But he seemed distracted, no doubt by his anxiousness to be quit of her; he'd gone to the window and was gazing down onto the garden. "I'll fetch the ring," she whispered, and escaped into Esmé's rooms.

Once there, she wiped her eyes with the back of her hand, took a deep breath, sought to calm her mad-beating heart. For an instant she opened the gray velvet box and looked down at the glittering stone she'd been so proud to wear. *I know it is only decayed vegetative matter*, he'd said when he gave it to her. And then they'd made love for the first time in the tall weeds beside the Wold, life in all its incomprehensible mystery buzzing about them, moving beneath them, passing overhead in the clear blue skies. . . . Useless to torture herself with that memory. She snapped the box shut with a sharp *click*. As she turned for the door, she caught a glimpse of her reflection in Esmé's mirror and paused to study it.

There is magic in this world, she thought: the sorcery that changes a naiad to a dragonfly, a caterpillar to a bright Vanessa. She had changed as well. If she went with her father now to Bath, she would collect suitors the way a captured *Endromidae* did, flocks and flocks of them. For she had discovered that what propelled the magic, what grew the wings and marvelous colors, was nature's insistence that life continue, that mate find a mate. Most of the animal world was hopelessly promiscuous. Males rutted; females acquiesced, more or less willingly. The human insistence on a single lifelong companion was really highly unnatural, born of who knew what tangle of need for protection and comfort and the perpetuation of the species. That the race had reached the state of accommodation it had was nothing short of miraculous. A stalwart, honest second lieutenant, contemplated from that angle, was not so bad. And yet . . . and yet . . .

When she returned, he was still at the window. Johnnie's excited cries floated up from the parterre beneath them.

"Here you are," she said, and bit her lip as she laid the gray velvet box on the sill.

He turned to look at her. "You've been very . . . understanding, Pris."

"I only ever wanted your happiness, Jack."

"Maybe that was the trouble. Maybe you ought to have thought about your own happiness instead."

She gave a little shrug. "For a time there, I thought yours and mine were the same."

He scooped the box up and slipped it into his coat. "There's one thing I'm certain of, the way I'm certain of death. You deserve better than me."

He was almost to the door when she reluctantly recalled Esmé's explicit instructions. It was all nonsense, of course, but she wanted to be able to reassure the maid she had followed them to the dot. "Jack?"

Very slowly he turned back. "Yes?"

"There is one thing more. Esmé asked . . . I fear you will find this presumptuous. But—the charm Camille gave you. The love token. Esmé asked if she might have it back, as a keepsake."

His hand went to his throat. "This? God, why would she want it? I don't even know why I have it on." He fumbled to loosen his collar, cigar-stained fingers moving awkwardly.

Pris clenched her eyes shut, her hands balled into fists. I don't *want* a second lieutenant. I want *you*, Jack Cantrell. I have from the first time I saw you. Even though it means I am a moth tumbling headlong into flame . . . Oh, if there is such a thing as magic, I summon it now, call on all the power of grace and goodness. *Love me again, Jack. I will it so, with all my heart and soul and mind . . .*

He pulled the chain up over his head. As it cleared his mouth, then his nose, then his forehead, a change came over his face. The lines of dissolution seemed to melt and soften; his brow unknotted, and his dull, blear eyes suddenly shone out again like the blue of a Caribbean sky. He stood for a moment with the charm clenched in his fist. Then he let out a sigh so deep and heartfelt that it seemed to rise from his very soul. "Pris," he whispered, the chain slipping from his fingers to the floor.

The transformation was so abrupt and utter that she could not speak; she simply stared in astonishment at this man who seconds before had been a stranger and now was once again her lover, her beloved, the other half to her whole. The sunlight bathed him, swathed him in its brightness; he seemed to drink it in as he stood there, to breathe it, let it envelop him and drive out every vestige of darkness that still clouded his mind and senses. He put up his hands to push back his tangled, soiled hair, brought them away and gazed down at them with distaste. "Christ!" He went to wipe his palms on his coat, realized that, too, was filthy. "Christ, where the devil have I been, to get in such a state?" He yanked out his handkerchief, turned up his nose at the crumpled wad of linen.

Pris found her voice at last. "You don't—remember?"

"The last thing I remember . . ." He paused, reflecting. "I can't remember the last thing I remember. No, wait. I do. I was on my way to—where was I on my way to? Where the *devil* have I been?"

"I'm not certain," Pris whispered, "but I think you may have been in hell."

He took a whiff of his coat sleeve. "Lord knows I stink like it! I must have fallen in a pigsty or something. Yech!" He tugged the coat off, found the shirt beneath it in no better shape. "And here you are in your wedding gown, all sweet and beautiful and clean . . ." His puzzled expression turned to one of alarm. "Bloody Christ! I know! Shropley's had me out for a last bachelor's night of debauchery, hasn't he? And I'm late for the wedding! Your father never will forgive me! I'll go and bathe straightaway!" He started to rush out, then whirled and came back to plant a kiss on her open mouth. "But you'll forgive me, won't you? You'll forgive anything. You are my bright angel."

"Oh, Jack—"

"Lord, now I've made you cry—and on your wedding day, too! No, don't hug me; you'll spoil that lovely gown. I'll be ready to head for the church in ten minutes. No, in five. Exactly how late *are* we?"

"There's still time," Pris told him, the tears of joy spilling over. "There is still time."

He'd no sooner sprinted out the nursery doors than Esmé came in through them, a smile of supreme satisfaction on her face. "*Eh bien,* all is well?"

"All is *more* than well," Pris assured her.

"Did I not say it would be?" She bent down to retrieve the love charm from the floor.

"Esmé, you would not have believed it! The moment he pulled that from his head, everything about him changed! He—he—I don't know how to explain it, but he started to *shine*."

"Ah, but I do believe." She bounced the token in her hand. "Let's look to see what has caused all the trouble, shall we?" Esmé loosed the sequence of latches that held the golden token closed and poured its contents into Pris's cupped palms. Amid the small pile of flower petals and dust and leaves and twigs and powdered lunar moths' wings lay a single long hank of hair, twisted in an intricate love knot. "*Zut alors!*" she breathed, almost in admiration. "She is clever, that one!" Gingerly she plucked the tress from Pris and raised it up, so that the dust fell away and the knot unfurled.

"I don't understand," Pris murmured. "Jack told me Camille had *black* hair. Curly *black* hair."

"She did," said Esmé, contemplating the gleaming auburn strand.

"A week?" Jack echoed in disbelief. He was in Shropley's bedchamber, freshly bathed, hair brushed, clad in a clean suit, listening in bewilderment as the solicitor, with occasional interjections from Esmé and Pris, did his best to explain what had happened to him. "I cannot have been there a week!"

"See for yourself, milord. Your unanswered correspondence goes back that far."

Jack put a dazed hand to his forehead, examining the stack of letters he was handed. "But what in God's name could have made me stay away so long?"

"You were bewitched," Esmé said from her perch on Bennett's bed.

Jack glanced at Pris, who was holding tight to his arm with a smile that would not go away. "Surely, love, *you* don't believe that."

She shrugged happily. "All I know, Jack, is what I told

you. You took the love charm off, and you—woke up, as it were."

"Ridiculous. Shropley, tell her it is ridiculous."

The solicitor groaned a bit, shifting on his bed. "A few weeks past, I would have said stuff and nonsense as well, milord. But experience has taught me not to scoff at what I don't understand. 'There are more things in heaven and earth,' as Hamlet told Horatio, 'than are dreamt of in your philosophy.'" Esmé beamed and fluffed his pillows up considerably.

"I think you've all gone completely daft," Jack said resolutely. "Especially you, Pris! Why, if what you tell me is true—that I have spent the last week wallowing in Vivienne Harpool's arms—you'd throw me out the door on my bum!"

"I'm very fond of your bum," Pris replied, with only a hint of a blush. "And it wasn't your fault, not really. You see, the love charm Camille had made up for you contained a lock of her hair. But somehow Lady Harpool managed to get hold of the token, take Camille's hair out, and put her own in instead."

Esmé was nodding agreement. "And that changed the spell to her. I still wonder how she knew it would do that. Perhaps she only guessed. Or her witch's instinct told her what to do."

Jack shook his head. "No. Vivienne never opened that charm. I would have seen her."

"You might have been asleep," Shropley suggested.

"But she would have had to come here, sneak into the house and accost me in my bed! I would have heard her. Or Pris would have."

"I meant—asleep in *her* bed," the solicitor corrected himself.

"But that would suppose I'd gone to the cottage to see her! Why would I go to see her? I knew how you disliked her, Pris." He paused. Something, some shard of distant memory, was nagging in his mind. He clenched his eyes shut, thinking back, past the days of drunken debauchery he could barely recall now, and saw Pris and Johnnie in his study, the boy at his knees, reaching for the shiny brass pull on a drawer. . . . "The letter," he said slowly. "She had sent me a letter."

"Suggesting a *folie* together?" Esmé asked in disapproval.

"No, no! It was nothing like that. She wrote . . ." He could picture the ecru vellum scented with jasmine, the words that had propelled him there, so certain he was safe. "That she'd become betrothed. To Lord Chomundley! And she wished to return the jewels Robert had given her. That was what she wrote."

"That was the day 'Phrina saw your horse behind her cottage." Pris was beginning to understand.

"Exactly! I went there to offer my congratulations. I was so relieved that she was to marry, that she would be out of my life at last. I went, and she was cleaning the house—to put it up for sale, she said. She spoke of how happy she was with Chomundley. She made rum fizzes. We drank a toast."

"*One* toast?" Pris had her brows raised. "You came home completely pickled! You slept the afternoon away."

"It *was* only one drink, love. You have got to believe me!"

"She put something into it," Esmé said matter-of-factly. "Poppy. Or mandragora. To make you sleep. And while you were asleep, she opened the love charm and substituted her hair."

"We quarreled when you awoke," Pris recalled, color rising in her cheeks. "I called you . . . horrible things."

"And now you know I deserved them." He could not meet her clear gaze. "To have behaved so on the very eve of our wedding—you must have been—I don't see how you can bear even to look at me. I broke every vow of our betrothal. I shamed you in front of your father, the world—"

"Lincolnshire is not the world, you know. It only thinks it is."

"So!" Bennett rubbed his hands together in anticipation. "There is to be a wedding after all, I take it? Once that is over with, milord, you and I can get cracking on these bills."

"You might allow them a little time for a honeymoon, *chéri*," Esmé chided.

"One night?" Bennett suggested, not exactly happily.

Esmé shook her head, bemused. "I honestly cannot say what I see in you. Where is your sense of romance?"

Jack listened to their fond banter with an uneasy sense that all was not resolved, that this happy ending was too quick, too facile. Then it dawned on him: Pris might be willing to forgive him this interlude with Vivienne, convinced as she was—against all sense and reason—that he'd been the victim of a magical spell. But what about that first tryst, in the grass of the abbey cemetery? There was no conceivable excuse for what he'd done that day. Wasn't that what had started all this nonsense with Vivienne, his awful moment of lust and need? He couldn't, he simply couldn't let her marry him now, under false pretenses. He would have to confess, though it would cost him her love. How could he live with himself any other way?

He touched her arm. "Pris. I must talk to you. In private."

"Of course!" She sounded taken aback at his solemn tone but followed willingly as he led her to his study.

"You had best sit down," he told her. Pris sank into a chair. He paced across the room, paced across again, hands clasped behind his back, while she looked at him wonderingly.

"This can't go on," he said abruptly. "I cannot let it go on."

"I . . . don't understand. Do you not wish to marry me?" she whispered.

"Christ, of course I do!" he exploded. "It's all I want in the world! I'd give everything I have to stand before that altar and speak those vows to you. But—it's not to be."

"Why?"

"Because there is something you don't know about me, Pris. Something horrible. Shameful." He stopped pacing at last, took a deep, quick breath. "For some reason known only to you and to God, you are willing to forgive what I did this past week."

"You were under a spell, love! Any fool could see—"

"Wait!" He held up his hand. "You don't know the whole story. I . . . when I . . . this time with Vivienne. It was not the first." He raised his eyes to hers, and the light had gone out of them. "I lay with her once before, you see. Once when there was no love charm or magic spell to excuse it. When there was no excuse at all, except that she was there, and offering herself, and I was wretchedly weak."

Pris sat silent for a moment. Then a corner of her mouth twitched. "You mean the time you had her in the graveyard at the abbey."

"I mean the time I had her in the graveyard at the—" He broke off, staring. "My God. You know about that?"

She nodded. "Esmé told me. Not long after it happened."

"You have known *all along*?"

"Aye."

"But—I—you—she—" He was too stunned for articulate speech.

"She *also* told me," Pris went on calmly, "that her coach was not five minutes behind yours. Scientifically speaking, therefore, the logical conclusion was that your mating was something less than romantic. Something, in fact, quite animal in nature. Rather like the coupling of the *Bombyci-dae*, which takes place in less than five *seconds*, according to Professor Eisenroth."

"I was right," Jack said in humble awe. "You *are* too good for me."

"Nonsense." Pris waved a dismissive hand. "Copulation is the driving force behind the whole natural world. I would not be much of a scientist if I denied that fact. Oh, I won't say I did not have some uncertain moments. When she returned to Lincolnshire this last time, I was terrified she might be carrying your child. Then it occurred to me that if she were, she would have made no secret of the fact. A man as noble as you would certainly have married her under those circumstances."

"Noble?" Jack sputtered.

"Yes, noble, Your reluctant Lordship," Pris insisted, giving her smile full rein. "What other sort of man would be so troubled by past sins? Or bother bringing his dead brother's former fiancée to London just to cheer her up—not to mention his shrew of an aunt and her outlandish daughters? Or, for that matter, come back to England at all to settle his family's scrambled affairs, or let himself be falsely accused of cheating on his university exams and hold his tongue about it? Face facts, Jack: You are noble to the depths of your soul."

"And *you* have the universe's most skewed sense of logic."

"On the contrary. I am a scientist. I merely observe and conclude."

"A scientist who believes in magic."

"That, too, is based on observation and conclusion."

"You're not a scientist. Do you know what you are?" Jack demanded. And then his voice softened, caught in a sob. "You are the most wondrous thing in all of God's creation." He fought for control and knelt at her feet. "Will you marry me, Priscilla Margaret Anne Wilcox? *Will* you marry me?"

"If you'll expend tonight helping me to learn those pesky vows once and for all."

"Sorry. I can't oblige you." He swept her from the chair into his arms, held her there and kissed her, so fiercely that she had to struggle to come up for breath. He grinned at her, his blue eyes keen with desire. "I have other plans for tonight."

Chapter

35

The marriage of John David Howard Cantrell, fifth earl of Avenleigh, to Miss Priscilla Wilcox took place, to the utter astonishment of every biddy in Lincolnshire, just as scheduled, on the twelfth of June. The bride's father presided over the nuptials. Pris was attended by Agnes and 'Phrina, Jack by Bennett Shropley and Johnnie, cradled in Esmé's arms. The only discordant note was struck by the groom's aunt, who sat in the first pew draped in black from head to toe, wearing a permanent scowl.

Nearly as worthy of remark as the fact the marriage was taking place at all, whispered the ladies present, was the appearance of the bride. "I never really noticed before how truly beautiful she is," Mrs. Blathersby murmured to Lady Ashton, who nodded agreement as Pris came down the aisle arm in arm with her new husband:

"She's quite the most breathtaking little thing I have ever seen."

The happy couple was showered with flower petals as

they emerged form the cathedral. Before Jack lifted Pris into the waiting carriage, she tossed her bouquet of pale roses and deep-blue larkspur into the crowd. It was caught by 'Phrina, who stared at it for a moment and then burst into blushing giggles while the onlookers cheered.

Cook outdid herself with the wedding feast, which was to say that some of the food was actually palatable. There was a sirloin of beef with horseradish and mustard, quail in a rather tasty Madeira sauce, creamed leeks and carrots, chicken pie, lamb cutlets, mushroom omelet, and a sideboard sagging beneath its display of ices and tarts and cakes. Aunt Bertrice only picked at the meal, but 'Phrina was in heaven, returning to the sweets table again and again, the bridal bouquet still gripped in her hand. Jack had brought out the best of his cellars, and Pris thought— though she was not certain—that she glimpsed her father surreptitiously sipping St. Émilion from a teacup. Johnnie loved the musicians his father had hired, and danced before them, clapping and laughing, each time they took up their instruments.

It was, all the guests agreed as they called for their carriages long after midnight, the most splendid wedding they ever had attended. Jack and Pris stood at the door to bid them farewell, with Johnnie sound asleep against Pris's shoulder. Agnes and Lord Cowper had long since gone off to bed, and no one had seen the groom's aunt since the start of the dancing. Esmé was in Bennett's lap in a corner of the dining room.

"I wonder," Pris said, then had to stifle a yawn.

"What?" Jack asked.

"Whether they will marry."

"Of course they will. He won't dare risk her putting another curse on him if they don't. Here, give him to me." He reached for Johnnie. "Where on earth is Jamalla?"

"Snoring in the nursery, I'll wager. She much enjoyed

the champagne." Pris paused briefly to survey the detritus around them. "Lord, what a mess. 'Twill take all night to clean up!"

"That's not your concern, though, Lady Avenleigh. It's all on the staff."

She perked up considerably. "My, my. The charms of *noblesse oblige*!"

"Exactly. So once we change this fellow's nappie and have him in his cradle. . . ."

"Yes?"

"*Then,*" Jack murmured, bending to nuzzle her ear, "we'll begin to truly celebrate!"

Just at that moment, 'Phrina wandered toward them with a plate of sweets in one hand and the bridal bouquet, somewhat worse for wear, in the other. "There are still tarts and cakes left," she noted happily, "if you'd like me to bring some up to your rooms."

"How very thoughtful of you," Pris began, and then caught Jack scowling so ferociously that she giggled. "But I've had enough. Darling, have you?"

"More than enough. Night, 'Phrina." He tugged Pris toward the stairs.

Johnnie didn't even stir while Pris changed him. Neither did Jamalla, who was sound asleep in her rocking chair, a champagne glass at her feet. "Should I wake her and send her to her bed?" Pris whispered, laying Johnnie in his cradle.

"She looks cozy enough. Leave her be." He bent over his son, gently smoothing his curls. "Congratulations, Johnnie. You've got yourself a mamma." He planted a kiss on the sleeping baby's forehead. "And I couldn't have done it without you. I am certain of that!"

"Oh, I don't know," Pris demurred.

"Confess it. You are more in love with him than you are with me."

"I can't imagine one of you without the other," she admitted, her fingers stroking Johnnie's tiny palm.

"I can't imagine him without you." Tears were shining in his blue eyes; he blinked them off, embarrassed. "Come," he said gruffly, pulling her close to his side. "High time we started in on a passel of siblings for him."

When they reached his rooms, he carried her over the threshold and straight to the bed. "Wait," she whispered, fighting off his urgent embrace.

"For what?"

"You'll see." She turned her back to him. "Would you undo the buttons for me?"

"Gladly. And everything else."

"Just the buttons will suffice." He unfastened them, planting kisses down her neck and shoulder blades as he did. Pris turned her head to meet his mouth, then skipped away.

"Where are you *going*?" he demanded, so woebegone that she had to laugh.

"Don't fret. I'll be right back." She vanished into his wardrobe room with a mysterious smile.

When the door opened again and she emerged, he burst out laughing. "How very alluring!"

"It is, don't you think?" she asked, pirouetting in Melchior's best suit and straw hat. "Esmé and Jamalla thought white silk. But I insisted on this."

"You were right." He took a step toward her, aroused beyond reason by the sight of her in the linen shirt, with her rosy nipples showing plainly against the weave. He unfastened the buttons at her throat. "God, if you knew how I wanted to do this, the night we were at the Egyptian Hall!"

"If you knew how I longed for you to," she whispered. He removed the hat, reached for the pins that held her chignon and pulled them out slowly, let that heavy golden mass fall in shimmering waves in the candlelight. Then he stood and stared at her for so long that Pris grew self-conscious.

"You mentioned something about siblings," she reminded him softly.

"You look . . . too beautiful to touch."

"Oh, heavens. Not me."

"You do." He stretched his fingers almost to her breast, then pulled his hand away. "I *don't* deserve you, Pris," he said with abject conviction. And she, staring at her image reflected in his wide eyes, was amazed by her own loveliness, by the woman, proud and strong and graceful, who looked back at her.

"Do you remember . . . once you said to me perhaps I had just not found the right man yet? The man who would make me beautiful?"

"I cannot remember you ever not looking beautiful," he said truthfully.

"Your love has made me so." She laughed suddenly, raising her arms so that the shirt fluttered in the air like wings. And she knew, deep in her soul, that she would never be afraid of losing him to anyone or anything again. " 'The two shall become as one,' " she whispered. "I *am* you, Jack." It was a mystery profound as life itself, eternal as God or science. "I am *you.*"

"As I am you, wife." A slow, gratified smile spread across his face at the realization. "Nothing can part us. Not even death."

"*There's* a cheerful notion for our wedding night."

"But it is true," he said stubbornly, emphatically. "We belong to one another for all time." He lifted his hand again, and this time stroked her cheek, traced the soft bow of her lips. "Forever. What a wondrous word." His fingers caught in her hair, drawing her toward him. "Forever," he whispered again, just before his mouth closed on hers.

Pris leaned against him, into him, felt the pounding of his heart and the throb of his manhood hard at her thighs. She twined her arms around his neck, returning the kiss as he caught her up and carried her to the bed. He lay her down gently, delicately, then stretched out beside her, head propped on his elbow, staring into her dove-gray eyes. "I love you, Pris."

"I love you, Jack."

"I never imagined . . . I would be so happy," he told her.

"Nor did I think I would be."

"Do we warrant it, do you suppose?"

"Oh, we must."

He nodded thoughtfully. "Aye. So we must."

He removed the breeches very gravely.

"Your hands are awfully steady," she observed softly, "after all that bacchanalia."

"I didn't drink. I didn't need to. You intoxicate me." He kissed her bare throat, inhaling her scent, sweet and warm and clean. Her hair drifted across the pillows like a silken net; he caught his hands in it, drawing her toward him. The shirt fell away, baring her breasts. He traced their rosy tips with his thumbs, felt them stiffen to his touch. Bowing his head, he kissed first one and then the other, slowly, lingeringly, making her tremble with desire.

She reached for *his* shirt buttons, undid them with an eagerness that made him laugh. "Greedy girl," he whispered, smoothing his hand over her belly and thighs. "Is that any way for a bishop's daughter to behave?"

She glanced up. "He took it rather well, don't you think? That we were going to be married after all?"

"Why not? You've had the poor man at his wits' end for months. And he knows you are my problem now."

"Why, you—" She grabbed for the bulge in his breeches. "A problem? Is that what I am?"

"A dreadful problem. I cannot get enough of you." He bent to put his mouth to her breast again, his tongue circling its taut bud, teasing her with gentleness. Pris had no patience for gentleness, though; she drew him against her, and obligingly he intensified his attentions, until her soft breathing turned to moans of pleasure.

"Oh, Jack. Oh!" He'd put his teeth to her nipple, drawing on it, sucking hard, while his hands caressed the curve of her buttocks. "Take off your clothes," she begged.

"I thought you'd never ask."

He stripped hurriedly while she lay back, arms behind her head, watching him and smiling. As he pulled down his breeches, his manhood sprang out like a rock-hard lance. She touched a finger to it, laughed to see how it responded.

"Mmm," Jack breathed. And then, apologetically: "I haven't got my boots off."

"I noticed that. Even Johnnie knows—shoes before clothes."

He sat up to yank them off. "You put my mind in a muddle."

"Jack," she began, while he still struggled with the Hessians. He turned to her, made wary by the tone of her voice. "Is every woman different?"

"Different—how?" he managed to ask.

"You know. To have . . . in bed."

He groaned. "God, Pris! The things you ask!"

"It's my scientific curiosity." She blushed. "You don't have to answer."

"I don't mind answering." He pulled the last boot free while pondering what to say. "But it's not as if I've had hundreds and hundreds of women. Despite what you think. Yes. Every woman is different. And no. Every one is the same."

"That's no answer," she scoffed.

"It is the best I can give you. Except to tell you this." He paused. "Camille was . . . well. You know what Camille was. She knew certain things . . . about men. How to arouse them. How to keep them aroused. They were lessons she'd learned."

"What about Vivienne?"

"Vivienne knew the lessons, too."

"I see." Her small face was crestfallen for an instant. Then she brightened. "But you could teach them to me!"

"Oh, Pris." He stroked her cheek. "That is what I am trying to explain. There isn't any need. What you haven't learned, you seem to . . . to stumble on naturally. It's that scientific curiosity, I suppose. And it is far more arousing that way. Knowing that you have never had another man"— He pushed his hair back, smiled down at her. "You'll never understand how precious that makes you to me. Precious, and a little frightening. You have no one to compare me to, true. But what if—what if someone else could have suited you more, made you more ecstatic?"

"Impossible to imagine." She pushed herself up on her elbows to kiss him. "And just think. We have the rest of our lives to explore one another."

"I am looking forward to that. Very much." He touched his mouth to hers, pressing her down into the pillows. "God. You are so sweet." He swung his leg over her, straddling her, and put his palm to her mound of Venus, fingers riffling the soft blond curls there. Her knees parted as she let out an involuntary sigh that set his loins afire. Fighting his aching need, he reached lower with his fingertips, found the bud of her desire, touched it, caressed it, his motions quickening with the quickening of her breath.

"Jack. Oh, Jack. Oh, dear God, Jack—" She bent beneath him, arching back. Her hair was a wild mass of gold, her eyes wide and frantic with need—and she was so breathtakingly lovely that he wanted to prolong the moment, to stroke her forever, see her parted lips and hear her murmured endearments and smell Castile soap until the end of his days.

Pris, however, was not so patient. She wrapped her arms around the small of his back, tugging him down to her, coaxing his manhood into her sheath. At the glorious sensation of entering her, he abandoned all vestiges of self-control, surrendered himself to the desire that was coursing in his blood, pounding in his head. "I—love—you," he grunted, matching each word with an urgent thrust. "I—want—you."

"Yes."

"Wife."

"Yes."

"My—dear—love."

"Jack. Yes. Jack. Yes! Yes!" She clung to him, eyes clenched tight, the room, the house, the world dissolving, the whole universe subsumed into this sublime secret of two made one, joined beyond body and soul.

They were moving together like the earth and the sea, like the sun and the sky. And then the earth spun on its axis, tilted; the sea burst forth; the sky tore open above them; the sun exploded into shattering rays of blinding-bright light. "Pris!" he cried, lost in the confusion of the cosmos ending, needing her to bring him back to the world.

"Here," she answered, holding tight to him as he thrust into her one last time, as his seed erupted in a blast of heat. "I always will be here."

After that, it was a long time before either of them spoke. They held to one another, silent and awed, while their ecstasy receded in shimmering waves. At long last Jack roused himself, rolling from atop her, sprawling on the bed. "Christ! If that's what married life brings," he managed to gasp out, "there's no way to explain the bachelors of the world."

"Nor nuns," Pris agreed, so solemnly that he burst out laughing.

He turned sober quickly, though. "What I said before . . .

about women being different, but all the same? It was a lie. I've never in my life felt anything like that."

"Really?" she asked dubiously.

"Really," he swore, and sealed it with a kiss.

"It's rather . . . magical, isn't it?" Pris murmured.

"The best sort of magic." He pulled her into his arms, pressed his lips to the soft sheen of her hair. "But—shame on you! You are a scientist. No doubt science teaches it's no more than—what did you call copulation the other night? 'The driving force behind the whole natural world.' "

"That may be. But I am not quite ready to relinquish my entire system of belief on account of one experience."

"No?" He sounded slightly offended.

"No," she affirmed, and laughed, her fingers trailing toward his manhood again. "It will take repeated experiments."

A long time later, sated with science and magic, Jack lay in their bed with Pris curled against him, watching her as she slept. Her face in repose was like an angel's, pale and beatific in its halo of loose gold hair. He shifted to his side to look at her more easily; she stirred and smiled, moving closer to him, burrowing into his chest. He put his arm around her, softly, softly, and held her to his heart.

It still seemed incomprehensible to him, the greatest miracle of all creation, that she was his and always would be. *I must have done something right in this life,* he thought. *I wonder what it was.* So many unlikely turns of fate had brought them to this point. A sudden shift in the breeze sent the draperies at the window rippling. Seeing them flutter, he was reminded of Camille's white bedroom, with jasmine unfurling on the trellises on a summer morn. *Are you looking down on us?* he wondered, staring at the night sky. *Do you see how she loves Johnnie, how good she is to him?* Better than Camille herself might have been, he realized, startled by the revelation. How would she ever have fit a child into her life at the Hôtel de I'Isle—or even into her heart? She must have known as much. Theirs had been a love fueled by idleness and passion, a youthful love, selfish and immature and shameless, just as they both were then. He tried to imagine what might have become of them in five, ten, fifteen years' time, and saw only the sameness: no change, no growth, only a great stretch of what had already been. And he wondered: *Did you know that, Camille? Is that why you sent me back here? More than for the hats and the jewels, was it to save my soul, cleanse me of my anger and bitterness toward my family?* It was possible—nay, more than possible. She, who'd never known any family to speak of, might have been more wise than he'd given her credit for, might have sensed he never could be happy without the ghosts of the past laid to rest.

His father—for the first time, with his new wife sleeping beside him, Jack thought of how awful the loss of his mother must have been to his father. As a child, he'd felt only his own desolation, the abrupt absence of her sheltering love, and all that had happened afterward had only served to harden his resentment along that fault, like a mortar crack that starts small and edges out. But really, the earl had not been such an ogre when he and Robert were small. It was after his wife's death that he'd pulled away, become withdrawn. She'd been only thirty when she died, he realized with true shock. Younger than he was now. The earl and she had had only—what? Nine years together, when they'd been promised a lifetime. If fate dealt with him the same way, snatched Pris from him—God forbid!—so unfairly, what would that do to him?

As for Robert . . . Jack felt nothing but sadness and pity for his brother, who'd had this treasure, this *angel*, in his grasp, and had let her go. Granted, Vivienne Harpool was a woman hell-bent on getting what she wanted—he shuddered, realizing how close he'd come to succumbing himself, miring his future in her sty of mindless pleasure. If her greed had not propelled him back to Avenleigh for the ring . . .

It shone now on Pris's hand, joined by the plain gold band he'd slipped onto her finger in the cathedral that morning. How damnably easy it is to go astray in this life, he mused; how very little space lay between the unlooked-for contentment he felt at this moment, with Pris in his arms, and what might have been. *Camille,* he said again to her, wherever she was, *you did know, didn't you? I am certain you did.* And through the parted curtains, impossibly, magically, the Lincolnshire wind wafted a whisper of scent that was unmistakably jasmine. Jack nearly laughed out loud. *You see? You did. I will love you, chérie, always, for that. And for our son.*

He leaned back against the pillows, closed his tired eyes. The dawn was coming all too soon, with its clatter and rush. He clasped his wife to his heart, cherishing this small space of time, this night of redemption and forgiveness, this woman who had crept into his life as unportentously as a caterpillar and by doing so had given him wings.

The last sound he heard before he drifted into sleep was 'Phrina's slow, shuffling footsteps moving along the hallway. And he realized, smiling against the soft swath of Pris's hair, that he would have missed them had they not been there.

*H*e awoke, in stark darkness, to a scream, quavering and terrified. Startled, he sat up in bed, put his hand out to Pris to make certain she was safe. She was. Another scream pierced the night, so shrill that the hairs along his neck pricked and tingled. The air, he suddenly noticed, was awash with jasmine. What the bloody hell—

He lunged for the tinderbox, lit a candle. Pris roused herself sleepily in its yellow glow. "Jack?" she murmured, pushing back her hair just as the third scream came, long and wordless and hollow. "Jesus!" she gasped, eyes widening in fear. "What was that?"

"I don't know." He was already pulling on his breeches; shirtless and barefoot, he stumbled toward the door. Pris followed, catching up Melchior's shirt and then a sheet to wind around her shoulders. Jack grabbed the door handle, yanked—then strode straight into the heavy wood when it refused to open.

"Is it stuck?" Pris demanded, bewildered.

He tugged at it again, then turned to her, his blue gaze narrowed. "It is locked, I think."

"Locked?" Another scream resounded in the distance. "Did *you* lock it?"

"I haven't even got a key."

Pris had her nose up, sniffing the air. "What is that smell?"

"Jasmine," he muttered.

"No, no. It is like . . . something burning." Jack caught a whiff of smoke then, too, beneath the flowery perfume.

"Christ!" he burst out, and threw himself headlong against the unbudging door, just as the awful screaming was replaced by a male voice, Bellows's voice, shouting from somewhere belowstairs:

"Fire! Fire! Everyone out of the house! Everyone out to the lawns!"

"Fire . . ." Pris caught Jack's arm. "My God. Johnnie. He's upstairs. With Jamalla."

"I know." He scanned the room, grabbed up a chair, and rushed the door with it. The chair broke apart with a crash, but the stout oak panels did not even quiver. "Damn! Dammit all!" He ran to the fireplace, took the heavy iron poker and pried at the hinges. Pris, meanwhile, had gone to the window and was staring into the darkness below.

"Bellows!" she cried, seeing the butler run across the grass with a lantern. "Bellows, where is the fire?"

"Get out! Get out!" he screeched back at her.

"Where is the fire?" she shouted again.

He threw his arm in a circle, the lantern light making a white splotch of his aghast face. "Everywhere!"

It was true. Leaning over the sill, she saw smoke curling from the windows all along the west wing, and a shimmer of red-gold flame in the dining hall below. Servants were spilling from the doorways, forlorn and half dressed.

Esmé appeared, dragged forcibly by a hobbling Bennett; she was arguing furiously with him.

"Esmé!" Pris cried, fighting to be heard above the rising clamor of voices. "Esmé, where is Jamalla? Where is Johnnie?" The maid broke off disputing with her lover long enough to point above Pris's head:

"Still in the nursery, m'amselle!"

"Dear God!" Pris felt her knees buckle. "Someone must go and fetch them!"

"It's no use, milady!" Bellows shouted at her. "Impossible to get through! The entire corridor, the stairs—it's a wall of flame!"

"Jack!" Pris turned to him, saw him sweating, still fighting frantically to force the door open.

"I heard," he said grimly, then threw the poker aside. "I can't get through. Let me get you out safely."

"But Johnnie—and Jamalla drank all that champagne! She may not even waken!"

"I'll get to them somehow. First I want you safe outside. I'll need that sheet." She tugged it from her shoulders, and he tied it tight around her waist, playing it out, gauging the distance. "Too short. I'll need the other, too." He paused, looking down at her hands as she tested the knot he'd made. "What's become of your ring?"

"Of my—" She, too, glanced down, saw the diamond was missing from her finger. "God, who knows? What does it matter? It fell off, I suppose. I am not about to look for it now." She wrenched at the covers, then screamed herself as they came free and revealed a face staring back at her from under the high oak bedstead. "Jack! Jesus, Jack!"

"Vivienne." Instinctively Jack moved to shield Pris, hide her behind him. "I might have known this mischief was of your making."

Vivienne Harpool crawled out from under the bed, shaking dust from her skirts. "Don't be a bloody fool, Jack.

I only came for the ring. You promised it to me. You *owed* it to me."

"You set fire to my home, risked the whole household's lives, for the sake of that damned ring?"

"Of course I didn't set any fire!" she snapped back in fury. "If I had, would I have locked myself inside?"

"But if you didn't . . . how . . ."

"Mayhaps your passion for your quaint little bride caused the conflagration," Vivienne suggested nastily. "Though I sincerely doubt it."

Jack moved to strike the smirk from her face, but Pris caught his arm. "Jack. Love. There isn't time. We have to get Johnnie. Lower me down, for God's sake! Perhaps the servants' stairs to the nursery are still clear."

He held the end of the second sheet and lowered her slowly, gingerly. The linen played out while she was still ten feet above the ground. "Wait!" he called down to her. "I'll add the coverlet on." But before he could, he felt the sheets go slack of her slight weight; she'd untied the knot at her waist and dropped to the lawn. Horrified, he looked down at her crumpled form. "Pris!"

"I'm fine!" she cried, scrambling to her feet. "I am going around now to the side doors!"

"My turn," Vivienne said brightly, hauling the sheets in.

"Go to hell," Jack spat. "It's where you've always belonged."

"Now, now, Jackie. You aren't the sort of man, are you, who'd abandon a lady in distress?" Her lashes fluttered coyly.

"You're no lady," he grunted—then braced himself against the wall below the sill as she crawled through the window. She flashed a smile back at him.

"Don't you dare drop me!"

"Don't tempt me." But he waited until she'd fallen

into the arms of Bellows and the footman before letting the sheet slip from his hands.

Pris had reappeared beneath the window. "Jack! Jack, Bellows was right. The fire is impassable. The stairs have already collapsed." She was white and drawn, frightened beyond tears. "Oh, God, what are we to do?"

"Only one thing to do." He stood on the sill, testing the stones of the outer wall with the bare toes of his right foot.

"Oh, milord!" Bellows's horrified voice drifted up to him from the lawn below. "You cannot possibly mean—"

"Shut up," Jack shouted down at him, "and fetch blankets from the stables. Hay as well. Anything to cushion them." He inched out along the thin line of mortar between the stones, heading for the corner, where the abutting edges would be easier to climb.

Agnes and Harry had joined the little throng in the yard, and so had 'Phrina. When she saw Jack scaling the sheer wall, she began to scream, and Jack, glancing down, realized it had been her shrill cry that wakened him from sleep. Agnes was staring dumbfounded at Vivienne; her astonished voice floated up to Jack as he climbed: "But . . . you were not even at the wedding!"

"No," Vivienne answered suavely, "I simply stopped by to drop off a gift."

The wall was hard going, the stones so old they threatened to break away beneath his toes and fingers. Jack thanked God for his sobriety and simultaneously cursed the architect of Avenleigh House, who'd made the ceilings unnecessarily high. Still, another few feet and he'd be within arm's reach of the nursery window—which, praise God, was open. "Jamalla!" he shouted as loudly as he could. "Wake up, Jamalla! Fire! *Le feu!*" She did not answer, but above the growing roar of the flames he heard a sound that made his heart stop beating: Johnnie crying in terror, babbling for Papa, for Mamma, for rescue from his cradle. "I am coming, son!" he shouted back. "I am coming for you!" He lunged upward, caught his fingertips on the windowsill, hung there while his bare toes fought for footing . . .

The sandstone sill shifted crazily, pulling free of the wall in a piece. Jack flailed wildly, grabbing at nothingness, and felt himself hurtling downward, his son's screams ringing in his ears.

The fall seemed to last a lifetime. Just before he landed, breathless, on the bales of hay the servants had hauled from the stables, he caught a glimpse of the small white-clad figure who'd been scaling the wall in his wake.

"Pris! Oh, God, Pris!" He fought to rise from the hay, found he could not stand on his left leg; it crumpled uselessly beneath him. "Pris. Don't." She was so horrifyingly high, clinging by her fingers, her soft, sweet fingers. "Pris! Damn you, Bellows! Send someone up in her stead!"

"No one else would dare try it, milord!" the butler gasped, his own eyes fixed on Pris as she climbed. And Jack, kneeling helplessly atop the hay bales, saw it was true; they were all hanging back, even Harry Cowper. Then Bennett Shropley staggered forward despite being hobbled by his bad back. Esmé started to stop him, reconsidered. But he got no farther than a few feet before he fell.

"I'm sorry," he told Jack forlornly. "God, I am so sorry."

"I appreciate the effort, Bennett." Still Pris climbed on, moving slowly, carefully, testing each outcrop of rock before resting her weight on it. She looked tiny as a caterpillar by now, above the second story.

And then Jamalla's broad, dazed face appeared in the window, surrounded by swirls of smoke. She had Johnnie in her arms. "Jump!" Jack bellowed at her, seeing flickers of flame behind her sturdy figure. "You have to jump!"

"Je ne peux pas!" she blubbered.

"Throw the baby down!" It was a voice that hadn't been heard yet; Jack swiveled and saw Aunt Bertrice, close beside Vivienne. And he noted curiously, in a corner of his mind not preoccupied with his son's grave danger, that she was fully dressed, unlike the rest of the household; she'd never changed out of her vulture's black. Now, why should that be? "Throw him down!" she urged again, her dark eyes agleam in the light of the fire.

"No!" Jack shouted, suddenly certain that whatever she wanted, planned, must be circumvented. "Jamalla, don't!" The nursemaid hesitated, poised by the window, tears streaming down her cheeks. Esmé was praying in some admixture of French and Caribe and English; Bennett was trying yet again to climb up the wall. And still Pris crept higher and higher, clinging by the tips of her fingers and toes to the outcrops of stone.

Tiny and frail, white shirt fluttering, she inched toward the window. A sudden crash of sparks made Jamalla screech and glance behind her. The room was an inferno of roiling red flame. Johnnie was silent; his blue eyes as Jamalla held him were trained on Pris. And Jack could do nothing but watch in impotent horror and fear, certain that all he loved, all his reason for living, was about to be subsumed by the fire licking just behind Jamalla's back.

Pris had found a toehold that would let her reach almost to the window. She inched sideways along the wall, eyes locked on Johnnie's. "Jamalla," she said as calmly as she could. "This is what you must do. Lower him down to me."

"Oh, m'amselle—"

"Do it, Jamalla!"

The nursemaid screamed, whirling about. "My skirts are on fire!"

"Jamalla! Give me the baby and then jump."

"It's too high! He'll die! We'll die!"

"Well, you certainly will if you stand there and blubber!" Pris cried furiously. After a moment's hesitation, Jamalla dangled Johnnie over the broken sill. "Baby," Pris whispered, seeing his wide blue eyes filled with terror. "Johnnie. Love. You must hold tight to Mamma. Can you hold tight to Mamma?" She extended her arm, reaching for him, gathering him in as his fists caught in her loose hair. "Jump, Jamalla!" she shouted again.

"*Oh, mon Dieu,* have mercy!" And Jamalla jumped, her bright skirts made brighter by flame. She landed with a *whoosh*; the servants rushed to beat out the sparks that fell from her clothing. The house was imploding; Pris could feel the wall swaying away from her, bending, bowing, dragging her with its great weight. She glanced downward.

"Jack?" she cried.

"I've got you," he promised, his voice hoarse with smoke.

She leaned back from the wall, both arms wrapped around Johnnie, and let go.

She fought to curl her body around him as they fell, cushion him, protect him. But the heat, her dizziness, the lack of air, made her lose her grip, and she watched in agonized dismay as he flew from her arms, sailed out from her, billowed free, all the while with a smile of the utmost trust stamped on his small face. He billowed free—and then, in the midst of their plunge, just as he seemed about to shoot into oblivion, hauled up short and drew back toward her, tight as a fish on a line.

He still had his fists caught in her hair.

Chapter
37

The dawn brought rain, welcome for once, that slashed onto the ruined bulk of Avenleigh House and sputtered on the embers. The occupants had gathered in the stables, where at least they still had a roof over their heads. Pris was holding Johnnie, who was sleeping contentedly, all his fear forgotten now that he was safe in her grasp. Jack's fears were not so easily quelled. Propped against the wall of a stall—he still could not put weight on his leg—he wrapped his wife and son in his arms as though he did not intend ever to let go.

" 'Phrina!" he called to where his cousin stood in her nightdress, clutching Pris's wedding bouquet despite all that had happened. "It was your screaming, wasn't it, that wakened me? As many times as I rued your midnight wanderings, I am grateful for them now."

"We all are," Bennett Shropley reiterated, his own arm around Esmé.

"Where did you first see the fire, 'Phrina?" Agnes

asked curiously. "Did it begin in the kitchens? In the dining hall?"

"Leave the poor girl be," Aunt Bertrice said sharply "Can't you see she is frightened out of her wits? All this turmoil, this upheaval . . ." She stretched out her hands to her daughter. " 'Phrina. Come here." 'Phrina, pale and dazed shrank back from her. "I said come here!" her mother said again. 'Phrina shook her head slowly, moving backward knuckles white on the stems of the bouquet. "You foolish chit!" Aunt Bertrice muttered. "What on earth has gotten into you? Send someone for Dr. Allison, Jack. She needs a sedative."

'Phrina's pale blue eyes widened; she turned to her sister, beseeching. "Don't let her give me anything, Aggie Don't let her give anything to me."

" 'Phrina. Pet." Agnes enveloped her in a hug. "I do think a spot of laudanum—"

"No!" 'Phrina cried in terror. "She only wants me to forget!"

"Of course I want you to forget," her mother said, her cold voice turned lulling, soothing. "You've had a terrible shock. All of us have. The best thing is to forget what has happened. There's no harm done; you know that." Jack was watching her in wonder. He'd never seen his aunt so solicitous. "If you carry on, 'Phrina, if you go telling wild tales, you know what will happen."

'Phrina started to cry, tears rolling down her smudged face. "No," she whispered, backing away from her mother blundering into Pris and Jack. "No. I'll be good. I swear."

"Of course you will," Aunt Bertrice purred. "You're my good girl, aren't you, 'Phrina? You and I—we're all that's left to one another now, aren't we? You and I . . ."

Vivienne Harpool, who was standing in the shadows inched toward the stable doors. "So long as everyone is safe, and all's well that ends well, I'll just be heading home to my cottage. Terribly sorry about the loss of the house, Jackie. And my apologies for . . . well. For dropping in so unexpectedly."

Jack's long arm shot out to catch her wrist as she crept past him. "Just one moment. I'll have that ring, please."

"Ring?" she echoed, so innocently that Pris started to laugh.

"Aye, the ring you stole from my sleeping wife's finger!" Jack bellowed at her.

"Oh, *that* ring! Do you know, I must have dropped it when I jumped from the window. No doubt you'll find it in the morning, there in the hay."

"Vivienne!"

From her expression, she was evidently considering brazening it out. Then, as she glanced at Pris cuddling Johnnie, she shrugged and reached into her sleeve. "Very well. If you insist. She earned some reward, I suppose, for that amazing climb." For a moment, the diamond clutched in her hand, she hesitated. "Hard to fathom why she would risk her life that way for a child that's not even her own."

"But he is," Pris said softly.

Vivienne Harpool tossed her auburn curls. "You know, you don't deserve her, Jack."

"I'm quite aware of that fact." He beamed down at Pris and slipped the ring Vivienne reluctantly relinquished back onto her hand. "So long as we are playing true confessions, Vivienne, let me ask you this. Why *did* you take up with my brother?"

Her hard olive eyes peered through the stable window at the smoldering ruins of Avenleigh. "I would have enjoyed being mistress of that house. I used to stare up at it when I was small and dream of what life inside it must be like. I thought I would have it with Robert. By the time Chester died, I had not many honorable options left to me. Robert did not care about my reputation. How could he afford to, considering his? He was a simple capture." Then she turned on Pris. "But you must have told Jack that, since he cast me off for you."

"Told me what?" Jack demanded.

Pris shook her head. "No. I never did. I saw no reason to."

"Told me *what*?" Jack asked again.

"My God." Vivienne was staring at Pris in wonder. "You had that weapon in your arsenal and never used it?"

Pris was blushing. "Please, Vivienne. Let's not speak of it."

"I think we had better," Jack said with an edge to his voice. "What did you know about her, Pris, that I didn't?" She was silent. "Vivienne?"

"Ask Sephrina," Vivienne said disdainfully. "She spies on everyone."

But 'Phrina was still cowering against Pris, head ducked low. Bennett Shropley spoke up then. "I imagine, sir, Lady Harpool is referring to Lady Avenleigh's knowledge of the affair between herself and your brother."

"Affair? But, Vivienne! You told me—"

Vivienne Harpool was still staring at Pris. "My God. You really didn't say a word, did you?"

"Do you mean to tell me," Jack began furiously, "that you *were* sleeping with him? And you knew about it, Pris? Why the devil didn't you say so?"

"I hoped I would not need to," she admitted, and smiled. "I was right, you see."

"Who else knew about it?" Jack demanded. "Did you, 'Phrina?" She hung her head. "Agnes?"

"I had my suspicions. But nothing solid to go on, other than 'Phrina's reports."

"And *everyone*," her mother put in abruptly, "knows that Sephrina isn't right in her head. Besides, what would the truth have mattered? You have no respect for this family, for the past. For all that Avenleigh stood for."

"What did it stand for, Aunt?" he asked bemusedly.

"For honor! For heritage! For decency! For everything that you, Jack Cantrell, have abandoned, with your bastard son and your wicked ways!"

There was a small space of silence, and then 'Phrina spoke up, very quietly. "Is that why you burned it down?"

Her mother whirled on her. "Didn't I warn you about telling wild tales? Didn't I say what would become of you? Do you want to be sent to the madhouse?" 'Phrina began to cry, wringing her hands. "Because that's what will happen if you spread such lies!"

"Don't send me to the bedlam, Mamma! Please don't send me!"

"Why not? You are mad, aren't you? Even Cousin Jack says so!"

"I'll be good!" Jack, appalled, saw 'Phrina drop to her knees in the filthy stable hay. "I'll be good, Mamma, from now on! I won't tell any tales!"

Pris, too, was looking on, aghast. She pressed Johnnie into his father's arms, took a step toward 'Phrina. " 'Phrina. What did you mean when you asked your mamma if that was why she burned the house down?"

"Nothing! I didn't mean anything by it!"

"You all know she's daft," Aunt Bertrice interjected coolly, her black eyes narrowed. "She always has been. You tell them, Agnes."

Instead Agnes left the shelter of Lord Cowper's embrace to come forward. " 'Phrina?"

"I don't want to be shut away with the lunatics!" her sister insisted. "She will do that. She will! She always says she will, if I'm not good!"

"No one is going to send you away, 'Phrina," Jack told her, challenging his aunt with his gaze. "Tell us what you saw."

"Nothing," she whispered cravenly.

"There, you see? She saw nothing." Aunt Bertrice smiled with complacence. "Now let's send for Dr. Allison. The poor girl is distraught."

"Someone locked the door to my bedchamber tonight." Jack's blue eyes sought out the butler. "Bellows. You have keys. Was it you?"

"No, milord!"

"Who else has keys to the household?"

"Only M-mrs. Gravesend, milord!" the butler stammered. "But surely you cannot believe—"

" 'Phrina." Jack knelt beside her in the hay, Johnnie clasped in his arms. "What did you see?"

"You don't understand," she whimpered, clutching her battered bouquet. "I'm not right in my head. Anyone but Mamma would send me away. Only Mamma would put up with me."

"Oh, Mother," Agnes whispered. "How could you? How could you tell her that?"

"It's God's truth!" Aunt Bertrice snapped, black eyes flashing. "You've seen it for yourself. She wanders about at night. She listens in, she eavesdrops."

"Because *you* told me to," 'Phrina protested. "You *told* me to, Mamma! You said if I didn't, you would send me to live with the lunatics!"

"Dear God in heaven," Vivienne Harpool murmured, fascinated. And Jamalla made the sign of the cross, very fearfully.

" 'Phrina." Jack fought his instinct to murder his aunt. " 'Phrina, no one is going to send you to a bedlam. Never. Not ever. You'll have a home with us, with Pris and me, for so long as you want one. Now tell me what you saw."

"He doesn't have a home himself anymore!" Aunt Bertrice said in disdain.

"Neither do you," Bennett Shropley noted shrewdly.

'Phrina's pale, round gaze widened. "He is right,

Mamma. What is to become of you?" Her voice rose in a wail. "What is to become of us? What have you done?"

"What did she do, 'Phrina?"

"She locked the doors! To your rooms, and to the nursery!"

"Liar! Crazy liar!"

"She poured turpentine—"

"Straight to bedlam, Sephrina!"

"Over the floors and the walls! And she lit—she lit—she lit—"

"You'll *die* there!" Aunt Bertrice screeched, lunging for her. Jack blocked her with his shoulder, shielding 'Phrina, protecting her.

"And she lit a match!"

"Liar!" Aunt Bertrice screamed, flailing at Jack, clawing at her daughter. "You're insane! Why would I do such a thing?"

'Phrina cringed. Bellows and Bennett Shropley bounded forward as one, to hold her mother back. "Because you want him to be a post-boy," 'Phrina said wonderingly, her hand reaching out to touch Johnnie's curls. "Not a gentleman. Only a post-boy. And you know Pris never would abide by that."

"She lies," Aunt Bertrice said again. Her face was tight and red above her vulture-black gown. "She lies and schemes and—" She broke off, catching her breath. Her clawed hands fluttered, moved to her bodice. "I—" she said. "I—"

"Madame?" Bellows, who had her by the shoulders, peered down at her in alarm. "Madame?"

Those coal eyes glinted, staring straight at Jack. "*Damn* you!" she cried out. "Damn you for ever coming back here!" And then she went limp in Bellows's grasp.

The funeral was held only three days after the wedding; Cook could have planned the luncheon around cold meats left over from the earlier feast, if she'd had a kitchen to prepare it in. After the interment, Bishop Wilcox approached Pris as she stood in the graveyard, staring down at the fresh-turned earth.

"Daughter. A terrible pity such grief had to intrude upon the family in so untimely a manner. You have my deepest condolences."

"Thank you kindly," Pris said.

"Everyone carrying on despite the adversity?"

"Quite."

He glanced across the thick grass to 'Phrina, who was clad in a crisp silk gown of blazing crimson and yellow stripes, topped off by a purple parasol and a shimmering emerald-green plumed bonnet. "Poor thing," he murmured. "Her mother's death seems to have unhinged her totally.

Did no one suggest that her new apparel was hardly suitable for mourning?"

"I don't believe anyone did." 'Phrina, noticing him staring, waved as elegantly as a queen, with a radiant smile.

The bishop nodded back, then unwound his tippet and folded it in his hands. "What do you propose to do now, Priscilla?"

"I scarcely know. There hasn't been time to think."

"But you'll rebuild, of course."

Jack, who was fending off a combined attack of sympathy from Mrs. Blathersby and Lady Ashton, winked at Pris above their black-bonneted heads. She started to laugh, saw her father's scandalized expression, and turned it into a cough. "I really couldn't say. Jack never was fond of the place."

Her father nodded again. "Unhappy memories and all that. They have a way, have they not, of seeping right into the stones? I've often thought that about Wilcox Hall." She glanced up at him in surprise. It was the closest she had ever heard him come to expressing regret about his own wife's death. He cleared his throat. "But the Lord has his reasons for all things, I suppose. No sense trying to fathom them."

Pris looked to 'Phrina, who was spinning her gaudy new parasol delightedly. " 'God moves in a mysterious way,' " she murmured, " 'his wonders to perform.' "

"Is that Isaiah?" the bishop inquired dubiously.

"Lord Cowper's cousin William, actually. He's quite a splendid poet. Jack has all his books."

"Ah. I have been contemplating expanding my choices of reading matter. Perhaps I shall assay this Cowper."

Her dove-gray eyes slanted toward hm. "Why, Father! Next I'll find you curled up beside the hearth with a glass of port!"

He smiled ruefully. "I'm afraid not. My responsibilities

to my flock forbid any such indulgence." Then he sighed, pressing his fingertips to the bridge of his nose. "Though I wonder of late whether I have taken those responsibilities too seriously. I could have been a better father to you."

"You could have been far worse," she told him very soberly, from the edge of Aunt Bertrice's new grave. "We were not an ideal match, you and I."

"You always were a master of understatement, my dear." He glanced at Jack, still dealing nobly with the avid lady mourners. "Your husband has a finely honed sense of responsibility."

"Do you know, Father, that's quite the nicest thing you've ever said about him."

"It's the *only* nice thing I've ever said about him," the bishop noted dryly.

"Well, yes. That too." She smiled up at him and saw with shock what might have been a trace of moisture in his flinty eyes.

"I have been wanting to explain to you, Priscilla . . ." He was silent for so long that she felt obliged to prompt him: "Yes, Father?"

"That upright young military sort I always pictured you married to . . . and even Robert Cantrell . . . the great majority of the human race expends its days on earth without ever finding a great passion. Someone they love so utterly, so completely, that life without that person is like life without air. Most of mankind is content to do without that. I'd always hoped . . . always prayed . . . that you would be, too."

She stared at him, astonished. "Oh, Father. *Why?*"

"Because living without air is very hard to do. Believe me. I have been gasping for it for the past twenty years."

She thought about that for a moment. "Even if that is so . . . would you truly forfeit what you shared with Mamma for the sake of some—some more comfortable affection?

Simply because it would not hurt so much when it was gone?"

He turned his eyes heavenward and sighed. "I've asked myself that question each night for more than two decades. And I nearly always answer it—yes."

"*Nearly* always."

"Yes. Nearly always. Except when I feel I would not trade my memories for the sake of my eternal soul. And that, of course, is blasphemy."

"Oh, Father," she whispered. "If we are not suited to one another, it is only because we are too much alike."

"I'm afraid you may be right. Breathe deeply while you can, daughter."

"I am," she assured him. "God. I am."

He cleared his throat, gave a last swipe at his eyes. "Well! Whatever you may decide to do about the future—" He paused. "I wanted you to know—you are welcome to come and stay at Wilcox Hall. For as long as you like."

"*All* of us?" she asked in astonishment. "Even Johnnie?"

"You could hardly come without him, could you? You'll have to warn the earl, though. Officially, at least, Wilcox Hall is still dry."

Pris stood on tiptoe to kiss his leathery cheek. "I shall let you know. But thank you, Father, for the invitation. And . . . for what you said about Jack."

"Well. Rather difficult to despise a man who's done what I never managed to."

"And what is that?"

"Make you happy," he said gruffly, and returned the kiss.

Jack broke free at last and strode across the graveyard to join them, leaning heavily on his cane. "Splendid eulogy you spoke for Aunt Bertrice, sir. Meant the world to all of us."

"One of the more difficult tasks I've ever set myself,"

the bishop responded, "considering she was such a miserable old battle-ax." He laughed as Jack's jaw dropped open. "Nearly as hard as composing your brother's. Your own eulogy, I am sure, will be far easier to pen. But that job won't be mine, thank heaven. You'll outlive me, both of you, by dozens of years. Well, I must be off. Sunday's sermon beckons. Remember my offer, Priscilla."

"Forever," she said, with a hitch in her voice that made Jack look at her askant.

"What offer was that?" he demanded, when the bishop was out of earshot.

"For us to come and live with him at Wilcox Hall." Jack stopped in midstep, staring. "*And* he'd like to borrow your volumes of Cowper."

"I'll be damned," said Jack.

"Father has come to believe otherwise, evidently."

The coachman had brought their carriage round and was waiting to take them to the Two Cats, where they'd put up temporarily. 'Phrina and Agnes and Harry climbed in, but Jack waved him off. "We'll walk," he declared, tucking Pris's arm into his. "That is, if you don't mind."

"Not at all." She fell into step beside him as he headed toward the village.

"Good. We need a bit of quiet. We must talk about the future, Pris."

"Aye. I know."

"Bennett thinks I should rebuild." His brow was furrowed.

"This *has* been Cantrell country for five hundred years."

" 'Cantrell country.' " He winced. "That's got such a medieval ring to it, don't you think? As though anyone can truly own the earth! And all of it held in fealty from the king—did you know that in the New World, anyone can buy land? Free and clear?"

"Anyone with money," she noted calmly. "It is Johnnie you are thinking of, isn't it?"

"Part of it is Johnnie. In France, perhaps he'd have a stab at it. But here? In *Lincolnshire*?"

"Yet Camille desired he be brought up as a proper English lord."

"Camille never knew a proper English lord."

"Yes she did. She knew you."

They walked on for a few paces. "What about 'Phrina?" Pris asked then.

"Agnes has invited her to help with the school she and Harry are setting up. For impoverished daughters of the gentry."

"And Bennett and Esmé?"

"They're still bickering. She does not want to stay here. Bennett is not at all sure he is ready to plunge into island life wholeheartedly. I have a notion, though, that she'll bring him around."

"You would have to find someone else to manage the estates, then."

"I've been thinking of that. Bellows has a nephew—" He broke off; she had burst out laughing.

"Bellows?"

"Who's at Lincoln College," Jack finished defiantly. "On scholarship. He's coming to meet with me next week." He glanced at her. "What? The man's been most faithful to the family. Even kept his mouth shut to the constable about Aunt Bertrice setting the fire."

"I'm sure his nephew will prove an exemplary sort."

"We'll see." Jack paused, leaning on the cane, and pulled out a cigar, nicking the tip off with his pocketknife. "We'll see. If he doesn't—" He stopped again. Pris had frozen in her tracks, staring at a stand of dame's rocket by the roadside. "What? What is it?"

"Gadfly hawk moth," she whispered, unwinding her

hairnet, advancing on the plumes of purple flowers stealthily. "Don't you *dare* light that cigar!"

He stood and watched as she bent low and crept toward the fluttering moth, with the net outstretched. "Got you!" she cried as she snagged it in the web of silk. "Got you at last, by damn! After all these years!" She bore it back to Jack triumphantly. "Oh, it's a beauty, isn't it?" And she stared down happily at the wispy creature. Then, inexplicably, she unwound the net and shook it to the winds, and the moth sailed away.

"A gadfly hawk moth," Jack said after a moment. "A few months past, you would have sold your soul for a specimen of that."

"So I would have," she admitted cheerfully. "Let it go. Let it fly! Let it procreate, find the one great passion of its life and make ten hundred thousand more gadfly hawk moths! I'm tired of specimens pinned to corkboard. All God's creatures deserve to be free."

He looked at her as she stood with her hair blowing loose in the wind. "Have I ever mentioned there are butterflies in St. Lucia?"

"You have, as I recall. You described them very precisely. Yellow ones, you said, and white ones with red stripes, and great big brown ones."

"I may have left out a few. Did I also mention there are palm trees in St. Lucia? And oceans so warm that stepping into them is like taking a bath? And sunshine all the time, with never any rain—except in rainy season," he amended. "But then there are the most glorious sunsets."

"It sounds heavenly."

Jack toed a bit of dirt with his boot. "I don't suppose . . . that you would like to go there?"

"I must admit," said Pris, "I have a certain scientific curiosity."

Chapter

39

$\mathcal{B}$eneath a moon that hung more huge and round than any she had ever seen, Pris lay in Jack's lap aboard a schooner called *Tradewinds*, her hair billowing in a brisk sea breeze. The hammock he'd strung between the gunwales swung gently back and forth, like a baby's cradle. She closed her eyes, lulled almost to unconsciousness by the rocking of the waves.

"Pris?" The murmur at her ear startled her, but she was soothed by the warm circle of his arms.

"Aye?"

"You've no regrets, have you?"

"None at all."

"Not about your father?"

"You must be jesting," she said sleepily. "Father and I have never been so close as we are now that we're apart." She struggled to sit up against him. "But what about you?"

"Mm. What about me?" He nuzzled the nape of her neck.

"Regrets. Vivienne Harpool, perhaps?"

"Only that I ever met her."

The answer satisfied her; she settled back against his chest. "I should go check on Johnnie," she murmured after a moment.

"Jamalla is with him. And he likes being aboard a ship."

"Likes hurtling up to the deck railings, you mean."

"He takes after me," Jack said complacently. "Living close to the edge."

"It's nothing to be proud of."

"It won me you."

"Hmph," said Pris, and shut her eyes again.

"Last chance for a glimpse of the lights of England," Jack announced, twisting to glance toward the stern.

"You look for me." Nonetheless, she roused and peered past his shoulder at the distant haze. A sudden flare above the city made Jack laugh. "What is it?" she demanded.

"Fireworks. At Vauxhall. The first time I ever kissed you. I don't suppose you recall." He wrapped his arms more tightly around her. "I fell in love with you that night."

"God. After I made such an ass of myself at Professor Eisenroth's lecture?"

"You did no such thing. He proved himself an ass. Look at what you taught him about *Bombycidae*."

"You stood up for me."

"Only after you stood up for yourself."

She sighed, clasped in his embrace. "I wonder sometimes . . ."

"What, love?"

"If the world will ever change. If we'll ever have the freedom men do."

"Each step any one of you takes is a step forward." He bent his head to kiss her wild hair. "And there are those of my sex, you know, who do not consider that prospect a threat."

"You. But you are unique."

"Thank you. There's also Bennett. And Harry Cowper. And, in his own way, your father. He *might*, you know, have locked you in a tower until you married the first reasonably attractive second lieutenant who came along."

"Wilcox Hall doesn't have any towers," she scoffed, but then softened. "It was so odd, Jack, finding out how he loved my mother. To think I lived with him all that time and had no idea. 'Gasping for breath for two decades . . .' " She shivered, and he tightened his grip.

"If I ever lost you," he murmured into her hair, "I would feel that same way."

"You *will* lose me, though, Jack, someday. Or I shall lose you. It is inevitable, just as Father said. Death will part us. It's in the marriage vows, for God's sake! Like—like some sort of warning. *Caveat emptor.* Let the newlyweds beware."

He looked past her into the heavens, into that thick, soft quilt of endless black stitched through with shining stars. "Death is no reason not to take what one can from life. And God is gracious. He left us with a stab at immortality."

"Life after death, you mean. Heaven. I've never been able to picture it at all properly. Wings and haloes and harps—and what exactly becomes of a man who's had two wives, or three wives? Do they all sit about contentedly with him, imbibing nectar and nibbling at manna? Don't they quarrel? 'I had him first.' 'He loved me more.' " Jack was laughing. "What? I am serious! If our souls are what make us human, why should we expect them to be able to exist eternally in perfect harmony?"

"You scientists! You are so literal. Actually, I was thinking of another sort of immortality."

"I can't think what *that* might be."

His fingertips brushed the tips of her breasts. "No? You played pat-a-cake for two hours today with a rather robust example of it."

"Mmm," she whispered. "There is that, of course."

"Which would explain why copulation is the driving force behind the entire natural world." He eased the bodice of her gown down slowly. She turned to him in the darkness, making the hammock career wildly. "We may never be certain what heaven above is like. Heaven on earth, however, I am very sure of." He kissed her, the imprint of his mouth like God's handmark, indelible and holy. "I have that right here." Then, abruptly, he raised his head. "What's that sound?"

"Gulls," Pris said dreamily, her eyes closed once more. She heard the beating of their wings, faint and buzzing. Jack had drawn away from her.

"Pris. Look," he said sharply.

"Look at what?"

"Pris. Love. At this."

Made anxious by his imperative tone, she opened her eyes. Coming across the water toward them was a wave of pale fog—no, a wave of pale birds. No, not birds, either. "Oh!" she cried, sitting up in delight as the massive cloud descended on them, enveloped them, as thousands, millions, billions of insubstantial fluttering creatures swarmed over the gunwales, surrounding Jack and Pris and covering them, flapping just above their heads. Then, that suddenly, they were gone, moving on in a shimmering moonlit mass.

Jack stared down at her. "My God. In all my times at sea, I've never seen that happen. You *have* got strong magic."

"I have," she whispered, "so long as I have you."